A Lesser Evil

LESLEY PEARSE

PENGUIN BOOKS

PENGUIN BOOKS

UK | USA | Canada | Ireland | Australia
India | New Zealand | South Africa

Penguin Books is part of the Penguin Random House group of companies
whose addresses can be found at global.penguinrandomhouse.com.

First published by Michael Joseph 2005
Published in Penguin Books 2006
Reissued in this edition 2011

6

Copyright © Lesley Pearse, 2005
All rights reserved

The moral right of the author has been asserted

Set in Monotype Garamond
Typeset by Rowland Phototypesetting Ltd, Bury St Edmunds, Suffolk
Printed in England by Clays Ltd, St Ives plc

ISBN: 978-0-141-04609-9

To Jo Prosser, for all the laughs, the shared triumphs and disasters over so many years. What would I do without you?

Special thanks to Claire Ledingham at Penguin for her wisdom, tact and patience. And to Emma Draude for her support, interest and friendship above and beyond the call of duty.

Chapter one

March 1962, Bristol

'I want to sit down, not eat you!'

At the young man's jocular remark Fifi blushed and quickly shut her gaping mouth. 'I'm sorry, I was miles away. Of course you can share the table.'

She had in fact been dumbstruck because the man was so incredibly good-looking. Men who looked like Red Indians didn't normally frequent Carwardines coffee shop. He might be wearing a donkey jacket, jeans and desert boots, but his face was pure Apache.

'So where were you?' he asked as he sat down. 'In the South of France? Dancing with Fred Astaire or planning a murder?'

Fifi giggled. 'Nothing so exciting, I'm afraid. The only thing I need to kill is some time till my friend gets here.'

'Well, you could kill it talking to me,' he said with a wide smile that revealed perfect white teeth. 'Or has your mother warned you about speaking to strange men?'

Fifi knew her mother would throw a fit if she saw her daughter talking to a man like this one. For a start, it was obvious from his clothes and callused hands that he did manual work. His hair was jet-black and a little too long; he had amazing angular cheekbones and a wide mouth that screamed to be kissed. An over-protective mother's worst nightmare!

'I think even she'd imagine I was safe enough in here,' Fifi replied, glancing round at the many middle-aged ladies who were having tea and a cake after a hard day's shopping.

'Got any idea where Gloucester Road is?' he asked. 'I was directed this way from the station and told to ask again.'

'It's sort of over that way,' Fifi replied, pointing in the rough direction. 'It's a long road, though – have you got any landmarks or other street names?'

He pulled a scrap of paper from his pocket and looked at it. 'Opposite the junction of Zetland Road,' he said. 'D'you know that?'

Fifi couldn't help but smile at him. His accent might be rough Wiltshire, but there was humour in everything he said, and such a wicked sparkle in his dark eyes. 'Yes, it's only a longish walk or a short bus ride. I could draw you a map if you like.'

'Great! I can make out I'm Dr Livingstone going up the Zambesi. Will the people around Zetland Road be cannibals?'

'Why, are you one?' she giggled.

'I could be tempted. You look good enough to eat,' he shot back, his dark eyes sweeping over her with appreciation. 'Anyone ever tell you that you look like Tuesday Weld?'

People often likened Fifi to the blonde American film star and it always made her glow with pleasure, for the actress was very pretty. But as Fifi's entire childhood had been overshadowed by being considered very strange-looking, she was never entirely convinced that she'd changed.

'It has been said by those who need glasses,' she joked. 'But has anyone told you that you look like a Red Indian?'

'Yeah, now and again. The truth is, I'm the Last of the Mohicans, abandoned as a baby in Swindon,' he said.

The waitress came over at that point and took his order for coffee.

'So you come from Swindon? What brings you to Bristol?' Fifi asked him.

'To seek my fortune,' he smiled. 'I'm starting work at a building site here. I'm a bricklayer. I've got a room to see in Gloucester Road. What's it like around there?'

'Okay. Good shops, pubs, plenty of buses, lots of students live there. It's not rough, but not smart either.'

'I bet you live somewhere smart!' he said, appraising her tailored office suit with a crisp white blouse beneath.

'Suburban. Roses in the gardens and lots of trees,' she said briefly, not inclined to talk about herself and her family. What she wanted was to find out everything about this intriguing man before Carol arrived. 'I'm Felicity Brown. But I'm always called Fifi. So what's your name?'

'Dan Reynolds,' he said. 'And Fifi suits you. Pretty, like a little fluffy poodle.'

'I'm not fluffy,' she said indignantly. Her blonde hair was poker-straight, she was five feet seven, and she didn't go in for fussy clothes. At twenty-two, she also had the distinction of being the youngest legal secretary ever to be taken on at Hodge, Barratt and Soames, one of the best solicitors in Bristol.

'I think the word I should have used was chic,' he said, but he pronounced it 'chick'.

Fifi smiled. She liked that description.

'So, Fifi, are you meeting a boyfriend?' he asked.

The waitress came back with Dan's coffee.

'No, just a girlfriend,' Fifi said, watching him stir in four spoonfuls of sugar. 'I usually meet her after work on

Thursdays and we go to the pictures.' She was already hoping that Carol wouldn't turn up or at least that she'd be late.

'Have you got a boyfriend?'

'No,' Fifi said truthfully. 'What about you?'

'No boyfriend,' he said, and laughed. 'I'm not that way inclined. I did have a girl a while back but she left me for a rich bloke.'

'And were you heartbroken?'

'My pride was bruised, but it wasn't going anywhere, just habit really.'

They chatted easily for some time after Dan had finished his coffee. He didn't use any of the normal chat-up lines, not asking her about what music she liked, films she'd seen or even what she did for a living. He didn't talk about himself either, instead he made observations about people around them and told her little fictitious stories about them to make her laugh.

Fifi's mother, Clara, was always saying that the most outstanding thing about her eldest child was her nosiness. She claimed that as soon as Fifi could talk she was asking questions about people, and it had caused her much embarrassment. Fifi was still every bit as nosy, but she had learned to phrase her questions in a way that sounded caring rather than prying. It was lovely to be with someone who appeared just as fascinated by others as herself.

When the waitress came back to clear their table and rather pointedly put down the bills, Dan said he would have to go or he might lose the room.

'Could you do that map for me?' he asked, casually picking up her bill and paying it along with his own.

Fifi thought fast. 'I could show you the way,' she said. 'It's on my way home.' It wasn't, but he wouldn't know that.

'But what about your friend?' he asked.

Fifi shrugged. 'She'd have been here by now if she was coming.'

That wasn't true either. Carol was often kept late at work, and she'd be disappointed when she got here and found Fifi had gone. And if she were to find out she'd been stood up for a complete stranger, Fifi doubted she'd ever speak to her again. But there was something so compelling about Dan that she was quite prepared to take that risk.

'If you're sure,' he said. 'I've only got to take a look at the room and grab it if it's okay. If you like, I could take you for a drink after?'

Fifi didn't want to look too keen, so she shrugged non-chalantly, but she had her coat on, and whisked Dan and his small duffel bag, which appeared to hold his entire worldly goods, swiftly out of the door before Carol could get there and prevent her.

'I'll wait for you over here,' Fifi said, sheltering from the rain in a haberdashery shop doorway. The guest house Dan was looking for was across the busy road, above a scruffy-looking newsagent's. The paint on the front door was peeling off, and the sign 'Avondale' looked as if the lettering had been done by a drunk. Judging by the dingy nets at the windows, it was not going to be a home from home.

'You can't wait here, it's too cold and wet,' Dan said, and looked around and spotted a pub further down the road. 'Go in there.'

'I can't go into a pub on my own,' Fifi said in horror. 'I'll be fine here.'

He faltered for a moment, as if thinking she might

disappear while he was gone. 'I won't be more than five minutes,' he said, and darted across the road.

Fifi got only the briefest glimpse of a gaunt woman in a flowery overall opening the door to Dan, then the door closed behind him and she turned to look at the window display.

The theme was 'Spring', with white-painted branches festooned with balls of knitting wool in pastel colours. There were samples of crochet work, knitted lambs and rabbits, and various embroidery kits. As always when Fifi saw such displays, she felt a little tremor of nervousness. Her mother was always saying that knitting and sewing, along with cooking, were skills needed to be a wife and mother, and Fifi was terrible at all three.

All her friends were desperate to get married, and every new man they went out with had them mooning over engagement rings and bridal magazines. Fifi didn't share her friends' desperation, but whether this was because she really liked being single, or because her mother was always pointing out her failings, she didn't know.

A hand on her shoulder made her jump.

It was Dan, and when he saw how startled she was, he laughed. 'Sorry. Were you off on planet knitting wool?' he asked.

'Hardly,' she giggled. 'I'm hopeless at knitting. You were quick! Did you get the room? What was it like?'

'A damp, cold cell, with mushrooms growing on the wallpaper,' he grinned, 'but I bit off the woman's arm to have it, just so I could get back to take you for a drink.'

'Is the room really that bad?' Fifi asked as they walked down to the pub.

'Worse,' he laughed. 'The landlady is called Mrs Chambers. I wanted to ask if it was a Death Chamber, but she looked and sounded like Olive Oyl, Popeye's girlfriend, and that threw me.' He impersonated the woman's voice, 'No female visitors at any time. No callers or radios after ten. Clean sheets once a fortnight, all breakages must be replaced.'

Fifi giggled. 'It sounds frightful!'

'Not as bad as some places I've stayed in,' he said with a shrug and that delicious impish grin which made Fifi's toes curl up. 'I stayed in a place in Birmingham once where they operated a shift system. As I got up, another bloke who worked nights came in and got in my bed.'

'I don't believe that.' Fifi laughed. 'You're making it up!'

'It's true,' he insisted. 'We became really good mates in the end – he said I was the best bed-warmer he'd ever known.'

Fifi shuddered. 'I couldn't sleep in someone else's sheets,' she said.

'I don't suppose you've ever had to,' he said, looking sideways at her appraisingly. 'You look as if you've been brought up in the lap of luxury.'

The lap of luxury was perhaps an exaggeration, but Fifi was aware that her family's standard of living was much higher than average. Their semi-detached house in Westbury-on-Trym, one of Bristol's most pleasant suburbs, was large and comfortable, and as her father was a lecturer at Bristol University, that placed them firmly in the upper-middle classes. Although they were not rich by any means, there had always been month-long holidays in Devon, bicycles, dancing and tennis lessons. Fifi had gone to a private secretarial college after leaving school. But she'd never really thought of herself as particularly fortunate because almost all her friends came from similar backgrounds.

'I don't get on that well with my mother,' she blurted out.

She didn't really know why she told him that, true though it was. Maybe it was a way of distancing herself from her background. 'I really ought to leave home and get a flat of my own.'

In the pub over a drink Fifi told Dan about her younger siblings, Patty, Robin and Peter, and that there were only fourteen to sixteen months between each of them. 'They are all more like Mum and Dad,' she explained. 'They're docile and obedient. I was a disappointment to Mum from the start because I was weird.'

'You don't look weird to me,' Dan said. 'Far from it.'

'You wouldn't say that if you could see the photos of me at five or six.' Fifi giggled. 'I was as thin as a rasher of bacon, my hair was snow-white like an albino's, and I had a huge mouth and bug eyes.'

To illustrate this she pulled at her eyes and lips to make herself grotesque, a trick she'd found always made people laugh.

'So the good fairy came along, did she?' Dan chuckled, sounding as if he didn't believe her. 'Or am I looking at you with magic eyes?'

'What's that?' Fifi asked.

'My one talent,' he said. 'I don't ever let myself be dis-appointed. Looking at things with magic eyes makes me see how they could be when I'd rearranged them, painted, repaired or tweaked them. Take that room up the road. I imagined it with nice wallpaper and a rug on the floor, then it wasn't so bad.'

Fifi thought that was a lovely idea. She wondered if she could apply it to her mother and see how she would be if her critical manner, her sarcasm and suspicion could be removed. 'So do I need tweaking or rearranging?'

Dan shook his head. 'No, you're just perfect. I can't really believe that on my first night in Bristol I've got such a pretty girl with me. Even if you did only come with me out of pity.'

It wasn't pity Fifi felt for him, far from it. It wasn't just that he was so handsome, it was the sparkle in his dark eyes, the fullness of his lips, the sheen on his skin, the lithe animal grace with which he moved. He made her giggle and her heart flutter. She couldn't remember any man having this effect on her before, but then the kind of men she normally dated were usually smooth, besuited office workers.

'Now, what makes you think I came out of pity?' she said archly, raising her eyebrows.

'So what was it then?' he grinned.

'Curiosity. I'm famous as a nosy parker. When I was a kid I used to embarrass my parents by asking total strangers the most personal questions.'

'Go on then, ask me one,' he dared her.

Fifi had a hundred questions she was dying to ask, but if she could only pick one it had to be something that would move things on to a more personal level.

'Have you got a hairy chest?' she asked.

He looked a bit stunned, but grinned and unbuttoned his shirt, just enough for her to see smooth, hairless skin, still retaining the remnants of a golden tan. 'Any good?' he asked.

'Perfect,' she laughed. 'I can't bear hairy men.'

'Can I ask one now?' he said.

'As long as it doesn't involve me unbuttoning my blouse.'

'Would you kiss a man in his working clothes?'

Fifi spluttered with laughter. It was true she'd noticed his clothes were a little grubby, but it hadn't put her off him one iota. In fact his checked flannelette shirt, worn jeans and donkey jacket suited him.

'It would depend on the man,' she said. She nodded towards a man standing up at the bar; he had a huge paunch hanging over paint-splattered trousers, and he was nearly bald. 'I wouldn't kiss him even if he was in a velvet smoking jacket. But you I might.'

It was after eleven when Fifi finally got home. Her mother came rushing out into the hall at the sound of the key in the door.

In the last two or three years people had begun remarking that Fifi was growing to look just like her mother. It was a compliment as Clara was a very pretty woman who looked much younger than her forty-four years. They were both tall, slender, blonde-haired and brown-eyed, with heart-shaped faces. But Fifi fervently hoped she would never inherit her mother's nature, for she flared up at nothing and could say such nasty, spiteful things, which were mainly directed at Fifi.

'Wherever have you been?' Clara asked, her eyes narrowed with suspicion and irritation. 'Carol's been on the phone asking why you weren't at Carwardines to meet her. I was really beginning to worry about you as it is such a cold night.'

'I rang her office and left a message for her,' Fifi lied. 'I suppose no one told her.'

'What was so sudden and important you had to let her down? Carol's such a nice girl,' Clara said tersely.

Fifi had her head so far up in the clouds after the evening with Dan that she hadn't even considered thinking up a plausible story for when she got home. She certainly couldn't tell the truth – her mother would have fifty fits if she thought she'd been picked up by a strange man.

'It was Hugh,' she said hastily, hanging up her coat on the hall stand. 'He rang me this morning and seemed in a bit of a state. I felt I had to meet him.'

Hugh was an old boyfriend who lived in Bath. Fifi's parents had liked him a great deal and probably hoped she'd marry him because he was doing his articles with a law firm and came from a very good family. They had split up just after Fifi's twenty-first birthday, over a year ago, but had remained friends. So she didn't think it was too terrible to use him as an alibi.

'What was the matter with him?'

Clara always used this deeply suspicious tone with Fifi. Patty, Peter or Robin could get away with just about anything, but for some unfathomable reason Clara always seemed to think the worst of her eldest child.

'Oh, just a girl who's messing him around,' Fifi said lightly. 'We had a couple of drinks and some supper. He was more cheerful when I left him. I'll phone Carol in the morning and explain; it's too late now.'

'You could have phoned me,' her mother snapped.

Fifi sighed. 'I didn't know Carol hadn't got the message. So why would I phone you? I wasn't expected home.'

'Most girls still living at home would let their mothers know where they were in case of an emergency. You treat this place like a hotel and your father and me as if we were caretakers.'

Fifi rolled her eyes at the same old line her mother trotted out with monotonous regularity. 'Mum, I'm tired and cold. I'm sorry I didn't phone you, that Carol didn't get my message and for anything else I may have done to upset you. Now may I go to bed?'

Clara Brown turned and flounced back to the sitting room

without so much as a goodnight. Fifi went straight upstairs, fervently hoping Patty was already asleep, as she didn't fancy another interrogation.

Fifi had made Dan laugh that night telling him just how difficult she'd been as a child, and she had no doubt he thought she was exaggerating. But in fact she'd played the truth down. It wasn't only that she was so strange-looking; she knew her parents had been seriously worried for a time that her peculiar behaviour was caused by a mental deficiency. She couldn't sit still or concentrate on anything for more than a few minutes; she threw tantrums and could scream for hours. She either stared balefully at people in complete silence, or she was firing personal questions at them. She didn't mix well with other children; she snatched their toys and pinched their arms or legs. She wouldn't eat or sleep and she talked to herself.

It hadn't helped that Patty, who was only fourteen months younger, was a cute, docile little poppet, with golden curls, plump pink cheeks and the kind of charm that made everyone want to pick her up and hug her.

Fifi could appreciate now how desperate her mother must have felt, particularly in the last year of the war, when she had three under-fives and her husband was away most of the time. Clara had been so worn out after Robin was born that they had to have a live-in nurse for a while. It was that nurse who had suggested that Fifi's brain might have been damaged by the forceps during her delivery.

The nurse was wrong, of course. By the time Fifi was ten she could read and write as well as any child in her class, and her behaviour was vastly improved. While her mother claimed that she was still very difficult at home, elsewhere she behaved in a relatively normal fashion.

Fifi went out of her way to tell people what a horrible child she'd been. But then, she could look in the mirror and see no trace of the peculiar, bug-eyed, skinny kid she'd once been. At twelve she'd begun to fill out, her white hair finally darkened to honey-blonde, and all at once her eyes and mouth were not just in proportion, but her two best features. She still remembered so well the first time someone remarked that she was pretty – it was like finding a crock of gold. Now she got on well with almost everyone; people remarked how much fun she was, and on her caring, easy-going nature.

All except her mother, who still had plenty to complain about. According to her, Fifi was lazy, wilful, self-centred, undomesticated and completely oblivious to others' feelings. Fifi felt her mother's nastiness to her was just jealousy, because she'd never had the freedom or fun her daughter enjoyed.

Clara married Harry when she was twenty-one, just as war broke out. Harry had been teaching mathematics when they married, but he spent the war code-breaking, and was away from home for months on end. Fifi was convinced that the reason her mother sniped at her about her job, her clothes, and going dancing every weekend, was purely because when Clara was the same age, she'd been stuck at home alone with a baby.

Patty was fast asleep, but she'd left the little bedside light between their twin beds on. Fifi undressed quickly and got into bed, lying there for a moment remembering how when they were little they always slept together in one of the beds. The room still held so many childhood memorabilia. Cuddly toys and dolls still sat among their Enid Blyton books, a picture of a princess painted by Patty at seven or eight was still on the wall, and there were dozens of photos of them both. Patty kept pictures of her favourite film stars in a tottering heap of scrapbooks. Fifi had gone through a stage when she wanted to be a fashion designer, and the cards she made, with a sketch and samples of dress material pinned to them, were arranged on the wall by the window.

It was a big, comfortable room, with flowery curtains, pinstriped wallpaper and a long teak dressing table with triple mirrors. Patty's side was neat and tidy, little china ballerinas carefully arranged alongside scent, hair lacquer and cosmetics. Fifi's side was the complete opposite, littered with tubes and pots with the tops left off, pens, old letters, reels of cotton all mixed up with her makeup. Patty moaned about it, but she stoically removed dirty cups and plates almost daily, and when she dusted her side, she did Fifi's too, just as she hung up her clothes and made her bed.

Dan had looked envious when Fifi told him about her brothers and sister. She had thought he was joking when he said he'd been abandoned as a baby in Swindon, but it turned out to be shockingly true. He'd spent his life in various children's homes, and was kicked out at fifteen to fend for himself.

Fifi glanced across at Patty, lying on her side with one plump arm protectively around her head, and she smiled affectionately. She loved Patty; they were friends and allies, even if they were as different as chalk and cheese. Patty was placid and patient, while Fifi was fiery and impetuous.

Pretty little Patty had become fat, plain Patty with awful acne as she got into her teens, yet she was still so sweet-natured. She was training to be an optician, and she had the patience of a saint with old people.

Fifi wished she was patient too, but she always wanted everything immediately. She couldn't bear to wait in queues;

she ran across busy roads instead of waiting for the lights to go green. She spent her wages mentally before she even got paid. She jumped into situations with both feet without stopping to think.

She was doing it again now with Dan. She'd only known him for six hours, but she was already convinced they were made for each other.

Getting excited over a new man wasn't a new experience; she'd done it many times before. She would hang round the phone willing it to ring, count the hours till they met, weave improbable fantasies about the life they'd have together. But these romances had always been shortlived.

She knew exactly why. It was because she always hid her real character behind a phoney one, trying to be whatever she believed the man wanted.

Hugh had wanted someone who would bolster up his self-image. Not too bright, not too stunning, a girl who would hang on his every word and be the perfect accessory of a would-be lawyer, never complaining or demanding anything of him.

She'd been so good at it too, until she got bored with stroking his ego and kowtowing to him.

Alan, the boyfriend before Hugh, had wanted a wild, arty girl. Fifi had been quite good at that too, wearing tight black slacks and baggy jumpers and tying her hair back in a pony-tail. She learned lots of obscure poems, pretended she liked jazz and red wine, and talked about going to live in the Latin Quarter in Paris.

That had been fun for a while, but she missed pretty clothes, and got tired of pretending to be a Bohemian. There had been other characters she'd played too; it seemed preferable to be anyone other than her real self.

*

Tonight, however, she'd just been herself. That was partly because of the way she and Dan met, when she wasn't dressed up. She had been in her work clothes, her hair needed a wash, there was a ladder in her stocking and she hadn't even put on any perfume. She didn't once try to impress Dan, nor did she build him up to be something he wasn't either.

It was all the laughing that made it so easy to be natural. Dan was neither a clown nor a joke-teller; he was just a funny person with his witty turn of phrase, his razor-sharp observations and ability to see humour in just about everything.

After his question about whether she'd kiss a man in his work clothes they had gone on to a couple of other pubs, so he could get an idea of the area he'd be living in. She found out that he was twenty-five and had done his National Service in the Army; although he never went out of the country, he had enjoyed it so much that he was tempted to sign on as a regular.

In the past he'd had a spell living rough; he'd spent six months in a leaky caravan in the middle of a field, and stayed in many other grim lodgings when the building firm he worked for sent him off to a different town.

His friends were the men he worked with, and it seemed to Fifi, by the affectionate way he spoke of them, that they were the nearest thing he had to family. He hadn't accumulated many personal belongings as he had never had a real base. But he said his boss would be bringing the rest of his stuff from Swindon tomorrow, a few more clothes, a radio and some tools.

'What I'd really like is to settle down and have a real home,' he said at one point, the only time in the whole evening when he sounded less than content with his lot.

'I'd like to decorate it myself and have furniture I'd chosen. To lock the door and know no one could barge in on me.'

Fifi turned off the bedside light and snuggled down under the covers. She had been moved by the simplicity of what Dan wanted. Most men coveted a smart car or a hand-tailored suit; they wouldn't care about a decent place to live. And she'd never known anything else. She took this warm and spacious four-bedroomed house, with its plethora of lovely antique furniture passed down from both her parents' families, for granted. However much her mother might irritate her, she was always there with whatever any of them needed, be it a meal, an ironed dress or a mended zip. Cleaning, cooking, washing were all done as if by magic; there were homemade cakes in the cake tin, sandwiches ready every morning for their lunch. If one of them was ill, their mother fussed over them.

As children, their home was open to all their friends. Fifi's father would erect tents for them in the garden, play cricket with them and hang ropes on the trees for them to swing on. Her mother never minded how many extra mouths she had to feed, and she would run up costumes for little shows they put on, hide Easter eggs in the garden, haul huge boxes back from the grocery shop for them to make into toys or houses. She was there bathing grazed knees, comforting them when they didn't get school prizes, celebrating when they did, always loving and caring.

Dan hadn't had any of that.

He didn't invite sympathy; he was too amusing, too manly and confident. Yet all the same Fifi knew that her parents would take one look at him and disapprove. What they wanted for her was a man from a similar background, well bred, with a good family and excellent prospects. Fifi didn't feel her father was a snob — he liked nothing better than getting students from working-class homes attending his lectures, and he made himself accessible to them to give them extra help. But neither he nor her mother would welcome a roaming bricklayer with a poor education for their daughter.

To be truthful, Fifi had always imagined herself marrying a man in one of the professions. She'd never been attracted to louts that hung around on street corners or stumbled drunkenly about dance halls. All her previous boyfriends had been friends of other friends; not one had been an unknown quantity. And she had been out with all of them in a group situation before she took the chance and met them alone. It was completely out of character for her to behave the way she had tonight. But it felt as if it was meant to be.

She knew Dan was special. He might not be educated, but he was clever, funny and strong. When he'd kissed her goodnight at the bus stop, she had almost cried because it was so heartstoppingly wonderful.

The few short hours she'd spent with him had been the most memorable and happy of her whole life. Just before they left the last pub, 'I Can't Help Falling in Love with You' sung by Elvis came on the jukebox. They'd kind of looked at each other and smiled, and Dan sang along with it in an amazingly good impersonation of Elvis, all the time looking right at her. She supposed that was pretty corny, but it had made her feel all fluttery inside.

Just remembering his kiss made her tingle too. No other man had ever stirred her that way or made her feel she could easily lose control. She and her friends often discussed whether they would go to bed with someone before they were married. Fifi had always been insistent that she wouldn't. But tonight she'd experienced real desire, and she realized that those feeble little flutterings she'd felt in the past with boys were nothing compared with how Dan made her feel.

What was she going to do? If she told her parents about him, they'd ask her to bring him home. That might frighten him off. If she saw him in secret and her parents found out, they'd assume she had something to be ashamed of.

'Wait and see how it turns out,' she murmured to herself. 'Maybe you won't feel the same tomorrow.'

'You look even more beautiful than I remembered,' Dan said as they met by the Odeon the following night.

'You look pretty handsome yourself,' Fifi retorted. She had rushed home from work, wolfed down her tea and spent an hour getting ready, so she had half expected him to comment on how good she looked. But he was transformed, wearing a brown pinstriped Italian suit with a fashionable short jacket, white shirt and highly polished shoes. She hoped she might run into one of her friends so she could show him off. No one she knew had a boyfriend as gorgeous as Dan.

'Are you sure you want to see this film?' Dan asked, looking apprehensively at the poster for *A Taste of Honey* with Rita Tushingham.

'My sister said it was brilliant,' Fifi said. 'She cried buckets.'

Dan grinned. 'Is that what makes a film good for girls?'

'I suppose so,' Fifi agreed. 'But we could go to another cinema if you like.'

'No, it's too cold to walk about.' He looked down at her winkle-picker stilettos. 'And I don't think you'd get far in those anyway.'

*

The film was unbearably sad, and even though Fifi tried hard not to cry because she was afraid her mascara would run, she couldn't help herself. As they came back out into the foyer, Dan pulled her over to one side, and using the handkerchief he'd had in the breast pocket of his suit jacket, he wiped her face clean.

'That's better,' he said when he'd finished, kissing her on the nose. 'You're a bit of a surprise! I thought you were too sophisticated to cry.'

'I felt so sorry for Jo; she was so plain and unloved,' Fifi said. 'And her mother was such an unfeeling cow.'

'They all reminded me of people I've met,' Dan said thoughtfully as they left the cinema. 'It was a bit too much of real life for me.'

'Is your room as bad as the one she lived in?' Fifi asked as they walked into a pub in the city centre for a drink before she had to catch the bus home. The pub was crowded, with nowhere to sit, and she wished they had somewhere they could go to be alone.

'It's a lot smaller,' Dan replied, waving a pound note at the barman. 'But the kitchen could star in a kitchen-sink drama – it doesn't look as if it's been cleaned for months.'

'You didn't say you'd got a kitchen,' Fifi said in surprise.

'I have to share it with everyone else,' he said. 'I won't make anything more than a cup of tea in there, I'd be afraid of catching something.'

Fifi had a Babycham and Dan a pint of bitter, and she began quizzing him anxiously about where he'd eat and do his washing.

'There's cafés and launderettes,' he said airily. 'I'm used to all that.'

On the bus ride home later, Fifi's mind kept alternating

between reliving Dan's kisses and thinking of him going home to that horrible room. It wasn't the first time she'd been in a daze over a man's kisses, though she'd never met anyone who kissed quite as wonderfully as Dan. But it was the first time she'd ever been troubled by how someone had to live.

It was the combination of wanting to be with Dan all the time and worrying about him that confirmed she really had fallen head over heels in love with him. She could think of nothing but their next meeting. Her heart pounded when she saw him and just the touch of his hand made her feel she was on fire. But the thought of him washing and ironing his own shirts, having to work outside in the pouring rain and going home without anyone to make him a cup of tea moved her to tears.

Every day after work she would rush to meet him in the café near where he lived. She didn't care that he was often caked with brick dust or cement, soaked through when it had been raining – she needed to see him. Just to sit with him over a cup of tea and talk for half an hour every day was better than having to wait two or three days for a proper date.

Dan felt the same way too. Sometimes he'd ring her from a call-box while she was at work, saying he just had to hear her voice. When she was with him she was floating on a cloud, but during the times they were apart she felt bereft. Keeping him a secret was so hard too, for she wanted to tell everyone about him, especially Patty, but she didn't dare in case her sister let it slip to their parents.

Almost daily she told herself that she was twenty-two, old enough to go out with whoever she wanted to. She even mentally rehearsed telling the family over the evening meal.

But every time she was about to break the news, her mother would say something sarcastic, or she was in a bad mood, and Fifi lost her nerve. The longer it went on, the worse it got as she had to tell lies about who she was going out with. She felt bad for Dan too, for he must surely guess why she hadn't given him her home phone number, and why she didn't invite him home or to meet any of her friends.

Yet Dan didn't ever ask her about that. He cursed that he hadn't got a car, because at least then they'd have somewhere warm and dry to be alone together. He couldn't take her to where he lived, and that left only pubs or the cinema. But they didn't want to drink or watch films, all they wanted was to talk, kiss and pet. The cold, wet weather lingered on, and they felt tormented that they had no privacy.

One Saturday morning, when Fifi had been going out with Dan for six weeks, she was doing some hand-washing at the kitchen sink. Her mother was sitting at the table cleaning the silver, talking about getting some new curtains for the boys' bedroom, but Fifi wasn't really listening; as usual, she was thinking about Dan.

'I don't know why you want to bother with new curtains,' Fifi said when she realized Clara was expecting some input from her. 'They'll never notice.'

'I suppose you think your father and I haven't noticed you've got a new boyfriend, either,' Clara retorted with a touch of acid. 'When are you going to tell us about him?'

Fifi gulped, and carried on squeezing her cardigan in the suds. She had expected that her mother would put two and two together before long. She always did. But Fifi didn't feel relieved that it could now be out in the open. She knew her mother would find fault.

'His name is Dan Reynolds, he's twenty-five, a bricklayer,

and he comes from Swindon,' she blurted out, still keeping her back to her mother.

'I see. So what's wrong with him that you couldn't tell us that before?'

'Nothing. I just didn't want to rush anything,' Fifi said, blushing when she thought of all those hours they'd spent in shop doorways and back alleys, kissing and caressing each other. At times she'd got so carried away that if Dan had taken her against the wall, or pushed her down on the ground, she didn't think she would've objected.

'And where does this bricklayer live? I assume you aren't catching the train to Swindon to meet him?'

'He lives in lodgings on the Gloucester Road.' Fifi's heart sank at the way her mother had said 'bricklayer'.

Clara sniffed in disdain.

'Don't do that, Mum.' Fifi whirled round from the sink. 'Judging someone before you meet them.'

'I'd say it was you who has already judged him, and that's why you haven't brought him home,' Clara retorted.

'I guessed you'd be like this,' Fifi said indignantly. 'You always make it so hard for me to tell you anything. I really like Dan; he's the nicest man I've ever met. So please don't spoil it for me.'

'How can I spoil anything when I haven't even caught a glimpse of him, let alone spoken to him? Really, Fifi, you are so peculiar sometimes!'

'I'm not peculiar, it's you being such a snob! You look down your nose at anyone that's not in one of the professions. Well, Dan is a bricklayer, he's an orphan too, brought up in a children's home. But he's a good man, he works hard, he doesn't get drunk and beat people up, he's not in trouble with the police, and I love him.'

She could have kicked herself for letting herself be pushed

into a defensive position. Now she had accidentally revealed what she really felt. She had planned to introduce Dan to her family gradually, letting his natural charm win them over before she admitted that they were serious about each other. Now she'd blown it.

'I suppose he's a Teddy boy?'

'No, he's not,' Fifi snapped. 'Why would you immediately imagine he's a lout in a drape jacket armed with a knuckle-duster?'

'If you'd brought him home when you first met him I wouldn't need to use my imagination.'

'I needed to get to know him myself before subjecting him to an inquisition,' Fifi retorted. 'I'll gladly bring him home, but please don't be fierce with him, Mum!'

'I can't imagine what you mean,' Clara said, putting her nose in the air. 'Have I browbeaten any of your other boyfriends?'

'Not exactly, but you can be a bit much. Look at the time I went out with Gerald, the medical student. You frightened him off with all those questions about his father.'

'I was only interested; his father was a top surgeon at Guy's, after all.'

'Yes, but Gerald felt so intimidated he didn't want to come here again. I think he thought you'd got our wedding all planned.'

'I can't be blamed for hoping my daughter will marry well.'

'I'd only been out with him a couple of times, Mum,' Fifi said in exasperation.

'Well, all that was a long time ago,' Clara said dismissively. 'Anyway, this young man is an entirely different can of worms. If he has no family I can't ask him questions about them, can I?'

'Why do you have to question him?' Fifi asked. 'You don't question my girlfriends, you just chat. Do that with him!'

'About what?'

'Oh, Mum,' Fifi exclaimed. 'Anything – television, film stars, favourite foods, a story in the news. He's really easy to talk to, it won't be difficult. Just don't act as if you're against, or suspicious of him.'

'You'd better ask him to tea tomorrow then,' Clara said.

'Does it have to be that formal?' Fifi asked hopefully. 'Can't I just get him to come and collect me tomorrow evening and have five minutes with you both before we go out?'

'You invite him round for tea,' Clara said firmly. 'If he can't cope with that, then there's something wrong with him. Now, for goodness' sake get that cardigan hung out on the line to dry. I shouldn't be surprised if it's shrunk to half the size now, you've had it in that water for far too long.'

Fifi had a heavy heart as she hung her washing on the line. Dan would be pleased he'd been invited to tea; to him that would mean her family had accepted he was important to her. But all it really meant was that he would be on parade for her mother, who'd be giving him marks out of ten for table manners, cleanliness, intelligence, and a dozen other items that she'd decide on the day.

It would be a veritable minefield for Dan. He'd only got to stick his knife in the jam pot, pick his bread and butter up with the wrong hand or fail to use his napkin, and no matter how sparkling his conversation was, he would be blackballed.

Dan's table manners weren't that good, but he tried; Fifi

had noticed him copying her on more than one occasion. She would have to hope he did it tomorrow too, for she certainly couldn't embarrass him by suggesting she give him a crash course in her mother's pet hates tonight.

It was a balmy day, and the garden looked lovely with all the blossom and spring flowers. With luck, if it was still nice tomorrow, her parents might suggest having tea out here. That would be far less daunting for Dan. He really appreciated pretty gardens, and he knew a surprising amount about plants as he used to help in the garden at the children's home. That might stop her parents from assuming he was some kind of villain.

'Don't worry, I'll be on my best behaviour,' Dan said later that afternoon as they sat up on the Downs above the Suspension Bridge, looking at the view of the Avon Gorge. 'I'll wash behind my ears, put on my best dazzling white shirt and polish my shoes.'

'Just don't let Mum keep asking you questions,' Fifi warned him. 'Ask her about plants, praise her cakes, and stuff like that. Patty will be lovely, she always is. Robin is mad about rugby and cricket and that's all he wants to talk about. Peter's not much of a talker, but he's interested in photography.'

'Of which I know nothing,' Dan smirked.

'You don't have to, just ask to see some of his work, you'll be his best mate then.'

'Are they both at college?'

'Yes, Robin's doing accountancy and Peter wants to be an architect. But don't worry about that, they aren't geniuses or anything.'

'Will your dad ask me if my intentions towards you are honourable?'

Fifi giggled. 'Of course he won't, he's not a heavy Victorian father. He's rather sweet, much gentler than Mum. Are your intentions honourable?'

'I'd give anything to go to bed with you,' Dan said, putting his arms round her and bending her backwards over the bench to kiss her neck. 'I suppose that's considered dishonourable?'

'My parents would think so,' she said, laughing and trying to extract herself from his clinch.

'Even if I said I wanted to marry you?'

'Do you?' Fifi asked, assuming it was just a joke.

'More than anything else in the world,' he said.

Fifi was shocked to see his eyes were swimming. He had told her he loved her after knowing her just two weeks, but in such a light way that it wasn't possible to gauge whether he'd said it out of affection or real to-die-for passion. Yet now she was left in no doubt.

'But we've only known each other six weeks,' she said, caressing his cheek tenderly.

'I knew on the first night you were the only girl for me,' he replied. 'All the other six weeks and two days has done is confirm it.'

Fifi held his face in her hands, loving his high cheekbones, his generous, sexy mouth and his chocolate-brown eyes. She felt exactly as he said he did – they were like twin souls – but she hadn't dared even think about marriage.

'Are you asking me to marry you?' she whispered. 'Or is this one of your jokes?'

'I'll say it's a joke if you refuse, just to keep face,' he said with a weak grin. 'I wouldn't blame you refusing, it's not as if I can offer you anything. I haven't got any money, not even a car or a decent place to live. But I love you, I'd look after you and I'd treasure you.'

Tears came into Fifi's eyes then. Dan's love was all she wanted. 'Let's see how tomorrow goes first,' she whispered. 'You might not want me after you've met my mother!'

Chapter two

Fifi looked around the table and not for the first time wondered why she was so different to the rest of her family.

Her father Harry, at the head of the table, was the personification of what everyone expected from an academic: tall and thin with stooping shoulders, glasses slightly askew on his nose, and a wide expanse of forehead which grew larger every year as his fair hair receded even further back. His maroon cardigan did nothing for his pale skin, but it had been knitted by his wife and as he had a very placid nature, it would never occur to him to abandon it for something more flattering.

Despite having a very strong bond with her father, Fifi didn't appear to have inherited anything from him, neither his looks nor his keen intelligence. She also wished he would take a stand on how he felt about family matters but he never did, just going along with his wife.

Fifi might look like her mother, but the similarity ended there. Right now Clara was poised like a graceful but ever watchful deer. She looked lovely in her best powder-blue wool dress and pearls, with her hair in a neat chignon, but the effect was spoiled by a fixed false smile. She was not a relaxed person at the best of times, but since Dan's arrival at three o'clock she had become extraordinarily tense.

Peter and Robin, nineteen and eighteen respectively, showed every sign of ending up looking just like their father.

They were fresh-faced and bright-eyed, their backs as straight as guardsmen's now; a framed photograph of their father as a young man, in full view on the sideboard, could have been mistaken for either of his sons. They didn't share their father's sharp intellect, though – studying came hard to them. They were a couple of life's plodders, amiable, gentle and without much fire.

Fifi could see that her brothers were both wishing they had a good reason to excuse themselves from the tea party. Although she doubted that their mother had confided in them her fears about Dan, the atmosphere she was creating had made these all too obvious.

Fifi felt her brothers liked Dan. They had laughed at many things he'd said during the afternoon, and now and again they'd looked admiringly at him, but they lacked the social skills or the nerve to bypass their mother's disapproval.

Patty, a born diplomat, had done her best. Although she was usually shy with strangers, mainly because she was aware of being fat and spotty, she'd made a great effort to make Dan feel comfortable. She had done her best to bring the conversation round to subjects that would give him and her brothers common ground. She asked about the houses he was building and his relationship with the architect, and then reminded him that Peter was training in architecture. To Fifi's disappointment Peter didn't seize the opportunity, almost certainly because he realized Dan had far more practical building knowledge than he had. Patty brought up cricket then, and for a while all the men talked animatedly about the sport, but her mother stamped that out by interrupting and beginning to question Dan again about where he lived.

Fifi could remember how when she was about seven, her mother took her to task for embarrassing another child she met in the park by commenting on the holes in the bottom of her shoes. Her mother had explained that the child's parents were probably very poor, and she should always be tactful and kinder to people less fortunate than herself.

What a hypocrite her mother had turned out to be! She'd always claimed she would like to see an end to the class system, declaring that bright children from poor homes should be given the same opportunities as the children of the wealthy. Yet now her daughter had taken up with a working-class man, all that tact and kindness had vanished.

Just from the way her mother had looked at Dan when he arrived today, Fifi had known he was never going to be able to win her round. She took in his shiny winkle-picker shoes and his pinstriped suit with its bum-freezer jacket as if that was all the evidence she needed to know he was a bad lot.

As it was raining there was little opportunity for Dan to show off his interest in and knowledge of plants, though he tried hard enough. He stood at the French windows in the sitting room and admired the magnolia tree which was in full bloom.

If her mother was surprised he could actually name it, she didn't show it, and almost immediately launched into an inquisition about his lodgings.

'Is it a guest house?' she asked.

'The landlady certainly doesn't treat us like guests,' Dan replied with one of his wide grins. 'More like lepers.'

Clara smiled, but it didn't reach her eyes, and Fifi could see she was getting agitated. 'What I meant was, does she provide breakfast and perhaps an evening meal?'

'No, all we get is the room, and what she calls "servicing" it. That only amounts to emptying the waste-paper basket and running a vacuum cleaner over the bits of the carpet that show.'

Clara wanted to know how Dan got his clothes washed and where he cooked meals. When he said he went to the launderette further up the road, and mostly ate in cafés, she launched into a lecture about the value of good nutrition and how he should learn to cook for himself.

'I can cook quite well,' Dan said. 'We were taught at the children's home. But I can't really be bothered after working all day.'

Fifi was relieved that Dan didn't reveal that the shared kitchen was overrun with mice, so dirty he could barely bring himself to make a cup of tea in there, and that the other lodgers would help themselves to any food he bought. Yet it was a shame that his explanation suggested he was bone idle.

From then on it seemed to Fifi that her mother was deliberately trying to make Dan feel gauche and ignorant. She brought up subjects as diverse as the invasion of Cuba, the building of the Berlin Wall, Ban the Bomb marches and Rudolf Nureyev's defection to the West.

Fifi expected that, like her, Dan wouldn't know enough about any of these things to discuss them, and her mother would be successful in making him look like a fool. But he did know something about each topic, enough at least to toss the ball into her father's court and get him to give his views.

He couldn't resist winding her mother up a little on the subject of Rudolf Nureyev, though. 'It would have been handy if he'd been a nuclear scientist or something useful, but a man who struts around the stage in tights showing off his carrot and onions doesn't seem much of a coup to me,' he said.

The boys laughed, Patty giggled, and even her father smiled. But her mother looked deeply offended and said snootily that she loved ballet and Rudolf was the greatest dancer of all time.

'Maybe, but I bet less than one per cent of the population ever go to the ballet, so why should he get to stay here? He probably lived like a king in Russia anyway.'

Fifi had noticed before that whenever Dan felt unsure of himself, he resorted to jokey remarks. To workmates or acquaintances in the pub this created the impression of a genial, easy-going person, but to articulate, serious-minded people like her parents, meeting him for the first time, it was more likely to come across as discourtesy.

By the time they sat down to tea, Fifi noticed that two red blotches had sprung up on her mother's cheeks, a sure sign she was boiling up to a rage. Fifi had no idea how to defuse the situation, for Dan was doing his best to be open, friendly and appreciative.

'Another piece of cake, Dan?' Clara asked towards the end of tea. She had pushed the boat out, showing off with home-cooked ham and salad, scones, cakes and trifle, and now she had the silver cake knife poised above the remains of the iced chocolate cake.

'I'd like to relieve you of it, but I haven't got any more room,' Dan said.

Fifi groaned inwardly. She knew her mother wouldn't take that in the spirit in which it was intended. Sure enough, she finally snapped.

'It's one of my best recipes, made with four eggs,' she said indignantly, her voice rising. 'I certainly don't need "relieving" of it, young man.'

'He wasn't being rude about your cake,' Patty said quickly.

'He meant he loved it, but he hadn't got room for any more. Isn't that right, Dan?'

'Yes, of course. I'm sorry if it came out all wrong, Mrs Brown,' Dan said apologetically.

'Every single thing you say comes out all wrong,' she snarled back at him. 'I've never met such an ignorant, cocky person as you.'

For a second there was complete silence in the dining room. Patty, Peter and Robin all stared at their mother in shock. Even their father looked stunned.

Fifi leaped to her feet so quickly she made all the china on the table rattle. 'And you are the rudest person I've ever met,' she spat at her mother. 'Come on, Dan, we'll go now.'

Dan didn't leap up; he rose from his chair calmly and slowly, wiping his lips on the napkin and placing it back on the table. His wide smile was gone and he looked devastated. 'If I seem ignorant and cocky, then I'm sorry,' he said, his voice a little shaky. 'But you'd decided I wasn't good enough for Fifi before you even met me, hadn't you?'

Dan only let Fifi go as far as the bus stop with him. There he kissed her goodbye and said she was to go home, despite her protestations. He knew that if she stayed out with him for the evening, it would only be more difficult for her when she returned. He also needed to be alone.

After waving goodbye to Fifi as the bus pulled away, he climbed up the stairs, got his cigarettes out of his pocket and lit one up. He felt sick with disappointment that the tea party had gone so badly wrong.

He hadn't expected the Browns to be overly welcoming. Fifi had said enough about her mother to give him the idea that she was something of a snob. He had been very aware of his rough accent, terrified that he'd slip up and lick his knife, or drop the dainty china tea cup. He knew he'd put Mrs Brown's back up when he joked about that ballet dancer, but he hadn't for one moment expected such vicious spite. He drew deeply on his cigarette and wondered what he should do.

He'd never been that struck on invitations to girlfriends' homes, and if anyone else had been like that to him, he would've said something cutting, then left, letting the girl decide whether it was to be him or her parents she cared about.

But Fifi was different. Right from the day he'd shared her table in that tea shop, he knew she was special. It wasn't just her looks, though he loved her silky blonde hair, those soft brown eyes and her slender yet shapely figure. She was different to other girls; she didn't rabbit on about her job, clothes or old boyfriends and, like him, lived for the moment. He knew perfectly well when she showed him where Gloucester Road was that it wasn't on her way home. She just wanted to make sure he found somewhere to live, and meanwhile get to know him better.

He loved the way she asked stuff like whether he'd got enough blankets on his bed or had had a proper dinner. When he had a bad cough she brought him medicine and told him he must wear a scarf when the wind was cold. She was thoughtful too about his money, never asking for the most expensive thing on the menu or expecting the best seats in the cinema.

Kissing her was like glimpsing heaven, and just the touch of her hand made him feel he'd lie down and die for her. But it was far more than fancying her like crazy. She'd filled all the lonely, empty places inside him; she made him think he could do anything, be anyone he wanted to be. He loved her classiness, her poise and warmth. But she wasn't tough;

she might insist he meant more to her than her parents, but once that mother of hers started to put the screws on, he doubted she'd be able to cope.

It was already difficult enough for them, for they had no place where they could go to be alone together. Snogging in doorways and bus shelters soon lost its appeal, especially when it was cold or wet.

Fifi had made it quite clear that she intended to remain a virgin until she got married, and he respected her for that, even if in the past he'd always got his way with girls. He wanted her desperately; sex was on his mind from first thing in the morning till he went to sleep, but because he loved her, he'd been prepared to wait.

But today he'd seen that her parents would never welcome him as a son-in-law. Fifi might be old enough not to need their consent and perhaps she'd say she didn't care about getting their blessing either. But he wouldn't feel right about that; in a few years' time it might come as a wedge between them.

He was left in a no-win situation. He wanted her for ever, and he supposed too that he really wanted to be part of her family.

Her brothers were okay, a bit dopey and lacking in any sparkle, but they might have improved after a couple of pints. Patty was every bit as sweet as Fifi said; she didn't have any side to her. As for her father, well, Dan had soon worked out how he could win him over, because he wasn't practical; he could've fixed the swaying back-garden fences for him, mended the roof on their summer house, and rebuilt the front-garden wall which was crumbling. Brainy blokes always appreciated anyone who could do such jobs.

But her mother was a very different kettle of fish. It wasn't just that she wanted Fifi to have a husband out of the top drawer, there was something much more behind her attitude. Dan would lay money on the fact that Clara married Harry Brown because her parents virtually selected him for her. She'd had four children in about six or seven years, probably never even enjoyed sex, and now when she saw her beautiful elder daughter in love she was probably riddled with jealousy.

The funny thing was that he felt for her. Clara had obviously been a very good mother, but now her children were all of an age where they would leave home, perhaps she was getting panicky about what she'd be left with. She was still quite young and very attractive, but if she'd never had any great passion, or even much fun, who could really blame her for thinking she'd been cheated?

Twice this afternoon she'd alluded to how difficult Fifi had been when she was little, which suggested Clara had never quite got over it. He'd wanted to ask her about it, but he hadn't quite dared. Fifi seemed to enjoy knowing she'd been such a pain, and that probably made the situation worse. Dan could see there were many issues that needed thrashing out between them, but sadly they were both equally stubborn and so he suspected they would never resolve their differences.

Dan wondered what was going on now. Clara could hardly ban Fifi from seeing him. He didn't think she'd be stupid enough to throw her out either, for she'd know Fifi would run straight to him. So all that was left was to give her the cold shoulder in an attempt to wear her down.

He sighed deeply. As a kid he'd had plenty of that kind of treatment, which was worse than being given a good hiding. And, as he remembered, it worked. In a few weeks Fifi would be putty in her mother's hands.

*

'It's only a shower. It'll stop soon,' Dan said optimistically. He wasn't that worried by the heavy rain, but he was concerned that Fifi hadn't said a word since they'd taken shelter under a large tree. He was afraid she was about to tell him that she didn't want to see him any more.

The awful tea party was months ago, and there were times when Dan wished he'd stuck to his guns when he had tried to end it a few days later. He had felt then that it would be best for Fifi as her mother wasn't ever going to accept him, and in the long run that would split them up anyway.

But Fifi had been adamant that her parents would come round before long, and that if they didn't she'd leave home anyway. Dan had wanted to believe her on both counts, but it was the end of August now, and they were no further on. Clara Brown hadn't budged an inch, and Fifi hadn't moved out.

As far as Dan was concerned, as long as Fifi loved him and he could still see her, he was content. But as the weeks passed he could tell she was growing more and more unhappy, however well she tried to hide it.

He guessed, though Fifi made light of it, that her mother was constantly on her back. On several Sunday mornings when he'd met her she'd had puffy eyes and a blotchy face and he knew that there had been a row at home the night before.

He could see she wasn't sleeping well as she often had shadows under her eyes; she picked at food and she had lost weight. He couldn't bear the thought that she was suffering because of him.

She had cut herself off from all her old friends. While this was partly because she wanted to be with him rather than with them, the main reason was because she felt she couldn't trust them. It seemed that one or two of them had passed a few confidences on to their mothers, and in turn they'd been repeated to Clara. Fifi felt betrayed by such disloyalty. Her brothers had accused her of causing trouble at home, and now the only person she had left on her side was Patty.

Today they'd come out to Leigh Woods for a walk. It had been bright sunshine when they got off the bus by the Suspension Bridge, but as soon as they entered the woods the heavens opened. Dan felt she was brooding now, almost certainly thinking that her whole life had gone wrong since she met him.

'A penny for them,' he said lightly, putting his arms around her and drawing her closer to him.

'They aren't worth a farthing,' she said glumly.

'That bad, eh?' he said. 'Can't we try doing magic eyes and see what that does?'

'I've tried that on Mum, but even if I could remove her snobbishness, tweak her suspicious nature and paint her dark soul sparkling white, I'd still be left with a carping dragon,' she said, trying hard to smile.

'I didn't mean doing magic eyes on her,' Dan said. 'I meant the other possibilities, like you getting a flat with some other girls. Or you just thinking about getting a bedsitter again. Just think how good it would be if we had somewhere nice to be alone together.'

'Umm,' Fifi murmured, burying her head in his chest. There was hardly an hour in the day when she didn't wish she was brave enough to throw all caution to the wind and get a room somewhere. She told Dan that her reasons for not doing so were because of the cost, because she was afraid of burning all her bridges with her family, and even that she was nervous of living alone. But while they were all considerations, they were also excuses, for her real reason for not leaving home was because she knew that the moment she was alone with Dan they would become lovers.

She dreamed of little else, she wanted him more than life itself, but she was afraid of what that might bring. Two girls from her school had had to get married because they were pregnant. She'd seen the hardships they'd had to go through, and their parents' disappointment, and she'd always vowed it would never happen to her. While she no longer cared about disappointing her parents, or even infuriating them, she certainly wasn't inclined to give her mother any further ammunition to shoot Dan down with. Nor did she want to start married life under a cloud.

It was intolerable at home now. There was no let-up in her mother's digs about Dan and her comments that Fifi was making the biggest mistake of her life. Mostly she managed to ignore her, but every now and then Fifi would retaliate, and it turned into a full-scale row. Each time it happened she was shocked by her mother's venom; anyone overhearing her would assume that Dan was a serial criminal, or had done something unspeakable to Clara. The only way to avoid these scenes was to stay out as much as possible.

All through this summer she had lived for the time spent with Dan, yet happy as they were together, the strain of knowing she'd have to go back home at night often spoiled the good times. Fifi had used all her ingenuity to find things to do together at the weekends that didn't cost much – picnics, long walks, a day trip to Weston-super-Mare or Bath. But when the weather was bad they were still stuck with pubs or the cinema.

Now it was raining again, here they were in a sopping-wet wood, and once more she was hiding what was really going on to spare Dan's feelings. She had cut herself off from her friends and her family because she loved him. But she didn't think she could live this way much longer.

'Give me a kiss then, I'll cheer you up,' he said, tilting her face up to his.

As always when Dan kissed her, Fifi was immediately aroused, and as his hands slid up beneath her blouse, groping for her bra fastening, she found herself arching against him, wanting the thrill of his touch. But she also knew what came with it; they became more and more excited, and when she was forced to back away, they were both left with a feeling of let-down.

'Don't, Dan,' she murmured, pushing his hands away from her breasts, but remaining glued to him.

'I'm only human, Fifi,' he said with a sigh. 'I can't think about anything else but touching you.'

Fifi wriggled away from him and got up from the ground, shaking off the damp leaves stuck to her skirt.

'What are we going to do?' she asked angrily. 'We spend all our time wandering around with nowhere to go. It's going to get even worse when winter comes. Couldn't we just get married and be done with it all?'

Dan got up and came up behind her, putting his arms around her waist and kissing the back of her neck. 'We could, but what about your parents?'

'I really don't care what they think any more,' Fifi sighed. The truth was that she felt she hated her mother now, but she couldn't bring herself to admit it openly. 'It's my life; I should be able to marry anyone I want. If they can't be happy with that, then there's something wrong with them.'

'We could go to the registry office and book a date,' Dan said. 'Maybe if you just told them when it was, they'd come round?'

Fifi shook her head. 'I could imagine my mum locking me in the bedroom on the day. If we were to do it, it would have to be in secret and we'd tell them afterwards.'

Even in her most desperate moments, this option had never presented itself, but the moment she'd said the words, she suddenly realized it was the answer to everything. She turned in Dan's arms, took his face between her two hands and smiled. 'Let's do it! What's to stop us? As soon as we've booked it – I think you have to give three weeks' notice – we could find a flat for us ready to move in afterwards.' All at once she was so excited that ideas came spilling out. 'Wouldn't it be lovely to have a home of our own? Me cooking for you, you doing the place up. We wouldn't waste so much money on going out for meals and drinks, we'd be snug as bugs all through the winter!'

Her excitement was infectious and Dan caught it. 'I can't think of anything better than waking up with you in the morning and coming home again at night to you,' he said, his eyes shining. 'We could save so much money if we didn't have to keep spending it on pictures and pubs.'

'I've got about thirty pounds in the bank now,' Fifi said excitedly. 'That's more than enough to buy some bed linen, crockery and stuff. Let's go down to the registry office now and ask about it!'

Dan kissed her. 'It's still pouring,' he reminded her, amused at her impetuosity. 'And they'll be really busy on a Saturday anyway. You could go in on Monday in your lunch hour. I don't suppose we need anything more than our birth certificates.'

Fifi's face clouded over for a moment, as she remembered her mother kept the whole family's in a box in her bedroom.

'Problem?' Dan asked.

'I'll have to raid Mum's special box. But that's okay, I

expect I can do it on Sunday while she's getting the lunch ready. But what about you? Have you got one?'

He nodded. 'Yeah, they gave me that, a bible and a fiver when I left the children's home. I've got the distinction of having two unknown parents. I was registered by the police, I think. I suppose one of them named me.'

Fifi looked at him askance. Even though she knew he'd been abandoned as a baby, it hadn't occurred to her what that really meant, or that his name had just been made up by someone else.

'Don't look like that,' he said, and laughed. 'It could have been worse; they could have called me Oliver Twist or something.'

'I wonder why your mother left you,' she said thoughtfully.

'Lack of money, I expect.' He sighed. 'It was 1937, the Depression and all that. I was only a couple of days old, so she must have been absolutely desperate. The police never traced her, so that suggests she had me all alone.'

Fifi shuddered. Just the thought of giving birth alone, without help, was too ghastly to dwell on, let alone thinking about his mother's state of mind. 'Oh, Dan,' she said softly, stroking his cheek tenderly. 'Poor you!'

'Poor me?' he chuckled. 'With someone as lovely as you going to be my wife? But you've got to give it some more thought, Fifi. It's a huge step, and you've got to be sure you want to do it for something more than putting two fingers up to your mother.'

'That's not why I want to do it,' she insisted, but laughed because she knew it was the ultimate revenge. 'It's only because I love you too much to want to waste any more time.'

'Even if your parents cut you off for ever?'

'The way they are at the moment I'd be quite glad,' she said firmly. 'Anyway, once they see a fait accompli, they'll come round.'

'I really hope so, sweetheart,' he said, cuddling her. 'But we can't count on it.'

'This one looks so very elegant, madam,' said the saleswoman in Bright's department store in Clifton as she zipped up the back of Fifi's dress. 'And with the little jacket you won't be chilly.'

Fifi put on the short fitted jacket and looked critically at herself in the mirror. It was by far the best outfit she'd seen, cream light-weight wool, and the dress had the little pleats around the bottom of the skirt that had become so fashionable since the Twist started. It didn't look obviously weddingy either, so she could wear it afterwards.

'I could hold it for a day or two if you want a friend's or your mother's opinion,' the woman said. She was about fifty and rather stout, with a flame-red beehive that made her look like a pantomime dame. She was beginning to look bored, clearly thinking Fifi was only a time-waster, for she'd tried on almost everything in her size, and she'd already had this one on twice before.

'No, I'll take it,' Fifi said. 'It's a bit more than I wanted to pay, but it *is* right.'

'Very wise, madam,' the woman said ingratiatingly. 'You looked lovely in all of them; you have such a good figure. But this one looks stunning.'

Fifi left the shop and hurried on down Park Street back to work. She'd managed to get two hours for lunch, but she'd have to make up the time tomorrow. Her head was reeling with all the things she still had to do with only a week to go, and the secrecy involved. But now she had her

44

wedding outfit and a flat, she thought she might be able to calm down.

No one, not even the people at work, knew she was planning to marry on 20 September. Dan had told his foreman, and he and his wife were going to be their witnesses. Tonight after work she'd take the new outfit up to the flat, along with a small bag of clothes she'd smuggled out from home this morning.

The flat was the biggest joy, for they'd been really lucky to get it. They'd been to see dozens, and most were horrible or far too expensive, and they were getting worried they wouldn't find anything in time. But two days ago it just happened that Mr Pettigrew, a landlord who used the firm of solicitors she worked for, came into the office, and she overheard him telling her boss that he had a vacant flat in one of his properties in Kingsdown.

Kingsdown was considered rough by some people, but only because it was all big old houses which had been divided up into flats, and lots of students lived there. But it was within walking distance down the hill from the city centre, and a lively place.

She waylaid Mr Pettigrew when he was leaving the office and asked if he'd consider her as a tenant. He seemed delighted to think he might not need to advertise the flat, and arranged to let her see it when she finished work.

It was only one room, with a tiny kitchen and bathroom, but it was clean and bright, with views right over Bristol. She paid the deposit and advance rent straight away and he gave her the keys. Fifi was so excited she ran almost the whole way down to Dan's in Gloucester Road, and arrived so out of breath she could barely speak.

This Saturday they intended to go shopping for all the things they needed in the flat. She could hardly wait to make up the double bed with their own sheets and blankets, put food in the cupboards and hang her clothes in the wardrobe. A week from today Dan would be carrying her over the threshold as his bride.

It was a bit sad they'd have no friends at the wedding, but having cut herself off from her old ones earlier in the summer when their mothers began talking to Clara, Fifi didn't dare contact them now, in case the same thing happened again. But maybe they could have a little party later on at the flat, so they could all get to know Dan.

She'd always imagined getting married in church, bells ringing, the organ playing and Patty as her bridesmaid. But she was so excited about leaving home for good, making meals for Dan and having a little home of their own, that the lack of wedding presents, a honeymoon and all the other trappings just didn't seem important.

There was a nip of autumn in the air now; the leaves on the trees were beginning to change to gold and russet. She couldn't wait to be snuggled up by the fire with Dan instead of walking around the streets or sitting in a smoky pub.

On the morning of 20 September, Fifi sat and ate her cornflakes for breakfast as if it was any other work day. Her father was sitting on the other side of the kitchen table reading his paper, and her mother was rushing about as she always did in the mornings, making toast, feeding the cat, opening mail, now and then going out into the hall to shout to Peter and Robin to make them hurry up. Patty had already gone to work.

Fifi had thought of nothing but this day ever since they booked the wedding at the registry office. But now it had come, and she knew she wouldn't be coming back this evening, she was scared. Everything suddenly seemed to be so dear to her. The larder door covered in old photographs, some right back from when she was a toddler. The drying rack up on the ceiling, as always full of drying or airing clothes. She knew that if she were to lift the lid of the three-tier cake tin it would hold flapjacks, gingerbread or maybe a Victoria sandwich. In future she'd have to make her own breakfast, wash and iron her clothes and Dan's too. Everything from toothpaste to washing powder would need to be bought by her.

She glanced at her mother. As always she was fully dressed, right down to proper shoes; she never slopped around in slippers and a dressing-gown. She was looking in the larder, making a list of things she needed from the grocer's. She had probably already decided what they would be having for the evening meal tonight.

Fifi wondered if she'd cry when she got the call to say her daughter was now Mrs Reynolds and wouldn't be coming home any more. It was odd that the thought of her mother being angry didn't bother her at all, but she couldn't bear the thought of tears.

'You'd better get a move on, Fifi, or you'll be late,' Clara said, for once without her more customary sharpness. 'You look a bit pale this morning. Are you feeling all right?'

'I'm fine,' Fifi replied, drinking the last of her tea and getting up. 'Thank goodness it's not raining this morning, I've got to work wet every day this week.'

She felt guilty now. She wasn't going into the office at all. First she was going to the hairdresser's, then to pick up her corsage of flowers, finally to the flat to change into her wedding clothes and wait for the taxi she'd ordered to take her to the registry office in Broadmead. Her father ought to be in that taxi with her, and Patty too, wearing a new dress. Could she really do it all on her own?

'I'm going to make a steak and kidney pie for dinner tonight, so for goodness' sake come straight home instead of hanging around to meet that worthless article.'

At that spiteful order from her mother Fifi snapped out of her sentimental mood. 'Why did you have to spoil the day by saying something so nasty?' she asked.

Clara looked at her contemptuously. 'You spoil every day for me by lusting after a piece of filth like that. But believe you me, the moment you tell him you're carrying his child, you won't see him for dust.'

For a second Fifi was tempted to slap her mother's face. But she resisted; what she intended to do later would hurt her far more. Besides, she didn't give a damn about this house or her parents any more. She was glad she would never have to spend another night here.

'You are so wrong about Dan,' she said, her eyes filling with tears. 'It makes me wonder what kinds of filth you mixed with before you met Dad; you seem to know an awful lot about it.'

'Only you would jump to that conclusion,' her mother retorted haughtily. 'Now get off to work or you'll be late.'

Later at the hairdresser's Fifi was nervous that someone who knew her would come in and ask why she wasn't at work. She painted her nails pink while she was under the dryer and tried very hard to think only about the night ahead with Dan. But her thoughts kept straying to Patty.

She would be very hurt that Fifi hadn't confided in her. She would probably never understand that it was because Fifi didn't want her in the firing line of her parents' anger.

At half past one, with just fifteen minutes until the taxi arrived, Fifi had stomach cramps with nervousness. Alone in her new flat, everything seemed so strange. She'd had a bath, put on her new outfit and makeup and pinned the pink rose spray to her jacket. But now, completely ready, her pink 'Jackie Kennedy' pill-box hat secured firmly to her hair, stockings and shoes on, she had suddenly become frightened.

The double bed, made up with new bed linen, and covered with a dark blue candlewick bedspread, seemed almost threatening. What if she didn't like sex? Suppose Dan did something to her that she didn't like?

She could remember a woman at work telling her and the other girls that on her wedding night her new husband wanted her to put his penis in her mouth. All the girls had laughed because she said, 'It wasn't his thing I minded so much, but all the attachments.'

Yet even through the laughter Fifi had felt disgusted that a man would want his wife to do that. She was sure she'd be sick.

Growing up with two brothers, Fifi had always known exactly what the male anatomy was like, and there had been several men, Dan included, who'd got her to hold their penises, so it wasn't going to be shock and horror when Dan stripped off. But suppose it wasn't lovely, as she imagined now? What if it really hurt?

To take her mind off such things, she opened the fridge and checked that the champagne Dan had bought at the weekend was really cold. It was funny looking at all the other stuff in there, butter, cheese, bacon and eggs. She hoped she wouldn't mess up the first breakfast she cooked him, she so much wanted everything to be perfect. But she knew she was a hopeless cook; her mother always said she couldn't even boil an egg. Maybe she should have warned Dan about that?

Right now that didn't seem to be as important as the clothes and personal belongings she'd left at home. So far she'd only been able to bring small bags of stuff so her mother wouldn't notice anything had gone. Would she let her back into the house later to collect more?

The doorbell made her jump; she grabbed her handbag and gloves and rushed to the door, only pausing momentarily to check once more in the mirror. She looked fine, though a bit pale. She just wished she had someone to go with her.

Chapter three

'You look gorgeous and I love you,' Dan whispered as the registrar pronounced them man and wife. 'Tonight I do intend to eat you.'

Fifi giggled at the reminder of Dan's very first words to her. 'You're supposed to kiss me, not talk dirty,' she whispered back.

All her stomach cramps and nervousness were gone. The moment she saw Dan in his new navy blue suit, waiting at the door of Quaker Friars registry office, all her doubts vanished. Now she was Mrs Reynolds and their life together was going to be wonderful.

Dan's foreman, Mike, a short but burly man in his forties, came forward to congratulate them both, with his wife Sheila, wearing a red hat, just one step behind him.

'Perhaps he'll be able to keep his mind on the job in future,' Mike joked. 'He's been off with the fairies for months.'

Sheila kissed Fifi's cheek. 'We both hope you'll have a long and happy life together,' she said. 'Dan's a good man, hardworking and very honest. He'll make a fine husband.'

'Husband': that word seemed so strange to Fifi. It was one she associated with older people in cardigans, with thinning hair, mowing the lawn. Dan looked like a film star today, his dark hair neat from a recent hair-cut, his cheeks as smooth as silk, and he smelled of Old Spice. She didn't think he'd ever succumb to slippers or cardigans.

'Put me down,' Fifi pleaded as Dan continued to carry her up the second flight of stairs. He was panting from the effort and she was afraid he was going to drop her.

'I'll carry you over both thresholds,' he insisted. 'Just be glad I'm not doing it caveman-style, dragging you by the hair.'

Fifi unlocked the door, and Dan turned sideways to get her in without banging her head or legs. Kicking the door shut behind him, he carried her across the room and dropped her on the bed.

'There you are, Mrs Reynolds, and there you will stay till Monday morning.'

Fifi laughed. 'I can't cook meals from here,' she said.

'I shall be waiting on you hand and foot,' he said, taking off his suit jacket and opening the fridge to get out the champagne. 'By Monday morning you will realize you have married a man of many talents.'

'You are extremely talented,' Fifi murmured sleepily a couple of hours later as she snuggled into his shoulder. It seemed ridiculous now that just this morning she'd been scared of making love. It had been wonderful, the best feeling in the whole world. She could happily stay in bed the whole three days till Monday.

They had drunk the champagne with Dan's radio playing softly in the background, and then he'd begun kissing her, peeling off her clothes bit by bit. She'd had many dreams since she met him of sensitive and gentle fingers stroking and probing her, and she'd wake to find she was touching herself. But Dan's touch was far more thrilling, just as sensitive and gentle, but confident, loving and so sensual that she found herself moaning with pleasure. There was a moment when she felt a stab of jealousy, for she knew he must have learned this skill from another woman. But that moment passed, for how could she be angry about how he gained his experience when he was transporting her to heaven?

By the time he moved on top of her to enter her, she wanted it as much as he did. It hurt a little, but not enough to put her off, and she wanted the glorious sensations to go on for ever.

'It takes a little practice for women to come,' he murmured lovingly afterwards. 'Please don't ever pretend it's happened to try and please me. We have to work at that together.'

Until he said that Fifi imagined that was as good as it got, but clearly he knew better. 'How would I know if it happened?' she whispered back.

'You'll know, I promise you,' he said with a low chuckle.

Fifi woke a little later, to see it was dark outside. They hadn't drawn the curtains earlier, but as the flat was high on a hill overlooking the centre of Bristol, there was plenty of golden light coming in from street lamps.

She looked at her watch and saw it was eight o'clock, and suddenly she thought of her parents waiting for her at home. She could just imagine her mother's face tight with irritation that she hadn't come straight home from work.

Reluctantly she crept out of bed, leaving Dan sleeping peacefully. If she didn't phone them now and get it over with, she'd never be able to relax tonight.

There was a pay-phone in the hall downstairs. She fumbled for her housecoat which she'd left on the floor, found some change and went barefoot down the stairs.

Patty answered the phone. 'You'd better have a good excuse for missing dinner, Mum's savage,' she warned Fifi.

She was tempted to ring off as Patty called her mother, but there was a mirror by the phone and her reflection gave her more confidence. Her hair, so neat earlier today, was all tousled, but there was a glow to her; she reminded herself her new name was Felicity Reynolds and resolved not to be intimidated.

'So where are you?' her mother said, without any preliminaries. 'I told you to come straight home.'

'Dan and I got married today, Mum,' Fifi said. 'We've got a new flat in Kingsdown.'

There was a sharp intake of breath, then silence.

'You married him?' her mother said eventually, as if she didn't believe what she'd heard.

'Yes, at quarter past two at Quaker Friars. I'm sorry if it's a shock. But it's what we wanted.'

'How could you throw your life away on him?' her mother exclaimed, her voice rising with agitation. 'He'll pull you down to his level.'

'Don't speak about Dan like that,' Fifi said, a flush of anger rising up within her. 'You don't know him, but I do, he's wonderful and I love him.'

'How could you do this to us?' her mother asked, her voice cracking. 'After all you put us through when you were a child! People said I should put you in an institution, but I didn't, and this is how you repay me for all my patience and care.'

The claim about an institution was something Fifi hadn't

heard before and she wanted to challenge it and find out if it was just an hysterical exaggeration or the truth. But her wedding night wasn't the time for such things, and a draughty hallway wasn't the right place either. 'I couldn't help how I was as a small child,' Fifi retorted. 'Any more than I could help falling in love with Dan.'

'Rubbish!' Clara snapped. 'It's not love. It's just animal sex! I know it is. I could see that written all over him.'

It was tempting to say the sex had been pretty good so far, but Fifi was suddenly too upset to make any clever retorts. 'You don't know what you are talking about, Mother,' she said sharply. 'Please don't try to make something grubby out of this. I told you I loved Dan months ago. He was the man I wanted to marry, and I've done it. I would've preferred to have had a blessing from you and Dad, but I can live without it.'

'You've made your bed, now you can lie in it,' her mother snapped. 'Don't come crying to us when he gets in trouble or he deserts you for some common tart more suitable for him. I'm finished with you.'

Fifi could only stare at the receiver as her mother slammed the phone down.

'Come back to bed, sweetheart.'

Fifi looked up and saw Dan above her on the stairs. He was wearing only his jeans and his deeply tanned, muscular chest looked powerful and reassuring. But the sad expression on his face told her he'd been there for long enough to get the gist of what had been said. Tears filled her eyes and she ran to his arms.

'She will come round, she's just shocked, that's all,' he said comfortingly as he hugged her tightly.

'I didn't do anything wrong, I just married the man I love,' she wept. 'Why is she so horrible about that?'

'Maybe she wasn't lucky enough to ever feel the way we do,' Dan suggested. 'But don't let her spoil what we've got, it's our honeymoon, remember.'

That night as Fifi lay in Dan's arms she told herself she didn't care about her parents. They were stupid snobs, and she could do perfectly well without them. She was glad she hadn't got to go home any more, she had her own one now and she was blissfully happy. She and Dan would prove to them that they were wrong.

Six weeks later, Patty sat back on the couch in the Kingsdown flat and grinned broadly at Fifi. 'Stop worrying about Mum's feelings,' she said in answer to her sister's question about how things were at home. 'Just think how happy you've made me by letting me have the bedroom all to myself.'

Fifi felt a surge of affection for her sister. If Patty was hurt she wasn't told about the wedding, she'd never showed it. On the Monday following, despite all hell having broken out at home following Fifi's phone call, and orders that no one was to break rank and speak to their sister, Patty turned up at Fifi's office, bringing her a canteen of cutlery for a present.

She hugged Fifi and wished her happiness, and said she had liked Dan right from the start. Then she'd asked what Fifi had worn, who was there and if they'd had any other presents. When Fifi admitted there were only two guests and all they'd had was an electric kettle from Dan's workmates, Patty hugged her again and said maybe they could have a blessing in church one day when Dan had proved he wasn't such a bad choice.

Since then Patty often popped in on her way home from

work, diplomatically skirting round what was being said at home, admiring everything they had done to their flat, and being happy for them.

Dan liked Patty a great deal, and it had pleased them both when she found a boyfriend herself. In just three weeks, she had begun to lose weight and her acne was getting better. Dan said he couldn't wait to meet the man responsible for it, but as yet Patty was too nervous to introduce him to anyone.

'Especially not Mum,' she laughed. 'I'm afraid she'll jinx it for me.'

'Make him carry garlic and a crucifix when he gets invited to tea,' Dan suggested. 'And maybe a couple of pints of holy water too.'

Fifi tried very hard to treat her mother's attitude in the same light-hearted way as Dan did, but she often shed a few tears about it in private. She felt so angry and indignant that he'd never been given a chance to show everyone what a wonderful person he was. Every time Patty came round she remarked on how homely the flat was, and much of that was down to Dan's efforts.

He was always bringing home things he'd found in junk shops. He liked a bargain, so he was always attracted to the damaged or ugly things that were cheap, and he did his magic eyes thing, believing he could transform them into something beautiful.

Sometimes he succeeded. A hideous old bookcase had been transformed with a coat of pale blue paint; a coffee table with a new tile top looked fabulously expensive, yet had cost him only three shillings. But Fifi was hoping he might accidentally break the china shepherdess ornament he was trying to mend, and that he'd decide the cuckoo clock was too irritating to keep.

She bought fresh flowers every Friday night to put on their little dining table, hand-sewed pretty curtains for the bathroom, and painted red spots on some white enamel storage jars to hold their coffee, tea and sugar. They'd bought a lovely picture of a bluebell wood, two table lamps, and bright cushions to put on the bed. Fifi often thought that if her parents were to unbend enough to visit, they'd get a pleasant surprise.

It was Patty who bit by bit brought Fifi's belongings to the flat, her record-player, clothes, shoes and books, each time making a joke about how it left more room for her in their old room. While Fifi was delighted to have all her old belongings back with her, it saddened her too. It was as though the memories of her were being permanently erased from her family home.

Patty had only just left one evening when Dan arrived home, and right away Fifi knew something was wrong because he seemed distracted. While he had a bath, she warmed up the stew she'd made for him, and once he was eating it, she tackled him.

'You know this estate in Horfield will be finished by Christmas?' he finally blurted out. 'Well, I thought we'd be moving straight on to the site in Kingswood. But there's been a setback there, some problem with the planning department and an access road, so now we've got to go down to Plymouth.'

'You mean move there?' Fifi exclaimed. 'You can't, we've only just got this place, and there's my job.'

'I know,' Dan sighed. 'I suppose I'll have to get digs and just come home at weekends.'

'Oh no. I couldn't bear that,' Fifi said.

'Nor me,' Dan agreed. 'I told the boss how it was, but he

said that's all he's got, the one job in Plymouth, take it or leave it.'

'You mean you get the sack if you won't go?'

Dan shrugged. 'I took the job with Jackson's on the understanding we worked all over the place. If I want to stay here, I'll have to find a local firm willing to take me on.'

'How hard will that be?'

'Easy, I should think. There's loads of new developments in Bristol.'

'Then there's no problem.' Fifi beamed. 'I get to keep you here.'

'Happy Christmas, sweetheart!'

Fifi forced her eyelids to open. Dan was standing by the bed with just a towel around his waist, and he had a tray in his hands. 'Come on, look joyful, it's breakfast-time!' he said with laughter in his voice. 'Don't panic, I haven't got you anything unsuitable for a princess with a hangover.'

Reluctantly Fifi sat up and Dan put the tray across her knees. It was just grapefruit segments in a little glass dish with a glacé cherry on top, toast and a pot of tea.

She had been on top of the world and slightly drunk when she got home yesterday after the office party. She had tinsel in her hair and a bag of small presents from the other girls. Dan had arrived home soon after, also a little tight as it was his last day with Jackson's, and they decided to go out for the remainder of the evening to the Cotham Porter's Stores, a pub just around the corner from their flat.

The Porter's Stores was a cider house, and a bit run down, but it always had a good atmosphere because of the wide range of people who drank there, from serious cider drinkers with red noses to hard-up students and the immediate locals. Maybe drinking rough cider wasn't such a good idea after drinking spirits at work, but Fifi was fine until Robin, her younger brother, came in with a group of friends.

Overjoyed to see him, she left Dan and rushed over to Robin, and because she was a bit drunk and assumed he'd come looking for her, she flung her arms round him.

'Don't embarrass me in front of my friends,' he said coldly, nudging her away.

Fifi was so deeply hurt she couldn't think of a clever or cutting remark. Instead she said something about how she was only pleased to see him, and it was Christmas after all. Robin retorted that he wasn't pleased to see her drunk, and obviously she was going downhill fast since she married Dan.

Robin had always been a bit of a prig. If Fifi had been sober she would have given as good as she got. But Robin turned on his heel and left the pub without having even one drink. Fifi returned to Dan's side and ordered another cider.

She didn't tell Dan what had been said, but her good humour vanished and she drank quickly and silently, not even talking to Dan.

Later, she vaguely remembered being carried up the stairs over Dan's shoulder, and the next thing she knew was she was kneeling on the bathroom floor, head over the toilet, vomiting and telling him to go away.

By the time she came out of the bathroom, much more sober now, Dan was fast asleep in bed, but she was wide awake, very much aware it was the early hours of Christmas morning and for the first time in her life she wouldn't be sitting down later to a family lunch.

She and Dan had bought a tree and put up decorations everywhere, and until then she'd thought the flat looked like an enchanted grotto. But as she sat huddled up on the couch wrapped in her dressing-gown, thinking about what Robin had said earlier, the twinkling lights, tinsel and paper streamers all looked so garish in comparison to the elegant decorations her parents went in for. There was only a hand-ful of Christmas cards too, just from girls at work, and suddenly she felt an enormous sense of loss.

Christmas at home was always so jolly and noisy. Even when they'd all got too big to have stockings, they still crowded into their parents' room quite early in the morning and insisted on opening the presents. Neighbours would pop in during the morning for a drink, and there would be a record of carols playing on the radiogram. Sometimes her maternal aunts, Rose and Lily, would come up from Somerset with their husbands and children; other times Uncle Ernest, her father's brother, would come with his wife and two boys who were a similar age to Robin and Peter. After a huge dinner they'd play games, charades, Monopoly or Ludo.

This year there would be just her and Dan, no carols playing, no games. She had believed until now that she would be glad to be alone with Dan, that family gatherings were boring, yet all at once they seemed so dear and precious. She began to cry because she felt forlorn and cut off. If Robin was against her, that meant Peter probably was too, her father would always side with her mother, and that left only Patty. Her family had shrunk to one person who wouldn't even be able to visit over the holiday.

'Would you like an aspirin?' Dan asked, looking concerned.

Fifi forced herself to smile. 'No, I'm fine,' she said. 'I'm sorry I got so legless last night, and Happy Christmas.'

'Santa's been,' Dan said, pulling a bulky stocking out from under the bed. It was one of the white net ones, trimmed with red crêpe paper, that Fifi had often had as a child, and peeping from the top was a teddy bear in a red woolly hat.

'Oh, Dan,' she exclaimed, all at once aware he must have planned this weeks ago. 'I didn't think to make you one.'

'I didn't expect one,' he said, sitting down beside her on the bed and pouring her some tea. 'You are all I want for Christmas.'

'I have got you presents,' she said. 'Just not the stocking. I intended to get up before you and put them all under the tree. They're still in the sideboard where I hid them.'

'Eat your breakfast, then we'll open them,' he said, kissing her on the cheek. 'Our first Christmas together, that's very special.'

Fifi's eyes filled with tears. She wiped them away and laughed, saying it was because he was so sweet, but the truth was that she felt ashamed of herself. She could have thought of making Dan a stocking. And she shouldn't have spent half the night thinking about her old home and feeling sorry for herself.

Dan was taken on by a Bristol building firm the day after Boxing Day. He was ecstatic when he returned home, for the job was building a new rank of shops, and the site he would be working on was right in town. Just a walk from home, and better money than he'd been earning with Jackson's. He was due to start work on New Year's Day.

On New Year's Eve Fifi hurried home from work with two steaks and a bottle of Blue Nun. They had no plans to go anywhere special to see the New Year in, but some of the girls at work had said it was always like a big party up at the Victoria Rooms in Clifton. Apparently the previous year someone had put detergent in the fountains and the bubbles went right across the road. Fifi thought if Dan was agreeable they might walk over there to have a look.

Dan had the chips cooking and the table laid when she got in. He'd lit candles and he had Little Eva's 'Locomotion' on the record-player. He took Fifi's coat and hung it up, then grabbed the steaks and began grilling them, all the time singing and dancing to the music.

This was a new party piece, it was usually Elvis Presley he liked to do. He knew the words of all his songs, and he had Elvis's voice, gyrating hips and mannerisms down to a T. Often he would get Fifi crying with laughter when he did 'Teddy Bear'.

'Come on, baby, do the Locomotion with me,' he sang as he put the bread on the table and coming up behind her, made her turn her arms like pistons.

'Where's Elvis tonight?' she asked laughingly as the record finished.

'New year on its way in, new music,' he said. 'I've got to work on Cliff Richard, or Duane Eddy.'

'Duane Eddy doesn't sing,' she giggled. 'And you don't look anything like Cliff.'

'Then perhaps I'll be Ray Charles,' he said, and turning away, swiftly picked up two beer-bottle tops as impromptu sunglasses and burst into 'I Can't Stop Loving You'.

'Idiot,' she said affectionately. 'But let those steaks burn and I'll stop loving you.'

'I'm too full to go anywhere,' Fifi said with a groan as she staggered away from the table an hour later. She lay down on the bed, undoing the waistband on her skirt.

Dan looked at her and laughed. 'I thought you wanted to dance in the fountains!'

63

'That was before steak, chips and mushrooms,' she said. 'Do you really want to go out?'

Dan went over to the window. 'Well, I thought I did,' he said, a note of surprise in his voice. 'But it's snowing!'

'No!' Fifi exclaimed. 'You're just saying that to make me get up.'

'It is, and it's heavy too,' Dan insisted. 'Come and see.'

Fifi got up reluctantly. 'If you are having me on I'll punish you,' she said. But as she got to the window she gasped when she saw Dan was telling the truth.

There had never been any snow to speak of in Bristol, not since 1947. Fifi was seven then and she remembered going sledging day after day because the schools were closed, and building a huge snowman in the garden. Grown-ups harped on about that terrible winter for years after, but it had never been repeated. If snow did fall it was light and usually gone within a day or two.

'Good God,' she exclaimed as she watched it swirling against the window. 'It's like a blizzard.'

As they were on the second floor and it was dark, they couldn't see if it was settling on the ground.

'I won't be able to lay bricks if it does settle,' Dan said. 'Let's hope it's cleared by morning.'

When they woke the following morning the light in the room was grey and sinister and there was no sound of traffic in the distance. Fifi got up, and to her astonishment a thick carpet of snow lay over the whole of Bristol.

Her initial reaction was delight, for everything looked so beautiful, like an old-fashioned Christmas card scene. She called excitedly to Dan to come and look.

Like her he was entranced, but he looked worried too.

'I'll go down to the site, but the chances are there'll be no one there as I doubt if there's any buses running. Damn, this would happen just as I was starting a new job.'

'It won't last,' Fifi reassured him. 'Shame I only have to walk to work, I've got no excuse for not being there. We could've gone to Redland Park and played in the snow.'

Bristol's centre was virtually deserted. No buses were running and few people had even attempted to drive in as many roads into the city were impassable. Fifi was amused to see how the few very determined people who had braved the snow to get to their work were reacting. Bundled up in thick coats, boots, hats and scarves, they were acting like intrepid pioneers, yelling out warnings to others about areas they'd passed through that morning.

Fifi enjoyed her walk to the office, taking a childish delight in making footprints in clean snow. Everything looked so pretty; even waste ground that was normally an eyesore of rubbish and weeds had become a winter wonderland. But the sky was like lead and everyone was predicting there was more snow to come.

Only one of the solicitors and Miss Phipps, the accountant, had managed to get into the office, so at three in the afternoon as it began to get dark, they went home.

Dan was already there when Fifi got home, making a stew for their dinner. He looked glum and anxious as he told her that the foreman on the building site had told him there would be no work for the rest of the week, and unless the weather improved dramatically, he doubted there'd be any the week after either.

'Never mind,' Fifi said comfortingly. 'We can manage on my money.'

'I'm supposed to provide for you,' he said grumpily. 'It's not a very good start to the new year.'

The bad weather continued for several weeks, with many more heavy snowfalls, and Dan's spirits sank lower and lower when he couldn't go to work. Fifi was very sympathetic at first because she knew it hurt his pride to live on her wages. But as time went on, and she had to battle her way through snow and ice daily while he was home in the warm flat, irritation began to set in.

She didn't care that he wasn't bringing any money in, she just missed him being jolly and fun. There were no more Elvis impersonations, he had nothing to talk about, and each night when she got home, he had a glum face. He did all the shopping, cleaned the flat and cooked the dinner, but that only seemed to emphasize her shortcomings because he was far better at cooking and cleaning than she was, and an expert at economical meals.

Whenever she suggested they went out for a change, he always pointed out how cold and miserable it was outside. He was right of course, but the real reason he didn't want to go was because of the money. She ached to be in a noisy, lively pub, to see other people and have some fun, and she really missed her old friends.

She wished she hadn't been so hasty in dropping them all when she met Dan. She had always despised girls who abandoned their mates the minute they found a new man, yet she'd done just that. While it was true that a couple of them had made indiscreet remarks to their mothers, which had got back to hers, mostly she'd kept Dan all to herself because she didn't want to share him with anyone.

She realized now what a mistake that had been, for they could have been allies. Almost all their mothers were friendly with hers, and if they'd liked Dan, they would've talked Clara round. But by cutting herself off from everyone she'd inadvertently created the impression that there was something suspicious about Dan.

Yet even though Fifi knew she alone was responsible for losing her friends, now that she was feeling miserable, she found herself blaming Dan because he hadn't been welcoming one night when they all called round to the flat.

It was just after they'd got married, and a whole gang of them, including Carol, the friend Fifi'd stood up the night she met Dan, turned up drunk, late one night after the pubs closed.

She and Dan were just about to go to bed, and the flat was a bit of a mess. Dan said her friends were rude, and that it was obvious they'd only called round to check him out. He was curt with them because they were all staggering about, knocking things over and making a great deal of noise. Fifi was embarrassed when Dan asked them to leave, and she'd heard them making sarcastic comments about him as they lurched off down the stairs. She hadn't seen any of them since.

Even Patty didn't drop by now. While Fifi knew full well that this was only because of the bad weather, not through ill-feeling, it still made her feel entirely marooned and friendless.

Two weeks crept into three and four, still with no sign of Dan being able to start working again. Fifi found herself thinking wistfully about her old home, of Sunday roasts, of having her clothes washed and ironed for her. In bad moments she even found herself regretting rushing into marriage.

Towards the end of February, after Dan had been off work for seven weeks, he had a letter from the building company telling him that they no longer wanted him when work resumed on the site. They stated that the long layoff had resulted in them needing to make cutbacks and the most productive way to do this was to offer their more senior men overtime when work commenced again.

Dan was savage about it. 'Bastards!' he exclaimed. 'I could've got a job working in a warehouse or something all this time. What am I supposed to do now?'

'Get a job in a warehouse?' Fifi suggested without any sympathy.

'I'm a bricklayer,' he snapped at her. 'And a bloody good one. I don't want to be loading lorries or sweeping floors.'

'This bad weather can't last much longer,' she said hopefully, although the forecast was that it was here to stay for a while yet. 'With spring coming on, all building work will start again soon.'

'And meanwhile I've got to live like a pimp on your wages,' he ranted, red in the face with anger. 'I can't even afford to buy a television or go and have a couple of pints. Your parents will be delighted to be proved right about me.'

All at once they were rowing. Fifi snapped at him and said she was sick of him moping when none of this was her fault. Dan said she was like a spoilt child expecting that everything should be like fairyland. At every retort they got nastier to each other, bringing up anything they could think of, Dan bringing home junk, and Fifi's lack of housewifely skills.

'You're so untidy and messy,' Dan shouted at her. 'You think you're so high and mighty because your father's a sodding professor, but if it wasn't for me cleaning up we'd be living in a pig sty.'

'That would be the right place for you,' she hurled back at him. 'You eat with your mouth open, your elbows all over the table. You can't even hold a knife and fork properly.'

She was shocked at herself for saying something quite so vicious, but he didn't give her a chance to take it back.

'Well, I'm sorry if I offend you, Little Miss Perfect Manners,' he hurled at her, his eyes blazing, 'but while you were learning all that at your cosy little tea parties, I was having to work in the children's home's laundry and out in the grounds. You've lived in cloud cuckoo land all your bloody life, never had one day's hardship.'

That night was the first time they went to bed without kissing goodnight. Fifi lay curled up with her back to Dan, seething with resentment that he had dared to criticize her. She fully expected that he'd apologize and cuddle her, and when he didn't she became even more resentful.

She hadn't been able to buy herself any new clothes or get her hair done. She was fed up with having no television, not even a trip to the pictures. She'd given up everything for Dan, and this was how he repaid her.

The next three weeks were so miserable that Fifi even thought of going home. Dan was out all day looking for work, and when he could find nothing, not even a warehouse job, he got steadily more morose and sullen. There were more rows and angry silences, and they even stopped making love.

One evening, the night before Fifi's payday, the electricity went off soon after she got in from work. Neither of them had any money for the meter; they couldn't heat up the leftover stew from the night before for their dinner, or make a cup of tea. Without heat or light they were forced to go to bed.

Fifi began to cry because she'd spent her last few shillings on some stockings and a couple of magazines that lunchtime.

She felt guilty now that her selfishness meant Dan had to go to bed hungry and would have to start the next day without a cup of tea, or even hot water to shave. She blurted this out to him and said how sorry she was.

When he cuddled her and said it didn't matter, she was surprised to find his face was wet with tears too. 'It's not your fault,' he said. 'I've lived this way most of my life, but now it seems I'm making you live that way too.'

He held her tightly, smoothing her hair and telling her how much he loved her. 'But look what I've done to you! Your family and friends have cut you off; you're keeping me. I'm useless.'

Fifi said that wasn't true and that she'd rather be with him, even if they were penniless, than with anyone else in the world.

'There's nothing for it but to go to London to work,' he said dejectedly. 'I saw work there advertised at the Labour Exchange today. I'll go and get the details tomorrow first thing.'

Fifi said she couldn't bear that, but he stopped her with a kiss.

'Look, Fifi,' he said. 'I've got to do something before things get even worse. Let's face it, nothing's worked out since we got married.'

'It's only the job that's gone wrong,' she said.

'It's not and you know it,' he said softly. 'You miss your folks terribly, and all those friends who've dropped you. I could say that none of them are worth a light if that's how little they really care about you, but that would only start another row.'

'You aren't trying to say you're going to leave me?' she asked in panic.

'Don't be daft. I'd even put up with your mother sleeping

here in our bed rather than lose you. But we've got to find a way out of all this. What if we both moved to London and started all over again?'

'I couldn't go. There's my job,' she protested.

'A legal secretary would get more money in London,' he said. 'And I'll be earning more too. Just suppose I went up there alone and found us a flat, then you joined me when you were ready?'

Fifi thought about it for a moment. The thought of moving to London was very appealing. It was busy, exciting and with so much more going on than there was in Bristol. Once she might have been afraid to leave her friends, but they'd all vanished anyway, and away from here she wouldn't be reminded about her parents so much either.

'It *would* be an adventure,' she said eventually. 'Imagine us walking through Hyde Park on a summer afternoon, or going to Petticoat Lane on a Sunday!'

'It's dirty, noisy and fast,' he reminded her. 'They call people from the West of England "Swedes" and think we go about in smocks with straws hanging out of our mouths.'

Fifi giggled. 'They couldn't think that about you. They're more likely to ask where your bow and arrow is.'

'So will you think about it?'

'I have,' she said. 'Yes, we'll go. Just as soon as you've found somewhere for us to live.'

Suddenly it didn't matter that they were lying in the dark unable to even have a cup of tea. It didn't matter either that her family didn't approve of Dan. He was here lying next to her, his skin as silky as a child's, and she loved him. They would go to London and make a wonderful life for themselves. And to hell with everyone.

Chapter four

Fifi walked slowly up the stairs of 4 Dale Street, looking with trepidation at the horrible orangey-brown varnish on the doors, and wallpaper so old it was impossible to see a pattern. Dan was bounding on ahead, enthusiastically listing the advantages of Kennington. These seemed to be mainly that it was so central, just a couple of stops on the tube to the West End.

Fifi could see that it had once been a very good area, judging by the many imposing large houses on the main road. But just as St Paul's in Bristol had once been a good address until the middle classes moved out, the same seemed to have happened here. The big houses were now very dilapidated, their front gardens full of rubbish, and judging by the number of people lounging around on the front steps, they were mainly divided up into rabbit warrens of small flats and bedsitters.

Elsewhere Fifi had noticed yawning gaps where houses had been bombed during the war, and instead of being rebuilt the sites had become dumping grounds for old furniture and mattresses. She had also observed that although there were many shops, they all looked grubby and tired. She thought the council might as well have erected a sign saying 'Only the poor live here', for there were no quality shops, just a depressingly large number of fish-and-chip places, pubs and second-hand shops.

But even if parts of Kennington appeared to have had a more elegant past, Dale Street didn't. It looked as if it had been designed in Victorian times to house as many people as possible in the smallest space. The houses didn't even have front gardens.

'Here we are!' Dan said unnecessarily as he reached the last flight of stairs. 'It's almost entirely self-contained. I think the other tenants are quiet all the time, I didn't hear a sound the time I came before either.'

Fifi had been looking down at the worn sisal runner up the stairs, wondering how long it had been there. The house was clean, in as much as there was no dust or rubbish anywhere, and, as Dan said, very quiet, but to her it was little better than a slum.

At his words she looked up, and there on the landing, at the top of the last run of stairs, were an ancient cooker and an equally old sink with a small geyser above. This, she had to assume, was her new kitchen.

'I can put up a cupboard on the wall for all our pots and pans,' Dan said happily. 'I thought maybe I could fix up a fold-down table-top too, for a surface to prepare food. Then a towel rail and a small shelf for our washing things.'

Fifi came up the last few stairs and caught hold of his arm. 'I am *not* washing myself in a kitchen sink,' she exclaimed indignantly.

'No one will come up here but us, and I could build a folding screen from here to there,' he said, putting one hand on the banisters and the other on the wall. 'We'd be quite private then.'

'It would still be a kitchen sink. It's for dirty dishes and straining cabbage,' she retorted. 'I'm sorry, Dan, but I can't possibly live here.'

Dan's face fell. 'I know it's not what you're used to, Felicity. But it was the best I could do.'

He only ever used her real name when he thought she was being a snob, and mostly it was with a teasing note. But this time it was with real reproach.

'Oh, come on, Dan,' she wheedled. 'I know it's cheap, and that flats in London are like gold dust, but look at it! You really can't expect me to live somewhere as squalid as this.'

She didn't even want to look at the two rooms. What she'd seen already was more than enough to make her want to run out.

'Please just try to look at it with magic eyes,' Dan pleaded, reaching out to smooth her cheek, the way he always did when he was trying to get round her.

Fifi's spirits dropped even lower, for she knew now that when something needed Dan's magic eyes most normal people would turn it down flat.

'I'm trying,' she said wearily. She supposed as it was the top flat no one would be coming up the last flight of stairs but them. 'But don't you dare tell me we've got to buy a tin bath, and the lav's outside.'

'Of course there's a bathroom,' Dan grinned boyishly. 'Would I expect Princess Felicity to go without one? It's downstairs, and the only reason I said about washing up here is because we have to share it with the other tenants.'

'Well, I just hope there aren't dozens of them,' Fifi retorted, for she'd seen at least six doors on the way up through the three-storey house.

Dan had left for London during the last week in February to start work on a large housing development in Stockwell. The weather was still every bit as bad then, the whole country still in the grip of ice and snow, but it seemed the foreman knew a good worker when he saw one, and he gave Dan other work inside the almost completed houses because he didn't want to lose him. He even arranged digs for him near the site, and paid his train fare home at weekends.

Fifi hadn't minded being alone during the week at first. She'd meet up with Patty one night, go to the pictures with one of the girls at work on another, and the remainder of the time she spent reading, making food for the weekend and doing chores. She was so excited at the prospect of moving to London, day-dreaming about all the things they could do there, and each weekend she expected Dan to arrive home with news that he'd found a place for them.

But as the weeks passed and Dan still hadn't found a flat, she began to feel they would be living apart for ever. It wasn't that Dan didn't try. He bought the *Evening Standard* every day, and rushed to see all the flats in their price range that same evening. But all too often the flat would be gone before he got there, and those that were left either had landlords who didn't want a married couple, or were so awful that Dan had to turn them down.

He had his name down with countless letting agencies too, but he got the idea that landlords discriminated against men with jobs like his. Perhaps, too, they didn't really believe he had a wife, and thought he would have a succession of women coming in and out. As the weeks went by Fifi had seen him getting more and more dejected at his failure to find a home for them.

It was now early May. Spring had finally arrived with much-longed-for sunshine, and when Dan had rung her earlier in the week and jubilantly said he'd found a place at last and could borrow a van at the weekend to move her and their belongings, Fifi was overjoyed. She spoke to the landlord and her boss at the solicitors the very next day, and although the landlord insisted she gave him another week's rent in lieu of notice, her boss was really nice about it and said she could finish up at the end of the week.

Dan had admitted that Kennington wasn't the best of areas, and the flat was a bit crummy, but always the optimist, she had assumed that all it would need was a bit of cheering up with pictures and perhaps a lick of paint.

But she had burned all her bridges by giving up the old flat and her job, so she knew she really didn't have any choice. She had to accept this was her new home.

Dan opened the door of the living room. 'After you, Princess,' he said, making a comic, sweeping bow.

Fifi stifled a gasp of horror and desperately scanned the room looking for some attractive feature that she could praise. But there was nothing. Twelve square feet of scruffy patterned lino, hideous old floral wallpaper, and the kind of worn-out furniture people left out for the dustman.

'I know it's pretty grim,' Dan said, his voice subdued and troubled. 'But I didn't want us to be apart any longer. We can make it nice. Can't we?'

Fifi's heart melted just as it always did when he looked at her with imploring spaniel eyes. 'Look, it gets the afternoon sun,' she said, trying very hard to do magic eyes. The faded orange curtains didn't even reach the sill of the dirty window, but she could replace those. 'Once we get our things in here it will look quite different.'

Dan smiled in relief and moved over to kiss her. But as his arms went round her, an angry shout from the street below made them both move over to the window.

A girl of about seven was running up the road, hotly

pursued by an overweight woman with her bleached blonde hair in curlers.

'Come back 'ere, yer little bleeder!' she yelled angrily.

The child stopped running. She was crying and looked terrified. The woman reached her, caught her by the shoulder and slapped her round the face so hard that Fifi winced.

''Ow many times'ave I got to tell yer?' the woman ranted, dragging the girl back down the street by her ear. 'You do's what I tell you or else.'

As they reached the house opposite Dan and Fifi, the woman gave the child another thump around the head, then pushed her in through the front door, kicking her up the backside as she went.

The front door slammed behind them and Fifi looked at Dan questioningly, deeply shocked by what they'd witnessed.

'I expect she's a little sod,' Dan said thoughtfully. 'But I hate it when people lay into children.'

Fifi thought such blatant brutality needed reporting, but she was too stunned to comment. Her parents had never resorted to hitting her or her brothers and sister. They might be punished by being sent to bed, or having their pocket money docked, but never by anything physical.

'I hope that isn't an indication of what we can expect here,' Fifi said quietly, still looking out of the window. Dan had often said she was entirely ignorant of what life was like for people living on low wages, in poor housing, but if that was how they behaved she'd rather stay in ignorance.

The view from the window held no cheer. It was of a cul-de-sac, ending in a coal yard behind big gates, with seven three-storey terraced houses on each side. Even though it was a sunny day, the houses were too tall and the street too narrow to let in much sunshine. From her vantage point on the second floor, Fifi could see behind the gates into the coal yard, where a man was shovelling coal into sacks held open by a young boy. It was almost a Dickensian scene, for they were both as dirty as chimney sweeps, and she noted that all the brickwork in the street had become black with soot over the years.

Every house looked neglected. The one the woman and child had gone into didn't even have proper curtains, just a blanket or some such thing hung over a piece of wire. There were no flowers in tubs, not even a tree; in fact the street had a sinister, almost malevolent air about it. Could she really bear to live here?

'Forget what's out there,' Dan said from behind her, sliding his arms around her and nuzzling his chin on her shoulder. 'Come and see the bedroom. We could christen it straight away!'

As Dan kissed the back of her neck, his hands cupping her breasts, Fifi began to tingle all over. Since Dan went to London they were like honeymooners every weekend, often staying in bed most of Saturday. He'd only arrived back in Bristol early this morning to collect her and all their stuff, and once they were on their way to London, he kept telling her all the naughty things he was going to do to her once they were alone in the flat. It had aroused her so much that it was all she could do not to suggest they pulled off into a quiet lane to make love.

'There aren't any bedclothes,' she protested feebly as he shuffled her into the room next door. It was every bit as miserable as the living room, but at least the mattress on the old bed looked brand-new. 'We should go down and get our stuff in first.'

But his fingers were already unzipping her jeans and she could feel his erection pressing against her bottom. Perhaps if she just let herself sink into the bliss of being made love to, she might start thinking of this horrible place as home.

'You are so beautiful,' Dan whispered as he slid into her. 'I wish I could give you everything you deserve.'

Whatever other disappointments they'd encountered since they got married, lovemaking always made up for them. Dan could whisk her away on a magic carpet ride every time. She loved his slim but muscular body, the silkiness of his skin, the sensitivity of his touch.

Fifi pulled him close to her, covering his face with frantic kisses. 'I've got everything I want, I've got you,' she whispered back. She meant it too. Maybe this flat wasn't what she'd expected, but she was in London at last and she and Dan could start afresh.

Right from when she was a child, visits to the cinema had given Fifi tantalizing images of America, with ultramodern houses, flashy cars and a standard of life so different to the post-war austerity she knew. By 1960, when she was twenty, she had got the idea from the news and magazines that London was becoming like this too. It infuriated her that new fashions, films or even music took such a long time to filter down to the West Country, and she'd resolved to move to London then so that she'd be at the hub of everything.

As it turned out, a secure job and various boyfriends sapped her desire to make the break. But now at last she'd made it here, and she just knew there were going to be untold opportunities for her and Dan. Wages were higher and there were far more prospects for advancement.

Yet it was the idea that they could start off all new and shiny, free from class snobbery, which appealed to her even more. No one knew her, or her parents, here. There was no one to whisper behind their hands that she, a professor's daughter, had married a bricklayer. They could live how they wanted, go where they wanted, with no one watching for them to fail.

She did of course hope that one day her parents would come round about Dan. But a hundred miles away from them, she wouldn't be holding her breath for it. London was going to be a huge adventure, and she would show her family just what she and Dan were made of.

Later that same afternoon Dan and Fifi were being watched from three separate windows in Dale Street as they unloaded the borrowed van.

Yvette Dupré in the ground-floor flat of number 12, across the street, was a dressmaker. With her sewing-machine in front of her window, she saw most of the comings and goings in the street.

Seeing such an attractive young couple moving in was a real event, but she was unsure whether it pleased or worried her. The blonde girl was so slim and elegant in her jeans and hand-knitted jumper. Her husband was devilishly handsome, gypsy-like with his dark hair and angular cheekbones. She could see they were deeply in love by the way they laughed together and touched each other. It made her smile just to watch them.

Yvette had little to smile about in her life. She was thirty-seven but looked far older. Her once thick dark hair was peppered with grey, and she pulled it back tightly from her face into a severe bun at the base of her neck. She wore old-fashioned, drab clothes, and lived a very reclusive and lonely life. Her only real pleasure was her work, which she took great pride in.

Like most of her neighbours, she'd come to live in Dale

Street out of desperation. Old Mrs Jarvis, who had lived at number 1 since the street was built in 1890, had told her that in those days everyone kept a maid. Yet Yvette found it hard to believe that it had ever been a smart address.

The young couple were laughing about a bag which had spilled its contents out on to the pavement and the sight reminded Yvette poignantly of similar scenes in her native Paris when she was a girl. She used to sit in the window, just as she was doing now, to watch people moving into the apartments in rue du Jardin. She would report back to her mama when she saw leather luggage, fur coats or beautiful hats, for these were signs that their owners might be likely candidates for needing a first-class dressmaker. Then at the first opportunity Mama would go round there with a bunch of flowers or a homemade cake to welcome them, always leaving one of her gold-edged cards.

Yvette supposed that on the outside at least, Dale Street and rue du Jardin had some similarities. Both were narrow, sunless cul-de-sacs, with tall, neglected old houses. Yet behind the peeling paint of the shutters and doors in rue du Jardin there were some beautiful apartments. Yvette remembered seeing chandeliers, opulent drapes, beautiful rugs, silver and alabaster when she went with her mama to do a dress fitting. She once asked why their apartment wasn't the same, and she got boxed round the ears instead of receiving a proper explanation.

There were no pleasant surprises behind the doors of Dale Street, except perhaps at the Boltons' next door on the left to Yvette's, which was luxurious. But then John Bolton was a villain, and the thick carpets, gilt-framed mirrors and brocade curtains were in keeping with his handmade suits, gold watch and the many visits he had from the police.

The smells and sounds which wafted out of the houses

here were of damp, fried food, crying children, adults squab-
bling and *Workers' Playtime* on the radio. Back in Paris it was
newly baked bread, garlic, Mozart or Edith Piaf, and when
adults raised their voices it was in greeting, not anger.

Remembering Paris always made Yvette feel shaky and
sick, and today was no exception. She turned away from the
window and went over to the turquoise cocktail dress on
her dressmaker's dummy. She had to set the sleeves in and
have it ready for a final fitting for Mrs Silverman in Chelsea
on Monday.

Forty-seven-year-old Ryszard Stanislav, known to everyone
in Dale Street as 'Stan the Pole', was also watching Fifi and
Dan from his bedsitter on the top floor of number 2. He
wanted to go down to offer to help them, but he knew
from experience that he would immediately be suspected of
having some sinister motive.

After fifteen years here his English was excellent, but try
as he might, he couldn't lose his Polish accent. It didn't help
either that he was a dustman and lived alone; this made
people think he was dirty and uncouth.

About ten years ago he'd rushed to help an old lady who
had collapsed in the street. Later, after she was taken away
in an ambulance, the police came, accusing him of stealing
her purse. He would never forget the way they spoke to
him, so bigoted, so full of hate, almost ready to string him
up without a shred of real evidence against him. It transpired
eventually that the old lady had left the purse at home – she
found it once she was discharged from the hospital. But the
police officer who came to tell Stan the charges against him
had been dropped didn't apologize. It was as if he imagined
that an immigrant with a funny accent couldn't have any
feelings.

Stan had learned to ignore slights and ignorance; that he had to be dim because he was a dustman; that he'd never known anywhere better than Dale Street; or that he liked being called 'Stan the Pole'. Sometimes he was tempted to grab people by their shoulders and insist they listen to his story before judging him. But he was only too aware that most people around here had no idea what had gone on in Poland during the war.

The truth was that he'd been a skilled carpenter with a wife and two beautiful daughters, until the Germans invaded. While he was off trying to defend his country, his wife and children were gunned down in the streets of Warsaw and his home destroyed. Stan felt he might as well have been killed too, for without his family he was nothing.

But the English didn't understand, and how could they? Their country had never been invaded. London might have been heavily bombed, but English people had never experienced soldiers crashing into their homes in the middle of the night, or seen innocent civilians shot in the street just because they were out after curfew. He was just Stan the Pole, the man with the funny accent, another one of those immigrants who ought to leave England for the English.

As he looked down at the couple in the street below, laughing because their pile of belongings was toppling over, he realized that his daughters, if they had lived, would have been around the same age as the young blonde girl. Sabine had been dark, taking after her mother, and Sofia blonde, after him. A tear trickled unchecked down his cheek as he remembered them.

Alfie Muckle at number 11, right opposite number 4 and next door to Yvette Dupré, was watching Fifi through a hole in the blanket which covered his bedroom window. As she bent over to pick up a box from the pavement, his cock stiffened at the sight of her pert backside in her tight jeans.

Alfie was the same age as Stan the Pole, but that was the only thing they had in common. Stan was tall and thin, with a face as sad and loose-skinned as a bloodhound's. Alfie was short and stocky, with a round, shiny face and receding sandy hair. Stan was an intelligent, honourable man, Alfie was a liar and a thief, and what he lacked in intelligence he made up for in low cunning.

Alfie's bedroom was representative of his entire house. Distempered walls were stained with everything from thrown food, blood and grease, and the furniture was equally knocked about. The double bed he shared with his wife, Molly, was unmade, the sheets unwashed for weeks on end. It smelled sour, of sweat, feet and cigarette smoke, and the bare wood floor was littered with dirty clothes. Alfie and his family weren't aware of either the mess or the odour, for they had never known any different.

'Whatcha doin'?'

At the sound of his wife's voice behind him, Alfie jumped.

Molly was forty-five, two years younger than Alfie, an overweight bleached blonde who, when she managed to take her hair out of curlers, put on some makeup and dress up, was still quite attractive in a garish way.

'Doggin' up the folk moving into number four,' he said.

Molly came over beside him and flicked the blanket back to look out of the window, then looked back at Alfie, her sharp eyes taking in the bulge in his trousers. 'You dirty bastard,' she exclaimed. 'You'd 'ave bin wanking over 'er if I 'adn't come in, wouldn't yer?'

There was no reproach in her voice, just a statement of fact.

Molly was seventeen when she married Alfie, already six months gone with their first child. They spent their wedding night in 1935 sharing a room with two of his four brothers, for back at that time Alfie's grandparents were living here, plus his parents and their four sons and two daughters. Molly went into labour prematurely when Alfie knocked her down the stairs for complaining that Fred, one of the brothers, wouldn't stop pestering her for sex. After twenty-eight years of marriage she had long since forgotten she once thought such behaviour unacceptable; she knew now that all Muckles were sex mad and violent. She had even become that way herself.

'Mind yer own fuckin' business,' Alfie retorted.

Molly flounced away from him without saying anything more. She wasn't concerned about what he got up to, but she liked him to know he didn't fool her.

Fifi and Dan were blissfully unaware of the scrutiny they were under as they carried their belongings indoors.

'We should go along to the corner shop and buy some groceries before we unpack,' Fifi said as she staggered up the stairs to the top floor with her Dansette record-player. 'I'm dying for a cup of tea, and they might close soon.'

'I'll go once we've got all our stuff up,' Dan said. 'Are you all right about this place now? Maybe I should have looked a bit more before taking it, but I wanted you to join me here so badly.'

Fifi couldn't bear to see him look so worried. 'It's fine,' she lied. 'Well, it will be once we've arranged all our things in it.'

Half an hour later, Fifi stood at the window looking out on to Dale Street, watching Dan going up to the shop on the corner. She could see how happy he was by the way he bounded rather than walked.

In the eight months they'd been married she'd come to see he needed only one thing to make him happy. He could get by without money, he'd eat anything, work harder and longer than any man she'd ever known, without complaint, just as long as he felt loved.

That was humbling for someone like her who had always taken love for granted. And here she was, looking at her new surroundings with distaste, wondering how she could survive a few weeks before they found somewhere she liked. She couldn't live with the awful orange curtains, and having no carpet on the floor appalled her, yet Dan would settle in here as if it were a palace, just because she loved him and would be sharing it with him.

How, with his bleak childhood, he'd ended up this way, she didn't know. She thought most people brought up as he was would become hard and cold, always on the take. If all he wanted in the whole world was to be with her, then the least she could do was show some real appreciation for the effort he'd made in finding them a home.

She would start by suggesting they went to the Rifleman, the pub on the opposite corner of the street to the shop, after they'd returned the van. That way it would show him she didn't think she was too grand to live here.

Yet as she continued to gaze out on to the miserable grey street, she didn't believe she would ever get to like it. As much as she told herself she no longer gave a damn what her parents thought about anything, she knew she'd sooner die than let them see her living here.

The moment she knew Dan had found a flat for them, she had written to her parents to tell them she was leaving her job and going to join him in London. Last night she had hoped they might come to say goodbye, and she wouldn't have felt ashamed for them to see the flat in Kingsdown.

But this place would shock them, and it would be just another thing to hold against Dan.

Yet if they couldn't unbend enough to go a couple of miles from their home to see her, they weren't likely ever to come here, so that was something she really didn't need to worry about.

Just as Fifi was about to return to the unpacking, the same little girl she'd seen crying earlier came out of her house. Although she wasn't crying now, her lethargic movements and the way her head hung down suggested she was still very unhappy. Fifi hadn't taken in much about the child's appearance earlier, but she could see now that she was as neglected as the house she lived in. Her dress looked like a hand-me-down from someone far older, her brown hair was fuzzy at the back, as if it hadn't been brushed, and her ill-fitting shoes slopped up and down on her heels as she walked in the direction of the corner shop. She was exactly the way Fifi had always imagined slum children, malnourished, dirty, pale and sickly.

She looked back to number 11, the child's home, noticing again the lack of proper curtains, and that one of the panes of glass in the ground-floor window was broken, boarded over with a piece of wood. It was by far the most dilapidated house in the street, the front door battered as if it was constantly kicked in. As her eyes flickered over the house, she saw a man on the top floor looking straight at her.

Fifi backed away in fright. She couldn't see him clearly as his house was in shadow, and he was only partially visible as he'd been holding back the cloth covering the window. But she sensed something unpleasant about him.

At eight that same evening they had returned the van and finished unpacking. With their own table lamps, a cloth and a vase of flowers on the ugly table, and their picture of the bluebell wood above the gas fire, the living room looked much better.

Dan was sitting in one of the fireside chairs smoking a cigarette and looking around him reflectively. 'We've got enough money saved to buy a square of carpet, some paint and new curtains. I reckon that would turn it into a little palace.'

Fifi half smiled. A little palace it would never be, but she liked the idea of attempting to beautify it. 'I think we'll have to get some net curtains too,' she replied as she arranged some books and a couple of ornaments on a shelf. She went on to tell him about the man she'd seen in the house opposite. 'I don't want someone like him gawping in at us.'

'You, the original nosy parker, complaining of someone watching you!' Dan exclaimed. 'If I spotted a gorgeous girl in the house opposite, I'd have my nose pressed up against the window too.'

'He gave me the creeps,' she said, tossing back her blonde hair. 'And you saw what that woman was like with the little girl. I saw the kid again, she looks terribly neglected.'

Dan got up and came over to her and lifting a strand of her hair he ran his fingers down it. 'What do you know about neglect?' he said teasingly. 'I bet you never even had a dirty face as a kid.'

'She looks half-starved, and her dress and shoes were too big,' Fifi replied indignantly.

'So her folks are poor, that's all. Now, let's go down to the pub and check out the rest of our new neighbours.'

The Rifleman was packed by the time Dan and Fifi got there. They squeezed through the crowd to the end of the bar where there was a little space, and while Dan waited to be served, Fifi looked around her eagerly.

She liked what she saw, for this was what she expected of a London pub. It had atmosphere, colour, jollity and a huge range of age groups from those barely old enough to drink, to the very elderly.

There were slickly suited young men with the latest college-boy hair-styles and winkle-picker shoes, girls with teetering beehive hair-dos, Cleopatra-style eye makeup and skirts so tight they could hardly walk. There were old stooped men with rheumy eyes, watching the proceedings from their seats in corners. Brassy women, mousy women, men still in working clothes who'd forgotten to go home for their tea, others who looked as though they hadn't got a home to go to, and a whole gang of men between twenty-five and forty wearing expensive suits and don't-mess-with-me expressions.

A thick-set man in his sixties smiled at Fifi. 'How are you settling in?' he asked. 'I'm Frank Ubley. I live downstairs to you on the ground floor. I saw you moving in, and I would've offered to help you carry your stuff up, but I'd just had a bath and I wasn't dressed.'

'I'm Fifi Reynolds and that's my husband, Dan,' Fifi said, pointing to Dan who was just paying for their drinks. 'We're more or less straight now, thank you. Though we'd like to paint the place. Is your wife with you tonight?'

'I'm a widower,' he said. 'My wife died four years ago.'

'I'm so sorry,' Fifi said, a little embarrassed. 'I just assumed a married couple lived on the ground floor as the net curtains are so white.'

'A man alone doesn't have to become a slob,' he said, and smiled. Fifi noticed he had nice eyes, grey with very dark lashes. 'I like to keep the place proper. My June was very particular, she washed the nets every two weeks without fail. She wouldn't like it if I let things go.'

Dan came over with their drinks then and she introduced him to Frank. 'Who lives on the first floor?' she went on to ask.

'Miss Diamond,' Frank replied. 'She works for the telephone company, and she rules the roost.'

'She's an ogre, is she?' Dan asked with a grin.

Frank chuckled. 'She can be if she doesn't like a body. She's particular, you see, just like my June was. You leave a ring round the bath, make too much noise or don't take your turn sweeping the stairs, then there's hell to pay.'

Fifi could see now why the bathroom had been so unexpectedly clean, the only nice surprise of the day. She approved of the pub too, and now meeting Frank cheered her still more as he looked and sounded a decent, rather fatherly type. A comforting person to have as a neighbour.

She made some remark about being glad she hadn't got to share the bathroom with messy people, and brought the subject round to the house across the street.

'I saw a little girl coming out of there. She looked sad.'

'She would be, with folks like them,' Frank said with a grimace. 'The Muckles are a disgrace. Filthy ways, lying, cheating curs.'

'You don't like them then?' Dan joked.

'Like them!' Frank's voice rose a couple of octaves. 'They need exterminating!'

'I can't believe anyone is called Muckle,' Fifi giggled. 'Maybe they are that way because of their name.'

'Their name is the only thing you can laugh about,' Frank said, grimacing with disgust. 'If I was a Catholic I'd be crossing myself whenever I heard it.'

A Polish man came along then, and Frank introduced him as his friend Stan and said he lived next door but one. Despite Stan's strong Polish accent he had the manner of an English gentleman, very correct, a little stiff but also rather charming, and his long, mournful face reminded Fifi of a stray dog she'd once taken home.

'You have such pretty hair,' he said appreciatively. 'It is good to see you leave it loose, I do not like this fashion they called the bird's nest.'

'Thank you.' Fifi blushed at the unexpected compliment. 'But I think the style you mean is called a beehive.'

'To me it looks like a bird's nest, and all stuck up with that lacquer,' he made a grimace, 'a man would never want to touch such a thing.'

Dan ran his fingers through a lock of Fifi's hair protectively, giving both Frank and Stan a clear message she could be admired, but not touched by anyone but him. 'Let me buy you both a drink to celebrate our first night in London together. We'd begun to think we'd never be able to find a flat here.'

Both Frank and Stan said they'd like a pint. 'I hope London will be good for you,' Frank said, looking from Fifi to Dan almost fondly. 'I'm glad to have young people in the house again. When my daughter lived nearby she was in and out all the time with her children. I miss all the laughter and chatter.'

'Where does she live now?' Fifi asked, as always wanting to know everything about her new neighbours.

'In Brisbane in Australia,' Frank replied sadly. 'June and I were intending to go out there and join them, but after she died I felt it was too late for me to uproot myself.'

By the time they were on their second drinks, Frank and Stan had pointed out several other neighbours and given Fifi and Dan a potted history of most of them. There were Cecil and Ivy Helass at number 6, solid, reliable folk who had the only phone in the road, and had four children aged from sixteen to twenty-two. John and Vera Bolton lived at number 13, and they were described as flashy. The names of the other neighbours and which houses they lived in went over Fifi's head, but the one family Frank kept coming back to was the Muckles. It was clear the man had a real grudge against the family, for as he told them the child Fifi had seen earlier in the day was called Angela, he looked fit to burst with something more.

As always when Fifi got a whiff of scandal or intrigue, she was desperate to know the whole story. Bit by bit she pumped both Frank and Stan for more.

It appeared that Angela was the youngest of eight children, four of whom still lived across the street, and that their mother Molly was what Frank called 'a woman of easy virtue'.

'Then there's the two half-wit relations, shacked up together,' he spat out. 'God help us all when they produce an offspring!'

Fifi looked at Dan and saw his lips were twitching with silent laughter.

When Stan intervened to say almost apologetically that everyone in Dale Street had good reason to hate the Muckles, and that but for them the street would be a good place to live, Dan asked why they hadn't been evicted.

'You can't evict people who own their house.' Frank shook his head sadly. 'That's the real problem. Alfie lords it over us. He knows there's nothing we can do about him.

The only place he can't come in is this pub, thank God. He was banned from here years ago and it will never be lifted.'

'How does someone like him get to buy a house?' Fifi asked.

'The legend goes that his grandfather won it from the man who built the street in a game of cards,' Frank said. 'Only Mrs Jarvis has lived here that long, and she was only a child at the time, so you can't say it's absolute truth. But the house was passed down to Alfie's father, and then to Alfie. The house ain't the only thing passed down through the generations, though.'

'What else?' Dan asked, his lean face alight with interest.

'None of the Muckle men has ever done an honest day's work, they chose women who became their punch-bags, and they pump out children at an indecent rate,' Frank said with indignation.

'They are not what you know as a family,' Stan chipped in. 'I would call them a tribe. Right now there is only Alfie, Molly and their four younger children, plus Dora and Alfie's nephew, Mike.'

'Dora is Molly's backward sister,' Frank interrupted. 'Completely doolally, and like a walking jumble sale. I once saw her going out in odd shoes and just a petticoat!'

Dan winked at Fifi. He was enjoying this, and she had no doubt he would be imitating both Frank and Stan when they got home.

'But it never stops at just the immediate family,' Stan went on, getting a little agitated now. 'This number can swell at any time. They have so many relatives who come and stay, and there's the card parties.'

Fifi couldn't be sure, but she thought she saw Frank send a warning glance at Stan.

'Card parties!' she said brightly. 'Like bridge or something?'

'Look, Stan, there's Ted over there,' Frank said suddenly, pointing to a fat man with a big red face at the other end of the bar. 'We must catch him and see when the next darts match is.' He turned back to Fifi and Dan and apologized for rushing off, but said if they needed any help or wanted to borrow any tools, they only had to ask.

'The Man Who Said Too Much,' Dan said in a mock chilling voice as the two older men left them. 'Maybe the card game is Happy Families and they won't let Frank or Stan play?'

'They sound a monstrous family,' Fifi said. 'But I suppose you think they were making it all up?'

'I suspect a bit of exaggeration,' he said with a grin. 'But I especially liked the bit about dopey Dora.'

By closing time Dan and Fifi had met several other neighbours, Cecil and Ivy Helass, Mrs Witherspoon from the corner shop, and a man called Wally who had only recently moved into a room below Stan, and they all had something more to add about the Muckles.

Mrs Witherspoon was a plump, seemingly kindly middle-aged woman, and she claimed they targeted any new people in the street, asking to borrow things and telling them hard-luck stories. She advised Fifi and Dan never to invite any of them in, as they would be back to rob them as soon as they got an opportunity.

Ivy Helass said that Stan had seen the two older children locked out of the house one afternoon when there was thick snow back in the winter, so he brought them in to get warm. Two days later he came home to find he'd been burgled, and two solid silver photograph frames taken.

'It was shameful,' Ivy said indignantly. 'That poor man lost his wife and two daughters in the Warsaw uprising, and all he had left was the two pictures of his family. They meant everything to him, and those children must have thrown the pictures away before they sold the frames.'

Wally said that Alfie was a peeping Tom.

Fifi didn't like the look of Wally at all. He had a beer gut spilled over his trousers, and food stains down his shirt. Although he was only about thirty, she thought she wouldn't be surprised to find he was a flasher himself.

But he claimed Alfie was in the habit of climbing along the wall at the backs of the houses, looking into lighted rooms. He warned her she should keep her curtains closed at night.

Despite the rather tedious repetitions about the Muckles, the warmth of the welcome from their new neighbours went a long way to reassure Fifi that Kennington wasn't such a bad place to live. By the time they got home after the pub had shut, with a bag of chips each, she was feeling much happier and a little drunk.

'It's beginning to grow on me,' she said as she sat down and looked about the living room. With just the light from the table lamps and all their things in place, it looked quite homely.

'Even with the monsters across the road?' Dan asked, raising one eyebrow. 'Or is that part of the attraction?'

Fifi giggled. Dan was always teasing her about her curiosity. 'They sound much too awful even for me,' she said. 'That woman with the black hair who said she lived next to the coal yard said their house is absolutely filthy. She said none of the children were ever toilet trained, and they'd just do it on the floor. She claimed the council has been round to fumigate the place loads of times. She said they have terrible fights in there, and there's always dodgy people coming and going.'

'Don't take it too seriously,' Dan said evenly. 'People do get a bit vindictive about anyone different from themselves.'

Fifi knew he was right about that. Her own parents had proved it by being so nasty about Dan.

'Perhaps I'll put them under close observation,' she joked. 'I could make a study of them. Log what they do and at what time. If they really are responsible for all the crime around here, it could be useful to the police.'

'Then you'd better have a chat with the French dress-maker,' Dan said with a wide grin.

He had been far more intrigued to hear about the woman from Paris who sat sewing by her window all day than by the more salacious stories about her next-door neighbours. Apparently she only went out to give fittings for her wealthy clients, but it was generally supposed she knew everything that happened in the street. 'She might do some shifts for you. Or maybe I should study her!'

'We could call ourselves "Super Snoops",' Fifi giggled. 'For a slogan we could have "Nothing gets past us".'

Dan laughed. He was so relieved Fifi seemed happier now. For a minute or two this afternoon he'd thought she was going to take the next train back to Bristol.

He loved her to pieces, just to look at her lovely face made his heart melt, and he still couldn't quite believe that a girl like her could love him. But there were times when she was like a spoiled child, expecting life to be one long picnic in the sun. He'd got her well away from her parents' influence at last, and though it would probably be another nail in his coffin that he'd brought her to live here, Fifi needed a dose of reality.

Chapter five

Fifi bounced along the street. She was happy because it was Saturday, a lovely sunny day, and once she'd got the shopping she and Dan were going out for a picnic in Hyde Park. As she reached Mrs Jarvis's house at the end of the street, on an impulse she knocked on her door.

'Hello,' she said as the old lady answered. 'I'm going down to Victor Values, is there anything I can get for you while I'm there?'

'Is that the new-fangled place where you have to serve yourself?'

Fifi smiled. Although Alice Jarvis was over eighty and very frail, she didn't miss much that was going on. Fifi had spoken to her for the first time a few days after they moved into Dale Street, a month ago now, and had been invited in for a cup of tea. The old lady lived in a Victorian time warp, still with the same heavy, highly polished or over-stuffed furniture her parents had brought with them when they moved in when she was a girl. She had four siblings, but she'd never left home as they did; when she married Mr Jarvis, he moved in with her and her parents.

Mrs Jarvis's one and only concession to modern times was the electric lighting, which she'd reluctantly agreed to have put in after the war, a short while after her husband died. Her home reflected the lives and personalities of all those who had lived there: a lace-trimmed tablecloth made by her mother, a grandfather clock that had been her father's pride and joy, dozens of framed sepia photographs of her brothers and sisters, and the piano in the parlour which they'd all played and sung around.

'Yes, you do serve yourself,' Fifi replied. 'But it's ever so much cheaper than the grocer's.'

'It sounds American to me.' Mrs Jarvis sniffed with disapproval. 'I don't hold with anything from there. And I like someone to serve me.'

'I'd rather save money,' Fifi said with a smile. 'And if I'm going for you, you're not going to miss being served personally.'

Mrs Jarvis wavered. She looked very stern in her old-fashioned black dress and thick stockings, with her white hair tied up tightly in a bun, but Fifi had discovered she was a warm and friendly person. 'Well, I could do with a quarter of tea and a packet of chocolate biscuits, if it's not too much trouble,' she said. 'I've got my niece and her husband coming tomorrow afternoon. They usually take me out to tea somewhere, but it's so nice out in the garden now, they might want to stay here.'

Fifi had a feeling Mrs Jarvis lived on little else but tea and biscuits; she hadn't seen any sign of food in her kitchen when she was in there last week. But she didn't know her well enough to start cross-examining her yet.

'Have you finished your painting?' Mrs Jarvis asked. The last time she had seen Fifi she'd remarked on the paint in her hair.

'Yes, it looks lovely,' Fifi said eagerly. 'The living room is pale green and the bedroom cream. We've bought a new carpet too. Miss Diamond thinks it very tasteful.'

'I hope she's kind to you?' Mrs Jarvis said anxiously. 'She can be very fierce.'

Fifi grinned. Miss Diamond in the rooms downstairs to her was a supervisor at the telephone exchange and quite formidable, laying down the law about everything. 'I can give as good as I get,' she said. 'She's got a good heart really. I'd rather have her living downstairs than certain people in this road.'

'Did you hear them last night?' Mrs Jarvis said, raising her hands in an expression of horror and alarm. 'Shouting and bawling, and the language!'

She was of course speaking about the Muckles. Hardly a night passed without something going on there. If it wasn't a fight between Molly and Alfie, children screaming or music blaring out, it was the Friday night cards party when seedy-looking men left in the small hours, banging car doors and honking horns.

Last Friday, Dan had wanted to go over there because one of the women was screaming as if she was being viciously beaten. But fortunately it stopped suddenly and Dan let it go.

'We thought everyone was exaggerating about them when we first moved in,' Fifi replied. 'I don't really believe that the police can't do anything about them. Surely they could charge them with disturbing the peace, if nothing else?'

'They say Alfie bribes the police to turn a blind eye,' Mrs Jarvis said conspiratorially. 'I wish I could bribe someone to burn that house down and them with it. Mr Jarvis went over there once to try and stop their noise and soon after he was attacked coming home one evening. We couldn't prove it was them, but everyone knew it was. They broke his jaw and his ribs – they are worse than animals.'

Although Fifi and Dan had found the stories about the Muckles a bit far-fetched when they first moved in, there was no doubt that some of the neighbours really were terrified of them. Mrs Jarvis's lips quivered and her voice shook as she spoke of them, and she always looked out of her window before opening her front door. Fifi thought it was awful that an old lady who had lived here for almost her entire life should spend her last years in such fear.

Fifi wasn't afraid of the Muckles, but she found watching them completely addictive. She knew she really shouldn't find them so fascinating, they were after all the absolute dregs of the earth. But they were a novelty, so far removed from the quiet gentility of the neighbours she'd grown up observing that she almost liked them for giving her so much entertainment.

Dan had bought a second-hand television, but Fifi watched the Muckles more often. It was like having a theatre on her doorstep, the family acting out a long-running serial. There was comedy when Dora, the backward sister-in-law, ran down the street wearing nothing but men's boots and a towel around her. She was running after Mike, the nephew, screaming that she loved him.

The serial had suspense when Molly and Alfie came home drunk; would it turn to a fight? Or would the night be filled with the sound of animalistic lovemaking later on? There was mystery when men arrived to play cards on a Friday night. Mainly they were as seedy-looking as Alfie, but some were smartly dressed, almost like businessmen, and Fifi was baffled as to why such men would want to play cards in such a grim place. Dan said that owning a handmade suit was in fact a hallmark of a villain, and however affluent these men appeared, they probably came from homes as rough as Alfie's. She was puzzled too that the police never seemed to act after complaints of noise and disturbance. Then there was tragedy as well, as the poor children all looked so neglected.

Where did Molly go when she went out in the evening, alone and dressed to kill? Why was it that the children took a pram full of washing to the council laundry every week, yet not one of the family other than Molly ever wore anything clean? Where did they get the money to buy all those boxes of drink they carried home, when no one in the family appeared to work?

Yet most intriguing of all was that the Muckles had so many visitors. Hardly a day went by without Fifi seeing someone new go in there. Maybe the couple of teenage girls she'd seen were the two older daughters who no longer lived at home, but she didn't think all the callers could be family members. No one in the street had anything good to say about Alfie, so how come he had so many friends?

She wondered about the Muckles all the time. She would give anything to be able to turn herself into a fly and go into that house to take a look around. She knew it would be filthy, she was sure they lived on nothing but fish and chips, but however much everyone kept telling her how dangerous they were, she couldn't really believe that. To her they were all idiots, often brutal, always coarse, but hardly dangerous.

After a little chat with Mrs Jarvis, Fifi went on to the shop. To her surprise she had come to like Kennington. It might not be what she was used to, but it had a kind of buzz about it, as though there were a million and one things going on right under her nose.

She even liked the flat now they'd done it up. It might have been very different if they'd had awful people downstairs, but no one could mind sharing a bathroom with either Miss Diamond or Frank Ubley. Dan laughingly called Miss Diamond the bathroom monitor, because on their second day she'd personally instructed Dan on cleaning the bath after he'd used it. She put plants on the windowsill, she went in for various things that made it smell nice, and she washed over the floor twice a week.

As for Frank on the ground floor, he was a gem, as keen as Miss Diamond about cleanliness, but also kind and very helpful. He had lent Dan tools and helped him put up some shelves. He advised them about the best places to get paint or timber cheaper, and he showed his pleasure in having younger people in the house by being delighted when they asked him up for a cup of tea and to inspect what they'd been doing to their flat.

It felt so safe living above such nice, decent people, and the low rent meant they didn't have to worry about money.

Yet it was the other neighbours who had really changed Fifi's mind about Dale Street, for they were all so fascinating. Back in Kingsdown in Bristol, none of the other tenants had ever spoken to Dan or Fifi. In her parents' street the neighbours had always seemed to lead such narrow lives, and though they were pleasant, they couldn't talk about any subject other than their homes, children and gardens. She hadn't thought anything of it when she was there, but now, after living here for a month, she realized that they were all afraid ever to let their real feelings show.

People around here didn't have that problem. If something good had happened to them, they wanted the world to know. They'd drag you in to show you their new television or three-piece suite, or a new baby. They aired their disapproval as well. Fifi had heard people ranting about their unscrupulous landlords, hated in-laws, and even children who had disappointed them. They liked to laugh at themselves too. Back at home no housewife would admit she'd made a cake and forgot the sugar in it, or burned her husband's dinner because she was chatting over the fence. But they did here, seeing no shame in showing they were flawed.

Fifi really liked that. It was real, it was good. She had always believed that the only way you could make real friends was if there was mutual opening up, seeing the differences in people and liking them for it.

Yvette the French dressmaker and Stan the Pole had come here in 1947 as refugees. Ivy Helass had been a dancer before she married Cecil, and it was said that John Bolton had robbed a bank and gone to prison for it. Fifi wanted to get to know everyone in the street, to hear their stories and make friends with them. But sadly, now she was working, she didn't get much opportunity.

She had been taken on by a firm of solicitors in Chancery Lane during her first week in London. She liked the work as it was more varied than back in Bristol. Sometimes, if there was no junior available to deliver documents to one of the barristers in their chambers at the Temple, or the law courts, she took them. Aside from this breaking up the day and providing a chance to be out in the fresh air, she found the Temple appealing because it was so ancient.

It was exciting living in London. Everything seemed to go at twice the speed of Bristol. Rush hour had been terrifying at first; she couldn't bring herself to elbow her way on to buses and the tube the way everyone else did. But she learned to, and now she could run after a bus and jump on the back as it was moving, leap off at traffic lights, even cross the road dodging through cars. She loved the incredible mixture of people too. Businessmen in bowler hats with furled umbrellas, strap-hanging on the tube alongside manual workers. Young girls in market-style clothing, their hair in beehives and Cleopatra-style eye makeup, mingling with women who looked as if they'd stepped out of the pages of *Vogue*.

There were so many different nationalities too. In just

one day she could hear Germans, French, Greeks, Australians and Americans, and see Africans, West Indians, Arabs, Chinese and Japanese. And the shops catered for everyone – in Kennington alone you could buy anything from a kebab to a yam, fantastic sari material or halal meat. She and Dan had been up to Soho a few times at night, and had been both shocked and amused by the number of strip clubs and dirty-book shops. Yet even more incredible was that it was theatreland too. As people in evening dress hailed cabs or went into the expensive restaurants, just around the corner there were prostitutes plying their trade.

Fifi really didn't miss Bristol, in fact sometimes she realized that days had gone past without her thinking about it at all. She had written home once, just to give her parents her new address. While she wrote to Patty every week, other friends had only got a postcard telling them how happy she was.

Happy didn't really adequately describe how she felt; she was joyful. Joining Dan in London had strengthened their marriage and bonded them even closer together. Here they were on an equal footing, both still rather wide-eyed tourists finding their way around.

Fifi loved shopping in Victor Values. Conventional grocers were so dark and cramped, but this shop had bright lights, with everything priced and arranged in wide aisles. Shops like this had been nicknamed 'supermarkets', and most people thought they were a five-minute wonder because they didn't see how they could keep the prices so low. Fifi didn't agree; she felt it would be the traditional shops that would be forced out of business.

She was on top of the world as she made her way home along the busy Kennington Park Road with two laden bags, enough food for the whole week. Dan had managed to get them a second-hand fridge the previous day, and she thought it would be bliss not to have to shop for meat and milk every day any more. She was also dying to get home to read the paper she'd bought. The on-going scandal about the call-girl Christine Keeler and John Profumo, the Minister for War, was so exciting. It had all started back in March when Christine's ex-lover had fired shots into the flat she was sharing with Mandy Rice-Davies, but now it seemed that John Profumo had been sleeping with a call-girl, and that she in turn was sleeping with Ivanov, a Russian attaché. Every day there was a new revelation. Dr Stephen Ward, a society osteopath, owned the flat, the two girls had swum naked in Lord Astor's swimming pool, there were suggestions of kinky sex and drug-taking, and goodness knows what else would be revealed before long.

About twenty yards before the turning to Dale Street there was a piece of waste ground where some houses had been demolished. As always, Fifi glanced through the broken fence panels because it was an improvised playground for the local children. There were usually dozens of children in there, building camps, playing pirates and occasionally lighting fires. Fifi's feelings were mixed about it. The child in her approved, for there were few places in London where children could have adventure and freedom. But her adult side worried, for it was after all a dangerous place, full of broken bottles, piles of rubble and other hazards.

To her surprise there were no children there today, despite the good weather. But as she walked on by she heard the sound of crying. Curious, she put down her shopping and stuck her head right through a hole in the fence to take another look.

One lone little girl was in there, sitting on the ground, hands covering her face, crying her heart out.

It was Angela, the youngest of the Muckle children.

As this was the child she'd seen being clouted by her mother on her first day in Dale Street, Fifi had put her under even closer scrutiny than anyone else in the family. It was clear she was the least favoured child. Her parents were always shouting at her, her older brother and sister bullied her, even her Aunt Dora appeared to have it in for her.

If Fifi had seen any of the other three children in apparent distress she would have walked on by. She had noticed the low cunning in their eyes and heard their foul language, and would suspect they were trying to trick her. They were known to snatch money from the hands of children on the way to the shop on a message and they'd slip into any open front door to steal. Fifi had seen them barge into old people, overturning dustbins and breaking milk bottles on the pavement. If reprimanded they would scream vicious abuse.

But Angela wasn't like the others. She was cowed, not cocky, thin and malnourished. If her eyes met those of an adult they were fearful. Fifi hesitated. Common sense told her it would be better to ignore the child, but her crying was a plaintive bleat which plucked at her heart strings. 'What's wrong, Angela?' she called out.

The child started, uncovering her face. 'Nothin',' she said.

But it wasn't nothing. She had been punched; the flesh around her eye was so livid and swollen that her eye had all but disappeared.

Fifi assumed it had been done by another child, and that was why no one else was playing there. Remembering times when she'd been bullied as a child herself, she felt she had to do something, if only offer some sympathy.

She went back to the place where the fence had been

broken down completely. 'Who did that to you?' she asked as she cautiously picked her way over the smashed-up fence panels.

The child's sharp features, the pallor of her skin, tangled dull hair, missing front teeth and dirty clothes made her an unappealing sight at the best of times, but with this injury to her eye she looked utterly pathetic. As Fifi came closer she started to get up as if intending to flee.

'Do you know who I am?' Fifi asked, assuming Angela was frightened at being approached and questioned by a stranger. 'I live opposite you at number four, my name's Fifi Reynolds, my husband is called Dan.'

The child nodded. 'I've seen you,' she whispered. 'You were painting the walls.'

Fifi felt that meant Angela had watched her from an upper window late in the evening. 'I used to watch people when I was a little girl,' she said in an effort to win the child's trust. 'I used to make up things about them. Nice things mostly, like they were princesses or ballet dancers. Do you do that?'

Angela made a kind of half-nod.

'So what did you make up about me?' Fifi asked.

There was no response, but that was hardly surprising given that Angela's injury had to be hurting a great deal. 'Come on,' Fifi insisted. 'It's just a game. I'd like to hear what you made up.'

'That you were my big sister,' Angela replied, hanging her head.

At that unexpected and touching admission a lump came up in Fifi's throat. She could guess where that little fantasy had taken the girl. A place of safety across the street, where there were no fights or rows. A place where everything was clean and bright, perhaps with a big sister washing and brushing her hair for her. Did she imagine someone there who cared enough to cuddle her and make a fuss of her?

'Who hit you, Angela?' she asked.

The child shrugged, as if it didn't matter who was responsible.

'You must tell me. If you let children carry on being bullies they just get worse and worse. I could talk to their mothers about it.'

'It weren't another kid,' Angela mumbled.

'Well, who was it then? Was it your mum or your dad?'

'Dad,' the child whispered, looking fearfully at Fifi. 'But don't you go saying nothin' or he'll lay into me twice as bad.'

A surge of anger welled up in Fifi. It was hideous that a grown man could punch a helpless child.

She faltered for a few moments. Her heart told her to take Angela home with her, put some ice on the swelling and get Dan to call the police and report Alfie Muckle. But she was afraid of the repercussions.

'Why did your dad hit you?' she asked.

'Cos I spilt a cuppa tea on 'im,' Angela said glumly. 'I couldn't 'elp it, 'e was in bed, see, I tripped up in the dark.'

Fifi got a nasty mental picture of Alfie lying there in his fetid bedroom, too lazy to work for a living, but energetic enough to lash out at a little girl. She knew then ,that she had to show Angela not everyone in this world was as uncaring. 'Come home with me and I'll bathe your eye,' she said impulsively.

'I can't do that! Dad might see me going in your 'ouse,' Angela said in horror. ''E'll 'urt you.'

'If he tries to do that, he'll be sorry,' Fifi said more calmly than she felt.

'You don't know what 'e's like. 'E wouldn't just come and 'it you, 'e'd do something sneaky. That's 'is way.'

Fifi was appalled that such a young child could already be so aware that her father was a devious thug. 'You let me worry about that,' she said firmly. 'Your eye needs some urgent attention. Now come with me.'

Fifi half expected Angela to run off once they got to Dale Street, but she didn't, not even when Yvette Dupré came out of the shop right in front of them.

''Ello, Fifi,' she said. ''Ow are you?'

Dan referred to her as the French mistress; he said her accent was the sexiest he'd ever heard. Fifi agreed, but it was the only sexy thing about the woman. Someone had said that she wasn't even forty, but she looked middle-aged in clothes left over from the war years. On the rare occasions when she went out she wore a grey mid-calf-length fitted coat and a felt hat. Dan called it her Resistance outfit, and said she wore it to hide her astoundingly voluptuous figure, which no man would be able to resist.

Fifi had called on her just a few days after they moved in to ask her to replace the zip in the skirt of the suit she needed for interviews. She found Yvette warm and friendly, and although she didn't invite her in, she said she would gladly replace the zip and bring it back later.

Dan was of course entirely wrong about her figure; she was very thin, no curves at all showing in a plain dark brown wool dress. Yet close up she was rather beautiful, with large, very dark eyes and a soft, full mouth. Fifi didn't understand why she pulled her hair back off her face so severely, and why when she made elegant, fashionable clothes for other people, she should choose to look so prim and frumpy herself. She hoped eventually to get to know the woman well enough to persuade her into covering up the grey in her hair with some dye, to wear makeup and change her style of clothes. But she hadn't got anywhere near close enough for that yet.

'I'm fine, thank you,' Fifi replied in answer to the question of how she was. Normally she was eager to stop to chat with Yvette because she was so intriguing, but with Angela in tow she needed to get home as quickly as possible.

'*Sacré bleu*,' Yvette exclaimed as she saw Angela's rapidly blackening eye. ''Oo did that to you?'

'Need you ask?' Fifi said. 'I'm taking her home with me to bathe it.'

'Ees that wise?' Yvette said softly.

In a previous conversation Yvette had told Fifi that it was hell living right next door to the Muckles. Her kitchen window was overlooked by theirs, and she heard and saw the most hideous things. Fifi hadn't yet managed to get the woman to divulge any details, not just because there had been no opportunity, but because Yvette appeared to be as frightened of the Muckles as Mrs Jarvis.

'Probably not, but I'm going to do it anyway,' Fifi said defiantly. Yvette made a gesture with her hands implying she thought such action was foolhardy, then she turned and walked away.

Fifi settled Angela in a chair holding some ice cubes in a bag over her eye, then indicated to Dan he was to come outside on to the landing with her.

'You must go to the police and report Alfie,' she whispered, turning on the cold tap so Angela couldn't hear what they were saying.

'We can't go grassing them up,' Dan said, shaking his head.

'Why ever not?' Fifi exclaimed. 'Surely you don't agree with a grown man punching a small child?'

'No, I don't,' Dan said, looking concerned. 'What he needs is a good kicking. But if the police go round there Alfie will make sure Angela tells a different story and nothing will happen to him. Then he'll lay into her again.'

'So what do you suggest we do?' Fifi asked with heavy sarcasm. 'Just patch her up and send her home? Then curse ourselves later when we hear more screaming?'

'I didn't say I wasn't going to do anything,' Dan said. His face darkened and his eyes glinted in a manner Fifi had never seen before. He was always so gentle with her, but she suddenly felt she was seeing a more dangerous side of him he'd kept hidden from her.

'You aren't going to hit him, are you?' she said in alarm. She knew that with his background, Dan was unlikely to walk away from a fight.

'No, I'll warn him,' he said quietly. 'I'll tell him I'm on his case and if it happens again he'll be sorry. There's only one way to deal with scum like him and that's to put the fear of God into him.'

He didn't stop to see if Fifi agreed or disagreed, he was off down the stairs taking them two at a time. Fifi felt a little sick; she'd heard so many stories about Alfie Muckle getting back at anyone who opposed him, and some of them at least had to be true.

Going back into the living room with a glass of squash for Angela, she looked out of the window. Dan was banging on the Muckles' door, and as she watched Molly answered it. Even though the window was open, Fifi couldn't hear what Dan was saying, but then his voice was soft and deep. But she did hear Molly bellow out for Alfie, and a second or two later he appeared beside her in the doorway. He had his braces over a grubby-looking vest, and the expression on his face was one of surprise to see Dan on his doorstep.

Fifi could hear Dan's voice now, but not what he was saying, and Alfie backed up into his hall as if afraid of being struck. He appeared to be protesting, perhaps denying he hit Angela, and Molly had got in behind him, her stance one of someone poised for flight.

Whether there was any substance to Alfie's fearsome reputation or not, next to Dan he looked pathetic. Dan was a good eight inches taller, fit, powerfully built and over twenty years younger. He looked capable of tearing Alfie apart, but he had said on many an occasion that he despised men who resorted to brutality to make a point. Yet on the other hand Fifi knew he felt very strongly about cruelty to children, because he'd been subjected to it himself. So when she saw him lunge forward and grab Alfie by the shoulders she involuntarily covered her face with her hands.

Hearing no shouting or sounds of fists, she peeped through her fingers and was astounded to see that Dan was merely shaking Alfie, their two faces close together. Then he let him go, and turned on his heel to return home.

The Muckles' door was immediately slammed shut, and Fifi flew back across the room and down the stairs to meet Dan in the hallway.

'Shush!' he said putting one finger to his mouth. 'We don't want Angela frightened.'

'What did you say to him?'

Dan shrugged. 'Just that if I ever see another injury on the kid again I'll break his neck.'

'But he'll take it out on her when she goes home!' Fifi exclaimed. 'You've made it worse for her.'

'No, I haven't. I know his sort, I meet them every day on the buildings, bloody bullies picking on people who can't defend themselves. But put them up against someone who can fight back and beat them and they shit themselves. He knows I'll have him if he lays another finger on Angela. He won't take the risk.'

Fifi wanted to believe him, but if it was that easy to make Alfie Muckle toe the line, why hadn't someone done it before?

Dan must have picked up on her disbelief. He put his arms around her and kissed her nose. 'Stop worrying. I told him Angela was staying with us for the rest of the day, so let's feed her up, play with her and give her a nice time. I'll take her home later and I promise you he won't lay into her.'

Dan took Angela home just after six. They'd had the picnic Fifi had planned in the flat, sitting on the floor, because Angela was in no fit state to be taken out. Later Fifi washed her hair for her and put it up in bunches with blue hair ribbons. They'd played snap, and Dan had put four nails into the end of a cotton reel and showed her how to do French knitting with some wool because they had no toys, children's books or even coloured pencils for her to use.

But Angela seemed happy just to be there. She didn't speak much but she snuggled up to Fifi and grinned shyly at Dan.

With clean, well-brushed hair she looked a lot better, but Fifi was appalled by the way she ate. She was like an animal, tearing at the food and stuffing it into her mouth which remained open as she chewed. Fifi wished she could bathe her and wash her filthy clothes for there was a sour smell wafting from her that made it hard to cuddle her.

Dan didn't seem to notice any of this. But as he said after he'd taken her home, '*She isn't so different to me at the same age.*'

He said that Molly had been quite pleasant. She admired Angela's new hair ribbons, asked if she'd had a good time, and then in an aside to Dan claimed that Alfie hadn't meant to hurt his daughter. She said he was burned by the hot tea and lashed out involuntarily.

Yet Fifi found Dan very subdued that evening, hardly saying a word. He rarely talked about his childhood, but he had once told her that right up till he was about ten, he believed that his mother would come looking for him one day. He said that he would drop off to sleep every night thinking about how pretty and kind she would be and the wonderful life they would have together. Fifi guessed that the day's events had reminded him of that, and perhaps other things he'd never told her.

She didn't want to upset him further by trying to get him to talk about it, but she hugged him tightly.

'I was really proud of you today,' she said. 'You were so considerate of Angela's feelings. And so controlled with her parents.'

'It took me a long while to learn how to do that,' he admitted. 'Right up till after I'd done my National Service, I used to lash out with my fists at anyone who upset me, and it didn't take much. It was my first boss, after the Army, the bricklayer I was apprenticed to that got me out of it. He took me to a boxing club and let me loose on a punch-bag. He was a really tough man, brought up in the slums of Glasgow, so he knew what he was talking about.'

'A father figure,' Fifi said reflectively. 'According to Mrs Jarvis, Alfie Muckle learned all his nasty ways from his father. I wonder what Angela will turn out like?'

'Her mother,' Dan said sadly. 'She'll go off with the first man who asks her, almost certainly another vicious animal like Alfie, and she'll bring another brood of unloved and neglected kids into this world.'

'Don't!' Fifi exclaimed, tears springing to her eyes. 'You

didn't end up like that, so it isn't a foregone conclusion.'

'If it hadn't been for my old boss and other men I worked with, I probably would've,' he said dourly. 'They were all hard men, but they were proud of their building skills and believed that nothing was of value unless they'd worked for it. They loved their wives and families too, I saw a softness in them when they boasted about them. So I began to look up to them rather than wide boys who lived on their wits. Then I met you, and all at once I felt as if I was the luckiest man alive.'

Fifi thought of her parents and their feelings about Dan. She supposed that if they could see Dale Street and people like Molly and Alfie Muckle they'd be even more convinced that he was intent on dragging her down.

'The luck was all mine,' she said, smiling, and kissed his cheek again. 'You are the best thing that's ever happened to me.'

The following morning, while Dan was out getting the Sunday papers, Yvette Dupré called unexpectedly carrying two cushions.

'I 'ope I am not intruding,' she said. 'But I wanted to geeve you these as a little welcome present.'

Fifi was so touched and surprised she hardly knew what to say. The cushions were simply beautiful, pale green ruched silk, the kind she'd only ever seen in glossy magazines.

'They are so lovely, what a kind thought,' Fifi gasped, running her fingers over the intricate ruching. 'Did you make them yourself?'

'Why, of course,' Yvette said with a faint blush of pleasure. 'I like to do this, it is, how you say?, my 'obby. I 'ope the colour is right for you.'

'I haven't got much of a colour scheme yet,' Fifi said, and

invited Yvette into the living room. 'I've been intending to replace those awful curtains, but I haven't seen any ready-made ones yet that I like.'

'If you find some material I will run them up for you,' Yvette said, wrinkling her nose at the hideous orange curtains. 'You must not spend much time looking at these, they are so ugly.'

Fifi said she couldn't trouble Yvette to sew curtains for her. Yvette said it would be a pleasure, even whipping a tape measure from her pocket and measuring the window.

Fifi offered her a cup of coffee and they chatted for a few minutes, then Yvette asked what had happened about Angela.

Fifi told her the gist of it, then finished up saying that Dan seemed to think Alfie wouldn't dare hurt her again.

'I think it is Dan who must watch out,' Yvette said warningly. 'Alfie is a bad man, and Molly, she is worse. They find it good to hurt people. You both must take good care.'

Fifi was in a very serene and happy mood as Dan had woken her with lovemaking, so she gently ribbed Yvette and asked if she wasn't over-reacting.

'I leeve next door to them.' Yvette reproved her with a stern look. 'I 'ear things I do not want to 'ear, all the time. You are young and pretty, your Dan is strong and handsome, they would take pleasure in spoiling the 'appiness you 'ave. Move away, Dale Street is not for you.'

Fifi could not take this seriously, it sounded such a melo-dramatic thing to say. But she was delighted to have Yvette visit her, and she wanted to know more about her, so she agreed she'd talk to Dan when he came home.

'Your concern is very touching,' Fifi said sincerely. 'But tell me about your customers. I see you in the window sewing at nights and I'm really curious about who wears the clothes you make.'

'They are grand ladies,' Yvette said with some pride. 'I used to work for a fashion 'ouse in Mayfair and I get to know some of them there. I do a little sewing and alterations on the side, but soon many ladies ask me to make clothes for them. So I leave the fashion 'ouse and now I make clothes only for them.'

'Have you got the whole ground floor?' Fifi asked. She knew perfectly well she had, as she made it her business to discover such things, but she hoped the question might make Yvette ask her over.

'Yes, it ees much like Frank's. The front room where I work, then there are double doors through to the bedroom at the back. Behind down the passage is the kitchen. I 'ave the garden too. But I cannot use it, not with them next door.' She paused, grimacing. 'I too should move away to a better place, but it is hard to make a move on my own.'

'How long have you lived here?' Fifi asked as they sipped their coffee.

'I come just before Christmas in 1946,' Yvette said. 'Eet was a very long, cold winter in 1947, I think sometimes I will die of the cold and I am so lonely because I know no English. But the Ubleys, the Jarvises and other people who have gone away now were kind to me. I even theenk then that Molly Muckle was my friend.'

'What did she do to you?' Fifi asked.

Yvette shrugged. 'She use me, and rob me. When I will not let her come into my flat any more she insult me. But I 'ave said enough, I must go now. Just you take care, even little Angela will steal from you if you let 'er in 'ere again. Molly will make 'er.'

Fifi did not tell Dan any more than that Yvette had made them the cushions as a housewarming present. She knew that he would not take her warning seriously. He would probably laugh and say Yvette was in need of a good rogering. That was his prescription for all troubled or neurotic women. Besides, Fifi couldn't really take it seriously either, Yvette was well-meaning but she spent too long on her own, and perhaps that made her brood on things other people would barely notice.

During the following week Fifi often saw Angela outside in the street during the evening. The swelling had gone down on her eye, but it was still very badly bruised. She looked listless, often just sitting on the kerb watching other children playing. But there were no other obvious injuries.

Two weeks later, however, Fifi had something more to worry about than what her neighbours were doing. Her period didn't arrive, and as she had always been regular, by the time she was a week late she was absolutely certain she was pregnant.

Having a baby was not part of their plan. They had talked about having children in the future, but not for a few years until they had a secure place to live and some money saved. They had always been so careful too. Dan had often joked that he ought to buy a gross of Durex at one go as they got through so many. But there had been a couple of times since they moved here when they'd got carried away and forgotten to take precautions.

Fifi viewed it as a calamity at first but she didn't tell Dan because she couldn't be absolutely certain. As the days ticked past and still nothing happened, she swung between dread and delight. It had been hard enough to find this flat, but to find one suitable for a baby would be ten times harder.

But then sometimes she found herself imagining walking a baby in a pram to the park, holding its hand as it took its first steps. She found herself looking in baby-shop windows and even observing heavily pregnant women with real interest.

But whether it was dread or delight she felt, she was afraid of giving up the life she had now. It was good working in Chancery Lane, the other secretaries and typists were fun, they went out shopping together in the lunch hour or sat gossiping in the sunshine. In the evenings she and Dan often went to the pub after their dinner and on Saturday afternoons they went off exploring London, usually eating out. On Sundays they stayed in bed until later. All that would end with a baby.

Then there were her parents. Would this heal the rift or make things even worse?

Chapter six

'Pregnant?' Dan repeated. His expression was one of deep shock.

'I knew you wouldn't like it,' Fifi said, and promptly burst into tears. She had waited a full month to make absolutely certain before telling him, and every day had been miserable for her.

'Who said I wouldn't like it?' he said, getting up from his chair and pulling her into his arms. 'I was just surprised, that's all. Give me a few seconds to take it in and I'll lead you in a joyful tango around the room.'

'You can't do a tango,' Fifi sobbed. 'Can you?'

'How hard can it be? You just lean the girl over like this,' he said, bending her backwards. 'And hold a rose between your teeth. I'll have to pop out for one of those.'

Fifi's sobs turned to a giggle.

She had felt sick almost all day, and that was what finally made her blurt the news out to Dan the minute she came in from work.

'That's better,' he said, holding her face between his two hands and showering kisses all over it. 'So we're going to have a little Reynolds. When will it be?'

'Early next March, I think I'm just on seven weeks,' she said. 'Aren't you cross?'

'Cross!' he exclaimed. 'Why should I be? It's great news, the best ever. I always wanted a son and heir.'

'It might be a girl and we've got nothing for him or her to inherit,' Fifi reminded him.

'Except our looks and brains,' he said, and his smile grew ever wider as he looked at her.

'But we can't have a baby here. Imagine having to pull a pram up all those stairs,' she said anxiously. 'And how will we find another place we can afford?'

'Old worry-guts,' he said with affection. 'We leave the pram in the hall in the time-honoured tradition of slum dwellers.'

Fifi looked stricken.

'I was joking.' He laughed. 'We'll find somewhere else. If I work all day Saturdays we'll soon have enough for a deposit on a house of our own. A bloke at work said he only put down two hundred. We could scrape that together.'

Fifi leaned into his arms. For a whole month she had been so worried and scared. But now Dan knew and seemed happy about it, she felt inclined to be that way too.

'We'll have to tell your parents,' Dan said thoughtfully as he held her. 'With luck it might even make them accept me.'

Fifi looked up at his words. He never mentioned her parents any more, but she realized then that he had been brooding about them. 'I'm sorry,' she said softly, suddenly seeing that she only ever considered how situations affected her, and rarely thought about how it was for him.

'Don't be,' he said, kissing her on the nose. 'I don't suppose I'll be too happy if my daughter wants to marry a guttersnipe either.'

'You aren't a guttersnipe,' she said quickly. 'Don't say such things.'

'There's only this much,' he said, holding up two fingers an inch apart, 'between me and the Muckles. If I'd married someone like Molly, there'd be even less.'

'Rubbish,' Fifi retorted. 'You've always worked, you aren't a thief or a bully, you've got a brain, for goodness' sake! There's a million miles between you.'

Dan shook his head. 'I'll only think that when I can carry you over the threshold of our own house.'

A month later, at the very end of July, Fifi sat in a chair by the open window knitting a little white baby jacket. Yvette had helped her get started, and though she still kept dropping stitches, she found it a rather soothing pastime.

It had been a scorching day, and though it was nine in the evening, it was still very hot and sticky, without any breeze. Dan was working late, as he had done every evening for the past two weeks. The office building he was working on was behind schedule, and all the men were doing overtime to catch up. Fifi didn't really mind being alone, but she was concerned that Dan was working too hard: last night he'd been so tired when he got home that he could barely speak.

She was finding her own journey to and from work hard. She felt she couldn't breathe on the tube, and although her stomach had only the slightest curve so far, the waistbands of her skirts were now too tight. Sometimes on the way home she had to get off the tube because she felt so giddy and sick in the crowds.

She wondered if this was something that would go as the pregnancy advanced, or whether it would get worse. Her mother would have been the right person to advise her, but her parents hadn't yet replied to the letter she wrote to inform them. That was over two weeks ago, so she could only suppose they thought a baby was another calamity.

Putting down her knitting, Fifi turned to look out of the window. All the children who had been playing in the street earlier had gone in now, but Angela was still outside, perched on her doorstep playing cat's cradle with a bit of wool, all by herself.

Fifi had been so preoccupied by her pregnancy that she hadn't thought much about Angela in the past weeks. She saw her often enough in the street, but Angela had very little to say, just a shy flickering smile, the odd halting question about where Fifi was going. The bruising around her eye was all gone now, but she still looked pitiful because she was so pale and thin.

Now the schools had broken up for the holiday, Fifi doubted the child got anything to eat at midday. Yvette had said she was pushed out of the house in the morning and stayed outside all day.

Fifi had become very friendly with Yvette since she made the curtains for her. They were only cheap cotton from the market, but the design of lilies on a pale green background was very pretty and they fitted from the ceiling right down to the floor and made the room look really swish. Each time Fifi looked at them she smiled because they were so lovely and she thought Yvette was very clever.

Yet she was puzzling too. Not just her frumpy clothes, or the hermit-like life she led, or even her flat which was a complete shambles – Fifi had got used to all that. The puzzling part about Yvette was that she gave nothing away about herself.

She had great warmth, she took others' troubles to heart and often refused to accept any payment for little sewing jobs she did for neighbours. She was also intensely interested in other people, so why didn't she ever reveal her hopes, dreams, past mistakes or glories?

Her ground-floor flat was overrun with pattern books, the walls almost hidden with fashion pictures cut from magazines. Boxes of fabrics and trimmings spilled out on to the floor, cards of buttons and reels of coloured thread covered almost every surface. Yet there appeared to be no personal belongings, not even a photograph. She fitted her clients in their own homes, admitting she would be embarrassed for them to come to her. Fifi could only assume, in the absence of any information, that Yvette had no family or real friends of her own. She appeared to live her entire life at second hand, listening to her clients talk about their families, holidays and social life.

Yet Fifi loved going over to see Yvette. She was so welcoming, so interested, and she had a kind of wisdom about life and people that was quite unique. That was why she was the first person after Dan that Fifi told about the expected baby.

'That ees wonderful,' Yvette exclaimed in delight, clapping her hands with joy. 'You must be so 'appy.'

Fifi had confided that she wasn't certain about that, and then went on to tell her about her parents disapproving of Dan, and how she was afraid if they didn't manage to get a house of their own they'd get stuck in Dale Street.

'Then you must, 'ow they say?, take the bull by the horns,' Yvette said with an enigmatic smile. 'Become the strong one.'

Fifi took that to mean Yvette thought she should push Dan harder. But that wasn't necessary – since she'd told him about the baby he wanted to work all the hours God sent. They'd stopped going out for meals and if they went for a drink it was only for one. He was taking fatherhood very seriously.

It occurred to Fifi that Yvette had misjudged Dan in much the same way her parents had. Why did they assume he was feckless and weak? That wasn't how he was at all.

*

Yvette glanced up at the windows across the street as she reached to draw her own curtains. She could see Fifi silhouetted in her window on the top floor and guessed she was alone again. She hoped Dan really was working late and not down the pub with his workmates.

Yvette really liked Fifi. But then she was the kind of girl almost anyone would like, for she was beautiful, sunny-natured and so full of life. She remembered how back in early June Fifi had come rushing in to tell her that Dr Stephen Ward, the osteopath at the centre of the big vice scandal, had committed suicide. Yvette had taken very little interest in the affair of Christine Keeler and John Profumo, for she'd known people back in France far worse, but Fifi knew every last thing about it, and the girl's passionate interest made her laugh. Yvette hoped for Fifi's sake that she'd move on soon, before this street changed her.

In the sixteen years Yvette had spent here, she'd observed how the street made people apathetic. It was almost as if there was something poisonous in the soot-laden air. No one of course really wanted to live here, except perhaps old Mrs Jarvis and the Muckles who'd never known anywhere else. Everyone said it was just a temporary place to live until they found something better. Yet almost all those who had arrived since the war ended were still here.

Stan the Pole had told her he was going to find work on a farm. Miss Diamond had her sights set on a place on Clapham Common. Frank and June Ubley were intending to join their daughter and grandchildren in Australia. But Stan was still a dustman and Miss Diamond was still complaining that it wasn't what she was used to. Sadly, June Ubley had died, but Frank stayed on, keeping his net curtains snowy-white in memory of his wife, when there was nothing to stop him going to Australia. There was always farm work available for a man like Stan, and as for Miss Diamond, surely she could reply to any of those advertisements for flats that required a mature business lady with good references?

Yet Yvette knew why they hadn't moved on, for the street had affected her too. She loathed everything about it – the meanness, squalor, lack of sunshine, the dust and noise from the coal yard, and the Muckles next door above all else. She could afford to live somewhere better, so why was she still here?

She had told Fifi it was because she couldn't face searching for another flat or packing up all her belongings. That was true to a point, but it was also the neighbours, with the exception of the Muckles, who kept her here.

In the absence of real family, these people had taken their place. As she sat sewing in her window, their familiar faces made her feel less alone. She knew they were like her, the flotsam and jetsam of humanity, tossed up here to live out the remainder of their damaged lives. Some had shared their stories with her, and it made her feel better about herself because they valued her ability to listen and comfort.

Without that, what would she have? Her clients were not friends; they might value her dressmaking skills, but not her as a person. If she lost her sight, or her fingers became crippled with arthritis, she would never hear from them again. But that wouldn't be true of her neighbours here, they'd care enough to call and ask if she needed shopping or a fire lit. They would invite her into their homes, for though being French set her apart from them a little, they sensed she was truly one of them.

She might ache to live somewhere clean, quiet and beautiful, but deep down she felt this was all she deserved.

In Fifi she saw something akin to that too. Intelligent,

pretty and from a very good family, she was a girl who should have had the world at her feet. Yet maybe because she had burned her bridges by marrying Dan, she had got into the mindset that she now belonged in the kind of world he came from.

Dan was certainly very handsome and he had a rough charm too with his ready smile and his irrepressible sense of humour. Yvette liked him very much. But the fact remained that he was a working-class man and he couldn't transform himself into anything else.

Yvette knew Fifi saw living in London as a bit of an adventure. She saw the people in this street as 'characters' rather than life's casualties. But once her baby was born, with only Dan's wages coming in, she was likely to view things very differently. Had she realized those characters were likely to complain about a crying baby? She would be lonely and bored stuck in those two small rooms all day, and once she started complaining, Dan might do exactly what other men in the street did – run off to the pub.

Yet worse still to Yvette's mind was that Fifi would lose that sparkle of hers, and that every day she'd find herself a little further alienated from her own family and the middle-class world she grew up in.

She deserved better than that.

Yvette knew these things because it was what her own mother had endured. She had run off with a man her parents considered a bad lot, and they were right about him too, for he did leave her when the going got tough after Yvette was born. Mama had sewed from first light until it was too dark to see, but they still often went to bed hungry. Yvette wondered what she would make of her daughter ending up in much the same situation, albeit without a child. She thought she had secured safety and the chance of a much better life for Yvette by sending her away when the Germans took Paris. Perhaps it was as well that she died before the war ended, for it would have killed her anyway if she'd known what happened to her child.

Yvette could remember her first night here in Dale Street very clearly. She was so glad to have a home of her own at last that she barely noticed it was virtually a slum. She was just twenty-one, and two years had passed since the war and all the horrors she'd endured during it.

She had next to nothing to unpack, just a change of clothes, a towel, a few shillings in her purse and a small bag of groceries. She knew no more than a dozen words of English and it was so cold that she had to wear all her clothes to bed. But she was happy because she'd been taken on as a seamstress in Mayfair, to start the following day, and she believed she'd left all the hurt and shame back in France.

Mr and Mrs Jarvis were the first to offer her a welcome. Mr Jarvis had been in France during the First War, and knew a little of the language, and he invited her over to share their Sunday lunch. Sadly, he died a few months later, but Yvette would always remember him fondly, for that Sunday he had taught her so many English words by naming things and making her repeat them.

Yet even through the cold and loneliness of that winter of 1947, she still found many reasons to be glad she'd come to London. First, she found she stopped dwelling on the past so much. The nightmares she'd had virtually every night for so long became less and less frequent. She liked the polite way the English queued for buses and their rations, never pushing in as they did in Paris. She liked their affection for the King and the Royal Family, and the way people tried to help her when they realized she was French. But above all she liked London itself. It might be battered from the war, with weed-strewn bomb sites everywhere, nothing much in the shops, and so many people living under terrible conditions, but there were still many beautiful buildings and wonderful parks. She found much to admire in the English, too, for they held themselves with pride. They grumbled of course, but she also saw that they pitched in to help one another, and the weak and the old in local communities were supported by their neighbours.

Yvette remembered how at the height of her loneliness, she brought scraps of silk and velvet home from the workshop. She would lie in her bed rubbing them comfortingly against her cheek, just as she used to do as a child with her mother's dressmaking scraps.

As a little girl the pieces of luxurious cloth had transported her into day-dreams. She would see herself and her mother living in a grand house; the table would be laden with every kind of expensive food and they'd be wearing beautiful clothes. Her mother was never toiling at her sewing-machine in these dreams, she would be playing a piano, dancing or picking roses in the garden. And she smiled all the time.

Yvette's adult day-dreams were far less fanciful. The touch and the smell of fine fabrics were merely reassurance that she had landed in a safe, female-only world. She might use her dressmaking skills to ensure her ladies got male attention at balls, parties and weddings, but she didn't have to suffer it herself.

Sometimes these same ladies told her she had beautiful eyes and they held their own clothes up to her, clearly suggesting that if only she'd dress in something more colourful and fashionable, she would soon have admirers. Yvette would giggle and blush, and let them think it was timidity that prevented her.

*

The sudden blaring of music next door made Yvette start. She was used to Molly shouting – the woman seemed unable to communicate with Alfie or her children in any other way – but music in that house went with drinking and that often led to a vicious fight with Alfie.

People in this street always claimed that Alfie was the worse half of the couple. But Yvette knew better. Alfie was more obviously reprehensible: ignorant, brutish, a thief and a perverted bully. But Yvette was inclined to see some of those traits in most men, and she could handle Alfie.

On the face of it Molly appeared to be nothing more than a harassed, downtrodden woman who had had the misfortune to marry the wrong man. But in fact she was far brighter than Alfie, the instigator of much of their mischief, and far more cunning. She drank and swore like a man, she showed no maternal feelings, and she was predatory and dangerous.

Molly was in her late twenties back in '47 when Yvette came to Dale Street. She had four children already, and four more would arrive over the next eight years, but back then she looked far younger than she really was, clear-skinned, shapely and attractive in a pin-up girl sort of way. There was also a spontaneity and jollity about her that was very appealing.

She seemed so kind in those early days. She acted as a go-between for Yvette and her landlord when the geyser didn't work or the fire smoked. She would often give Yvette a couple of rashers of bacon or an egg when all her rations were gone. Her children supplied wood for Yvette's fire in that first bitter winter, and Molly often brought her in a glass of brandy to warm her up. All Yvette could do in return was offer to make Molly a dress.

She could see Molly now when she came in for the first

fitting. It was around seven in the evening in early May, and it had been the first warm day of the year. She had on her usual everyday skirt, a worn hound's-tooth black and white check, but instead of the customary stained blue jumper, she was wearing a cream crêpe de Chine blouse, and her face was flushed pink from the sun.

'*Très jolie*,' Yvette said, not knowing the English then for 'You look pretty'.

She thought Molly understood it was a compliment as she smiled, and Yvette remembered thinking that she wished she knew the words to say that Molly should smile more, as it made her look beautiful.

She had a voluptuous, very curvy figure with a small waist and full breasts, and the cream blouse emphasized her shape and gave a becoming glow to her complexion. Even her peroxide-blonde hair looked lovely that night, for she'd just washed and curled it.

Yvette indicated that Molly was to take off her clothes, and stood waiting with the blue and white summer dress she was about to fit in her hands. She noticed an old scar above Molly's right breast when she had stripped down to her petticoat, but it wasn't until she turned for the back of the bodice to be pinned in place that Yvette saw all the other scars.

Livid red ones and old faded brown ones criss-crossed her back and Yvette was so shocked she almost stuck a pin into Molly's flesh.

She had no English words for 'What has happened to you?' but she didn't need to ask that anyway. She knew they were the scars of beatings, almost certainly achieved with a thin cane, because she had such scars herself.

She had tears in her eye as she fitted the dress, and Molly saw them and wiped them away tenderly with her finger, smiling at her. She said something Yvette couldn't understand, but by the tone of her voice she felt Molly was assuring her it was nothing.

Yvette knew now to her cost that Molly saw sympathy as weakness and gullibility. She was soon asking to borrow money which she never repaid, and to dump her children on Yvette for her to look after. She should've refused and backed away as soon as she saw she was being used, but she felt sorry for Molly and indebted to her too.

Yvette knew now that Molly was never the victim she took her for. The truth was, for every blow she received from Alfie, he got one back, and she got some kind of perverted thrill from violence.

In sixteen years Yvette must have witnessed and overheard hundreds of shocking and depraved scenes, and she knew now that even if Molly were to meet a rich man who would overlook her drinking and sluttish ways, she couldn't leave Alfie. They were joined in some unholy bond which had nothing to do with love.

But Yvette didn't know any of that back in the late forties. She learned it gradually as her understanding of English improved and the gossip from the street began to filter through to her. Sadly, by then she had already become trapped in Molly's web.

Yvette could still remember the day the woman boasted that she and Alfie frequently had other sexual partners. Yvette was so shocked she listened in silence as her neighbour gleefully described the thrill they got out of watching each other with someone else. Her language was graphic, intended to upset and disgust Yvette. Molly was in fact doing to Yvette what she so often did to Alfie – trying to provoke a fight.

Yvette had made so many excuses for Molly up until that

point. But that day she suddenly realized that this wasn't a woman who was merely overstretched and unable to cope. She actually thrived on chaos and she had a black heart. She was also trying her best to recruit Yvette into her sordid games.

It was only then that Yvette attempted to distance herself from the entire Muckle family. She didn't answer the door to the children, and ignored Molly calling to her over the back fence. Even when Angela, the last child, was born, she didn't weaken and offer any help. But living in such close proximity, she couldn't block out what went on next door.

In the Muckle household bodies were shared like food and drink. Molly had sex with two of Alfie's brothers while he looked on, and Alfie regularly used Dora, Molly's backward sister. Recently, Mike, Alfie's young nephew, had come to live with them, and now it was he who had laid claim to Dora. But Yvette had heard Mike rutting noisily out in the backyard with Molly on several occasions since then, when the children were watching television in the front room. The four oldest children had left home: the two boys were always in and out of prison, and the two girls left when they were heavily pregnant, never to return.

Yvette had no illusions left about Molly or Alfie now. They were totally amoral in every aspect of their lives; they would steal anything from anyone, intimidate anyone who opposed them, neglected and hurt their children and lived in utter squalor. Each time the police came to the house Yvette prayed that whatever their latest crime was, it would be serious enough for them to be sent to prison for a long stretch. Yet this never happened. Somehow they always seemed to wriggle out of it, and they were getting worse as the years went by.

Yvette was stuck now with having to be on her guard all

the time. She had to remember not just to keep the back door locked so one of the children couldn't jump the back fence and steal something from the kitchen, but also never to confront or upset Molly in any way.

Back in the early years she had foolishly told Molly a little of what happened to her during the war. She knew that if she were ever to cross her, Molly would use this against her, and she just couldn't take that risk.

This was why she didn't dare go to the social workers and report Molly and Alfie for what they did to their children. She hadn't even found enough courage to warn Dan that she'd overheard Alfie saying he'd get even with him for threatening him about Angela.

Yvette sighed deeply as she slipped the bodice of the dress she was making on to her dressmaker's dummy. It was too hot to sew any more tonight, her sweaty hands might mark the fabric. She would turn up her radio a little louder and try to blot out the sounds from next door. Perhaps if she had a little brandy she'd fall asleep before things got really nasty.

Frank Ubley shut his window as the music blared out, picked up a book and went into the bedroom at the back of the house. He had only to see Molly and he got angry, but when he saw her dancing around to music, drinking, laughing and shouting, he felt murderous.

The bedroom was just as it was when June died. He hadn't even had the heart to get rid of her clothes. They had bought the new divan in 1953, the day before Coronation Day, and they were so thrilled finally to get rid of the old one they'd inherited from June's mother that they joked they were going to spend all day in it.

June was a real home-maker. With a pot of paint and a

few yards of material she could transform any room, however dismal, into a little palace. She found this place when Frank was waiting to be demobbed from the Army. He came home briefly on a twenty-four hour pass, took one look at it and wanted to run out the door, just the way young Fifi upstairs said she had.

But June insisted she could make it nice, and by the time he got his demob three months later, she had. She'd painted and papered everywhere, even though no one else could get decorating materials for love or money. Green and white stripes in the front room, the bedroom pale pink, and the kitchen all yellow and white. But it wasn't just decorating she was good at, she made things so comfortable and nice. A little table with a lamp on by his chair, a pouffe to put his feet on, and within ten minutes of getting home his dinner was always on the table.

If she hadn't been such a perfect wife in every way, maybe he would have been able to admit what had happened with Molly. But he couldn't hurt her that way, it would have broken her heart.

If only he hadn't made out he was on guard duty at the camp that weekend when he was really in Soho. But all his mates wanted to celebrate the end of the war, and if he'd come home drunk in the early hours June wouldn't have liked it. He didn't think much of himself for having sex in an alley with the blonde who talked dirty; as soon as he sobered up he was ashamed. But all the lads got up to much the same, it was the combination of the drink and the thrill of the war ending.

He had been back with June three days before he discovered that the blonde also lived in Dale Street, right opposite them.

As he walked down the street to the shop, she'd come

out of her door. It was so strange that he thought he had no recollection of what the woman in the alley looked like, but the moment they came face to face, he knew it was her. But what was worse, she recognized him too.

Of all the women in London, why did that one have to be living right across the street? And why did she have to turn out to be the most evil bitch in God's creation?

At first he thought his secret was safe as Molly was married too. But by the time she demanded money for her silence, Frank had been told by dozens of people that Alfie actively encouraged his wife to go with other men. He might give a man a kicking for doing so, but that was just part of the sport.

Frank was forty-nine in 1945. He landed a job as a mechanic at the bus station right after his demob, and he thought he and June were sitting pretty. Their only daughter Wendy was married to an electrician, and the couple had a home of their own and a baby on the way. Frank believed the years until he retired were going to be the best years yet for him and June.

Molly ruined all that.

It was like living with an unexploded bomb. A few weeks, sometimes months, passed between her demands for money, and he'd begin to think it was all over. Then she'd sidle up to him in the street and once again she was threatening to tell June. He wanted to move away, he tried desperately to find another flat, but with thousands of people homeless after the war, there was nothing. And June didn't want to leave anyway; Dale Street suited her as Wendy and her husband Ted were only down the road in Elephant and Castle and of course she wanted to see John, their little grandson, frequently.

John was quickly followed by Martin and then Susan, and

in 1953, Wendy and Ted decided to emigrate to Australia. Frank and June intended to follow them out there, but June must have told someone in the street and it got back to Molly. This time she demanded fifty pounds to keep quiet.

Frank boiled over every time he thought about it. June was already upset that her daughter and grandchildren were leaving England, and she was living on her nerves because she was afraid she and Frank wouldn't be allowed to go too because of their ages. If Molly dropped her bombshell, Frank knew that would be catastrophic.

He had about a hundred pounds saved up, but they'd need that in Australia until he found a job and somewhere to live.

He tried to be tough with Molly, saying he didn't have the money and that he'd go to the police if she persisted. But she just laughed at him and said he'd be sorry if he did. A couple of days later, while Frank was at work and June out shopping, they were burgled. They didn't have much of value for anyone to take, just a few bits of silver that had belonged to June's grandmother's, and some odd bits of jewellery, but it was all gone when June got home.

Everyone suspected the Muckles. Who else but them would see June leave the house and know there was no one else about? But this was confirmed as far as Frank was concerned when June showed him that his Post Office savings book had been taken out of the drawer in their bedroom and left on the chest of drawers. He knew that was Molly's way of telling him that she knew how much money he'd got and she intended to go ahead with her threat unless he paid up.

Nothing could be proved. The police searched the Muckles' house and found nothing. Frank had to pay

Molly, and it wasn't long after that June became ill. They found she had cancer while performing a hysterectomy.

In the two years before June finally died, Molly slowly bled their savings dry, yet he had to keep her silence. He couldn't bear the thought of June passing away knowing he'd been unfaithful.

He had to give up his job to nurse June towards the end. Too old now to apply for an assisted passage to Australia, and with no money left to pay his fare, through that evil bitch of a woman he'd never see his daughter and grand-children again. He hated Molly Muckle so much he would happily kill her and her brats, and never mind if he had to swing for it.

'Get up to bed, you little shits,' Molly yelled at her children because they were arguing. Angela had crept off the minute she'd come in from the street, but the three older ones had ignored her previous order.

'I wanna see *Quatermass*,' Alan, the fourteen-year-old, said belligerently. 'I always watch it.'

'I'll give you Quatermass with the back of my hand if you don't fuck off,' Molly retorted, rising somewhat unsteadily out of her chair.

The three children shuffled nervously backwards towards the door.

They were all remarkably alike, with the same dirty, straw-coloured hair, pinched pale faces, light brown eyes and sharp features. Alan, the eldest, had a squint. Mary, though only thirteen, had big breasts which were stretching her grubby blouse to bursting point. Joan, who was ten, had large buck teeth.

'Go on, piss off.' Molly took a threatening step towards them. 'Mike and I want a bit of peace.'

'You said we could 'ave some chips,' Alan said, trying to look tough and eyeing Mike, his father's nephew, with deep suspicion. 'And where's our Dora?'

'If you don't sodding well fuck off I'll brain you,' Molly screamed out. 'And tell that half-wit upstairs to have a piss. If she wets the bed again I'll belt 'er so 'ard she won't be able to sit on 'er arse for a week.'

Realizing their luck had run out, the two younger ones fled. Alan hung on a second or two longer, but as his mother stepped threateningly towards him, he backed away and scampered upstairs.

'That's more like it.' Molly slammed the door shut and returned to the couch. 'Get us another drink, Mike.'

Mike got up, picked up her glass and walked towards the kitchen. He had an identical build to Alfie and all his brothers; five feet eight, bull-necked, broad-shouldered and muscular. His sandy hair was already receding, and he had the start of a beer gut. He was what his mother called 'homely', which he took to mean he was no Cary Grant.

Stopping in the kitchen doorway, he looked back. 'Where's Dora?' he asked.

'Gone to the flicks.'

'Who wiv?'

'On 'er tod.'

'She don't like going nowhere on 'er tod!'

'She does if I tell 'er to,' Molly retorted. 'Now get us a beer.'

Mike was twenty-five and had lived with his Aunt Molly and Uncle Alfie since coming out of prison two years ago. He'd only got six months for breaking into a sweet shop, but his mother wouldn't let him back in the house again. Within a few weeks he'd realized that there were some serious drawbacks to living here; it was like a madhouse most of the time, but he'd got nowhere else to go.

He was pretty certain Molly had got rid of Dora and the kids tonight because she was feeling randy, and just the thought of that turned his stomach.

It wasn't very smart of him to start having it off with Dora. She was ugly, thirty-five and backward to boot, but getting his leg over was his first priority when he got out of the nick, and Dora was there, like a bitch on heat. To be fair to her she was kind of sweet, always eager and grateful, idolizing him and prepared to do anything he asked. But it was a bit sickening to know Alfie screwed her too whenever he felt like it.

It might not have been clever to get involved with Dora, but it was total insanity giving Molly one too. She was old, fat and as vicious as a rabid dog, and he never knew when she was going to pounce next. Weeks could go by and she wouldn't come near him, then out of the blue she'd start touching him up, coming on strong. And she even did it in front of Dora and Alfie.

Mike stood for a moment in the kitchen, looking at the mess. It wasn't any worse than usual, but perhaps because he knew what Molly had in mind tonight, he suddenly saw how filthy it really was.

The sink was full of dirty dishes that had been there for days, the table was strewn with more, along with sauce and beer bottles, chip papers and other bits of rubbish. The floor, never washed, was so dirty he couldn't make out the pattern on the worn lino. Empty bottles, rubbish, dirty clothes and even engine parts were strewn around. A dead mouse in a trap had been there so long it was putrefying. The smell was sickening, worse than a sewer.

His mum had always said Molly was a dirty slut. She used

to say other stuff too, until his dad gave her a back-hander to shut her up. But his mum didn't know the half of it and she'd have fifty fits if she was to find out.

Mike picked up the bottle of beer from the floor and filled Molly's glass. He wondered if he dared just give it to her and then go on out.

As he hesitated, Bill Haley's 'Rock Around the Clock' suddenly blared out on the gramophone.

Molly's usual taste in music when she was randy was Bobby Vee or Billy Fury. Bill Haley was Alfie's favourite. Mike looked round the door to see what she was doing, and found she'd turned the sound down on the telly and was gyrating around to the music. She looked disgusting; he could see her belly and tits wobbling around under her tight yellow dress.

'I've got to go and see me mate,' he shouted over the music as he handed her the beer.

He was halfway to the front door when she caught hold of his arm. 'You ain't goin' nowhere,' she said. 'We gotta make a lot of noise. Make out Alfie's in 'ere too.'

Mike was confused now. 'Why?' he asked.

'Cos he's up to summat.' She tapped her nose to imply it was a secret. 'Come on, dance wiv me fer a bit, then we'll start shouting and bawling. If them nosy bastards across the street look out their winders they'll think you're 'im.'

'You mean like an alibi?' Mike shouted over the deafening music. He had often looked at the window from outside, and knew that the thin cloth tacked up inside became opaque when the light was on. It wouldn't give anyone a clear view, but they'd get a pretty good idea of what was going on inside. And he and Alfie were very close in size and height.

''E finally got it!' she said sarcastically, and grabbing his hand she made him jive with her.

Alfie and Molly often danced together when they were drunk. When Mike first moved in he'd thought it was kind of nice. But he'd soon found out it was usually the first step towards a fight, and their fights were bloody ones, neither giving in till one of them went down.

In two years he'd seen them breaking bottles over each other's heads, punching each other like heavyweight boxers. Alfie once pushed Molly's head right through the glass in the window. But even more sickening was what came after. Violence turned them on, they could be bleeding like stuck pigs, then all of a sudden they'd be fucking. They didn't care who else was there. Alfie would push Molly down over the back of the couch or doggy-fashion on the floor, and the noise they'd make was unbelievable.

So Mike was very apprehensive as he danced with Molly, assuming she would expect him to run through the usual ritual completely. As the first record finished and the second, Elvis's 'Jailhouse Rock', fell down on to the turntable, she turned up the volume.

'We'll start fighting as this one ends,' she said in his ear because the music was so loud. 'You start pushing me about, I'll scream and throw stuff at you, then you pick up the poker and make out you're hitting me wiv it. We gotta make a lot of noise. We want everyone in the street to know we're 'aving a ding-dong and we gotta make it look real.'

Mike sincerely hoped that a pretend fight wouldn't have the same effect on her as a real one usually did, but he went along with it anyway. As the record ended he began pushing her, and she wrestled with him while shouting out obscenities.

'What if Alan comes down?' he asked, as he pushed her down on to the couch and rained punches down on to the cushion beside her.

''E won't do that,' she said between a couple of ear-piercing screams. 'The kid's a fuckin' coward. 'E'd be scared 'e'd cop it an' all.'

Mike found there was something profoundly satisfying about whacking a poker down on the couch, yelling out the kind of insults he had always wanted to throw at Molly. He overturned the coffee table in just the way he'd seen Alfie do, hurled an empty beer bottle at the hearth and got Molly in a half-Nelson. He was actually enjoying it.

'You fuckin' fat bitch,' he yelled at her, for a moment tempted to hit her for real. 'You're a slag, a fuckin' slag, and I'm gonna kill you.'

He had to admit Molly played a blinder. She screamed, shouted, swore, then got away from him and ran up and down the stairs. At one point she was clawing at the front door as if trying to get out. She was so good it would fool anyone into thinking she was being murdered. Yet the fact that no one came banging on the door spoke volumes. Mike reckoned the neighbours would love it if she was to be found dead.

'No, Alfie, no,' she yelled out in the kitchen, and threw a few dirty pans on the floor for good measure.

Mike could well imagine the effect it was having on their neighbours. Dozens of times in the past there had been real fights like this one, and he'd looked out of the window and seen people opening the windows, coming out on to the street, getting into little confabs about what they should do to stop it. As it was a hot night and everyone had their windows open, they'd all be getting steamed up about it by now.

Molly made Mike keep it up for a good three-quarters of an hour, then she signalled to him to turn off the music and go upstairs as if to bed. As he left the room, Molly slumped down on the couch and sobbed noisily.

Mike was well used to following Molly's orders without question, but as he went upstairs he couldn't help but wonder what his mother would have to say about this situation. She was no angel, she'd done her share of lying to the police to keep her husband and Mike out of the nick, yet she would never even think of staging something like this. But then, his parents didn't hit each other, or argue that much; they certainly didn't go in for sex with an audience. He could see now that his own childhood had been idyllic compared with that of his cousins.

He turned the light on in Molly and Alfie's bedroom at the front of the house, then turned it off again as if he'd gone to bed. He stayed sitting in the dark, listening to Molly sobbing downstairs.

He wondered how she could do it so easily, it sounded exactly like the real thing. But then he supposed she'd had a lot of practice in acting over the years, and that was why she got benefits she wasn't entitled to, and the coppers hardly ever managed to nick Alfie for anything.

The bedroom had a blanket over the window, and through a hole in it Mike could see the blonde girl opposite, staring out of the window. She wasn't watching the Muckles' house, but looking up the road. He supposed she was waiting for her husband to come home.

Mike felt sorry for himself then, wishing he had a girl like her waiting for him. She was so beautiful; he could see her profile with the light behind her, a neat little straight nose, a long slender neck, and her hair down over her shoulders.

He'd come in here once and caught Alfie wanking as he watched her cleaning her windows. Mike had been sickened by that, though he had to pretend he thought it was funny. It was all right to wank over women in magazines, but not someone real.

But Alfie had stopped drooling over the blonde since she took Angela in when she had a black eye. He seemed to think she or her husband had tried to grass him up.

All of a sudden, like a light switched on in a dark room, Mike put Alfie's absence, the need for an alibi, and the girl watching out for her husband, together. To his horror he realized that Alfie had gone to fill in the bloke!

A year ago he would've loved it. He'd have been one hundred per cent behind Alfie, but not now. Molly and Alfie always went too far. It was going to come down on top of them one of these days, and Mike had a feeling that if he was still living here then, he'd cop it too.

Molly stopped her pretend crying suddenly, then he heard her speak. Curious, Mike went to the top of the stairs to listen. To his surprise he realized that Alfie was back – he must have climbed along the wall out the back and come in through the kitchen door.

'Did you do what I said?' he was asking Molly.

'Course I did. The whole street will say you was 'ere. Did you collar 'im?'

'Yeah. But I think I 'it 'im too 'ard. 'E went down like a ton of bricks.'

Mike went on down the stairs. 'What you done?' he asked, thinking Alfie looked scared. 'Was it the geyser across the road?'

Alfie nodded, and grinned humourlessly. 'Reckon I might 'ave finished 'im off and all. 'E looked as dead as a doornail when I left 'im. You get off now down the back way and meet our Dora, she'll be waiting outside the Odeon. Anyone asks, you've bin wiv 'er all night.'

Chapter seven

Dan came round sufficiently to know he was lying on the ground, but when he tried to move, sharp pains shot through both his head and his ribs.

He lay still for a moment, trying to work out where he was and what had happened to him. He remembered leaving the building site with the other men clearly enough. It was almost dark and as they got to the alleyway which was a short cut to the tube station, the others said they were going for a pint. They asked him to go with them, but he turned them down because Fifi was waiting for him.

The last thing he could recall as he turned into the alley was Owen the chippie shouting out for him to mind the dog shit as the smell of it on a man's boots killed any woman's passion.

That was it. Nothing more, and he guessed he was still in the alley as it was so dark. And he could smell dog shit. Therefore, it stood to reason someone must have crept up behind him and hit him hard on the head. But why? It was a Thursday, not pay day, and he hadn't fallen out with anyone. Perhaps whoever did it thought he was someone else?

He attempted to get up, but the pain in his head was so bad he couldn't. Then he heard the sound of footsteps coming towards him.

'Are you all right, mate?' a male voice enquired.

Dan could see two people but they were indistinct and out of focus. He managed to tell them he'd been attacked.

They lifted him up on to his feet and then, supporting him between them, they helped him walk down the alley towards the main road at the end of it. They asked him where he was hurt, where he lived and who attacked him, but he was in such pain he couldn't answer.

'Christ Almighty!' one of them exclaimed once they reached the lights on the main road and they could see him properly. 'You've been given a right going over. We'd better call an ambulance.'

'My wife!' Dan managed to get out. 'Got to get home.'

'She'll have fifty fits if you go home like that,' the man said. 'You've got blood all over you. You need a doctor.'

Fifi's eyes kept moving from the clock to the window. She was growing ever more anxious about Dan. He couldn't work once it was dark, and she didn't think he would go off to the pub with the other men, not when she was expecting him home.

It was after eleven now and thankfully all quiet again over at the Muckles'. The fight had begun soon after it got dark, and because they had only the thinnest of covering over their window she had seen it all.

She had watched the silhouettes of Alfie and Molly laying into each other like maniacs, with blaring music accompanying them. At the height of it all she'd been so frightened she'd gone down to see Miss Diamond, to ask if she thought they should call the police.

Fifi was always wary of bothering Miss Diamond as she seemed to be the kind of person who wanted to maintain her distance from other people. She always spoke if she ran into Fifi or Dan on the landings, but it was invariably a brief interchange. Fifi was as curious about this big, striking woman with dark brown hair as she was about Yvette. She was about forty, exceptionally well groomed with an elaborate beehive which looked as if it had been glued in place, she never had visitors, and aside from going to work at the telephone exchange, she rarely went out. Dan joked that she was related to Attila the Hun.

Fifi had caught glimpses of her flat when the doors were open. The front room was her sitting room, her furnishing style plain but rather classy with a cream fitted carpet. The bedroom, which was beneath Fifi and Dan's, was lovely, with a pale blue flounced bedspread and white-painted furniture. Even the kitchen, which was right at the back of the house, was attractive, with sunshine-yellow cupboards and the work surface tiled in white. It seemed odd that a woman with so much style, and obviously coming from a good background, should choose to live here. Since Fifi met her for the first time, she'd been determined to find out all about her, but as yet she'd had no success.

Fifi's mind wasn't on prying, however, when she knocked on the woman's door around ten o'clock, only on the disturbance over the road. Miss Diamond came to the door wearing a long, loose emerald-green garment that wasn't quite a dressing-gown or a dress. She looked tense and angry at all the noise, but her hair was still as immaculate as always.

'Mrs Helass usually rings the police,' she said. 'She's the only one in the street with a phone. Much good it does though. Really, that family are just the end! They need locking up and the key thrown away.'

She ranted about what she'd seen and heard so far, and Fifi said she was afraid Alfie was going to kill Molly.

'I wish he would,' the older woman said with a weary

sigh. 'Then once he was locked up perhaps we'd all get some peace. I really can't stand much more of this.'

Miss Diamond offered Fifi a cup of tea, but even as they chatted about the Muckles in her kitchen, they could still hear the row continuing across the street. By the time Fifi went back upstairs, however, it had grown quieter. While looking out the window to see if Dan was coming down the street, she saw the light come on in the Muckles' bedroom, and momentarily saw Alfie silhouetted before it was switched off.

Molly was still downstairs. Fifi could see her on the settee and hear her crying. She wondered about the children, particularly Angela, for it had to be terrifying hearing such battles. But she supposed they happened so often they'd just got used to them and might even think them quite normal.

Later, as she continued to look out for Dan, she saw Dora come down the street with Mike, Alfie's nephew. They were arm-in-arm, chatting quite happily. Fifi assumed they'd been out for the evening and felt a little sorry for them that it would be spoilt the moment they got indoors.

Everyone in the street talked about the relationship between Mike the nephew and Dora. Strangely, the ten-year age gap was rarely mentioned, only that Dora was simple. Yvette had said that she was damaged at birth through a forceps delivery. Apparently she looked upon Molly as a mother, for her own had died when she was around five or six and Molly had taken care of her ever since.

Fifi watched as they went indoors. For a short while they were standing in the front room, and she assumed they were talking to Molly, although she could no longer see her. The light went out in the room, and a few seconds later another

149

came on right at the top of the house. Presumably they were all going to bed.

Fifi wanted to go to bed too, but she felt she had to stay up and wait for Dan. The street was quiet now, and one by one all the lights that had been on in the houses on the other side of the road went out. She thought that Dan must have gone home with one of his workmates, for he wouldn't be able to go on to a club after the pub, not in his working clothes. Perhaps he'd gone to look at some job the man wanted help with. A few beers and he'd lost track of time. Maybe he'd even got too drunk to make his way home.

At midnight she was too tired to wait any longer, so turning off the lights she went to bed.

She woke at the sound of a bell. Fumbling for the alarm clock, she saw it was seven o'clock, but it wasn't the alarm clock ringing, it was the front-door bell. Then she remembered Dan hadn't come home.

Frank Ubley's voice wafted up the stairs, and she could hear another male voice. All at once she was wide awake, sensing that the caller had come to see her.

She jumped out of bed and grabbed her dressing-gown, putting it on over her nightdress as she flew down the stairs.

When she saw a policeman in the hall with Frank she clasped a hand over her mouth in horror. 'Is it Dan?' she asked.

'It's okay, Mrs Reynolds,' the policeman said, coming up a few stairs to meet her. 'I just called to tell you that your husband was taken to St James's Hospital last night. Someone attacked him.'

'Who attacked him? Is he badly hurt?' Fifi asked, all at once feeling sick with fright.

There wasn't much more the policeman could tell her as he hadn't seen Dan himself, he was only passing on the message the local police had been given.

'But his injuries can't be very serious or the hospital would've asked us to call on you last night to take you to your husband,' he said soothingly. 'So don't get all worked up, Mrs Reynolds, I expect they only kept him in overnight for observation.'

He went on to tell her where the hospital was in Tooting, and suggested she phoned before going there to check if they wanted her to bring anything with her, like clean clothes or pyjamas. Then, after apologizing for giving her such a shock, he said he had to go back on his beat.

Fifi burst into tears after he'd gone and Frank took her into his kitchen to give her a cup of tea.

Both Fifi and Dan had come to like Frank a great deal. He always greeted them warmly when they came home, he'd give Fifi little bunches of flowers from his garden, and he took her milk in every day and put it in her fridge so it wouldn't turn sour. He was obviously lonely with his only daughter and her family in Australia, but he never made a nuisance of himself. He just took a friendly and kindly interest in them, and if they asked him up for a cup of tea, or bought him a drink at the pub, he was always delighted to accept, but never outstayed his welcome.

'Why would anyone attack Dan?' Fifi sobbed out. 'Everyone likes him. He isn't a troublemaker.'

Frank put his arms around her and comforted her. 'It must have been robbery, I suppose. But a bloke like Dan wouldn't have been my choice to rob, he's young, fit and strong. I'd have gone for an easier target.'

'They wouldn't have found anything on him worth stealing,' Fifi said tearfully. 'He never has any money left by Thursday, he doesn't even wear a watch.'

Frank was still in his dressing-gown too, so Fifi drank her tea, then said she was going to get dressed so she could go and phone the hospital.

'Want me to come with you?' Frank asked. 'You look a bit shaky to me.'

'I'll be fine once I know he's all right,' she said. 'But thank you for being so kind.'

Frank patted her on the shoulder. 'Come and tell me how he is when you get back. I could make you a bit of breakfast.'

'The ward sister said he's quite comfortable,' Fifi told Frank when she got back from the phone. 'He got a blow to the back of his head and another in the ribs. The police are going to talk to him this morning to find out what happened.'

'You'll take the day off then?' Frank asked. 'Would you like me to ring your office at nine and explain for you?'

His fatherly manner was touching. He'd dressed and shaved while she was making the phone call, and he smelled of soap and toothpaste. He'd already laid the table for breakfast for them both in his tiny kitchen, and with the back door open and a huge pot of colourful petunias right outside it, it felt very homely and comforting.

'I can do that on the way to the hospital,' Fifi said. 'They only allow visiting between two and three and five and six, but maybe if I go there with his pyjamas they'll let me see him straight away.'

'So they're keeping him in then?'

Fifi nodded. 'Yes, the sister said they have to monitor

him for brain damage as he was knocked unconscious. But he can't be that badly hurt. She said Dan made a joke about how they'll have to check he's got a brain first.'

Frank smiled. 'I can just hear him saying that. He's the kind that finds summat funny in everything. You know he's even charmed Miss Diamond, don't you? She knocked before she went to work because she'd heard the policeman earlier. Upset she was! Said if there was anything she could do, you'd only got to ask.'

'That was very kind of her,' Fifi said. She was feeling a bit better now that she'd spoken to the hospital, and it was so nice to know her neighbours cared. 'I spoke to her last night when all that noise was going on over the road. Did you hear it?'

Frank nodded grimly. 'If the whole street hadn't heard them at it hammer and tongs I might have thought Alfie was behind this attack on your Dan. But as he was over there giving Molly a pasting it can't have been him.'

Fifi remembered Yvette's warning and frowned in consternation. 'Why would you think he might be responsible?'

'Alfie ain't one to let anyone get the better of him,' Frank said with a shrug. 'Your Dan marked his card when he hurt Angela. That's enough reason for Alfie to get some revenge, and walloping someone over the head in the dark is just his style.'

At the hospital the ward sister did soften and let Fifi in for ten minutes, just so she'd be reassured Dan was all right. But Fifi wasn't reassured, not when she saw Dan with his head bandaged and his face unnaturally pale. He grinned as she came up the ward, but it was forced, so she knew he was in pain.

'I'm as sound as a pound,' he insisted. 'They're only

keeping me here as a precaution, not cos I need to stay in bed. I've a good mind to get up and come home with you.'

'You'll do nothing of the sort,' Fifi said sharply, sniffing back her tears. 'They don't put bandages that big on someone for no reason.'

She asked him how it happened, and he explained that he couldn't remember anything after Owen called out to him. 'Whoever did it must have been in the alley already,' he said. 'There's gates into backyards where he could hide.'

'But why?' Fifi asked. 'Are you sure you haven't got on the wrong side of someone?'

Dan sighed. 'That's what the police asked me when they came a while back. They wanted to know if I owed anyone money, or if someone had a grudge against me. They even asked if I'd been playing around with another woman! I told them to have a look at you, then they'd know I wouldn't be messing with anyone else.'

Fifi liked that. Sometimes Dan could be so charming. 'Frank thought it sounded like Alfie Muckle's work,' she said. 'But it couldn't have been him, he and Molly were in their house fighting, everyone heard them.'

'The Dale Street Obsession,' Dan exclaimed, rolling his eyes. 'Everything that happens to anyone is always down to Alfie Muckle. If Martians landed in London that would be his fault too.'

'They've had years of bitter experience with him,' Fifi said indignantly. 'You should have heard the row last night! He's a monster.'

'I agree he's a wife and child beater, a slob and a lazy thieving bastard, but that still doesn't make him responsible for every single crime committed in the neighbourhood.'

'Maybe not, but Frank, Stan, Yvette and even Miss Diamond all say –'

'He's the son of Satan, I suppose.' Dan cut in before she could finish. 'You shouldn't listen to them, Fifi. They're all losers too.'

'They aren't,' Fifi said incredulously. 'What a horrible thing to say! I thought you saw them all as friends?'

Dan shrugged. 'I do, but it doesn't blind me to their faults. If they had anything about them at all they would've moved away years ago. But they stay, and moan about the Muckles. And you know why? Because that family make them feel better about themselves.'

'Dan! That's a wicked thing to say. Maybe they can't afford to move, perhaps they've tried and can't find anywhere. I don't believe for one moment that they feel better about themselves just because they have ghastly neighbours.'

Dan gave her one of his looks that said he thought she was naive. 'I know how it is for them, sweetheart, because I'm guilty of it myself. Your parents look down on the way I speak, the way I look, and my job, and let's face it, I've justified their belief I'd bring you down to my level by taking you to live in Dale Street. But I feel at home there. I can look across to the Muckles and see the blankets across their windows and feel dead smug because we've got nice curtains. No one looks down on me there for working on a building site. I'm even the envy of every other man in the street because I've got a gorgeous wife.'

'I don't see what you're getting at,' Fifi said peevishly. She hated it when he put himself down. 'That bang on the head must have done you more damage than I thought.'

'You're the one who's always studying the neighbours,' he said. 'I would've thought you'd seen it by now.'

Fifi decided that it was anxiety and pain that were making him look at things with such jaundiced eyes. In a day or two he'd probably regain his normal optimism, so there was no point in her arguing with him. 'So when did they say you could come home?' she asked.

'Not for a couple of days at least,' he said. 'Look, why don't you make the most of having today off, and go home to your parents for the weekend?'

'Home to them!' Fifi exclaimed, thinking the bump on the head must be worse than he thought. 'They haven't even answered my letter about the baby. They won't want to see me!'

Dan took her hand in his and caressed it, his dark eyes boring into hers. 'You don't know that! I was thinking about it before you arrived. Maybe they've been waiting for you to make the first move? I don't like the thought of you alone all weekend in the flat, and it will be a darned sight easier for you to make it up with them without me around.'

'Mum will just be nasty,' Fifi said stubbornly. 'I know she will.'

'You don't know that for sure,' Dan said firmly. 'Ring them and see what they say. If they blank you off you've lost nothing. At least you've been big enough to give it a try.'

As Fifi had always considered she was the wronged party, she believed that it should be her parents who should offer the olive branch. But she liked the idea of being magnanimous – her father at least would see it as a sign she'd grown up. And if she made it clear she was coming home alone, her mother wouldn't be so edgy. Once there, with Patty getting all excited about the baby, it would be hard for her mother to stay on her high horse.

'But even if Mum was agreeable, how could I go and leave you in here?'

'Why not? Normal visiting hours are only an hour, twice a day, it would be daft staying in London just for that.'

'But you'd hate not having a visitor,' Fifi argued.

'It's the weekend, some of the blokes from work might come,' he said with a shrug. 'And even if they don't, I won't mind. I can chat to the nurses or the other patients. Or just catch up on some sleep.'

Dan never said anything he didn't mean, so Fifi knew he really would be happy enough here alone. Her mother had always claimed that Fifi was as stubborn as a mule, so it would take the wind out of her sails just getting a phone call. She really did want to make the peace now with a baby coming, and perhaps this was the golden opportunity to call a truce.

Dan was right, she didn't relish the weekend stuck alone in the flat, especially when it was so hot. She could see the garden at home in her mind's eye, the lush grass, the trees and flowers, and she could imagine herself lying on a blanket reading a magazine, with her mother bringing her out a glass of her homemade lemonade. It would be so nice to sleep in her old room, to see her brothers and sister, maybe catch up with a few old friends on Saturday night.

'Ring her,' Dan said firmly, perhaps sensing she was wavering. 'You're having their grandchild, for heaven's sake! You'll want them in the picture when he or she is born. Then there's Patty and your brothers, they're going to be aunty and uncles, and they'll be thrilled to see you. I don't want you to be home alone all weekend either, so please, do it for me!'

Fifi felt a surge of love for Dan. He was hurt, yet he wasn't thinking of himself, only her. If their positions were reversed she knew she wouldn't be that noble or generous. She really did have to go along with his idea.

'Okay, I'll phone, but I'll only go if she's nice. I'm not going all that way just for more rows.'

He took her hand and squeezed it. 'Meet her halfway,' he

said. 'But just don't get to like it at home so much you decide to stay.'

'As if I could live without you,' she said, leaning forward to kiss him. 'And a couple of days of Mum and Dad bending my ear will be more than enough to send me scooting back to you.'

Frank and Stan met up on Friday evening in the Rifleman. As always at the weekend it was packed to capacity, and because it was a warm night, the doors were propped open and many people had taken their drinks outside.

The news of Dan being attacked had been passed around, and Frank had found himself the centre of attention since he arrived in the pub because he lived downstairs to the couple.

Frank told them all he knew, and as always when there was trouble in the street, Alfie's name was put in the frame, but Cecil Helass was quick to point out that Alfie had been too busy thrashing Molly to be held responsible.

'He could've ordered that half-wit nephew of his to do it,' Frank said contemptuously.

Someone said that he'd seen Mike come home with Dora after the fight was over, and a couple more people confirmed they'd seen that too.

'But young Fifi! Who is watching out for her while her husband is in hospital?' Stan asked nervously.

'She's gone home to Bristol,' Frank said. 'Dan made her go.'

Stan waited until the other men had moved away from him and Frank before questioning his friend more closely.

'Fifi tell me she fall out with her family over Dan,' he said in puzzlement. 'It is good that she is not alone now, but I think this put Dan more in bad light with her parents.'

Frank nodded, knowing exactly what his friend meant. 'I can see why they didn't think much of him. I thought he were a bit of a wide boy when he moved in.'

'Wide boy?' Stan repeated. 'What is that?'

'A bit fly, a rascal,' Frank explained, and chuckled. 'But I were wrong about him, Dan's a decent sort, even Miss Diamond hasn't found anything to complain about.'

Stan smirked. He knew how fussy the woman upstairs to Frank was, she was considered to be a fire-eating dragon by almost everyone in the street. 'So Dan is worried the man who attacked him might hurt Fifi too?'

'I reckon that's about the size of it.'

Stan mulled this over for a moment. 'But when Fifi tell her family Dan has been beaten up, they will be certain he is a bad man.'

Frank sighed. 'Yeah, maybe, their sort always think the worst of everyone. They can't believe a working man can be honest or have much the same values as them.'

'This is how it is for me too,' Stan replied sadly. 'Because my English not so good, they suspect me of many bad things.'

Frank put his hand on his friend's shoulder in sympathy. 'You should ignore them, pal. They wink about Yvette being a sex-pot just because she's French. Danny O'Connor, at number nine, gets treated like he's thick just because he's Irish. I've never seen Yvette with a man and Danny has a degree in engineering. Daft prejudice, that's what it is.'

The two men nursed their pints in silence for some little time, both immersed in their private thoughts.

'We must do something about the Muckles,' Stan suddenly burst out. 'It is not right for so many to live in fear of them.'

'What can we do?' Frank shrugged despairingly. 'I'm too

old to give Alfie a good hiding and anyway, Molly is the one behind most of their villainy.'

'Perhaps we frame them for a crime?' Stan said, his doleful expression brightening. 'We plan something that would put them away for a long time?'

Cecil Helass and his drinking partner Bob Osbourne, who lived at number 7, had been standing close enough to Frank and Stan to overhear what Stan had said.

'Now you're talking!' Bob said with a wide grin. He and Cecil had both recently retired and they spent more time in the Rifleman than their wives liked, often reeling home so drunk they could barely walk. 'We'll give you a hand.'

'It would have to be murder to be sure they would go for good,' Frank said laughingly. 'I'd cheerfully kill anyone in their family, even the kids.'

Stan nodded in agreement before adding jokingly, 'Then perhaps we kill one of their children? We make it seem like Alfie and Molly did it.'

'Brilliant idea.' Frank laughed. 'That should sort out the problem.'

'Now, now,' Rosa the aging barmaid piped up from behind the bar. 'You can't plot murder in here!'

'We don't mean it, Rosa,' Stan said quickly, regretting his bad joke.

'That's a shame,' she laughed. 'I might've been tempted to help you.'

Fifi sat at the kitchen table eating the sandwich her mother had given her, but she was tense, knowing by the way Clara was rattling dishes in the sink that she was boiling up for something.

Everything had looked so hopeful at first. When Fifi

telephoned that morning and asked if she could come on her own for the weekend, Clara hadn't hesitated in agreeing, in fact she'd sounded delighted. Fifi purposefully didn't mention what had happened to Dan, it was too hard to explain on the phone, but perhaps that was her first mistake, as maybe her mother got the idea she was walking out on him.

When Fifi arrived, she took it as a good omen that her mother was wearing the pale blue linen dress Fifi had always said she looked so pretty in. While she didn't hug her daughter, Clara did say what a lovely surprise the phone call was, and that she'd made up the bed for her.

It was a bit disappointing to find that Patty had gone to a friend's for the weekend. Her brothers were at cricket practice and her father had gone to see an old friend and wouldn't be back till much later. But the house was as sun-filled and peaceful as she remembered, and Fifi felt that the time alone with her mother would be good for them both.

Over a cup of tea Fifi explained about Dan being in hospital and why. When there was no real reaction, good or bad, she moved on to tell her mother about her job and the girls she'd made friends with at work.

It was only when she said that she and Dan had been hoping to buy a little house before the baby arrived, but she supposed Dan might not be able to go back to work for a while, that her mother got up from the table to make the sandwich. She shot a few terse questions over her shoulder at Fifi – had she seen a doctor yet? Where would she go for antenatal care? – but it wasn't until she gave her the sandwich and moved over to the sink, making far more noise than was normal, that Fifi realized trouble was brewing.

'So why was he beaten up?' Clara asked suddenly, her voice tight with disapproval.

'I told you already, we don't know,' Fifi said evenly. 'He's well liked, he wasn't robbed of anything, it's a mystery.'

Clara sniffed and turned back to the sink.

Whenever Fifi thought about her mother, she always pictured her here in the kitchen as it held all her best childhood memories. Baking cakes with her mother, painting with Patty at the table, playing Scrabble with her brothers too. It had always been the heart of the house, a warm, inviting place, with her mother at the centre of it.

It hadn't changed in any way since she left to marry Dan. Pretty china on the dresser, family snapshots covering the larder door, the three-tier cake tin with a small Perspex window in each tier was still stocked with scones, flapjacks and a Victoria sandwich, just as it always had been. The yellow walls needed repainting and the checked curtains were faded, but it had been that way for years, and as her mother always said, it was clean, even if a bit shabby.

But even though Fifi's old photos were still on the larder door, she felt that was an oversight and they would have been removed if her mother had noticed them. Likewise, Fifi didn't feel able to get up and help herself to something from the cake tin as she always had. She didn't feel she was family any more, but just a visitor, and as such she must abide by the same rules that would apply to anyone visiting.

'How do you and Dad feel about becoming grand-parents?' Fifi asked. She knew in her heart it was probably unwise to ask, but she couldn't help herself.

'Feel about it?' Clara said, wheeling round from the sink to look at her daughter.

'Pleased, angry, indifferent?' Fifi suggested weakly.

'What is there to be pleased about? You are living in a couple of rooms, your husband has no prospects, and it strikes me you have been thoroughly irresponsible.'

Fifi had made up her mind on the long train ride home that she would be sweet, generous and tactful, whatever her mother threw at her. But there was no way she could deal with that spiteful statement except with more spite.

'It could be said you were irresponsible having four children while there was a war on,' she snapped back. 'And as I remember, you and Dad were helped to buy this house by his parents. Where would you have been living if not for that?'

'Don't answer me back,' Clara hissed. 'You go off and marry a worthless labourer who has neither brains nor breeding and expect us to be glad that you are producing his offspring!'

Fifi reeled at the vitriol in her mother's voice. 'He is not worthless,' she retorted, getting to her feet. 'And he is a skilled bricklayer, not a labourer. And if breeding is what makes you so nasty, then I'm glad he hasn't got any.'

'Nasty! I'm just speaking the truth, my girl.'

It was all too obvious that time hadn't mellowed her mother's views on Dan one iota, and out of loyalty to her husband Fifi knew she must make the final stand, even if that meant losing her family for good.

'You aren't speaking the truth,' she hissed at Clara. 'You are just airing your stupid prejudices and snobbery and showing how ignorant you are! You haven't attempted to get to know Dan, if you had you might have found out how wrong you are about him. Well, I love him, I'm glad I'm having his baby, and as it was a mistake to come here, I'm going right back to him.'

'Don't be so hasty,' her mother called after her as Fifi

sped out to the hall and picked up her weekend bag. 'You can't go back to London now, it's too late.'

'It's too late for you to show any concern about me,' Fifi threw back at her, then opened the door and left.

Clara Brown stood for a moment in the hall, tempted to run after her daughter and apologize. She knew she shouldn't have been so outspoken, but when Fifi rang this morning and asked if she could visit, her immediate thought was that her daughter's marriage was on the rocks.

But the moment Fifi came through the door, she knew that wasn't so. Her daughter had a glow about her, and a calm that Clara recognized as the kind women had when they felt secure and happy. For a little while it had eased all Clara's fears, but the moment Fifi told her what had happened to Dan, they all came back a hundredfold.

Maybe it was true that Dan didn't know his assailant, but she thought it far more likely he was involved in something unpleasant, maybe even criminal. Long before she actually met Dan she had an idea there was something shady about him. The story about him being abandoned as a baby sounded preposterous. She thought it far more likely that he'd spent his youth in approved schools and invented such a story to gain sympathy. When he and Fifi got married in secret, that was all the confirmation she needed. A convenient way of hiding his real origins.

Of course she might have been less suspicious if Dan hadn't been so handsome, but any man with filmstar looks would have made her question his motives in going after her daughter. She had voiced her misgivings later to Harry, and he had asked why she thought their beautiful daughter couldn't attract an equally beautiful man. She hadn't been able to explain that. But the truth was, she had retained an image of Fifi as plain and anti-social, the way she was when she was a child. And just as she'd wanted to protect her from harm then, she still did.

No one fully appreciated what she'd been through with Fifi when she was little, not even Harry as he was away so much in the war years. As a baby she hardly slept, screaming her head off half the night, and when Patty was born Clara had to watch like a hawk because Fifi was always prodding and poking her. She'd throw her dinner on the floor, disobey every order, and she never allowed herself to be cuddled. Every single milestone – walking, talking and toilet training – she reached later than any other child.

In the first few years of school, Clara had to listen almost daily to complaints from Fifi's teacher that she couldn't concentrate and disrupted the class. Clara remembered biting back tears because she couldn't bear the fact that her oldest child was so much trouble. No one, neither teachers nor doctors, had any practical advice to offer.

Clara had no choice but to battle away on her own with Fifi, making time to help her with reading and writing, at the expense of the other children. No one fully appreciated how exhausting it was, or what a thankless task it seemed. She had three perfect, completely lovable children, but the eldest, who had such a special place in her heart, drove her almost mad, and prevented her from enjoying the other three.

By eight or nine Fifi became more stable, and by ten she had caught up with other children of the same age. But Clara found it impossible to forget the havoc Fifi had wreaked in those early years. Perhaps that was why she was always so hard on her. Was it her unconscious way of getting back at Fifi for all the unhappiness and anxiety she'd caused in the past?

As she turned back to the kitchen, she began to cry. Harry would be cross with her when he found Fifi had gone off in a huff. Only yesterday he'd said that they should write to her and congratulate her about the baby. He'd also said it was high time they accepted Dan, for if Fifi loved him that was all that mattered. Clara guessed he'd be concerned about Dan's injuries too; he wouldn't jump to the conclusion, as she had, that Dan was involved with crooks and thugs. But most of all he'd be horrified that his wife had forced Fifi to rush back to London in an emotional state when she was pregnant.

Chapter eight

Fifi was on the way to the corner shop on Saturday morning when she saw Molly Muckle coming along the street towards her. Her heart sank, for she was in no mood for being accosted by anyone, especially someone like Molly.

Last night's train journey home to London had seemed endless, and she'd had to fight back tears all the way. It was nearly midnight when she got to Paddington, and the tube on to Kennington was packed with drunks. By the time she got back to Dale Street she was completely wrung out. The flat was hot and airless, and when she opened the windows dozens of moths flew in towards the lights. The more she flapped at them with a newspaper, the more seemed to come in, and she finally burst into tears.

She had never felt so desperately alone. She wasn't just angry with her mother, she felt a real sense of abandonment. While she hadn't expected that just one visit would put everything absolutely right immediately, she had believed that the baby coming would make her mother soften. But now there was no way back. She had lost her family for good.

She might have told herself countless times that she didn't need anyone but Dan, but now that was all she had, it didn't seem anywhere near enough.

She couldn't sleep because it was so hot, and her mind kept going over and over the nasty things her mother had said.

It was a relief when the sun finally came up, but the thought of a weekend all alone made her want to weep again. She didn't want to have to tell Dan what had happened in Bristol, but if she just turned up to visit him and said she'd changed her mind about going home, he'd suspect something and keep on until she told him the truth. Nor could she stay away from him and pretend she was in Bristol, as when he came home he'd soon find out she'd been here all along.

The anxiety made her sick. She had to run to the bathroom and was in there for over half an hour until Miss Diamond hammered on the door and reminded her the bathroom wasn't hers alone.

But by eleven, and feeling a bit better, Fifi decided to go out and buy a newspaper. When she saw Molly she wished she'd stayed indoors, or at least stayed on her own side of the street, for if she crossed back now to avoid the woman it would be all too obvious.

''Ow's yer old man?' Molly bawled out, still some ten feet from Fifi. 'I 'eard 'e 'ad a bit of bother.'

'He's not too bad now, thank you,' Fifi replied politely, hoping that would be the end of it.

''E's still up the 'ospital then?'

Fifi groaned inwardly. 'Yes, but he'll be out soon.' She could see a glint in the woman's eyes that looked all too much like malice and she wanted to get away from her as quickly as possible. Molly was wearing a sleeveless pink cotton dress which had food stains down the front and her fat bare arms were mottled like sausagemeat. As usual her hair was in curlers and she had rings of the previous night's mascara around her eyes.

'I 'ear you're up the spout an' all,' Molly said. 'When's it due?'

Fifi couldn't imagine how Molly had found out about her pregnancy. She had only told Frank and Yvette, and neither of them would gossip about it.

'How did you come to hear that?' she asked.

'I gets to 'ear everything.' Molly grinned, showing yellow teeth. 'Me old man calls me the ears of the world. You ain't showing yet though, you feeling all right?'

'I'm fine, thank you,' Fifi said starchily, hating the way the woman was looking her up and down. 'The baby's due in March. But I must go now, I've got to meet someone.'

'You look after yerself,' Molly said. 'I 'ope yer 'ubby ain't in the 'ospital long. You need 'im around to watch out fer you.'

It was only after getting the paper and then going on to the greengrocer's to buy some fruit that it suddenly occurred to Fifi that she'd seen no bruises on Molly. Surely anyone taking a beating like the one she'd heard would have some visible injuries?

The more she thought about it, the stranger it seemed, and Molly's parting shot, '*You need him around to watch out for you*', seemed to hold a warning too.

When Fifi got home she could see that the back door through to the garden in Frank's kitchen was open, so she called out to him.

'So it *was* you I heard earlier!' he exclaimed when he saw her. He was in his gardening clothes, old khaki shorts, a vest and a battered panama hat. 'I thought you'd gone home for the whole weekend.'

Fifi explained that she'd thought better of staying in Bristol. Frank invited her to come outside as he was doing some weeding.

'I just saw Molly Muckle,' Fifi said once she was sitting down. Frank's garden was very pretty, with masses of flowers. He had said it had been his saviour since June died as he could forget himself while working on it.

She went on to tell him about her conversation with Molly, and how she had been surprised to see that the woman looked uninjured.

'How could she be unhurt?' she asked him. 'We heard all the screaming and thumping, it was terrible. Either Alfie was hitting someone else, or it was all fake. And how does she know I'm having a baby? I haven't told anyone but you and Yvette.'

'Well, I did tell Stan on Friday night,' he admitted. 'But only because of what happened to Dan, and I know he wouldn't have passed it on, he isn't that sort. I couldn't see Yvette speaking to Molly either, she steers well clear of her like I do. I suppose the police could have said something. They were over there just after you left for Bristol.'

'About Dan?' Fifi asked, immediately thinking that it was even odder Molly should have spoken to her if she had cause to blame her for something.

Frank nodded. 'They came over here afterwards to talk to you and I said you'd gone home for the weekend.'

'Did they tell you anything?'

'Only that they had found a length of lead pipe in the alley where Dan was attacked. They think it was used to hit him.'

'Any fingerprints?'

'They didn't say. But they did ask me if I could confirm Alfie was at home on Friday night. I had to say I thought he was. Maybe they told Alfie and Molly not to upset or harass you in any way as you were having a baby.'

Fifi raised her eyebrows. 'As if that would deter them!'

They discussed it for a little while and Fifi said she wondered if the fight had been staged to give Alfie an alibi. After all, she hadn't actually seen Alfie, only the outline of someone in the window who looked like him.

'He's crafty enough for that,' Frank said thoughtfully. 'Maybe you'd better tell the police what you think.'

'I can't,' Fifi sighed. 'Dan was a bit sarcastic about the Muckles getting blamed for everything. It's going to be hard enough telling him why I came home so quickly.'

She blurted out then how her mother had been.

Frank listened sympathetically, at times shaking his head sadly as if shocked her mother could be so hard. 'I'm sorry, Fifi,' he sighed as she finished. 'She's being daft about Dan, but it isn't easy to accept your little girl is grown-up enough to marry, and even harder when you think she's made the wrong choice. I expect she wanted you to marry someone just like your dad.'

'Dan isn't really that different,' Fifi said sadly. 'He's honest, hard-working, loves kids and has a kind heart. He just didn't have the kind of education and upbringing that meant he could go to university.'

'Maybe you should write to her and tell her that,' Frank said, getting up from his weeding and coming closer to her. 'Don't let this come between you, Fifi, you'll need your family when the baby comes.'

Fifi went to visit Dan that afternoon. She was feeling utterly miserable, but she had a bath, washed her hair, made up her face and put on her prettiest dress because she didn't want him to sense anything was wrong. When she got to the hospital she told him she'd come back from Bristol that morning because she wanted to be with him.

'You must be mad,' he said, but looked pleased anyway.

'I know I'd sooner be out of London in this heat. Are you sure you didn't have a fight with them about me?'

'No,' she lied, and smiled to reassure him. 'I just felt strange away from you, and Patty wasn't there to keep me company. I didn't like the thought of you all alone without a visitor.'

He looked at her doubtfully, perhaps wondering why she wasn't full of what had been said at home, but he didn't attempt to cross-examine her.

'They might let me out on Monday,' he said. 'But I won't be able to work for a week or two. Maybe next weekend, after my stitches have been taken out, we could go to Brighton or somewhere by the sea?'

Fifi didn't say they couldn't afford to go anywhere while he wasn't being paid. Instead, she just said they'd wait and see how he was feeling.

Dan appeared to be back to his usual self, making jokes about other men in the ward and telling Fifi things he'd found out about some of the nurses. If he was worried about who had hurt him, he didn't show it. When Fifi had to leave at the end of visiting he told her he loved her and that he was glad she was back in London.

Fifi hadn't been home for more than five minutes when the police called. Frank opened the door to them downstairs and they came on up to her flat.

'Sorry to disturb you, Mrs Reynolds,' the older one said. 'But we wanted to ask you a few questions about Thursday night. We understand you were here all evening?'

Fifi confirmed that she was, and the policeman asked her to tell him what she'd seen and heard that evening.

While Fifi was explaining about the fight over the road, the younger man was looking out of her living-room window as if to ascertain how well she could see the Muckles' house.

'What makes you think the man fighting with Mrs Muckle was her husband?' the older man asked.

'I just assumed it was,' Fifi said. 'I could only see his silhouette in the window and he was the same height and size as Alfie.'

'His nephew is a similar height and size. Could it have been him?'

'I don't know. I suppose so, but I saw him coming home later with Dora. Do you think it was Alfie who attacked Dan?' she asked.

The older policeman smiled. 'Let's just say we are still making enquiries.'

Fifi blurted out that she found it odd Molly had no visible injuries.

'That didn't escape us either,' the policeman said with a knowing look.

Fifi went back to the hospital in the evening to see Dan again. It was very hot and sticky outside, but hotter still in the ward, and Dan looked sweaty and uncomfortable.

'Shall I wet a flannel and at least cool your face and hands down?' Fifi suggested.

'It's you making me hot,' he said suggestively, looking at her cleavage.

Fifi blushed. Since she became pregnant her breasts had got bigger, and her dress had a low neck. 'If you're well enough to think dirty thoughts you're on the mend,' she said, then went on to tell him about all the people who had asked after him.

Later they heard a distant rumble of thunder and noticed how dark the sky had become.

'You'd better go before it starts to rain,' Dan said. 'I reckon we're in for a big storm.'

Fifi did leave before visiting time was over when she saw the first spots of rain. But by the time she was halfway to the tube station the rain had turned heavy and her thin dress was soaked. When she got out at Kennington it was a deluge. She stood for a moment in the entrance to the station, watching the rain bouncing off the pavements and turning the gutters into gushing streams. There was no light in the sky at all, and it was all too obvious by the rumbling thunder that this was far more than a brief summer shower, so she had no choice but to run for home.

The streets were completely deserted, cars slowing down to a crawl in the driving rain, and the pavements were slippery after the long dry spell. She was soaked to the skin and out of breath when she turned the corner into Dale Street and suddenly she slid on something and fell flat on her face.

She banged one knee very hard, and jarred her hand and arm as she tried to break her fall. The shock made her cry out. She felt someone grab her arm to help her up, but her wet hair was all over her face and she didn't know who it was until she heard his voice.

'You shouldn't be running like a mad thing in your condition,' he said. 'A drop of rain won't 'urt you.'

It was Alfie Muckle. As she brushed her hair back off her face she saw he was leering at her and she realized that her thin dress was stuck to her body and he'd probably seen right up to her knickers when she fell.

She backed away from him instinctively.

'Well, that's nice,' he said, his pale blue eyes travelling up and down her body. 'Not a word of thanks that I helped you up!'

'I didn't mean to be rude,' she said quickly. 'I'm a bit shaken up, that's all. Thank you.'

'You'll be all alone with the old man up the 'ospital,' he said, moving closer and putting his hand on her elbow. 'Come over to my place and I'll fix your leg up.'

From anyone else that offer would have touched her, for when she looked down she saw blood streaming from her knee. But coming from him it sounded menacing. 'I'll be fine,' she said, moving away from him. 'Thank you anyway.'

She hobbled the rest of the way home, aware he was still standing under the shelter of the corner-shop blind watching her.

Once indoors, her wet clothes stripped off and in her dressing-gown, Fifi found herself shivering with shock. Her right knee was badly grazed, as was the palm of her hand. All at once everything – Dan's injuries, the visit to her mother, her fall, being touched by Alfie and the prospect of a night alone – blew up in her mind to astronomic proportions and she felt vulnerable and fearful.

A loud clap of thunder, quickly followed by a flash of lightning, made her feel even more nervy, for she'd always been frightened by thunderstorms. She pulled the curtains shut and switched on a lamp and the television, but at each further clap of thunder she shook, and she could barely hear the television for the drumming of rain on the roof and windows.

Cold, shaken and frightened, she went to bed. But the thunder seemed even louder there, and as darkness fell outside, each flash of lightning lit up the room. She burrowed under the covers and even put Dan's pillow over her head, but she could still hear the storm and she became more and more scared.

As a child she had been terrified of storms, to the extent

that sometimes her mother thought she was about to take a fit. She felt herself going that way again, for she was rigid with fear and struggling to breathe. She felt as if she was marooned in a high tower with the storm raging all around her, and that any moment the roof would come crashing in and she'd be killed.

Through the paralysing fear, a memory of her father came to her. She saw herself as a small girl being held safe in his arms as he got her to watch the storm with him from the bedroom window. She remembered that watching what was happening outside wasn't as frightening as imagining it, and often she fell asleep in her father's arms.

Although far from convinced it would work alone, she forced herself to get out of bed and wrap a blanket round herself. Then she pulled back the curtains.

It wasn't as black outside as she'd expected. Although the rain was very heavy, she could see a faint yellow glow from street lighting in the road behind Dale Street, and there were lights in many of the windows in the backs of the houses to remind her that there were people all around her.

Another crash of thunder made her jump, but the lightning which quickly followed it lit up the darkness, and for a second or two the heavy rain looked golden and beautiful like sparks from a firework. At each successive flash of lightning Frank's garden below was lit up, and she could even see the pink roses climbing over his shed.

Her heart was racing and she felt sick, but remembering how her father used to reassure her that the storm was gradually moving away, she began to count from the clap of thunder until the lightning flashed. At first it came after two seconds, but the next was three, and by the time the gap was six and then seven seconds, her heartbeat was gradually slowing back to normal.

Another crash came and she peered down at Frank's shed again as she counted while awaiting the flash.

It came on the count of ten, illuminating not just the shed but the wall at the end of the garden. There, standing on the wall, was a man looking up at her, his face as clear as if lit by bright sunshine. It was Alfie Muckle!

She backed away from the window in terror, and a sudden tightness in her chest and throat made it hard for her to breathe again. An instinctive need for protection made her run for the stairs, calling for Frank.

She didn't stop to switch on the light, just flew down the stairs, forgetting in her panic that she was wearing only her nightdress. But as she reached the top of the last flight of stairs, her bare feet slipped on the worn carpet. She tried to stop herself falling by grabbing the banister but a sudden sharp pain in the arm she'd hurt earlier prevented her, and she toppled down the stairs.

Frank was sitting up in bed reading a book when he heard Fifi call his name. He threw back the covers immediately, sensing her panic, but even before he'd put his feet on the floor he heard the ominous sound, like a sack of coal falling down, thumping on each stair. He wrenched his door open just in time to see Fifi land at the bottom, her blonde hair bright against the floor in the dark hallway, arms and legs splayed out grotesquely.

The light came on just as he reached her, and Miss Diamond appeared at the top of the stairs in a long white nightgown. 'Oh, my God!' she exclaimed as she hurtled down the stairs towards them. 'Why was she screaming?' she asked. Then, bending down beside Frank, she pulled Fifi's nightdress over her bare thighs. 'She's not dead, is she, Frank?' she whispered.

Frank had enough knowledge of first aid to find Fifi's pulse and tell his neighbour she was alive but had been knocked unconscious. 'I'll run and phone an ambulance,' he said. 'Stay with her, but don't move her. If she comes round, talk to her and make her keep still. She's having a baby, and that will probably be the first thing she asks about. I'll bring a blanket for her after I've got my shoes and coat on.'

Nora Diamond sat on the stairs beside Fifi while she waited for Frank to come back from the phone, all her usual composure gone. To her, the awkward way the girl had landed suggested serious injuries, and with her husband in hospital too, things couldn't look blacker for the young couple.

Nora rarely took to anyone young, but she had to these two. They were a warm couple, always smiling and joyful, yet not noisy or dirty in their habits like so many of the previous tenants. She wished Fifi had told her she was pregnant, then she wouldn't have shouted at her this morning. She felt awful that she'd assumed the vomiting she'd heard was a result of drinking the night before.

What could have frightened Fifi tonight? Was it just being alone without Dan during the storm, or something more? Would she have been sympathetic if Fifi had come to her for comfort?

Deep down she doubted it. She had gone to bed early with a book and she always hated being disturbed. In fact, had she realized Fifi's sickness this morning was due to pregnancy, she would almost certainly have been alarmed at the prospect of crying babies above her head, or wet nappies hanging in the bathroom. The chances were she'd already have been planning a letter to the landlord asking him to evict the couple well before the birth.

But now, as she looked down at the beautiful girl lying at her feet, seemingly lifeless, for the first time in many years she felt ashamed of her bitterness and intolerance.

At Fifi's age she'd been just like her, vivacious, enthusiastic, warm and generous, despite having been orphaned at the age of eight and sent away by her guardians to boarding school. She had been popular with both teachers and pupils all through her schooldays, and though her guardians were distant and chilly, she was shown a great deal of affection by her schoolfriends' parents who often invited her to their homes for the holidays.

If she had fallen in love with anyone but Reggie Soames she might have stayed that way. But she married him at twenty-two, refusing to listen to all who suggested he was only interested in her sizable inheritance. But it turned out that they were right. Reggie was not only a womanizing fortune hunter but a swindler, a thief and a liar. The war made it all too easy for him to fool her. While she was tucked away in Dorset, doing her bit for the war effort, growing vegetables and helping out at the local hospital, she really believed Reggie was doing top secret work for the War Office.

In fact he was using her inheritance to support his playboy life-style in London. While she was worrying that he could be in terrible danger in Germany, he was gambling and drinking away her money, sleeping with other women and laughing up his sleeve at her naivety.

It was only when the war ended, and he showed no sign of returning permanently to Dorset, that she began to be a little suspicious. She had got to know many other women with husbands involved in secret war work, but they were all coming home and settling down again. She tackled him about it when she found she was pregnant, and he promised that he would be back for good within the month.

He never returned.

She found out then that he had forged her signature on her trust fund and plundered it. The family jewellery was gone from the safe deposit box, and every penny had been cleared from the bank account. She lost her baby when angry creditors began calling on her.

A great deal more happened before she ended up here in Dale Street, but she knew it was the loss of her baby which started the fundamental change in her nature. The girls who worked under her, neighbours and even local shopkeepers were intimidated by her, and that was how she wanted it.

The funny thing was that Fifi and Dan were the only people who didn't seem nervous of her. On many an occasion they had knocked on her door and asked if she needed anything when they were going to the shops, and they'd invited her up to their flat to see how they had decorated it. Dan had mended her coffee table when the leg broke off, and Fifi often invited her up for a cup of tea when he was working late. Nora told herself it was only good manners to accept these invitations from time to time, but it was more than that really. She had wanted the couple to stay at number 4 because she liked and trusted them.

Whatever the outcome at the hospital tonight, Nora had no doubt they would move on now, and that both saddened and frightened her. Since they moved in she had felt happier, less aware of all she had lost. And they had become the closest she could get to family.

'Are we feeling better now, Mrs Reynolds?'

Fifi opened her eyes and looked at the nurse bending over her. She was West Indian, her plump face shiny like a conker.

'Better than what?' she asked with some difficulty as her mouth was as dry as a desert. She knew she was in a hospital, she remembered Frank telling her she was in an ambulance with him because she'd fallen down the stairs, and later being examined by a doctor.

Yet she was confused by seeing it was daylight now. It seemed as if there was a great deal of time unaccounted for.

'Any pain?' the nurse asked, and offered her a drink of water from a cup with a spout. 'You had a little operation, you see, you've just come round from the anaesthetic.'

Fifi mentally checked herself. She seemed to be aching all over, but she supposed she would if she'd fallen down the stairs.

'Not real pain, just aches,' she said. 'Did I break something?'

'I'm afraid so, your right wrist,' the nurse said. 'Can't you feel the plaster?'

Fifi looked down and saw the plaster cast lying across her chest, her fingers coming out of the end looking swollen and discoloured. She wiggled them and felt a stab of pain run up her arm, but she thought she'd got off lightly if that was the extent of her injuries. 'What about the baby?' she asked, almost as an afterthought.

When the nurse hesitated Fifi became wide awake immediately. 'Have I lost it?'

'I'm so very sorry, Mrs Reynolds,' the nurse said in her curious sing-song voice. 'I'm afraid you miscarried and we had to give you a D and C too. But your husband will be coming down to see you soon, he'll tell you all about it.'

Fifi was too stunned to say anything. She closed her eyes and allowed the nurse to assume she was falling asleep again.

So she'd lost her baby, and what hadn't come away naturally had been scraped away. And who would mourn that little life? Her parents hadn't welcomed it, she hadn't even welcomed it herself, not at first. Dan was the only person who was one hundred per cent joyful about it.

So why was it that when she could barely feel the plaster on her arm, she could feel her heart breaking?

Dan was brought to her bedside later in a wheelchair. When she heard him say her name she opened her eyes to see his swimming in tears.

'They didn't tell me till this morning that you'd been brought in,' he said brokenly. 'They wouldn't bring me to you then because they said you were having an operation. I thought it must be on your broken wrist. They only told me an hour ago that you'd lost the baby.'

Fifi wept then, and Dan moved his wheelchair closer so he could hold her and cry with her.

Later Fifi tried to tell him how it had all come about: falling down in the street, her fright at the storm, and finally seeing Alfie on the garden wall.

'I suppose I must have thought he was coming to hurt me,' she finished up. 'But I don't really remember what I thought, or what happened after. Apart from Frank being in the ambulance with me.'

'Frank came to see me this morning, just after they told me you'd been brought in last night,' Dan said. 'He looked rough, I think he'd been here all night, and they didn't want to let him in as it wasn't visiting hour, but he insisted. He said that the first thing you said when you came round in the ambulance was that Alfie was on the back wall.'

'I suppose you both think I imagined that,' she said tearfully. 'But I didn't, I saw him as clear as day in a flash of lightning. Why would he climb along that wall in a thunderstorm unless it was for something bad?'

'Frank doesn't think you imagined it. He was going home to check if the honeysuckle that grows up on the wall was trampled on. But Alfie was probably only doing a bit of peeping Tom. He couldn't hope to get into the house that way, Frank keeps his back door locked and bolted. But Frank told me that you came back from Bristol on Friday night, not Saturday. Why didn't you tell me that, Fifi?'

Fifi was sorry he had to learn it through Frank, but she supposed she'd have had to tell him eventually.

'Because I had a row with my mum and I didn't want you to worry about it.'

She saw in his face that he knew the row was about him. 'I hope she'll be proud of herself when I ring her to tell her what's happened to you.'

'She didn't make it happen.'

'She let you come home all upset and alone,' he said. 'Don't tell me that wasn't the start of it all, because I know it was. You weren't yourself yesterday, I knew something had upset you. And now we've lost our baby, and that's going to take longer for you to get over than breaking your wrist.'

Dr Hendry came back the following morning to see Fifi and found her feeling very sorry for herself. He wasn't surprised; she probably hadn't slept well because of the pain in her wrist, and her body was bruised and battered. But it was clear to him that her aches and pains were secondary to losing her baby.

'It wasn't a planned baby,' she blurted out to him, almost as if she felt she had miscarried as a kind of judgment. 'I'd only just started to feel glad about it. What was wrong with me that I lost my grip in a thunderstorm? Aren't pregnant women supposed to stay calm and protect their baby from harm?'

Hendry was over sixty, and in half a lifetime of medicine he'd seen many women blaming themselves this way after losing a child.

'My experience is that miscarriages happen regardless of how well cared for the mother is,' he said gently. 'I've seen women deliver healthy babies after far worse accidents than yours, and, contrary-wise, lose them for no apparent reason at all. You mustn't blame yourself, Mrs Reynolds, and there is absolutely no reason to suppose that in a few months' time you can't carry another baby to full term.'

He went on to say he wanted to keep her in under observation for a week.

'I can't stay here that long,' Fifi exclaimed in horror. 'Dan's going home tomorrow and he needs someone to look after him.'

Hendry had already spoken to Dan Reynolds, and although he knew about the vicious attack, and that this attractive young couple didn't live under the best of conditions, he had to smile at Mrs Reynolds' belief her husband couldn't cope without her. To him, Dan Reynolds looked the type to sail through any amount of disasters and still keep smiling and cracking jokes.

'Your husband doesn't strike me as the kind of man who needs looking after, but anyway, we're going to keep him in for another day or two,' he said. 'You've both had too much to cope with all at once – you need rest before you start trying to get back to normal.'

On Monday afternoon Fifi lay in the hospital bed waiting for Dan to visit her. It had rained heavily all day on Sunday, but the sun was shining again now, showing up the rain-smeared windows. She'd grown used to the weight of the plaster on her arm, though not to washing her face or cleaning her teeth with her left hand. But the loss of her baby was just as raw; each time she put her hand on her stomach she was reminded that there was no little person growing in there any more.

She knew now that her ward was a gynaecology ward, all twelve women either waiting for an operation, hysterectomies in the main, or recovering from one. The youngest patient was eighteen; she had come over to talk to Fifi and said she had a cyst on one of her ovaries which they'd be operating on tomorrow. The oldest was in her sixties.

As Fifi had never been in hospital before she had no way of knowing whether this ward was better or worse than other kinds, but one of the nurses had said it was her favourite as the patients were usually cheerful and rarely desperately ill.

Fifi had wondered whether that was a gentle way of telling her to buck up and be jolly because she wasn't ill, but she couldn't summon the will to chat or laugh as most of the other women were doing. Frank had visited her the previous evening with Yvette, bringing the nightdress, dressing-gown and toiletries Fifi had asked Miss Diamond to get for her. Frank had brought some flowers from his garden and a box of Roses chocolates, Yvette some glossy magazines and a little bottle of flowery-smelling French cologne. They had brought get-well cards from various people in the street, and Stan had put together a little basket of fruit. Miss Diamond had written on her card that she would be happy to help Fifi with dressing and anything else she couldn't do one-handed when she got home, and that if she wanted any shopping she had only to give Frank a list.

It was very touching to see so many people cared about her and Dan, yet all the fussing, questions and attention just made Fifi feel worse. She thought she would give anything to be tucked away in a room by herself, where the only visitor was Dan.

The ward door opened and visitors came surging through, smiling and waving as they spotted their mother, wife, sister or friend.

All at once Fifi saw her mother and father among them. She could hardly believe her eyes, for they were the last people she'd expected to visit.

Her father normally wore an old tweed jacket with his pipe tucked into the breast pocket, corduroy trousers and brown leather brogues, and he looked right in them. But today he was wearing what he considered to be his best suit, a dark grey pinstripe. Fifi and Patty had always sniggered about it behind his back for it was a wartime style with wide lapels and very baggy trousers.

That he'd chosen to wear it to visit her was an indication of his state of mind, for he only ever dressed up when he was anxious about something.

Her mother was dressed up too, in a pale blue costume with high heels, gloves and a boater-style straw hat. But this was quite normal for her when she went out for the day.

Fifi didn't know how she felt about them coming. She'd told Dan not to ring them, but clearly he'd done so anyway.

'You poor darling,' Clara exclaimed, swooping over to the bed in a flamboyant display of maternal affection. 'What a terrible ordeal you've been through. We are so sorry.'

'Why are you?' Fifi asked sharply. She thought her mother had to be the most insincere woman on the planet. 'You should be glad there is no baby any more.'

'Don't be like that,' her father said testily. 'Your mother's been distraught ever since Dan phoned.'

'I'm surprised she could even bring herself to speak to him,' Fifi said sullenly.

'It was me who spoke to him,' her father said reprovingly. 'And I'm sure Dan will assure you that I was very upset to hear about your fall and the subsequent miscarriage. If we'd got the call earlier yesterday we would have come right away.'

'If only you hadn't run off in a huff on Friday,' Clara butted in, 'this might not have happened.'

'What you should be saying is, "If only I hadn't been so nasty to you",' Fifi corrected her. 'I'm a married woman now. If you can't accept Dan and try to like him, then I don't want anything to do with you.'

'I understand how you feel,' her father said quickly, glancing at his wife as if warning her not to retaliate. 'But you must try and understand what you put us through by getting married in secret. We couldn't help but think badly of Dan, it was all so furtive. However, when I spoke to him on the telephone yesterday I was pleasantly surprised by how sensitive he is, and it was obvious to me that he loves you. So I'm very sorry I misjudged him and in future I shall try to get to know him better.'

Fifi was very glad to hear that, but she could see by her mother's tight expression that this wasn't a joint change of heart. 'Well, perhaps you could start by going to see him while you are here?' she said.

'Of course we will,' her father said. 'I was going to suggest to him that you both come home to recuperate when you leave the hospital. You are going to find it quite hard going without the use of your right hand, and Patty and the boys will be delighted to see you and help you.'

Fifi was very taken aback by this U-turn, and moved that her father was doing his best to make everything right between them. She almost wanted to agree to his suggestion, if only to show him she didn't bear a grudge. But she knew that neither she nor Dan could cope with all the stuff that would come with being at home.

'That's very sweet of you, Dad,' she said. 'I appreciate the thought, but I think we'll manage all right in our flat. The neighbours are very kind, and I'll need to pop into the office too. I know I can't type but I could show willing by offering to do filing or something.'

'Don't be ridiculous!' Clara exclaimed. 'You won't be fit for work for weeks. And they won't keep your job open for you anyway, so there's nothing to keep you in London.'

'There's our home,' Fifi said sharply, astounded that her mother could be so grossly insensitive. 'And I think they will keep my job open. If you're thinking we haven't got any money to live on, we have. We've got some savings. You see, we *were* responsible.'

'I can see there's no talking to you,' Clara said curtly. 'We might as well have stayed at home.'

At that Fifi began to cry. All she wanted was a hug and some sympathy that she'd lost her baby, surely any woman would understand that?

'There now, Fifi.' Her father took out his handkerchief and tried to dry her eyes. He looked ill at ease and awkward, but he'd never been much good at emotional scenes. 'I don't really know what to say. I'm so sorry about the baby, and so is your mother, but she's a bit overwrought at the moment.'

'Go home,' Fifi said, still crying. 'I'm overwrought too, with a lot more reason than Mum. And don't let her any-where near Dan, he's been through enough already.'

Clara turned and walked away, her slender back stiff with indignation. Harry just stood there, looking completely out of his depth.

'You'd better go after her, Dad,' Fifi said, sniffing back her tears. 'Or she'll be making your life hell too.'

'It's guilt that makes her that way,' he said sadly, bending over to kiss Fifi's forehead. 'She's blaming herself for you losing the baby, but she can't unbend enough to say so.'

'I don't think I care enough about her any more to try and understand,' Fifi said brokenly. 'All I did was marry the man I love. Was that so very terrible?'

Fifi walked slowly up the stairs behind Dan who was carrying her small bag containing the things she'd had brought into the hospital.

'Everything's spotless,' he said, turning to look at her. 'Yvette came over yesterday and removed all signs of the mess I'd made while I was on my own. She even cleaned the cooker.'

Fifi could smell polish and cleaning fluids, and she knew that the flat bore no resemblance to how it was the day they moved in back in May. But she had the same feeling of trepidation she'd experienced that day; she didn't feel glad she was home.

'That was kind of her,' she said stiffly. 'I'm amazed she knows how to clean as she never does her own place.' She knew that was a shabby jibe, but she couldn't help herself.

'Everyone's been very kind,' Dan said with just a hint of reproach in his voice. 'Miss Diamond has made us a beef casserole for supper, I've only got to heat it up.' Fifi sniffed disdainfully at this, but Dan went on, 'Stan's brought you flowers, and Frank's brought you some magazines to read.'

Fifi said nothing more, just went into the living room and sat down. It was, as Dan had claimed, spotless. The flowers from Stan were beautiful, roses and pink carnations, clearly arranged in the vase by Yvette.

'Cup of tea?' Dan asked. Fifi nodded. She didn't want to

be like this, all sullen and hateful, especially to Dan who had been so brave and uncomplaining about his injuries, but she felt so miserable she just couldn't help it.

While Dan was out on the landing putting the kettle on, she glanced out of the window and saw Molly Muckle coming out of her house with Mary, the oldest girl. Molly yelled at the top of her voice to Alan, Joan and Angela who were playing down the end of the street by the coal yard. The stridency of her voice made Fifi wince and she wished she had agreed to go home to her parents' house. How on earth was she going to fill the days here until her plaster came off? She couldn't use her right hand, and even if she could, what was there to do?

She thought she'd probably go mad with boredom cooped up in the flat. At least at home she could have sunbathed in the garden and gone to see a few old friends. Dale Street looked so dirty and depressing, and she didn't want to see any of her neighbours because she knew they'd all be clucking with sympathy over her. How could she explain to anyone how hopeless she felt?

If she looked back, her whole life seemed to have had no point to it, and she could see nothing ahead but more of the same. A baby would have changed everything, they would have moved from here and had all the excitement of turning the new place into a home. The savings they'd got were going to be eaten up while neither she nor Dan could work, and it would probably be another couple of years before they'd be in a position again to buy a place.

'Here you are,' Dan said, coming in with a cup of tea and a jam doughnut for her. He put them down on the coffee table and sat down on the other armchair. 'It's lovely to have you back home. I hated going to bed without you.'

Fifi began to cry and Dan immediately looked stricken. 'What's wrong?' he asked, coming over and kneeling in front of her. 'Are you feeling ill?'

'I don't know what's wrong,' she sobbed out. That was true; how could she explain that everything which had once been dear to her no longer seemed to matter? She wanted to be alone, but she knew that if she was she'd hate it. She didn't want to be fussed over, but if people didn't fuss, that would hurt her too. Everything was contradictory, except her sorrow at losing the baby. That was the only constant thing.

'Dr Hendry told me you would be weepy for a while,' Dan said gently, trying to cuddle her. 'He said there was no quick cure for it, but to make sure you got rest, good food and a bit of exercise. Why don't you lie down for a bit? I'll make us some soup or something for lunch, then we could go for a walk in the park.'

'I don't want to walk around that scabby park, my insides feel as if they're falling out,' she snapped. That wasn't true. It had felt that way when she first got up in hospital, but the sensation had gone within twenty-four hours. Yet she preferred to have a medical reason for feeling so down, rather than allowing anyone to think she was going a bit crazy.

'Okay,' Dan shrugged, 'we'll stay here. Why don't we both go and lie down? It's a long time since we had a cuddle.'

'I'm not in a fit state for sex,' she roared at him. 'Don't you ever think of anything else?'

Dan got up and walked away. He turned at the door and looked back at her, his face a picture of hurt and sorrow. 'Yes, I do think of other things,' he said. 'Like how sorry I am we lost our baby, that I couldn't bring you home today to a nicer place, and that I can't afford to buy a car so I could drive you somewhere beautiful. I think about how lucky we are that our neighbours have all been so kind. I also think there must be something badly wrong with you if you imagine I'd be after sex when you are so unhappy.'

Chapter nine

Fifi carried her mug of tea into the living room and switched on the radio to hear the eight o'clock news, then sat down by the window. It was three weeks since her miscarriage, and at long last she seemed to have come out of the depressed and miserable state she'd been in. It was Saturday, another beautiful morning, and she thought she would get washed and dressed after her tea, then walk to the shops.

Eva Price, the red-headed woman who lived at number 8, the house next to the coal yard, was on her way to work at the launderette. She was a divorcee and lived alone with her ten-year-old son. She looked very fresh in a pale green dress, with white shoes and handbag, Fifi had noticed she was looking very much smarter lately and wondered if that was because she'd got a new man in her life.

Fifi smiled to herself, remembering how a few days earlier Dan had teased her that she was getting like an old busybody, taking up a grandstand seat to watch the neighbours behind the net curtains.

He was right, she was becoming a first-class busybody. Since coming home from hospital she'd done little else but monitor the comings and goings of everyone in the street. And, of course, upset Dan hundreds of times with her gloom, sarcasm and plain nastiness.

She was very ashamed of that now. Dan certainly didn't deserve what she'd put him through – he washed her, dressed her, cooked and cleaned. And all the time he'd been so comforting and understanding, even when she was impossible and he wasn't a hundred per cent himself. But thankfully now, aside from the limitations of her arm being in plaster, she felt like her old self again.

The doctor had given Dan the all-clear at the end of last week. Apart from the bald patch on the back of his head where they'd shaved it to stitch the wound, and some bruising on his chest, he seemed none the worse for his ordeal, and he'd gone back to work on Monday. Fifi missed him; the days seemed very long and empty without him around. She wished he hadn't agreed to work all day today, but he said they needed the money and she supposed he was only being sensible.

But being alone had forced her to do things herself. She'd even mastered peeling potatoes with her left hand, and writing letters, though they looked as though a child had written them, and cleaning up. She could use the fingers on her right hand to support things, but they were stiff still and her arm ached if she used them for too long.

Despite her mother's gloomy prediction, her job had been kept open for her, in fact she'd had flowers and a very sympathetic letter from her boss. She hoped that she could go back at the beginning of September when the plaster came off.

A child crying somewhere made Fifi lean forward in her seat, but she couldn't see the child outside, or work out which house the crying might be coming from. The milk float came rattling along and drowned it out. She watched the milkman leap out, grab a handful of bottles, then run from door to door depositing them and picking up the empties.

Frank's voice wafted up to her as he called to the milkman to ask if he had any eggs on the float. Then another male voice joined theirs, asking Frank if he had last night's *Evening Standard*. She guessed it was Mr Helass, two doors down, but without leaning out of the window she couldn't see her side of the street.

One good thing to come out of both her and Dan ending up in hospital was that they'd got to know so many of their neighbours far better. As Dan had pointed out to her, all of them had been incredibly kind. Miss Diamond had made several meals for them, including the beef casserole Fifi had been mean enough to mock on her first day home. Stan had got their shopping, and lots of other neighbours had brought them newspapers, magazines, fruit and chocolates. Frank and Miss Diamond had been running up and down stairs constantly for the first few days, wanting to help in any way they could.

Yet it was Yvette Fifi felt most indebted to. She came over every day for the first two weeks. She did whatever she saw needed doing, whether that was changing the sheets on the bed or a bit of washing up or ironing, in a gentle, unpushy way that didn't make them feel awkward. But it was the comfort she gave Fifi when she was at her lowest that helped the most.

Whoever would have thought that a distinctly odd French spinster would be the only person capable of getting her to talk about how she felt? Yvette alone seemed to understand all the conflicting feelings Fifi had experienced when she found she was pregnant. She didn't pooh-pooh Fifi's belief that it was her fault she lost the baby. Instead she talked through these things, making Fifi see that imagining it was a punishment because she hadn't been ecstatic with delight right from conception was ridiculous, but at the same time quite normal, and that most women who miscarried felt much the same.

She was equally wise about the rift between Fifi and her mother, and suggested that the causes were almost certainly based on something in Fifi's childhood.

'If she always had to worry about you and protect you as a leetle girl, she cannot just stop because you are big now,' Yvette said. 'She is frightened you will be hurt. It is hard for any mother to let go.'

As Fifi continued to gaze out of the window, she remembered how awful she thought this street was when they first came here, and how that feeling came back after she came out of hospital. It looked okay again now. It would be nice of course if there were a few trees, or the coal yard closed down, but if she and Dan left, and he'd been saying they should when her arm was better, she was going to miss the friends she'd made here.

Granted, the Muckles were still over the road, 'ze worm in ze apple', as Yvette humorously described them, but they had been quieter lately. They still had their regular Friday night card parties, but last night Fifi hadn't heard anything much because she and Dan had gone to bed early.

She wondered if maybe Alfie had got nervous when the police questioned him about Dan's attack. Or could it be that they'd finally grown tired of everyone loathing them?

If only the police could find out who attacked Dan! She didn't like things left in the air. But there were no fingerprints on the iron bar he was hit with. No one living in the houses and flats along the alley where it happened had seen anyone behaving suspiciously. The police hadn't officially closed the case as far as she knew, but it didn't look as if they were doing anything else about it.

Dan had always been convinced that he was merely mistaken for someone else. As he pointed out, the time he left work varied from day to day.

Being realistic, Fifi doubted Alfie was really capable of planning such an elaborate revenge anyway. She was even inclined to believe she'd imagined him standing on the garden wall that night of the storm too. She was distraught, after all. Would anyone, even a weirdo like Alfie, attempt prowling around on garden walls in such weather?

'Fifi! Are you up and about?'

At the sound of Frank calling her, Fifi got up from her chair and went out on to the landing. Frank was standing down on the stairs, her pint of milk in his hands.

'You look smart,' Fifi said. He was wearing a navy blue suit and a white shirt and tie. 'Where are you off to?'

'To visit June's grave, then on to see my sister,' he said, coming further up the stairs and putting the milk bottle down. 'I'll be gone all day and I wondered if you'd like to sit out in my garden in the sun.'

'I'd love to,' she said, smiling down at him. 'You are sweet, Frank!'

Frank had made this offer before, saying he didn't like the thought of her and Dan being cooped up in the flat. But they'd never taken him up on it as while Dan was home they could go to the park together. Fifi wasn't that keen on going alone to the park, and besides, it wasn't very comfortable sitting on the grass reading. Frank had a nice padded chair, and in the privacy of his garden she could wear shorts or even a swimsuit.

'Well, you just go on out there when you're ready,' he said, turning to go back downstairs. 'It's going to be a scorcher today. Make yourself drinks in the kitchen, you don't want to be running up and down the stairs. But when you come back in, remember to lock the kitchen door.'

'I'll do some weeding for you,' she said. 'That's one thing I can do with my left hand.'

'Pull up any flowers and I'll clip you round the ear when I get home,' he laughed.

Fifi washed herself and put on a pair of white shorts and a sun top, then made herself a boiled egg and some toast. It was infuriating how long it took to do the simplest tasks one-handed. Doing up her bra had been impossible at first, as was spreading butter on toast, and striking matches to light the gas. Dan had got round this by buying a battery-operated gadget, and as time went on she found ways round the other problem areas, especially when her broken wrist became stronger and she found she could use the fingers enough to support things.

She had just got her breakfast on to the table when she heard Alfie Muckle's voice out in the road. It was only nine o'clock, extraordinarily early for him to surface, especially after a card party, so Fifi went to the window to see what he was up to.

Alfie was dressed amazingly smartly for him in a shirt and grey trousers instead of his usual grubby vest with braces over it. With him were the three older children, Alan, the sulky-looking teenager, equally tidy, Mary and Joan in clean dresses and white socks. All of them were carrying bags full of what looked like towels and picnic things.

'Come on,' Alfie shouted back to Molly who was dithering in the doorway. 'You wanted the bloody day out. If we don't get out now it won't be worth going.'

Molly seemed to be arguing with him about something. She kept looking back in to the hall, but her voice was too indistinct to make out what she was saying.

'Serves 'er bloody well right,' Alfie bawled out. 'Now, come on or I'll change me mind about it.'

Molly looked the way she did when she went out alone in the evenings, wearing a pink dress with a full skirt and no curlers. As Fifi watched, Dora and Mike appeared too. Only Angela was missing.

The front door was slammed behind them, and Fifi watched in fascination as the family made their way up the road.

They were a hilarious sight en masse. Alfie tried to swagger, but it looked more like a waddle; Molly teetered unsteadily on her high heels, and the children were slinking along in the gutter, heads down. Dora was wearing a garish bright yellow dress with a full skirt and a kind of sailor collar trimmed with red. Fifi wondered where on earth she managed to get such a frightful outfit, and had some sympathy with Mike who was trying to distance himself from her as she tried possessively to hold his arm.

They had turned the corner when Fifi remembered about the crying child earlier, and she wondered if it could have been Angela. Had they left her alone in the house as a punishment when they were having a day out somewhere?

As she ate her breakfast Fifi watched the Muckles' house. Angela spent a great deal of time looking out of the top bedroom window, but she wasn't there now. The usual blanket was covering it, and Fifi couldn't hear any crying. It was of course possible she'd been sent to a friend or relative for the day, but Fifi couldn't imagine Alfie and Molly being that well organized.

It was lovely out in Frank's garden, a tiny oasis of beauty and peace. Although Fifi could hear traffic in the distance and the sounds of children playing in the streets and other back gardens, it was possible to forget she was in a big city.

As she lay back on the comfortable chair, the sun burning down reminding her of days she'd spent like this back home in Bristol, her thoughts turned naturally to her parents. Her mother had written a very cold and distant letter a few days after Fifi got home from hospital. It was clear from the stilted tone that she hadn't had any real change of heart. While she agreed a miscarriage was upsetting, she felt they always happened 'for the best'. She said she thought it was churlish of Fifi to refuse the offer of a period of convalescence at home, and she didn't know what more she could do.

The letter couldn't have come at a worse time. Fifi was already so weepy and miserable, and all it had done was push her further into gloom and despair. There were other letters around the same time, a sweet and totally sympathetic one from Patty, a joint one from her brothers, and indeed a very warm one from her father, but her mother's undid all the good the others might have done.

Dan had written back on Fifi's behalf, explaining that she couldn't write herself just then, and that their decision to stay in London was made not out of churlishness at all, but for practical reasons. He pointed out that neither of them had felt up to a long train journey or the pressures of being surrounded by other people. He said that neither of them believed losing a baby was 'for the best', and they both found it upsetting that anyone could view it as such.

Once Fifi had adjusted to writing with her left hand, she'd sent a brief letter saying little more than her job had been kept open for her and Dan was going back to work. But there had been no reply from her mother. Fifi felt now that she just had to accept her mother was never going to change her opinions, and that she should stop hoping she would.

At two o'clock the sun was too hot to stay outside any longer. Fifi locked Frank's back door and went upstairs, thinking she would go to the shops to get something for their evening meal. It was only when she changed into a dress that she thought about Angela again.

There was still no sight of her at the window, and it worried her to think the little girl might be all alone in the house, upset that she'd been left behind and possibly with nothing to eat. She decided to go across to Yvette and ask if she'd seen or heard her.

Fifi rang Yvette's bell and tapped on the front window, but there was no reply. She thought the dressmaker must be out at one of her clients' homes doing a fitting. Only a couple of days earlier she'd said she was close to completing an outfit for a bride's mother.

By the time Fifi had bought some pork chops, vegetables and a few other items, an hour had passed. Before taking her shopping indoors she rang Yvette's bell again, but she still hadn't come home. Along by the coal-yard gates, four boys all aged about nine or ten were idly kicking a football around. Recognizing one of them as Matthew, the son of the red-headed woman from the end house, she walked over to him.

'Have you seen Angela Muckle today, Matthew?' she asked him.

'No, she's gone to Southend with the rest of them,' he replied.

'She wasn't with them when they left this morning,' Fifi said. 'I think they left her at home.'

'She said she were going with them yesterday,' Matthew said. 'All excited she were. But she ain't been out here today, leastways not since we come back from the park. But if her mum told her she was to stay in, she wouldn't dare come out.'

Fifi thanked Matthew and gave him sixpence to go and buy himself and his friends ice lollies. But as she walked home she looked back at the Muckles' house. All the windows were shut, and their coverings in place; she could hear no radio playing and it now seemed extremely odd that Angela wasn't looking out watching the children playing as she usually did.

Fifi took her shopping in, put the chops in the fridge and glanced out of the window again, willing Angela to look out so she would know she was all right. But there was still no sign of her, the blanket on the window didn't look as if it had been moved all day, and on an impulse she went back downstairs, crossed over the road and knocked at the door. There was no reply, so Fifi peered through the letter-box. There was a fetid smell, but she could see nothing, as something appeared to be hanging over the inside of the door. 'Angela,' she yelled. 'Can you hear me? It's Mrs Reynolds from across the road.'

No reply, not even a sound of scurrying feet.

Fifi was worried now. Not just the anxious 'what if' kind of worry, but a nasty feeling in the pit of her stomach, almost of foreboding. She stood there in the road looking up at the windows of the Muckles' house and thought about what she'd heard Alfie say that morning. 'Serves her bloody well right' kept coming back to her. Could he have beaten her, or locked her in the bedroom?

'What's up, Mrs Reynolds?'

Fifi was startled by the question from young Matthew as she hadn't heard him come up to her.

She looked down and smiled at the ten-year-old. He was an attractive child with a sprinkling of freckles across the bridge of his nose, and periwinkle eyes. He was licking the lolly he'd bought with the money she gave him and his lips had gone green with the colouring.

'I'm a bit worried Angela might be hurt or ill,' she said.

'If Miss Dupré was in, I'd try to get over her fence to take a look, but she's gone out.'

'You could go along the wall at the back of our place,' he suggested.

Fifi smiled. It was common knowledge that Alfie used that wall all the time to spy on people and as an escape route if necessary. 'I don't think I could manage it with a broken arm,' she said.

'I could go for you,' Matthew volunteered. 'I've been along it loads of times with Alan. It's dead easy from our yard.'

Fifi was tempted. If he could get in the back way and open the front door for her, she could just check on the child, give her something to eat, and put her own mind at rest. But she had a feeling his mother wouldn't like it. She'd either got to do it herself or wait until Dan got home.

'No, your mum wouldn't like it,' she said reluctantly. 'I'll go myself. Can you show me the dead-easy way?'

She didn't even have to go through the boy's flat. There was a gate next to the coal yard that led straight out into his backyard. It was devoid of any plants or trees, just a well-swept space with a washing line and the brick wall along the back.

'You can climb up on the coal bunker,' Matthew said, and obligingly got a wooden beer crate and stood it beside the bunker.

Fifi had no trouble at all getting on to the wall, and once she looked along it, she understood why Alfie had no difficulty using it as his private route. The wall was at least fifteen inches wide, and though there were trees and shrubs on both sides of it, there were no obstacles between this end of the street and the far end by the corner shop.

'Stay there for a little while, just in case I can't get in through the back door,' she said, looking down at Matthew. 'Is there something in their backyard to climb down on?'

'Loads of stuff,' he said with a wide grin. 'But it's right mucky.'

If Fifi hadn't been worried about Angela, she would've got a childish delight in making her way along the wall because it reminded her of going scrumping for apples as a child. She was hidden from anyone looking out of their windows, yet if she parted the leaves she could see into the back gardens, and even into rooms that had no net curtains. Number 10, next to the Muckles, had a very overgrown garden, full of bramble bushes. The elderly couple who owned the house had been taken away to a nursing home soon after Fifi and Dan moved here. Their son came once a week to check on the house, and he'd told Frank he wasn't going to clear the brambles because it deterred the Muckle children from attempting to break in. Fifi hoped it wasn't the same in the Muckles' garden, because she wasn't keen on getting scratched to pieces.

Luckily, although there were some brambles on both Yvette's and number 10's side, a wide area had been hacked clear in the centre of the Muckles' garden. As Matthew had said, there was plenty to climb down on, almost a staircase of wooden beer crates and planks. She made her way down very cautiously though, for she wasn't certain the structure was safe and all around it were broken bottles, tin cans with jagged tops and other junk.

She reached the ground safely, wrinkled her nose at the smell of rotting rubbish and urine, and gingerly picked her way to the back door, past old car seats and a mattress with the springs coming through. The door was unlocked, but she had to push it hard as there was something behind it.

This was just a crate of beer: once she got the door open slightly she could see it and push it out of the way. Then she went in.

She almost turned and went straight back out because the smell made her gag, but she covered her nose with her hand and tried hard not to look at the filth.

She had never in her life seen anything like it. Dirty dishes, empty beer bottles, fish-and-chip papers, cigarette stubs, milk turned sour in bottles and cans of food with jagged tops lay everywhere. The sink and draining board were full of dirty dishes, cigarettes ends stubbed out on them. Burnt saucepans sat on the floor alongside clothes, shoes and old newspapers. She couldn't imagine how any-one could even make a cup of tea in there, let alone cook a meal. But not wanting to linger, she passed through it into the hall.

It was eerily quiet, the only sound a buzzing of flies somewhere. She pushed open the back-room door and saw a rectangular table strewn with beer bottles, dirty glasses, a half-full bottle of Scotch and several overloaded ashtrays. Eight chairs were set around it, and this had to be where they held the card games.

She knew the front room quite well from looking into it so often from her flat, yet close up it proved far more disgusting. Dirty cups and plates littered the floor and the battered and stained couch and chairs were strewn with clothing. The television was a big one, and there was a long, low walnut veneer radiogram, its top scarred with cigarette burns and rings from cups and glasses.

On she went, up the stairs, peeping briefly into each of the three bedrooms. All were vile; there were beds that looked like heaps of dirty rags, a smell that made sure she kept her hand clamped over her nose, and the light filtering through the covering on the windows was grey. She couldn't bear even to look into the bathroom.

Finally she got to the last flight of stairs. There had been no carpet anywhere except in the downstairs front room where the television was, and her footsteps rang out on the bare boards. Balls of fluff, refuse and even crusts of bread were everywhere.

'Angela!' she called out. 'It's me, Fifi!' Her voice echoed alarmingly, and her heart pounded with fear that the front door would open and Alfie would catch her in there.

She could smell stale urine on top of the other putrid smells now, and the buzzing of flies was much louder. She went first to the front room, as she'd seen Angela look out from that window so often, but it was empty except for two double beds pushed up close to each other, and the now all too predictable filthy bedding. A naked rubber doll with one arm missing lay on the floor, the only toy she'd seen in the entire house.

There was only one more room now, and she had a really bad feeling about opening that last door.

She braced herself as she pushed it open, but recoiled momentarily at the frenzied buzz of flies that flew at her. Her eyes met the end of an old-fashioned black iron bed with fancy brass knobs, and through the rails she could see a shape under a surprisingly clean sheet.

'Angela!' Fifi called, creeping hesitantly closer.

It had to be her under the sheet, the mound was the right size and there was even a little tow-coloured hair by the head rails. But even so, Fifi was afraid to pull the sheet back. Goosebumps came up on her limbs and her heartbeat accelerated with fear. She wanted to flee without looking, but she knew she must.

The smell which filled the whole house was much worse

in here, rank and heavy with overtones of urine, sweat and mould. But there was another smell too, something she couldn't define, and this disgusted her most.

But she had to get this over with, so she grabbed the sheet and pulled it back sharply.

'Oh no!' she exclaimed, clamping her hand over her mouth in horror.

It was Angela, stark naked.

Her arms and legs were all splayed out like a starfish, and her mouth was gaping open. There were smears of blood and bruising on her thighs and stomach. Even without touching her, Fifi knew she was dead.

For a second Fifi could only stare at the child in horror. Her eyes were shut, but her features were set in an expression of anguish. Such a thin little body, every bone visible through her pale skin, and her little vulva was swollen and red.

As she began to heave, Fifi turned and ran down the stairs, wrenching open the front door.

The heat of the sun hit her like opening an oven door. 'Did you find her, Mrs Reynolds?' she heard Matthew call out. She knew she was going to be sick, but some sort of instinct made her hide it from the boy.

'Yes, I'm just going to the shop to get her something,' she managed to croak out. Then, taking a deep breath to try and calm herself enough to fool him at least temporarily, she began walking quickly to the end of the street and the phone.

It seemed like an hour before the police came, although in reality it couldn't have been longer than ten minutes. She managed to report the crime, give her name and address and walk swiftly back to her flat. Fortunately Matthew and the other boys had gone from the street, for if they'd come over to her she might well have blurted out what she'd seen. She needed someone, anyone would have done, for it was far too big a shock to contain it. But the entire street was deserted, and she knew too that the right thing to do was to keep it to herself at least until the police had been.

She only just got to the bathroom before she was sick. Her legs felt like rubber, she was shaking like a leaf and as cold as if it were suddenly the middle of winter. She hauled herself back up to her flat, wrapped her dressing-gown round herself and waited.

It was so strange that she'd spent so much time recently looking out of the window but couldn't look now. The picture of Angela lying on that bed, the accompanying smell and the sound of the flies were all she could see, smell and hear. She was beyond crying; what she felt was white-hot rage.

Even when the first police car came roaring down the road, pulling up with a squeal of brakes, she couldn't move to look. She'd left the Muckles' door on the latch, and she could imagine the policemen seeing everything she'd seen as they went up through the house.

As a child she was always wishing she could be involved in a huge drama. She would imagine herself rescuing an old lady from a burning house or jumping into a frozen river to save a drowning dog. She wanted to be a heroine, to have everyone applaud her courage, to be looked up to and talked about.

Maybe she could have that kind of attention now, but she certainly didn't want it. She wished this was just a terrible nightmare and that she'd wake up to see Angela out playing with other children in the street.

When she'd sat at the window this morning, the sun had been on that side of the street. She'd felt happy, giggling to herself at how the Muckle family looked in their best clothes. They'd looked bizarre but not evil, not even dangerous. Yet they must have prepared for their day out while Angela was already dead or dying.

Her horror wasn't so much that Angela was dead. If she'd heard the child had been killed in a road accident she'd be upset, but at least that would be understandable. But how could she ever get over what had been done to that little girl before she died?

The sound of car doors slamming, heavy boots ringing out on the pavement and other neighbours' voices as they came out to see what was going on upset her still further. She had to go into the bedroom, draw the curtains and lie down. She wanted Dan. If only he'd come home right now.

She lay on the bed waiting for the inevitable ring at the doorbell. Even though she'd shut both the living-room and bedroom doors, she could still hear the ever-increasing noise from the street. She so much wished that she could be on the same level as the other neighbours, curious, eager, gossiping and trying to work out what was going on in number 11. She was certain that not one of them could even guess at the real horror the police would be confronted with.

The ring on the doorbell came at ten to five. Fifi knew she must answer it, but all she really wanted to do was to pull the covers over her head and ignore it. She got up, her legs stiff and wooden, and slowly made her way downstairs.

'Come in,' she said to the two police officers. She'd never seen either of them before. The smaller, older one was in plain clothes, his dark suit crumpled and shabby, his hair like a rough wire brush. The uniformed one was well over six feet tall, with washed-out blue eyes and rather prominent teeth.

They were introducing themselves, but she was too aware of the neighbours crowding around just behind them to take in what the men were saying.

'You are Mrs Felicity Reynolds?' the older man asked as the door closed behind him. Fifi could only nod and lead the way upstairs.

Once in her living room, Fifi took the chair furthest from the window. 'I don't know if I can tell you,' she said, feeling as if she might be sick again at any minute. 'It's too terrible.'

'Take your time, Mrs Reynolds,' the older officer said gently. 'We understand you are in shock. I'm Detective Inspector Roper, and this is Sergeant Wallis. We have of course been in there; we just want you to tell us what you saw.'

All at once she was blurting it out in one long flood of words, crying at the same time. They were gentle with her: Roper even took her hand and patted it, telling her that she was doing just fine, while the younger man made her tea.

After Fifi had drunk it, Roper went back over what she'd told them, getting her to explain how and why she went into the Muckles' house in the first place. His voice was calm and soothing as he asked her questions, and Wallis took notes.

As Fifi told them about seeing the Muckles leaving at nine that morning, and what she'd overheard, the noise level from the street was growing. She could identify some of the voices, sharp and questioning, perhaps wanting to know why the police were in with Fifi.

'I shouldn't have gone in there. I should have called you,' Fifi said, breaking down again. 'I wish to God I'd never seen it.'

'But we couldn't have gone in there straight away without any evidence of a crime,' Roper said evenly. 'What you did was perhaps foolhardy, but none the less brave. You have at least prevented the little girl's death being concealed.'

'What would he have done with her body?' Fifi asked, then shuddered at the possibilities that brought into her mind.

Fifi knew the moment Dan turned into the street as the voices outside grew louder still and she heard people running down the road.

'Do they know what's happened?' Fifi asked fearfully. 'If that's my husband they are running to, what will they tell him?'

'They know that Angela Muckle is dead and they've probably guessed that you found her,' Roper said. He looked hot, running his finger around the collar of his shirt as if he longed to unbutton it. 'We won't be telling anyone anything else, and we have to ask that you don't discuss anything that you saw with anyone, as it might prejudice our investigation.'

Even beneath the grime from the building site, Dan looked pale and apprehensive as he came up the stairs. Fifi ran into his arms crying and he held her tightly, looking at the two police officers for an explanation.

Roper told him the gist of it, then said they would have to leave now to continue with their investigation. 'Obviously your wife will need to talk to you about it,' he said, looking sternly at Dan. 'But I have to ask that you keep it between yourselves. Until we have made an arrest, and all the evidence has been examined, it is imperative that no one else knows the details your wife has given us.'

'How did Angela die?' Dan asked, his voice rasping with emotion.

'We can't be absolutely certain until the pathologist has examined her. But it appears to be asphyxiation.'

'The bastard,' Dan spat out. 'I should have ripped his throat out the last time he hurt her.'

'Don't, Dan,' Fifi implored him, knowing he was now going to blame himself for not going to the police then. 'We couldn't have known it would come to this.'

'He might have been doing a runner this morning!' Dan said, his dark eyes wide with horror.

'We don't think so,' Roper said firmly. 'It's like a tip over there, but it doesn't appear to have been abandoned. Don't you worry, we'll get him. We'll have officers everywhere around here waiting for him to come home. Now, Mrs Reynolds, we'll need to take a formal statement from you soon,' he went on to say. 'Not tomorrow, you need to calm yourself first. Monday morning will do, if you wouldn't mind coming down to the station at about ten.' He looked at Dan then, who was still holding Fifi tightly. 'I think you should call the doctor to your wife. She's had a terrible shock.'

A terrible shock! That was how anyone would describe it, yet it didn't come even close to describing what had happened to Fifi. Deep down inside her she had expected to find something nasty in number 11. But what she had found was way beyond any horror she was capable of imagining.

After the police had gone, she wanted to talk to Dan about what she'd seen, but she couldn't. The bare bones of it she could manage, but she couldn't convey the gut-wrenching disgust she'd felt, or even come close to describing the evil she'd seen, smelled and felt. The policemen understood, she'd seen it in their faces, but they'd been there, seen it, and Dan hadn't.

He didn't know what to say to her. He kept clutching her

to him, rubbing her back as she cried, kissing her face, even apologizing for not knowing what to say.

'I don't know what to say either,' she cried, clinging to him.

He washed and changed his clothes, then made them both a cup of tea and sat down with her on his lap, but his eyes constantly strayed to the window. There were five police cars in the road now and the area along the front of number 11 was cordoned off. As the police searched the house, more and more people were arriving in the street to look, and the noise they made wafted up to Dan and Fifi and engulfed them both.

They heard Frank arrive back, and voices shrill with an ugly kind of excitement telling him what had happened. Soon afterwards Miss Diamond came home too, and it was all repeated.

'They are all feeding on it,' Fifi whispered. 'Like sharks coming in for the kill. A little girl is dead, and they can't even be quiet and show a little respect.'

Both Frank and Miss Diamond at least came in quickly. Dan and Fifi could hear their muffled voices down in the hall.

'I don't want to see them,' Fifi said in panic, knowing they were probably discussing whether they should come up to her or not.

'I'll go,' Dan said, lifting her up in his arms. He put her back in the chair and ruffled her hair affectionately. 'I'll ring the doctor while I'm at it.'

'I don't need a doctor, only you,' Fifi said, looking up at him with tear-filled eyes. 'What can he do but give me something to sleep?'

'Maybe that's what you need,' Dan said, looking very anxious.

Fifi shook her head. 'No, I want to be awake when *they* get back.'

Dan slipped down to Frank and Miss Diamond. He spoke in a low voice and although Fifi could not hear what anyone was saying, she sensed the tone of sympathy in both Frank and Miss Diamond's replies.

Dan came back with a brandy bottle. 'Frank said you're to have some of this,' he said. 'Miss Diamond has gone in with him, they're both shaky and stunned and neither of them wants to be alone.'

Fifi had never liked the taste of brandy, but she drank it anyway, grateful for the way it soothed the jitters inside her. Dan made himself a sandwich but found he couldn't eat it. He stood at the window looking down at the people in the street and a tear rolled down his cheek.

'I should never have brought you here,' he said after a few moments of silence. 'In fact I should have disappeared after that day I went to tea at your house. I've brought you nothing but misery.'

'That's not true,' Fifi retorted. 'I've had more happiness since I met you than I had in my whole life before. What happened over there is nothing to do with us, Dan. If I hadn't been such a busybody someone else would've found her.'

'I wish it hadn't been you,' he said, looking round at her. 'I'm afraid of what it will do to you.'

They sat in silence by the window, watching as daylight gradually faded. It was a beautiful sunset, the sky turning red, with shades of purple through to mauve and pink.

They didn't turn on any lights, just stayed rooted in their chairs holding hands. As it became dark they could see into the Muckles' house, for all the lights were on there. Figures flitted from room to room, presumably conducting a thorough search. A little later they saw bright flashes in the top window, perhaps from a camera, and a man who could have been a police doctor, as he had a kind of medical bag, left and drove away. An ambulance arrived, two men went into the house and emerged only minutes later carrying a covered stretcher. Two policemen positioned outside the house spoke harshly to the onlookers who had come closer to look, and they melted back as if ashamed of themselves.

One by one the lights at number 11 were turned off. The two police at the door ordered people off the street, and they walked away too.

To all intents and purposes, it looked as if the house was now deserted. But there had been at least a dozen men inside it earlier, and less than half had left. Fifi felt for those left inside that stinking house of hell. Two of them slipped out and went down to the coal yard, presumably to lie in wait for Alfie in case he tried to escape that way. She had to assume there were more police positioned up by the shop and pub, and in the road behind Dale Street.

Every one of Fifi's muscles grew tauter as if she were preparing to run a race as the clock slowly moved on past ten o'clock. Dan was the same, leaning forward in his chair, eyes fixed on the corner shop.

There was no one left out in the street now, but Fifi was very aware that almost everyone was watching and waiting as they were, for windows that were usually brightly lit were in darkness.

A tripping sound of footsteps made Fifi lean forward.

'It's Yvette,' Dan whispered. 'I'd forgotten about her! Has she been out all day? If so, she won't know what's going on.'

Fifi had told the police Yvette had been out when she

knocked earlier, but she hadn't given her a thought since. She whispered this to Dan, and added that Mr and Mrs Balstrode, who lived above her, would soon fill her in with the news.

'Poor woman, she looks so weary,' Dan said.

He was right, Fifi thought. Yvette looked as if she was finding it hard to put one foot in front of the other. 'She must have been finishing off the wedding outfit she was working on in her client's home,' Fifi said. 'She never stays out after dark normally because she's so nervous.'

'Living next door to the Muckles must be more dangerous than being out in the dark,' Dan said grimly. 'I wonder if she heard anything this morning?'

They watched Yvette go in through the front door. She switched on her light and they saw her illuminated in the window for a couple of moments while she drew the curtains.

Ten minutes later, just as Fifi's attention was beginning to waver because of the brandy she'd drunk, Dan gripped her knee.

'They're coming,' he hissed.

Fifi was immediately tense again. She got up to see better, and sure enough there were the Muckles coming down the road, both Alfie and Molly wearing some kind of seaside hat. They were arm-in-arm, perhaps drunk, the three children trailing behind them and Dora and Mike, carrying the bags, bringing up the rear.

Seeing Alfie walking down the street apparently without a care in the world, when she knew he'd raped and killed his youngest daughter just that morning, was too much for Fifi. If Dan hadn't suddenly grabbed her, perhaps realizing what she might do, she would have run down the stairs, out on to the street and attacked him.

'No, sweetheart,' he whispered, holding her tightly. 'He'll hang for what he's done, and the police will give him the kicking of his life before that. Just watch him get captured, with me.'

'Bloody quiet tonight,' they heard Alfie say to Molly. 'Reckon we ought to liven things up, girl.'

Molly cackled with laughter, and the sound was an even bigger affront to Fifi's senses.

She held her breath as the Muckles approached their front door. Out of the corner of her eye she saw the officer down by the coal yard come out of the shadows, and at the same time a police car turned into the top of the road.

Alfie unlocked his door and went in. A light came on in the hall, and suddenly the silence of the street was broken by yelling, swearing and scuffling.

That noise was the signal for everyone to turn on their lights and spill out on to the street again, many of them shouting abuse and waving fists at number 11.

Alan Muckle had not yet got through the front door, and hearing the noise and commotion he tried to run for it. He was swiftly caught by the man at number 14 who twisted his arm up behind his back and brought him back to be handed to the police.

'Child killers!' someone shouted, and suddenly everyone was chanting it, over and over again.

'If they knew what else they'd done they'd tear them apart with bare hands,' Fifi exclaimed.

The three children were immediately put into the police car and driven off at speed. As the car turned the corner, someone hurled a brick through the windows of number 11, and the chanting grew louder and uglier.

A Black Maria came screaming down the street. Two policemen jumped out, pushing back the crowd and yelling that anyone stepping over the line would be arrested too.

After what seemed like hours, but was perhaps only ten or fifteen minutes, Molly and Dora were brought out hand-cuffed and shoved into the Black Maria, quickly followed by Alfie and Mike. The van drove off to screams of abuse, people running behind it, their faces ugly with hatred.

Fifi broke down and sobbed then. All the fears she'd had for Angela the time she intervened before had been justified. So why hadn't she gone to the police then, or even the social services afterwards, and reported the Muckles? She'd hardly given the poor kid a thought once she knew she was pregnant, and today she'd been sunbathing when just across the road Angela was dying.

'You are not in any way responsible,' Dan said, as always quick to pick up on what she was thinking. 'You couldn't have done any more than you did.'

They went to bed then, but couldn't sleep. Fifi wondered what asphyxiation actually meant. She'd heard the word often enough, but did it mean strangling or suffocation? She thought about the clean sheet over the child. Was that some kind of apology? Was Molly in on it all? She had to be; no man could go upstairs and do those hideous things to a seven-year-old without a mother sensing something.

But why kill her? Maybe in a way it was better that they had, for the poor little thing would surely never recover from the rape. Had Angela threatened to tell?

Fifi couldn't imagine the child doing so. She was too fearful and cowed already. And why didn't Alfie choose Mary or Joan, the older girls? Mary was already well developed for a thirteen-year-old. Or maybe he'd already done it to them too?

But over and above everything else, Fifi just couldn't

imagine how anyone could kill a child, then calmly take the rest of the family out for the day. What was Alfie intending to do with her when he got home? Bury her in the garden?

She knew Dan was awake too, even though he was pretending otherwise. The arm around her was tense, his whole body felt stiff. She sensed he was angry with himself for thinking that the warning of a good kicking would prevent Alfie from harming Angela again. He was probably dwelling too on what her parents would think about a man who exposed his wife to such dangerous characters.

But Fifi hadn't got anything left inside her to comfort or reassure Dan. Her head was too full of the horror of what she'd seen that day to make room for anything else.

Chapter ten

'Where are you going?' Fifi asked as Dan got out of bed on Monday morning.

'I've got to go to work,' he said.

She sat up sharply. 'You can't,' she said in disbelief. 'Tell me you're joking?'

They had spent Sunday in a kind of daze, hardly speaking because they didn't know what to say to each other. They didn't dare even go out for a walk because they didn't want anyone questioning them. They silently prepared a roast dinner, but couldn't eat it. Frank came up, and Miss Diamond later on, both asking if there was anything they could do, but it seemed as if they too had withdrawn into themselves, for they didn't try to linger or talk.

It was the longest day Fifi had ever known. She felt unable to watch the television or read a book. She was just marking time until she could get back to bed, craving oblivion.

But they barely slept at all, tossing and turning, getting up for cups of tea twice, and it had never crossed Fifi's mind that Dan would even consider going to work today. Surely he realized this was one time when she really needed him by her side?

Dan sat down on the edge of the bed, pulling on the pants he'd left on the floor the night before, then turned to her.

'I have to, Fifi,' he said gently, reaching out to caress her cheek. 'I've only just gone back after two weeks off, that held everyone up. I've got a wall to finish so they can start doing the roof. If I don't go in, it will hold the whole job up again.'

'I don't believe what I'm hearing,' she said coldly, pushing his hand away. 'You're not the only bricklayer they've got.'

Dan sighed and rubbed his eyes. He looked as if he hadn't slept for days, not just two disturbed nights. 'No, I'm not the only bricklayer, but I'm the only one who's already been off for two weeks, and was lucky I wasn't permanently replaced. If I go in now, with luck when I tell them what's happened they might send me home. If I don't show, the boss will be pissed off with me.'

'It doesn't matter that I'm pissed off then?'

'I have to go, sweetheart,' he said pleadingly, reaching for his shirt. 'Please don't make it harder for me.'

'You just don't care about me and my feelings,' Fifi said indignantly, and lay back down with a thump.

'You know perfectly well that isn't true,' he said wearily. 'The building trade isn't like the Civil Service, there's no such thing as sick pay or compassionate leave cos your wife is upset about something. I can't make anything better for you by just being here, all it means is there will be less money coming in, and I might get fired.'

'But something might happen, and I've got to go and make a statement,' she argued.

'Yvette's over the road, Frank's downstairs if you need help. Even if I was to stay home and go with you to the police station, they wouldn't let me sit in with you while you make the statement. You could be in there for hours. What sense is there in me sitting there twiddling my thumbs when I could just be finishing the job everyone's expecting me to do today?'

'Oh, go to work,' Fifi said irritably. 'Stay and do overtime too! You wouldn't be any good to me anyway, you haven't a clue how I feel.'

'Haven't I?' he said, arching one eyebrow. 'Just because I'm not a bloody psychiatrist doesn't mean I'm stupid. It's just a few hours, for goodness' sake! Go back to sleep now, then go and make your statement. I'll be back as early as possible.'

Fifi turned her face into the pillow. She could hear him getting dressed, and then he made a cup of tea. She ignored him when he put her cup on the bedside table, and stiffened when he tried to kiss her goodbye.

'I love you, Fifi,' she heard him say from the doorway. 'I'm not doing this because I want to, but because I must.'

It was his slow, heavy step on the stairs that pricked her conscience. He usually bounded down them two at a time, and so it was clear he was troubled at leaving her. One of the reasons she fell in love with him was because he was so uncompromisingly masculine. He saw his role as that of sole provider and protector and he wouldn't take a day off work even if he had a raging temperature. But although she admired his strength and sense of duty, she still thought that in this case he ought to have put her needs first.

She must have fallen asleep again soon, for the next time she looked at the clock it was after nine. It was another hot day, and it seemed almost obscene that the sun should still be shining when something so awful had happened, but she found she wasn't cross with Dan any more. He couldn't make anything better by staying home with her; with or without him the pictures in her head were going to be the same, and perhaps it was wise to keep his boss sweet.

She had a quick bath, put on a plain blue dress and fixed

her hair up in a ponytail. She was very pale, and her eyes looked awful, piggy, with dark circles beneath them; they still felt kind of tender from so much crying. But she supposed she'd be crying again once she had to tell everything again at the police station, so there was no point in putting on any mascara.

The interview room at the police station was small, hot and airless, painted a hideous mustard colour, and it stank of stale cigarettes. Detective Inspector Roper had a young policewoman with him to take down her statement, and without any preamble he asked Fifi to start right at the beginning when she first got up on Saturday morning.

Fifi related everything carefully. Now and then Roper would ask her to explain something a little more clearly, who she'd seen or talked to, the exact time of day, and the policewoman wrote it down.

By the time she got to the part when she entered the Muckles' house and made her way upstairs, it was already noon and so hot she had perspiration running down her face. When they had a break for a cup of tea and for her to go to the lavatory, she was actually glad Dan hadn't come with her. There really would have been no point in him sitting outside the interview room just waiting for her.

As they resumed the statement and she got to where she opened the door to the room where Angela was, she broke down. It was too much having to go through all that terrible part again. Roper got her a glass of water, and the policewoman comforted her. Roper waited patiently until she'd composed herself before continuing.

But finally it was over, she was given the statement to read herself, and she had to sign it to confirm it was an accurate account of the day's events.

'May I go now?' she asked, very relieved it was over.

'Just one more thing before you go,' Roper said. 'You said Mr Ubley was out all day?'

'Yes, he went to visit his wife's grave, and then to see his sister,' Fifi said.

'What time did he leave the house?'

Fifi shrugged. 'I don't know.'

'Well, was it straight after he came up with your milk and said you could sit in his garden?'

'I wouldn't know. I got washed and dressed and that took some time. He was gone by the time I went down to his garden.'

'So you didn't see him walk up the street?'

Fifi thought that a very odd question. 'No, otherwise I would've known when he left, wouldn't I?'

'But it was after you saw the Muckles leave?'

'Yes. No. Oh, I don't know,' she said irritably. 'He came upstairs with the milk before the Muckles went off, but I don't know when he left the house. Why are you asking me about him anyway?'

Roper shrugged. 'In a case like this we have to find out where everyone around was, and at what time, that's all.'

Fifi couldn't see why Frank's movements should interest them. After all, they hadn't asked her about Eva Price or Mr Helass, who had also been out in the road that morning.

'Where are the other Muckle children?' she asked.

'They've been taken to a place of safety,' Roper said. 'Don't you worry your head about them.'

That sounded a little patronizing to Fifi, and she bristled. 'I just hope you don't let any of the adults back to their house, they're likely to be lynched,' she said tartly.

Roper nodded but made no reply.

'How did Angela die?' Fifi blurted out suddenly. 'Was she strangled?'

'No.' He paused as if considering whether to divulge the cause of death or not. 'Unless something else comes up in her post mortem, we think she was suffocated, probably with a pillow.'

'Really!' Fifi said in surprise. 'Do you know yet what time she died?'

'Between eight-thirty and ten-thirty a.m.,' Roper said tersely, as if she had no business to ask.

Fifi wanted to ask a great deal more but didn't quite dare. 'What will happen now? Will I have to be a witness in court?'

'Almost certainly,' he said. 'But don't trouble yourself about that now, a trial is a long way off.'

Fifi thought 'a trial' was a very vague statement, almost as if he hadn't yet decided who had murdered Angela. But then she knew from her work in a solicitors' office that police and lawyers always hedged their bets and were careful to be seen to be impartial.

'Thank you for coming in so promptly, Mrs Reynolds,' Roper said, getting to his feet to signify the interview was at an end. 'I know this has all been very distressing for you, but do try not to let it prey on your mind. Obviously if you should decide to move away from Dale Street, please let us know your new address so we can contact you.'

It was even hotter outside the police station than it had been inside. Fifi bought a newspaper, then went into a café for a cold drink. As she flicked through the daily paper a headline on the second page caught her eye: 'Child murdered in Kennington'. Her stomach lurched; she hadn't expected it to be in a national newspaper.

The report said very little, just giving Angela's name and age, and stating that her body was discovered by a neighbour during yesterday afternoon, and that the child's parents were being held for questioning.

Fifi guessed that at the time the paper went to press, that was all the information available. But by now journalists would be sniffing around, and there would be dozens of people only too willing to tell them everything they knew about the Muckles, and indeed which neighbour found Angela.

She wasn't concerned so much that reporters might pester her, she could always refuse to say anything. But they might name her, and her parents might see it. She could just imagine what her mother would say. 'This is *his* fault. He took my daughter to live in a place where that sort of thing goes on!'

No one would be able to convince Clara Brown that 'that sort of thing' could happen anywhere.

Dan did come home early, bringing with him some ham and salad stuff for their tea. After a quick bath he prepared the meal and suggested they went out for a drink later, just for a change of scene.

He didn't apologize further about going to work, nor did he ask her much about making her statement. Fifi wanted him to, she needed some kind of outlet for her feelings, but without some prompting from him she felt unable to begin. He wasn't at all sulky, just quiet, and after they'd eaten the salad and cleared away and she said she thought they ought to stay in, he didn't argue, but began tinkering with an old clock he'd found in a junk shop.

What she had meant was that she wasn't sure it was appropriate to go out and drink so soon after Angela's death. She supposed she wanted his reassurance it was okay, and she certainly didn't want to sit there watching him playing with a clock or being reminded of the child whenever she looked out of the window.

It was hot and airless in the flat and Fifi wanted to suggest going to Hyde Park for a walk. She thought she'd feel better getting some fresh air, seeing grass and trees, but Dan seemed to be engrossed in his clock and quite happy to stay in.

Around eight, Fifi glanced out of the window and saw a couple standing outside number 11, looking up at it.

'Do you think they are journalists?' she asked.

Dan came over to the window and looked. 'I shouldn't think so,' he said. 'More like pathetic horror seekers.' He grimaced in disgust and went back to his clock. 'I suppose we're going to have lots more of them,' he added a few seconds later. 'I really wonder at the mentality of some people. What do they hope to see? A corpse hanging out the window?'

Fifi went into the bedroom and lay down on the bed, convinced then that Dan had already put the matter behind him, and he thought she should too. But she didn't see how she could ever put it behind her.

She didn't hear Dan get up the following morning. She woke at eight to find he had already gone to work, and she felt hurt he hadn't woken her to say goodbye.

By eleven the heat in the flat was oppressive, the police were over the road again and she was feeling very weepy, so she decided to go down and talk to Frank.

From the hall she could see through to his kitchen, and as the back door to the garden was open, she knew he was out there.

'Frank,' she called out. 'Could you stand a visitor?'

'Come on out, Fifi,' he replied.

He found him perched on a stool mending a pair of old

boots, and right away she knew he was upset too because he didn't get up to greet her or ask how she was feeling.

'Are you feeling miserable too?' she asked, putting her hand on his shoulder. 'It's awful, isn't it? I still can't really believe it's for real. But you must have got such a shock when you came home on Saturday and were told about it.'

'You can say that again,' he said dolefully.

'Thank you for the brandy you sent up. It helped,' she said. 'But I can't keep on drinking to numb it. I don't know what to do with myself today. At least yesterday I had my statement to make.'

She spoke about how hot it was in the police station, about it being in the paper and how she supposed her mother would read it, then suddenly became aware Frank was barely listening. He seemed to be in a world of his own.

'What's up?' she asked, kneeling down beside his stool.

'Nothing,' he said.

'There is,' she insisted. Normally he would have made a fuss of her, made her tea, even given her a fatherly cuddle. But he had gone right into himself, the same way she'd been all weekend. 'Tell me, Frank, we're friends, aren't we?'

'You've got enough on your plate without my worries too,' he said.

'Is it something to do with your daughter?' Fifi asked. 'Did you get a letter from her today?'

He sighed. 'No, it's nothing to do with her,' he said. 'It's just the bloody police.'

'What have they done?'

'They came at midday yesterday. While you were still down the nick.'

'Well, they would come, they talk to everyone when something like this happens.'

He just looked at her, and it seemed to Fifi that any

moment he was going to cry. It was clear something had been said that was worrying the life out of him.

'Just tell me, you'll feel better if you share it.'

'It's that evil bitch Molly,' he hissed. 'I reckon she's told them it was me who killed Angela.'

'Oh, Frank.' She half smiled. 'I don't doubt Molly has tried to blame half the people in the street, but the police aren't going to believe her, not about you. You wouldn't hurt a fly, and anyone around here would vouch for that.'

'I've been tempted to kill Molly several times in the past,' he said brokenly. 'She knows that, and now she's up to her neck in this, she's trying to wriggle out of it by pinning it on me.'

Fifi might have laughed if Frank hadn't sounded so completely serious.

'I think you've misunderstood what the police said –'

'That slag told them stuff about her and me,' Frank interrupted her before she could finish. 'She told them we'd been having an affair and that I wanted her to leave Alfie. She reckons I killed Angela because she turned me down.'

Fifi did laugh then, she couldn't help it. 'I'm sorry, Frank,' she said, putting her hand over her mouth. 'I didn't think anything could make me laugh today, but that is so absurd!'

'It might make me laugh too if it wasn't for the fact someone else told them that I was overheard saying I was going to kill one of her children so it looked like Alfie's work.'

Fifi sat down heavily on a garden chair. 'No, Frank, no one would say something like that about you!'

'It wasn't a lie, it was true, at least partly.' Frank hung his head. 'It was a sort of joke with Stan. We were in the pub the night after Dan was attacked, everyone was saying Alfie must have been in on it and that. I said I'd cheerfully kill any of the Muckles, even their kids. Stan said something about we could kill one of them and let Alfie get blamed for it.'

'Who told the police this?' Fifi asked.

Frank shrugged his shoulders. 'God knows, someone who was in the pub that night, I suppose. It were just a joke. I can't stand any of that family, not even the kids, but I wouldn't kill them.'

'Of course you wouldn't,' Fifi said soothingly. 'Everyone around here makes remarks like that. I've even heard Mrs Jarvis saying she wished someone would set fire to their house with them all in it. If the police took all the death threats made about the Muckles seriously they'd need the entire London police force here in Kennington to deal with them. But you mustn't worry about this, Frank. The police like to shake people up. It's the way they get information.'

'Well, they shook me right enough,' he retorted. 'I mean, if they can find out about a joke you made a few weeks ago, what else can they dig up? I'm really worried about it.'

'You mustn't be. For a start, if they thought you'd had any kind of hand in this, they'd have taken you down to the station for questioning.'

'But they asked me stuff about being in the Army during the war. I got the idea they wanted to know if I'd ever killed anyone.'

'Had you?'

'I don't know for sure. You fire your gun and you see men fall, but there's lots of others shooting too. You don't know if it was one of your bullets necessarily.'

'Well, Angela wasn't killed with a gun,' Fifi said. 'Did they tell you how she was killed?'

Frank shook his head.

'Well, they think she was smothered with a pillow. That's

hardly the work of an old soldier, is it? Now, let me make you a cup of tea.'

Fifi made the tea, and sat down again in the garden to drinks hers. She wanted to go now, Frank's gloom was making her feel even worse than she had before. But her customary curiosity wouldn't quite let her excuse herself and leave. She could see there was something more on his mind, and she felt compelled to winkle it out of him.

'Tell me what's bothering you,' she said after a little while. 'You know what they say, "A trouble shared" and all that.'

'If I tell you, will you promise to keep it to yourself?' he asked.

Fifi promised.

Frank stumbled, faltered and at times stopped altogether as he told her the story of how he'd met Molly on the night of VE Day in Soho. Fifi forgot her own troubles as she listened, hardly believing that staid, rather prim Frank could have sex in a back alley with anyone. But as his story unfolded and he told her of the coincidence that he'd come to live right across the road to the woman, who then blackmailed him, all at once she knew it was entirely true.

'She snatched everything from me,' he said bitterly. 'My savings, the chance of happiness with my daughter and grandchildren in Australia. I could just about forgive all that if she'd left me with peace of mind while June was dying. But she never let up taunting me. Every day I expected that she'd tell June and break her heart.'

'Are you saying she told the police about this?' Fifi asked incredulously.

'Not the truth, so I had to tell them. Like I said before, she said we'd had an affair and I asked her to leave Alfie and run away with me. She claims that I never stopped pestering her, and then when she wouldn't do as I asked, I got bitter and kept making trouble for her. She reckons I saw them go out for the day and I slipped round the back and killed Angela to spite her.'

'That is the most preposterous thing I've ever heard,' Fifi exclaimed. 'But you really mustn't worry about this. The police know what Molly's like, and they'll see this story of hers for what it is, a desperate attempt to blame someone else. If they really thought you'd done it they would've arrested you.' She felt very sorry for Frank and gave him a hug, saying that the police would have to find his finger-prints or some other evidence to prove he'd been in that house.

'How were you supposed to know they were going out for the day and leaving Angela behind anyway?' she said firmly. 'Even if you had known, and wanted to kill her, you weren't likely to risk going in there first thing in the morning when so many people might spot you.'

He didn't respond to that, just sat there with his head hanging down, a picture of misery.

'You've been very kind, Fifi,' he said eventually. 'But leave me alone now, there's a good girl. I don't want to talk about it any more.'

That felt like a real rebuff, and it hurt because she was only trying to help him. She wanted to ask Frank how the police had left it, whether he was a real suspect or not. But she realized that she wasn't going to get any real sense out of him, and feeling even sorrier for herself than she had earlier, she went over to see Yvette.

When she didn't answer the door, Fifi tapped on the window. She could hear the radio so she knew she was in.

Yvette came to the front door eventually, but she only opened it a crack, and her eyes were red with crying. 'Oh, Fifi!' she said. 'I cannot talk to you now, I am too upset, ze police have been 'ere, and all the time they are banging and moving things next door. I must go out to get away.'

'Come over to my flat then,' Fifi suggested. 'I'll make you some tea and we can talk.'

'*Non*, I cannot,' she said, her hands fluttering in agitation. 'I 'ave the need to be alone.'

It seemed to Fifi that everyone needed to be alone but her. 'Okay,' she said. 'But if you change your mind, you know where I am.'

A little later Fifi went along to the corner shop to get some bread, and walked into a coven of half a dozen middle-aged woman all gossiping about Angela's death. None of them actually lived in Dale Street, but all their faces were ones she'd seen around the area.

A woman with a headscarf tied round her curlers and a cigarette dangling from the corner of her mouth was holding forth about Alfie. 'He's been doing it to his girls for years,' she said with authority. 'He got the two older ones up the spout and then threw them out. A man that does that ought to be hung up by his feet and a bit chopped off him every day.'

When she saw Fifi, her eyes lit up. 'You found the kid, didn't you? What did she look like? How did he kill her?'

Fifi could understand curiosity, but the phrasing of this woman's questions was utterly repellent and ghoulish. 'If you've got any questions, go and ask the police,' she said snootily.

The woman was so surprised that the cigarette fell out of her mouth on to the floor. 'Hoity-toity,' she said as she picked it up. 'I suppose your shit don't stink either.'

Fifi turned on her heel and left the shop without any bread, her face burning. Until yesterday she had felt at home here, now it was as though she was an alien. If it was true that Alfie had got his two older daughters pregnant, why hadn't someone reported it? What was the matter with everyone round here? Why were they all so spineless?

As she marched indignantly up the street she could see a man at the door of number 3 talking to Mrs Blackstock who lived on the ground floor. She and her husband were frail and elderly, and Fifi had only spoken to them once or twice as they rarely came out of their house.

She guessed the man was a journalist. He was short and thin, with glasses and a very cheap baggy suit.

'I don't know anything,' Mrs Blackstock was saying. 'My husband and I keep ourselves to ourselves.'

Fifi could see Mrs Blackstock felt intimidated. She was holding on to her walking stick so hard that her knuckles were white.

Fifi tapped the reporter on the shoulder. 'Leave her alone,' she said. 'And I don't think you should be pestering people for information when a little girl has just died,' she added as he turned to face her.

'Would you be Felicity Reynolds?' he asked, his eyes lighting up behind his glasses. 'You found her, didn't you? Would you like to tell me about it?'

'No, I wouldn't,' Fifi said. 'Now clear off back to whatever cesspit you crawled out of and leave this lady in peace.'

He looked surprised and backed away. Mrs Blackstock quickly shut her front door and Fifi went home.

As she closed the front door behind her and walked up the stairs she began to cry.

She couldn't cope with all this, the horror in her own head, police questions, journalists and now other people trying to put their anxieties on to her. She'd lost her baby, got a broken arm, her parents had disowned her, and even Dan wouldn't stay home to look after her.

What had happened to her life? Before she met Dan it was all so easy and nice. She liked her job, she had good friends, she came home every evening to a hot dinner and even her clothes were washed and ironed for her. Now she was living in a slum, and everything was falling around her ears.

And it wasn't going to get any better either. She'd have to go to court when the trial began, forced to give evidence with that monster Alfie sitting there in the dock looking at her.

Why was all this happening to her? Cut off from her family just because she chose a man they didn't approve of, no one to turn to for comfort or advice. She wanted Patty, but she couldn't even phone her and tell her what had happened without having to go through her mother and she knew she wouldn't get any sympathy from that quarter.

Once upstairs she flung herself on to her bed and cried bitterly.

She was still lying there sobbing when Dan came home. 'What on earth's the matter?' he asked. 'Has something else happened?'

'Fat lot you'd care if it had,' she sobbed out. 'Nobody cares about me.'

'I'm knackered and hungry, Fifi,' he said, his voice strained and weary. 'If you've got some grievance, spit it out now. Then I'll go and get some fish and chips for us both.'

'Grievance?' Fifi spat at him. 'I've had a horrible day, everyone's been mean to me. And all you think about is eating fish and chips!'

'Can't you just think about someone else for a change?' he snapped at her. 'Look at me, I'm filthy, I've been working in eighty degrees for ten hours. I'll try to be sympathetic when I've had a bath, changed and had some food.'

He didn't wait for her reply but grabbed a bath towel and stomped off down to the bathroom.

Fifi could only cry harder then. If Dan had no time for her, there was no one left.

Chapter eleven

'Fer fuck's sake slow down, Dan, it ain't a bleedin' race!' Chas exclaimed as Dan snatched a brick from the hod before Chas had even had a chance to take the bricks out and stack them.

Dan looked askance at his labourer. He had been so immersed in thinking about Fifi he hadn't been aware he'd been laying the bricks like a madman.

'Sorry, mate,' he said. 'I'll stop for a fag.'

Once Dan had sat down on the edge of the scaffolding platform, his legs dangling over the side, he lit up a cigarette. Chas sat down beside him. 'What's up with you anyway? You've been on another planet for days now. Is the old woman giving you grief?'

Dan didn't like Chas Bovey. He thought the man was a lazy and dishonest thug who would sell his own grandmother for a few bob. He only did labouring work in the summer because he liked to build up muscle and get a suntan. The rest of the year he probably spent housebreaking or stealing cars. But Dan always did his best to get on with workmates, so he held out a cigarette to him. 'I wouldn't say she's giving me grief,' he sighed. 'But she ain't herself. That kid being killed has knocked her for six.'

A fortnight ago tomorrow, Dan had been looking forward to surprising Fifi by taking her to Brighton. He could remember wondering where she kept her swimsuit, and how he could manage to pack it into a bag with his trunks and two towels without her seeing it. He decided he couldn't, so instead he'd make out they were going to a swimming pool. He wasn't going to tell her where they were really going until they were on the tube heading for Victoria.

Two hours later that same day as he had made his way home, he was still trying to dream up a good excuse for setting off so early in the morning. Then he'd turned into Dale Street to be confronted with the sight of police cars and a hysterical horde of neighbours.

As soon as he was told that Angela was dead and Fifi had found her body, his first thought had been that this was way too much for her so soon after losing the baby.

Now, a fortnight later, he just didn't know what to do for the best. Fifi was either locked into brooding silence or going on and on about the murder to the point where he felt he might scream. Moving away from Dale Street was clearly vital, but it would take time to find another place, and any decent accommodation required a hefty deposit and advance rent. As their savings had taken a hammering in the two weeks he was off work without pay, they just didn't have that kind of money right now.

The only way to get some extra money was to go back to working all day Saturdays. But as Fifi's moods were so unpredictable, she might go spare when he told her. Only the other night she'd said that if he'd come home at lunchtime that day as he always used to on Saturdays, she wouldn't have been the one that found Angela.

He classed the evening of that day as the very worst in his life. On top of all the noise and police activity out in the street, Fifi's distress and the tension in the air as they waited for the Muckles to come home, he was tormented with guilt.

He should have gone to the police and the NSPCC when Angela was hurt before. But he'd smugly thought that the kid would be safe once he marked Alfie's card. How could anyone be so stupid as to believe a nutcase like that could be stopped by just the threat of a good kicking?

Alfie and Molly had been charged jointly with the murder and were remanded in Brixton and Holloway prisons respectively. Mike was also in Brixton, charged with being an accessory. No one knew for certain where Dora was, but it was generally thought she had been placed in a mental institution. Dan really hoped that Alfie and Molly would be hanged, but he would always be ashamed of himself for not having done more to protect Angela.

The more Fifi told him about what had happened to her, the angrier he felt with himself. He knew the right thing was to let Fifi talk and talk about it until she'd got it out of her system, but he couldn't bear to hear it.

'You two ain't havin' much luck lately,' Chas remarked, breaking Dan's reverie.

'You can say that again,' Dan said with a weary sigh.

Just a few weeks ago in the first spell of hot weather, he could remember sitting up on some scaffolding, just like he and Chas were doing now, smoking a fag and basking in the sunshine. Down below was all the usual chaos of a building site, the churning of cement-mixers, clonking of scaffolding poles, buzz of saws, shouted banter between the men and the occasional wolf whistle when a pretty girl walked past the site. He thought that day that he was the man who had everything. A beautiful wife, a baby on the way, a job he loved, good mates, and he hoped he'd soon have enough money for a deposit on a house of their own.

Then he was attacked, and Fifi lost their baby. Then Angela's death.

Now it looked as though their marriage was falling apart.

'If I was you, mate, I'd slap 'er and pack 'er off to her mum's for a while,' Chas said with a chuckle. 'You could come down the pub with us of an evening, pull a few birds, 'ave a laugh.'

Dan bristled. Chas often talked about slapping women and by his own admission he'd abandoned his wife and two children. He was older than Dan, in his mid-thirties, but with his Beatle-style haircut and seemingly innocent-looking blue eyes he looked far younger, and young girls made a beeline for him. 'I've done all the bird-pulling I want to do,' Dan said sharply. 'And I've never slapped a woman in my life. I despise blokes that do.'

He got up then and went back to the bricklaying, leaving Chas staring at him open-mouthed.

As Dan carried on laying his bricks and mentally calculating how many Saturday afternoons he'd have to work to get the money they needed, Fifi was crying.

She had spent a lot of time crying in the past two weeks. Anything could start it. The frustration of not being able to use her right hand, brooding on something Dan had said or not said. That there was still no letter from her mother, and because she wanted to tell her family about what she was going through, but couldn't. Sometimes she was afraid she was going mad.

Ray Charles's 'Take These Chains from My Heart' was playing on the radio, and that's just how she felt, as if she was chained. She might be able to get up and walk about, she could go out if she wanted to, but her mind was chained to this hideous business.

She could actually feel the suspicion, hate and fear in Dale Street. People who had always been gregarious were now scuttling by without so much as a hello or a smile. Those who had always lingered outside their doors gossiping hurried indoors now. Children had stopped playing in the street, and when the pub turned out at night there was no jovial laughter or loud goodbyes.

Malevolence wafted out from number 11, even though it lay empty. Police were still coming and going there, often carrying out boxes or bags which could possibly be evidence. Reporters came to the street frequently, searching for people who would talk to them. Then there were the sightseers, some even taking photographs of the house.

After two weeks there should have been signs that people were recovering from the shock, but the continuing unease and gloom left an impression that the neighbourhood had been permanently shattered.

Part of this was because the police were still questioning anyone with a known grudge against the Muckles. Frank had been carried off to the police station and questioned again for four hours. Stan had been kept even longer. Neither man had revealed what had been said, and that had been further cause for gossip. It appeared, too, that the police were still trying to establish the identity of the card players who had been at Alfie's on the Friday night before the murder.

As Detective Inspector Roper had stated that Angela was killed on Saturday morning, long after the card players had left, Fifi couldn't see why they had any importance in the investigation. But she supposed the police had to speak to everyone to try to establish Alfie and Molly's mood the previous evening.

Fifi and Dan had gone along to the pub last week in an

effort to cheer themselves up. But it only made them feel worse, for instead of jollity, all they found was that a great many of the regulars had turned into bar-room lawyers, arguing about whether Alfie would hang or get life imprisonment. There were also those who boasted that they had inside information about the case.

One of these men, Johnny Milkins, a hard case with a big scaffolding company, claimed to have friends in the police force, and he said that the police were not entirely convinced that Alfie or even Molly had killed Angela. Everyone poohpoohed that, of course; they didn't even believe Johnny had friends in the force. But Fifi knew he must have, for something he'd said could only have come from one of the officers who attended the scene of the crime.

Johnny's actual words were, 'A bloke that's twisted enough to fuck his own seven-year-old wouldn't bother getting a clean sheet to cover her. Someone else did that, after they smothered her.'

The facts about the sexual abuse had filtered out very quickly after the event. It was this which had sent everyone into a spin of savage hatred and disgust. But the sheet had never been mentioned.

Fifi had mentally trawled over every last detail of what she saw that day in number 11. The clean sheet was the one thing which didn't fit in. Every bed in that house was like a filthy rat's nest, so why would Alfie even think to search out a clean sheet to cover the child? Fifi had considered that it could have been done in a moment of remorse at what he'd done. Or maybe it was just an attempt to conceal Angela should any of his family open the door. But whatever the reason was, it was uncharacteristic behaviour.

Fifi began to fear that if Angela hadn't been killed by one of her parents, that meant the real killer was still at large.

He could be walking around amongst them, drinking in the pub, using the corner shop. Any child in the neighbourhood could be his next victim!

She did her best to suppress this vague fear as it did appear to be entirely groundless, but the more she analysed things Johnny Milkins had said, the more anxious she became.

Johnny certainly seemed to know a great deal about the police investigation. He claimed that in Alfie's statement he'd said he was so drunk at the card game the night before that he went to bed early, leaving the other men, whom he refused to name, still playing. As the other players often dossed down at his house, Alfie insisted that it was quite possible for one of them to have gone up to the top-floor bedroom and got into bed with the child.

Alfie also said that he'd told Angela the day before that she wouldn't be going to the seaside with the rest of the family because she'd been naughty. When he heard her crying the following morning he ignored her, and never even looked in her bedroom before leaving the house.

Several people in Dale Street had confirmed that Alfie had four or five men in for the card game the night before. There were also people who had heard some of them leave around two-thirty, but agreed it was possible that one or two of them could have remained in Alfie's house. It was possible, too, that they might still have been there after Alfie and his family left for the day. Apparently the police had found quite a few different sets of fingerprints in the room where Angela was found, and some didn't belong to any of the Muckles.

'No one wants to believe Alfie done it more than me,' Johnny said, thumping his big fists down on the bar. 'But it certainly ain't cut 'n' dried that 'e did. The Old Bill took fingerprints from all the bleedin' glasses in the card room, but so far they ain't matched them up wiv any names. Why's that? Surely any mate of Alfie's would 'ave a record? And why would a piece of shit like Alfie shield those geezers? 'E must be scared of 'em, that's why.'

Fifi didn't get to hear the rest of Johnny's thoughts on the investigation because Dan whisked her out of the pub in a hurry. He said he'd heard quite enough on the subject and Fifi was to stop dwelling on it.

But she couldn't stop dwelling on it. It was on her mind from the moment she woke up in the morning until she fell asleep. She went over and over what she'd seen that day, and analysed it painstakingly. Yet there were still more questions than there were answers, and Johnny had only added to them.

She tried to picture the scene at number 11 that morning. Angela lying in bed crying because she was hurt. The rest of the family calmly getting dressed up in their best clothes to go out for the day.

Alfie was a brute, there was no question about that, but was it humanly possible for him to have gone upstairs just before they left, put a pillow over Angela's face and smothered her, then gone off for a picnic at the seaside?

Somehow a pillow seemed the most unlikely weapon for a man who normally used fists, pokers or sticks.

Yet if Alfie was innocent of this charge, why on earth was he refusing to name the other men? She would have expected a rat like him to squeal immediately when his own life was at risk. That suggested to her that there was something far bigger behind all this, or that Alfie knew the police didn't have enough evidence to convict him.

The police had come back to her just a few days ago, asking if she knew or would recognize any of the men she had seen going into one of Alfie's card parties. The only one she remembered reasonably well was a big man of perhaps fifty or so. But she couldn't recall his face, only that he wore a very smart grey suit and it seemed incongruous to be wearing it to go slumming at Alfie's. But she hadn't seen anyone arrive for that last card game because she and Dan were watching television and the evening sun was so bright they'd pulled the curtains over to get a better picture.

Fifi had asked the police point-blank if it was true they thought Alfie and Molly might be innocent. To her disappointment they would not offer a personal opinion. One officer said in a very tight-lipped manner that everyone was innocent until proved guilty and they were still following various lines of enquiry. That hadn't been any help at all.

It didn't help either that Dan wouldn't discuss any of this with her. Every time she mentioned it he went all silent on her. A few times he'd actually stomped off out. And she worried that one night he wouldn't come back.

'I'm going to work all day tomorrow,' Dan announced that night as they were getting ready for bed.

Fifi was just pulling her nightdress over her head, and as soon as she'd got it on properly, she rounded on him and asked why.

'For the extra money of course, sweetheart,' he said wearily, as if that was obvious. 'We can't move away without it. Why don't you spend the day going round some flat-letting agencies and putting our name down?'

One side of Fifi's mind told her Dan was being sensible, but the other side was suspicious of him. Saturday afternoons had always been special to them. Dan would have a bath and change when he got home at noon, then they'd have some lunch together and often go out somewhere.

Even when she was pregnant and he was working late for extra money, he wouldn't work on Saturday afternoons because he said the time with Fifi was far more important. The only occasion he'd ever worked a Saturday afternoon before was the day Angela was murdered, and he only did it then as a favour because his boss had been good enough to keep his job open for him while he was off sick.

'If that's what you want,' she said in a sullen tone, and climbed into bed, lying down with her face to the wall. She expected him to get in and try to cuddle her. But he didn't. He faced the other way and they lay there with their backs to each other.

As usual he fell asleep very quickly, and that made Fifi even more annoyed. She couldn't understand why he'd changed so much. He didn't even seem to like her any more, yet alone love her. Was he regretting marrying her now? Did he think he'd be happier single, going down to the pub every night with his workmates?

She felt him bound out of bed the following morning, and once again she was reminded of how things used to be. Before Angela's death he had always been reluctant to get up, he would cuddle up closer and say he'd give anything to stay there with her. Now it was as if he couldn't wait to get away from her.

Fifi lay there crying after he'd gone. It was raining hard, and the thought of another long day cooped up alone in the flat was almost unbearable. August was nearly over, the whole summer had gone without so much as one day at the seaside. Next month would bring their first anniversary, and she couldn't help but think what they'd been like with each other when they first got married. They couldn't keep their hands off each other, often jumping into bed as soon

as they got home from work, making love far more important than meals.

Dan used to want to know every last thing about her
then. Stories from her childhood, about her friends, the
people at work. He wanted to know what she was thinking, what she day-dreamed about. And she was the same
about him.

They had only made love once since she lost the baby.
Maybe that was down to her more than him; she was weepy
and the plaster on her arm put her off. But Dan hadn't tried
very hard to get her interested. Since the murder there had
been nothing; even his cuddles seemed half-hearted. She
guessed that he was afraid that intimacy would open the
floodgates to how she felt about the murder. And he didn't
want to hear that.

But how could she deal with the images of that day
trapped inside her head, if no one would let her describe
them? She also needed to know what had happened, who
was responsible and why, and until she did, none of it would
fade. Once, Dan had understood everything about her, so
why couldn't he now?

But it wasn't just Dan who didn't want to talk to her.
Miss Diamond said she was in a hurry every time Fifi saw
her. Frank wouldn't answer the door when she knocked.
Stan would smile sadly but could not be drawn into conversation, and Yvette never seemed to be at home any
more.

Surely they all had the same sort of thoughts and questions
as she did about it all? If the Muckles had killed Angela,
what were they intending to do with her body when they
got home that evening? Were they going to bury it in their
garden? Borrow a car or van and dump it somewhere?
What story were they intending to put about to explain her

disappearance? Would anyone have cared enough about the child to question it?

And if it wasn't the Muckles who killed her, what was going on over at number 11? Who were these people Alfie wouldn't name? It was all too much having this milling around in her head.

Just after nine Fifi heard Miss Diamond sweeping the stairs. She had always done it every Saturday morning, from her landing down to the front door. When they first moved in Fifi used to volunteer to do it, but the older woman said it was her job. When Fifi broke her wrist, her neighbour had started coming right up to their flat and doing the stairs all the way down.

Desperate to talk to someone, Fifi got up, pulled on some jeans and a blouse and opened the bedroom door. Miss Diamond was a couple of steps down from Fifi's landing, working with a small stiff brush and dustpan. She had on the blue nylon overall she always wore for household chores, but her hair was as immaculate as usual.

'I'll be able to do this part just as soon as the plaster comes off,' Fifi said. 'And I'll do it all the way down to make up for you doing it all this time.'

'It won't be long coming off now, will it?' the older woman said, looking up and smiling at Fifi. 'I'm sure you can't wait.'

'Only just over a week now,' Fifi replied. 'I'm so much looking forward to wallowing in the bath, it's not the same when you've got to keep one arm out the water. And it'll be good to go back to work.'

'I often think it would be nice not to have to go to work.' Miss Diamond paused reflectively in her sweeping. 'But however good it appears to be able to just potter about all day, I'm sure I'd be bored with it in no time. I think I'd miss my colleagues too, even though I'm always grousing about them.'

Fifi felt very relieved and pleased that her neighbour seemed in the mood for a chat.

'I really miss having people to talk to,' she admitted. 'Actually, I've been quite desperate since Angela's death. It plays on my mind.'

Miss Diamond gave her a sharp look. 'You must snap out of that,' she said briskly. 'The Muckles are an appalling bunch, they aren't worth a moment's thought.'

'Don't you want to know exactly what happened? Don't you ask yourself questions about it? You must have seen people coming and going over there. Can't you give the police some descriptions of people you've seen?'

'No, I don't want to know what went on there.' The older woman sounded very indignant. 'I have gone out of my way to ignore them and all their visitors. That family are absolute scum, animals that need putting down. Of course it's awful that the little girl is dead, but at least she won't have to endure any more. And we've finally got some peace.'

Fifi was very shocked at such a cynical view. 'How can you enjoy peace that was won by a child's death?' she asked.

Miss Diamond leaned on the banister and looked intently at Fifi. 'You remind me of myself at your age,' she said. 'Champion of the underdog, a lover of lost causes. It's admirable to have compassion, Fifi, but you have to temper it with realism.'

'I *am* very realistic,' Fifi said indignantly.

Miss Diamond shook her head. 'No you aren't, dear. If you had been you wouldn't have trusted Dan to find you a flat in London, and ended up here. I heard you laughing when you first moved in. You thought it was romantic living somewhere so crummy. That's about as unrealistic as anyone can get.'

Fifi bristled. 'I couldn't come up here and look for a flat, and this was the only place Dan could find that we could afford. Why shouldn't I trust my husband to find a place for us anyway? Are you saying there's something wrong with him?'

'There's nothing wrong with him, he's a decent, very likeable man,' Miss Diamond said with a shrug. 'But he hasn't had the advantages you've had, Fifi. If you'd been doing the looking, you would've turned this place down, wouldn't you?'

'I expect so,' Fifi agreed. 'But he was getting frantic for us to be together, and so I made the best of it. So what's your excuse for coming to live here? I don't mean to be rude, but it sounds to me like the pot calling the kettle black!'

The older woman narrowed her eyes. 'I certainly wasn't as fortunate as you,' she said with acid in her voice. 'I was desperate for a roof over my head, and I had to sell my only warm coat just to get the advance rent. Until I got a job I was living on bread and marge, I didn't even have a shilling for the gas. But I don't suppose you can possibly imagine that kind of hardship.'

Fifi was stung by the implication that she was a spoiled little rich girl who swam through life without a thought for those less fortunate. But she had come up against this kind of prejudice before and knew the only way to handle it was to carry on, and hope that by showing interest in the other person she would prove herself to be sensitive and caring.

'It's hard to believe you've ever had hard times. I mean, you've got such a good job, you're so well dressed.' She paused, not knowing quite what else to say. 'And you're a real lady.'

'I was brought up to be one, certainly. Just as you were, Fifi. But I made the mistake of falling for the wrong man and it nearly destroyed me.'

Fifi's inherent curiosity reared up at that statement. In four months she'd made absolutely no headway in finding out anything about this woman, and even though that hadn't been her aim today, she wasn't going to let an opportunity like this slip away. She sat down on the top of the stairs. 'Tell me about it?' she asked.

Miss Diamond bent down again, carrying on with her sweeping. 'It's not something I like to talk about or even think about,' she said crisply. 'Let's just say he was a complete bounder.'

'Really?' Fifi was intrigued. 'Do tell me about him, Miss Diamond. If you don't I'll be wondering about it all day.'

The woman looked up again, a ghost of a smile playing at her lips. 'You can be such a child, Fifi,' she exclaimed. 'So curious about everything. Me, what went on over the road. Anything and anybody. My aunt used to say, "Curiosity killed the cat".'

'Mum used to say that all the time,' Fifi chuckled. 'But being interested in other people isn't such a bad thing, is it? Not if it helps to understand them.'

'Perhaps. I suppose we *are* the end product of what has happened to us,' Miss Diamond replied thoughtfully. 'I was once warm, trusting and full of fun. If I'd married a decent man I might have stayed that way instead of turning into a humourless Tartar.'

'You aren't a Tartar,' Fifi insisted, even though that name summed the woman up remarkably well. 'You were very kind to me after I lost my baby.'

'That was because I knew how you felt. I lost a baby myself after my husband ran out on me.'

Fifi saw the hurt in Miss Diamond's dark eyes and guessed this was something she wasn't in the habit of divulging.

'You poor thing,' Fifi exclaimed. 'I'm so sorry. No wonder you call him a bounder, though I'd be calling him something much worse than that.'

'I've called him all sorts over the years, but I've learned to live with what he did to me by blaming myself for being so headstrong. A great many people warned me about him, but I refused to listen.'

'I can't imagine you being fooled by anyone,' Fifi said. 'You seem so sure of yourself.'

'I am now,' Miss Diamond smiled wryly. 'But when I was your age, my heart ruled my head, just like yours does.'

Fifi thought there was a warning in that confidence. 'You don't think Dan's like your husband, do you?'

'Of course not,' Miss Diamond said quickly. 'He's a good man, with many very fine qualities. But I suspect that your family aren't enamoured with him?'

Fifi nodded sadly. 'And I don't think my mum is ever going to come round about him,' she said dolefully. 'But then Dan's being so funny with me, I shouldn't be surprised if we split up.'

'Oh dear.' Miss Diamond frowned. 'I'm sorry to hear that, Fifi. You seemed so close last time I came up and had a coffee with you.'

'Everything was fine till Angela was killed,' Fifi explained. 'But he seems to be cross with me all the time now.'

The older woman looked hard at Fifi. 'Is that because you keep talking about the murder and the Muckles?'

'I suppose so,' Fifi admitted somewhat reluctantly.

'Then I can't say I blame him for being cross. If I were

Dan I'd find your morbid fascination with the lower classes quite offensive.'

Fifi looked at her neighbour in puzzlement. 'Whatever do you mean?'

'I've watched you, Fifi,' Miss Diamond said crisply. 'You try to prove to everyone in this street that you are one of them. Though why you should want to be considered on a level with such riff-raff I can't imagine!'

'Don't call them that! You sound like my mother,' Fifi exclaimed.

'Of course! That's what's behind it, isn't it?' her neighbour said almost triumphantly. 'Your mother doesn't approve of Dan, so you've gone all out to try and join the other side.'

'I don't know what you mean,' Fifi said indignantly. 'I haven't tried to join anything. I believe in being nice to people. Just because they are poor doesn't mean they are worth less than other people.'

'I don't take exception to anyone just for being poor,' Miss Diamond said firmly. 'But let me tell you that most of the people in this street have as much money coming in as you or I do. They just can't manage it. You see them going down to the fish-and-chip shop night after night. If they cooked at home they'd save pounds every week. If they didn't drink so much they could afford to buy their children's clothes outright, instead of getting those Provident cheques which they never finish paying off. They wouldn't need to pawn things every week either. Oh, I could go on and on, but I think I've made my point.'

'You certainly have, you're a crashing snob,' Fifi exclaimed. 'Maybe some of the people around here are a bit feckless and disorganized, but life shouldn't be just about being careful with your money, it's for living. I don't see you having much fun, for all you've got a nice flat and a good job.'

The older woman shrugged. 'Fun, if that means going to the pub and getting blazing drunk, isn't something I'd want to do. But believe me, Fifi, these people around here will never enhance your life, they'll laugh at you behind your back, suck you dry and drag you down with them.'

'That's rubbish,' Fifi insisted.

'It's not.' Miss Diamond shook her head. 'It's just a fact of life. They resent you for being educated and beautiful, for all the good things in you that they sense lacking in themselves. They resent you even more now because you had the courage to go into that house and find Angela.'

'That's not true.' Fifi began to cry.

'Of course it's true! Wise up, girl. They feel guilty because they know they should've done something years ago. Of course they'll tell you it's their code of never informing on anyone, but that's just hot air. The truth is almost certainly that most of the people in this street have something to hide themselves, so they wouldn't dare speak out against a neighbour for fear of it coming out.'

'So I can't win then?' Fifi said through her tears. 'I've been cast out by my own family for marrying a working-class man, but I'm not welcome with his sort either! So what am I supposed to do?'

'From what I've gathered, Dan has no allegiance to anyone but you. So get away from here. Make friends with intelligent, free-thinking people. Stop feeling sorry for yourself, and most of all stop dwelling on what went on across the road. You'll lose Dan if you don't.'

With that Miss Diamond turned and swept off down the stairs, leaving Fifi completely astounded.

*

Nora Diamond felt shaky after her words with her neighbour, and instead of finishing the stairs, then moving on to clean the bathroom as she'd intended, she went into her kitchen and got out her bottle of sherry. She didn't approve of drinking during the day, but Fifi had rattled her, and a small glass of sherry and a cigarette would calm her down.

She hadn't meant to be so harsh with the girl, but that remark of hers, '*You must have seen people coming and going over there*', had cut right through her, making her defensive. She knew all too well she should go to the police and give them the name of the man she had recognized going into number 11 on several occasions. But how could she? They would ask how she knew him and she couldn't tell them that. Besides, she hadn't seen any of the card players on the night of the last game. Why should she put herself in jeopardy for something which might not even help the investigation?

The sweet sherry calmed her, but she still felt ashamed of how she'd spoken to Fifi. She was a sweet girl and it was clear she was deeply troubled by what she'd witnessed over the road. But Nora couldn't help her, she had her own troubles, and unlike Fifi she didn't have a man to protect her.

Later that morning as Fifi tidied up the living room, she found herself blushing with shame at everything Miss Diamond had said to her.

She wanted to discount it all – after all, what did the woman know, she was still living here, for all her good breeding and hoity-toity ways.

But she couldn't discount everything. Miss Diamond had as good as said that Fifi was silly, weak and misguided. More or less what her mother thought about her. Surely she wasn't like that? Was she?

Looking out on to the dreary rain-washed street, Fifi couldn't help but wish she could go back to the beginning and start again, this time thinking things through at every step. She could have told her mother when she first met Dan, got him to call for her so it didn't look as though she was hiding something shameful. She certainly shouldn't have rushed into marrying him the way she did.

Miss Diamond was definitely right in saying it should have been her who looked for the flat, not Dan. People were wary of him because he looked so tough, but she could have got round a very cautious landlord.

But she couldn't go back, so what was she to do now?

Glancing out of the window, she saw Yvette going through her front door, so she thought she would call on her and get her opinion.

'Ah, Fifi!' Yvette exclaimed as she opened the front door and found her neighbour standing there. ''Ow are you?'

'Fine, thank you,' Fifi replied, even though she was close to tears. 'Could I come in for a chat? You've been out every time I've called over.'

'I am a leetle busy,' Yvette replied.

'Just for a few minutes,' Fifi pleaded. 'I've missed you.'

She observed that Yvette was pale and drawn, the dark circles under her eyes suggesting she hadn't slept much recently. She took this to mean the dressmaker was as troubled by what had happened next door as herself.

'Okay,' Yvette sighed. 'I was just going to make some coffee anyway.'

Number 12 was exactly the same as all the houses in the street, and Yvette's flat was identical to Frank's, with two adjoining rooms and the kitchen at the end of a communal long hallway. But number 12 was very dirty and neglected.

The wallpaper on the stairs must have been put up before the war and it was worn away where people rubbed against it. The hall floor didn't look as if it had been swept or washed for years. Mr and Mrs Balstrode who lived upstairs were elderly, so perhaps they couldn't manage cleaning, but Fifi wondered why Yvette didn't do it.

But it was obvious from her kitchen that Yvette didn't care much about her surroundings. Although not dirty, it was dingy and disorganized. She took a percolator down from a shelf, filled the bottom with water, put a couple of tablespoons of fresh ground coffee in the top and lit the gas beneath it.

'You will have the plaster taken off soon?' she asked.

Fifi thought it funny that people asked about that all the time, as if it was really important, but didn't want to discuss more serious problems. 'Just another week,' she said. 'I wish I could get over all this other stuff as easily. Are you finding it hard too?'

Yvette nodded, glancing out of the window towards the Muckles' kitchen window which faced hers beyond a six-foot fence. 'I find it hard to live 'ere any more.'

'At least it's quiet now,' Fifi said, but realizing how callous that sounded she blushed. 'Oops, I shouldn't have said that!'

'We should say it how it is.' Yvette shrugged. 'It is quiet now, that is good. I do not miss all the trouble, the fighting, the insults. I weesh to forget.'

'I want to too,' Fifi said. 'But I can't stop thinking about them.'

'You must, Fifi,' Yvette said reprovingly. 'They are not worth a moment's thought. You and your Dan, you should go out and 'ave good time together. Find a new home and move away.'

'But I will be a witness at the trial,' Fifi said. 'Until that is over I can't forget about them.'

The water in the percolator began to boil and bubble up and the aroma of coffee filled the small kitchen. Yvette put some dainty china on a tray and milk in a jug. 'Just because you 'ave to be witness does not mean you have to halt your life. You 'ave had much sadness losing your baby, Fifi. Do not bring more sadness into your life by wasting a moment of it on that family.'

Yvette put the percolator on the tray and then lifted the whole thing. 'We will go into the front room,' she said. 'You have a cup of coffee, a leetle chat, then you go home.'

It was a great disappointment to find Yvette wasn't her usual warm, interested self. In the past she had always asked so many questions, keen to hear about even the dullest of day-to-day incidents. She merely shrugged when Fifi repeated what Miss Diamond had said to her, and when Fifi launched into telling her how Dan didn't want to talk about Angela's death, she sighed.

'Why should he?' she said. 'In the war we saw terrible things, but after we 'ave to put them aside and go on. It is like that now. Angela is better in heaven, and the other children happier in new homes. I expect Dan feels there is no more to say.'

'I can't see it that way,' Fifi said heatedly. 'There is so much that doesn't fit right. We don't even know for certain it was Alfie that did it, the police won't say. I heard a woman in the shop say Alfie's two oldest daughters had babies by him. Is that true?'

'I don't know,' Yvette said, looking away as if wishing she'd never let Fifi in. 'But you should not be worrying about this, Fifi.'

'Someone should, if it is true!' Fifi's voice rose with anger.

'If people had really thought he'd done that to the older girls, and done something then, Angela might not have died.'

'Perhaps,' Yvette said. 'But Alfie will be answerable to a higher authority one day, just as you and I will.'

Fifi started to cry. She had expected Yvette to feel as she did. 'Don't you sense all the nastiness in this street?' she sobbed out. 'We are all partly responsible for what happened. But we were too cowardly to stand up to Molly and Alfie.'

Yvette gave another of her Gallic shrugs. 'The nastiness was always in this street, there are many damaged people.'

'What do you mean by that?' Fifi sniffed.

'They may all be hurting over something in their past. They cannot feel the way you do about Angela because they have used up all their tears on themselves.'

Fifi stopped to think about that for a moment. 'Are you that way too?' she asked eventually.

'I theenk so,' Yvette nodded. 'But you, Fifi, you have so much, love, youth, beauty and intelligence, your life is good.'

This sounded like a re-run of what Miss Diamond had said. 'It doesn't feel good,' Fifi blubbed through tears.

'I think it is time you grow up and look at 'ow lucky you are,' Yvette said archly. 'Many of us 'ave 'ad to live without parents. Yes, you lost your baby, but that happens to many women and one day you'll 'ave another. Go home now, think about all you 'ave, and be glad.'

Fifi felt completely demoralized. Dan had lost patience with her, Miss Diamond had been dismissive, and now Yvette was packing her off with a message that she should be grateful for what she had.

'I'm sorry I took up your time,' she said weakly, getting to her feet and brushing away her tears. 'I didn't mean to be a nuisance.'

Chapter twelve

Fifi was singing along with 'She Loves You', a new release from the Beatles, on the radio as she changed the sheets on the bed. It was an awkward job with a plastered arm, and when she heard the front-door bell ring she ignored it, thinking it was for Frank. But when it rang long and hard again, she dropped the blankets and went downstairs.

She was feeling happier today than she'd felt for a very long time. Part of it was due to some fantastic lovemaking last night. But that had only come about because after the miserable Saturday with both Miss Diamond and Yvette telling her what was wrong with her, she had decided to try to modify her behaviour.

On Sunday afternoon she and Dan had gone to Hyde Park for a walk, and she didn't mention Dale Street or the murder once. Out in the sunshine in a place she associated with the happy times when they first came to London, it was easy to be her old self. Dan seemed relaxed and happier too, and they looked out an *Evening Standard* and sat on the grass ringing round each of the flat-letting agencies that seemed to have plenty of flats on their books.

In the evening they went to see *The Day of the Triffids* at Leicester Square and when they got home Fifi was too scared to go downstairs alone to use the lavatory, so Dan had to go with her. That made them both laugh until they were almost crying, and from then on things had got better and better.

She'd spent all day Monday and Tuesday going to register at flat agencies, and most of them had seemed quite hopeful, particularly if she and Dan were prepared to move a few miles further out of central London.

But the main thing which was making Fifi feel happy was that the following day the plaster cast was coming off. On Monday, in five days' time, she could return to work. She had an appointment later on that day to have her hair done, and she thought she'd make a special meal tomorrow night to celebrate.

The bell rang a third time as she reached the last flight of stairs.

'All right, I'm coming,' she called out. She hoped it wasn't the police again; now that she had begun to try to put all that business behind her, she didn't want anyone bringing it up again.

She opened the door and to her astonishment there stood her mother, wearing a pink two-piece. Fifi was so surprised she was rendered speechless.

'Well, say something,' Clara said. '"Come in" would be nice.'

'I'm sorry, I'm just so taken aback,' Fifi said, almost stammering with shock. 'What are you doing in London?'

'Your father had to go and see someone at King's College, so I thought I'd take the opportunity to come and visit you.'

Ever since they moved into Dale Street, a surprise visit from her parents had always been Fifi's greatest fear. While she felt some relief that she'd cleaned the living room that morning, she dreaded to think what her mother would make of the kitchen on the landing.

Fifi invited her in, even kissed her cheek, and then led the way upstairs. Clara seemed surprised her arm was still in plaster, as she seemed to think it had been broken much longer than six weeks ago.

'How nice,' Clara said as Fifi showed her into the living room. But it didn't sound a sincere compliment, only a display of the good manners she had always prided herself on. 'It is a rather grim street,' she added, going over to the window to look out. 'Which house was the child murdered in?'

Fifi's heart sank. 'You heard about it then?' she asked.

'Well, of course I did, it was in all the nationals,' Clara said tersely. 'You could have told us yourself, we shouldn't have had to read of your involvement in the papers.'

'As you weren't particularly sympathetic about me losing my baby, I didn't think you'd be interested in hearing about the death of a complete stranger,' Fifi said cuttingly.

'Ghastly business,' Clara continued, almost as if she hadn't heard what her daughter had said. 'Is it that house? The one with no curtains?' she asked, pointing at number 11. 'Do they know yet whether it was the mother or father?'

'Yes, it was that house, and no, we don't know for sure which of them did it, or even if it was someone else. But I'd rather not talk about that, Mum, I'm trying to forget about it. How is Patty? Is she still going out with Michael?'

Fifi had received a very funny letter from her sister on Monday. She said she was getting bored with Michael because he only ever wanted to stay in and watch television with her. She said he hadn't even got it in him to try to seduce her.

'Michael's a good boy,' Clara said vaguely, without turning away from the window. 'Oh! A coal yard so close to you! How dreadful.'

'Okay, Mum.' Fifi thought she'd try humour. 'The street, complete with coal yard and resident child murderer, is grim. Most of the other neighbours are what you'd call "Not Our Sort". I will have to be a witness at the trial too. But looking on the bright side, Dan and I are looking for a new flat. My plaster comes off tomorrow and I'm going back to work next week.'

'It's no joking matter.' Clara turned to face her daughter, her face tight with disapproval. 'Whatever were you thinking of coming to live in a place like this?'

'It was cheap and available.' Fifi shrugged. 'Now, would you like tea or coffee? Could I make you a sandwich? Or would you rather go somewhere more salubrious?'

Clara sat down. She looked as if she wanted confrontation but knew it wasn't the best course. 'Tea would be nice,' she said brightly. 'The curtains are very pretty. Did you make them?'

Fifi nipped out and lit the gas under the kettle. 'No, Yvette, the lady across the road, made them for me,' she called back. 'She's French, and a fabulous dressmaker. She makes clothes for rich women in Chelsea and Kensington. She gave me those silk cushions for a house-warming present.'

As Fifi came back into the room she found her mother examining one of the cushions.

'If she can sew like this and has wealthy clients, why does she live here?' Clara asked.

'It's very difficult to find flats in London,' Fifi said. 'I've been to several letting agencies in the last few days. It's almost impossible to find anywhere central for less than fifteen pounds a week.'

'Fifteen pounds a week!' Clara exclaimed. 'You could rent a mansion in Bristol for that.'

Over tea, Fifi learned that Robin had got a girlfriend called Anna, who her mother thought was gormless. Peter was drinking too much in her opinion and she didn't understand why Patty was growing tired of Michael.

Fifi had to smile. It was a first to hear her mother complaining about her other children.

'It's sensible to stay in and save money if you want to get married,' Clara went on about Patty. 'She doesn't know when she's well off. Most young men these days want flashy cars. Michael is so sensible, he rides a bike.'

'I don't think "sensible" is very attractive to many girls,' Fifi said, trying hard to keep a straight face. 'Besides, I don't think Patty wants to marry Michael.'

'I can't think why not! He's got a good job in a bank, he's steady and reliable.'

Patty had described Michael as pudding-faced, unadventurous and inclined to smell of BO because he wore nylon shirts. Now Fifi knew he rode a bike, and was considered steady and reliable by her mother, she thought she'd hate him on sight.

'Getting married isn't the be-all and end-all for girls these days,' she said. 'I'm glad Patty doesn't think she has to marry the first man that asks her.'

'Like you did?' Clara said waspishly.

'Dan wasn't the first to ask me. Hugh did too,' Fifi said evenly, telling herself she mustn't rise to her mother's bait. 'And I certainly don't regret marrying him. We are very happy together – it's our first anniversary next month.'

'I am well aware of that. From the day you got married I stopped being able to sleep at nights. I had to go to the doctor in the end for some tablets. I wish I could make you see what you've done to our family.'

Fifi found she couldn't ignore that.

'What exactly have I done to our family?' she asked.

'The boys hardly come home any more, Patty's not the same, and your father blames me for it all.'

'It's not my fault that the boys have got out from under your thumb, it's a sign they are growing up. Patty is changing too for the same reason. If you can't sleep at night just because I married a man I love, then perhaps you need to see a psychiatrist!'

'Are you saying I'm mad?' Clara's voice rose to a squeak. 'Any mother would be worried sick when her daughter's husband mixes with people who attack him in dark alleys, and she consorts with murderers.'

Fifi felt like asking why, if her mother was so worried, she didn't write to her. There hadn't been one letter since the curt one after she lost the baby. But instead she decided to deal with more recent issues.

'Even the police don't know who attacked Dan, and I do not consort with murderers. Why did you come here today, Mum? I thought for a brief moment it might be because you wanted to make it up. But it isn't, is it? I bet Dad suggested you came, and you felt you had to go through the motions or he'd be cross with you. What are you going to tell him? That I was impossible as usual?'

'You are. There's no talking to you.'

Fifi shook her head despairingly. 'Mum, you've only been here just twenty minutes and yet in that short time you've accused me of being a bad influence on Patty and the boys. Of forcing you to take sleeping tablets. You make snide suggestions about Dan and claim I consort with murderers. It's you who are impossible!'

There was sudden silence. Fifi decided she wasn't going to be the one to break it.

She looked objectively at her mother. She was a very

pretty woman, with a good figure and smooth, clear skin. She had tied her blonde hair back loosely at the nape of her neck with a pink ribbon to match her two-piece. She really didn't look old enough to have a daughter of Fifi's age. She had a good life, with a husband who adored her. So why was she so confrontational about everything?

'What will you do if you can't find another flat?' Clara broke the silence first.

'We'll stay here until we've got enough for a deposit to buy a house,' Fifi said. 'That won't take long once I get back to work.'

'There are some nice new little houses in Horfield,' Clara said.

Fifi wondered if that was a suggestion they come back to Bristol. 'I expect they are the ones Dan was working on,' she said. 'It would be lovely to come back and live in Bristol but he couldn't be sure of getting work there, not like here where they are crying out for skilled bricklayers.'

'I wish you would come back,' Clara said unexpectedly. 'Patty and your father miss you.'

'What about you?' Fifi asked hesitantly.

'Of course I do. It's not right to have one of my children so far away.'

'And Dan? Would you be prepared to see him as part of our family?'

'I'd try,' Clara said. 'I can't say fairer than that.'

Fifi's heart leaped for it seemed as if at last her mother wanted to build bridges. 'It's a start,' she said, and her smile was a joyous one. 'I've missed all of you, and I've hated the way it's been between us. Maybe when the trial is over and we've got on our feet again, we can come down to Bristol and give moving back some thought.'

Clara looked at her reflectively, perhaps surprised her

daughter had met her halfway. 'Now will you tell me about this murder?' she asked, clearly anxious to move on to safer ground. 'Maybe if I understood about it all I wouldn't be so frightened by it. No one I know has ever been a witness to anything like this.'

It seemed quite ironic to Fifi that she'd been unable to get any of the people she classed as friends around here to discuss the ins and outs of the case, yet her mother was desperately eager to hear it all.

She could be a good listener when she chose, and Fifi found herself pouring out all the detail, how it had affected her, and the aspects which were still baffling.

Every now and then Clara would stop her to question something. She winced from time to time at the more graphic descriptions, but she didn't interrupt with any opinions or snobby remarks.

'It's been good to talk it over with you,' Fifi finished up. 'I really struggled just after it happened. Dan didn't want to talk about it, and I'd sort of got everything stuck in my head.'

It was in fact the first heart-to-heart talk she'd ever had with her mother, and it felt good, as though they'd taken a huge leap forward.

'Your father never wants to discuss things either. I think it's a male thing. Maybe by refusing to talk they think it will go away. But what an ordeal for you, darling! It must have been appalling.'

'I'm well over the worst of it now,' Fifi said. 'I just hope to God it really was Alfie and the police can prove it.'

As Fifi said this, she realized that in fact it was this slim possibility that Alfie was innocent which was causing most of her anxiety. Once she knew for absolute certain that it was him, she felt she'd be able to put it all aside. She admitted as much to her mother.

'It must have been him,' Clara said firmly. 'If it was one of those other men at the card game, or one of your neighbours, the police would have found out by now. I bet he's only trying to muddy the waters by not admitting who was there with him that night. Look at it logically, Fifi, why would anyone else kill her? And how can the couple claim they loved the child if they were prepared to leave her alone in the house while they swanned off to the seaside? They are evil people and they deserve to be hung, drawn and quartered.'

Fifi made them both a ham sandwich and more tea and at long last Clara began to behave as if she was glad to be there. She helped Fifi finish making the bed and admired the bookcase Dan had found in a junk shop and painted. She even praised the cleanliness of the bathroom after visiting it.

Clara had to leave and meet her husband about the time Fifi had her hair appointment. She offered to cancel it and go with her mother, but Clara wouldn't hear of it.

'It's not worth you coming with me for just five minutes with your father, we've got to catch the train at five,' she said pleasantly. 'You keep your hair appointment, it will make you feel good about yourself tomorrow when the plaster comes off.'

'I feel good just because you came,' Fifi said, impulsively hugging Clara. 'I really am sorry I caused you both such distress, I hope we can start again now.'

Clara took Fifi's face between her two hands and kissed her forehead, just the way she did when Fifi was a little girl. 'It was good to see you,' she said. 'A mother always worries about her eldest child the most, and perhaps expects too much. You'll find that out when you have children. I don't know if I'll ever really like Dan, but I will promise to try. If he can get a long weekend off work, then come home to see us.'

On the way to the tube station Fifi felt she had to ask her mother to explain the remark she'd made on the evening of her wedding day.

'Did people really say you should put me in an institution when I was little?'

Clara blushed. 'I never meant to tell you that,' she said. 'I was angry.'

'But was it true?'

'Yes and no. Child guidance did suggest a special school, but that made me so angry I never took you to them again. But that was the only suggestion, and I'm ashamed I told you in such a nasty way.'

'I must have given you a very hard time,' Fifi said thoughtfully. A year ago her childhood problems had seemed funny and she'd never seriously considered how worrying it must have been for her parents.

'You couldn't help it, dear,' Clara said. 'Now, don't let's bring up any more unpleasant things we've said to one another. We need to forgive and forget.'

They parted at the tube station, where Clara bought a big bunch of flowers which she gave to Fifi. 'I could see you'd made a great effort to make your flat a real home, that pleased me. Now ring me, and if you haven't got enough change for the phone I can always ring you back so we can have a chat. I hope the trial won't be too long off, it must be dragging you down worrying about it. If you want us there to support you, just ask.'

Fifi's eyes filled with tears at such sweetness from her mother. 'Thank you, Mummy,' she said, feeling like a little girl again. 'Give Dad, Patty and the boys my love. I feel all hopeful now.'

That evening Dan listened to Fifi's jubilant tale about the visit with a wry smirk. 'It's nice to see you so happy to be thrown crumbs from the table,' he said.

'What do you mean, "crumbs from the table"?' she asked indignantly. 'She was really nice!'

'She had to be to get the lowdown on the murder, and to get in here to inspect the flat. I wouldn't mind betting that as we speak she's telling your father that she's almost persuaded you to come back to Bristol, and once you're back where you belong it will only be a matter of time before I get the big elbow.'

'Don't be so nasty,' Fifi snapped. 'Can't you just be glad she's coming round?'

'No, because I don't believe it,' he said. 'You said yourself she was snotty when she first arrived. She only warmed up once you gave her all the dirt about over the road. You told her that I was fed up with you talking about it, I expect, and she saw that as a chink in the armour.'

'Rubbish,' Fifi said indignantly.

'Okay, we'll wait and see,' he said. 'I bet you get a letter from her in a day or two suggesting you come down alone for a weekend. She'll dress it up saying she and your father want some time alone with you, or some such excuse.'

Fifi flounced out of the room into the bedroom. She thought Dan was actually a bit jealous. He probably felt powerful when she had no one but him to turn to.

She lay on the bed reading a magazine, and Dan didn't come in for over an hour. When he did, he was grinning from ear to ear.

'Who's a sulky girl then?' he taunted her.

'I'm not sulking,' she said airily, even though she was.

He caught hold of one of her bare feet and tickled the sole, making her giggle. 'You aren't allowed to sulk,' he said. 'Come on, let's go down the pub and celebrate the last night of the plaster.'

'What's to celebrate about that?' she asked.

'There isn't much, but you've had your hair done and you look pretty, so I'm looking for an excuse to show you off. Besides, we haven't tuned into the grapevine lately.'

Fifi found it impossible to be cross with Dan for long. One look at his handsome grinning face, those dark eyes and angular cheekbones and she was putty in his hands.

'Okay then.' She got up and put on her shoes and some lipstick. 'But don't say anything more about my mum or I'll come straight home.'

Fifi was laughing as she walked into the pub. Dan had been doing an impersonation of Stan as they walked up the road. He had caught his hangdog expression, the stiff-backed walk and the accent perfectly.

'Nice to see a pretty girl laughing,' Johnny Milkins said, turning on his bar stool to look at Fifi. 'Tell us the joke, I could do with a laugh.'

The pub was very quiet, no more than fifteen or sixteen people in all. But then it was often that way on a Wednesday night.

'Dan was doing an impression of Stan,' Fifi said. She tugged at Dan's arm. 'Go on, do it for Johnny!'

Dan arranged his face appropriately. 'I may not go to the Rifleman until all theese bad feelings are gone,' he said, getting the Polish accent perfectly. Then he walked up to the bar with Stan's special walk.

Johnny roared with laughter, his huge belly which

slouched over his trousers wobbling like a jelly. 'You've got him to a T,' he said through his laughter. 'Can you do anyone else?'

'I could do you, mate, if I had a big enough pillow to stick under my shirt,' Dan replied.

Johnny roared again, slapped Dan on the back and insisted on buying him and Fifi a drink.

Fifi liked Johnny. He was a huge man in every way, well over six feet tall, weighing around twenty stone, and with a personality to match. His hair was going grey but he had masses of it, standing up on end like a thick brush. With his deep, dark tan from working outside, and vivid blue eyes, he was attractive despite his immense bulk.

He was the man who claimed to have a close friend in the police force and had related the information about the clean sheet covering Angela.

Dan liked Johnny too, but said a man who wore half of England's gold reserves around his neck and wrist yet lived in a council flat had to be a bit thick.

'You don't normally come in here midweek,' Johnny said, giving Fifi one of his lecherous winks. 'Special occasion?'

'My plaster's coming off tomorrow,' Fifi replied. 'I can't wait, it itches underneath. I have to poke a knitting needle up it to scratch it.'

'You're gonna have to hang that arm out yer window to brown it up,' Johnny said. 'My missis broke 'er arm once and I nearly pissed meself when the plaster come off. I said she ought to audition for the Black and White Minstrels.'

'I'll wear long sleeves,' Fifi said. 'Or put gravy browning on it like they did in the war.'

Over the first drink Johnny entertained them with various funny stories connected with his scaffolding business, including an hilarious one about a man who fell asleep sunbathing in his lunch hour, three floors up, turned over in his sleep and fell off.

'Luckiest man alive,' Johnny chortled. 'Fell into a heap of sand. Not a scratch on him.'

They were on a third drink when Fifi asked Johnny if Frank or Stan had started to come back to the pub yet.

Both men had stopped coming in after they were hauled in for police questioning. They were not the only ones who'd absented themselves. Mike Skinner from number 7, Ralph Jackson who lived on the top floor of Yvette's house, and John Bolton at number 13 had not been seen in the pub either. They were all men who had been known to have been at card games at number 11 in the past, and they'd all been pulled in for questioning. None of them had been at the last game, but feelings were running so high about Alfie that any associates of his were not welcome in the pub.

'You haven't heard about Stan?' Johnny asked, looking surprised. 'I thought you must've when Dan was taking him off.'

'What about him?' Fifi asked.

'He's been taken down the cop shop again.'

'Oh, for goodness' sake,' Fifi exclaimed. 'Why can't they leave him alone?'

'A woman over in Brixton reported he'd molested her daughter,' Johnny said. 'Seems kosher too. She were seven, same age as Angela. And 'e weren't at work that morning she died neither. 'E never showed up.'

Fifi was so shocked she could only stare at Johnny in disbelief.

'Are you sure about this, mate?' Dan asked, suddenly very serious and ashamed he'd been mimicking the man. 'I can't believe that of Stan. His own little girls were gunned down in the war.'

'Yeah, I know,' Johnny said, rubbing his chin thoughtfully. 'I'd have staked me life on 'im being as straight as a die where kids is concerned. But it looks black fer 'im. He lied about being at work that morning, and he empties the bins around Brixton. Then there's that stuff him and Frank said about killing one of the kids and making it look like Alfie done it.'

'But that was just a black joke, they weren't serious,' Fifi said indignantly.

'No one wants Alfie to swing for it more than me,' Johnny said, gesticulating with his hands. 'I 'ates the geezer. The boys up the nick are sure he'd done stuff to all his girls, so no one wants 'im to walk away from this. But if 'e didn't actually kill Angela, then someone else did. And the Old Bill 'ave got to nab 'im.'

'Of course it was Alfie,' Dan said impatiently. 'It's as plain as the nose on your face.'

'That's just because you want to believe that,' Johnny said. 'We all do.'

'It couldn't be Stan,' Fifi said stubbornly. 'I just know it.'

'I certainly don't wanna believe Stan is a nonce. It just don't fit right to me,' Johnny said. 'But it could be 'e's never bin right in the 'ead since 'e lost his wife and kids.'

'Do you know why he didn't admit he wasn't at work that morning?' Dan asked.

'Stan reckons 'e overslept and 'e didn't own up to it cos another bloke 'ad clocked 'im in. 'E reckons they do it all the time for one another when they're late, to save 'em getting their money docked. 'E didn't want anyone to get into trouble for covering for 'im.'

'What time did he get into work then?' Fifi asked. Her

good mood had vanished and the old fear and anxiety were coming back.

''E joined 'is dustcart around eleven,' Johnny said.

Fifi and Dan went home after that drink, both subdued and shocked.

'I don't, I won't believe it,' Dan burst out once they got indoors. 'Stan's a decent man.'

'What about the word of the woman in Brixton?' Fifi said in a small voice. She was remembering all the times Stan had got shopping for her when she first came home from hospital. She found it impossible to believe such a kind man could molest a child, but if he had really done it, perhaps he had another side she and Dan hadn't seen.

'This information could have come from someone who owes the Muckles a favour,' Dan said grimly. 'Or just some hysterical woman who's remembered seeing Stan playing with her kid. I've seen him out in the road talking to kids plenty of times. He's just a lonely man who likes to see children playing.'

It was Fifi who lapsed into silence this time, saying nothing while Dan ranted about how he reckoned Alfie had been in the habit of giving the police backhanders, and this was why they were looking for someone else to frame.

'Look at the times he's got away with stuff that would get anyone else locked up immediately,' he said. 'If it's Detective Inspector Roper he's got in his pocket, Alfie could easily get him to pin this on someone else. Stan's the perfect patsy, he's a Pole for a start, with no family. Who's going to stick up for him?'

Fifi had been brought up to respect the law, and to trust the police to apprehend criminals and bring them to trial. She hadn't liked Roper much, but she didn't believe he would take bribes or frame an innocent man, not even to protect himself. Yet she knew Dan was far more worldly-wise than she was, and Roper did seem to be pulling out all the stops to find someone other than Alfie to pin the crime on.

It was unthinkable that Alfie just might be released without charge. Even if he hadn't actually killed Angela, he'd treated her and all his children shamefully, and once home again, he'd continue to do so. He would also be wanting revenge against anyone who had spoken out against him. Herself included!

Fifi left the hospital at noon the following day, feeling like a new woman without the plaster, though just as Johnny had said, her arm did look odd being so white. It was thinner too, and it felt weak; she supposed some of the muscle had wasted while not being used. But it felt so good to be able to stretch out her fingers, to know that she could dress herself quickly again, and cuddle Dan without clonking him on the head!

As she drew close to Dale Street she spotted Frank going into the pub. She hadn't as much as caught sight of him for days, but assuming he had come out of his hermit-like state, she thought she would go in too and see how he was.

After the glare of the sunshine, the pub seemed very gloomy. There was only a handful of people in there, and Frank was at the bar waiting for his pint to be pulled.

'Hello, how nice to see you,' she said brightly, as if surprised to find him there. 'I've just had the plaster off my arm, so I thought I'd get a drink to celebrate. Let me buy you that pint too.'

'No, you're all right,' he said, looking as if he wished she would go away.

Fifi had sensed when he began hiding himself away from her that he wished he hadn't told her all that stuff about Molly. She had kept her promise of silence, she hadn't even told Dan about it. But maybe he didn't believe that.

She wasn't going to back away now; she was determined to make him talk to her. 'I insist,' she said. 'I'll be back at work on Monday, so it's my last chance to be a bit naughty and drink during the day.'

He tried to produce a smile, but it was a weak, forlorn one. 'Was that your mum I saw you leaving with yesterday?' he asked. 'If so, she looks young enough to be your sister.'

'Yes, it was Mum, a surprise visit. I'll tell her what you said. That will make her day.'

She thought Frank looked ill. He'd lost weight and his normal good colour. Once she'd got her drink and paid for them, she suggested they sat over in the corner.

'Now why have you been avoiding me?' she asked teasingly. 'I thought we were friends.'

Frank shrugged. 'I've been down in the dumps. I couldn't face talking to anyone.'

'Well, it was a good job you didn't run into me,' Fifi said. 'I was down too, but it affected me the other way. I was talking non-stop to anyone that would let me.'

'It just seems to be getting worse rather than better,' he said wearily. 'And now they've got Stan again.'

'So we heard,' Fifi replied, putting her hand over Frank's. 'Dan and I think it sounds like a load of old rubbish.'

Frank looked as if he was going to cry. 'I've just been up to the nick to see if they'd let me see him, but they wouldn't. They'll have to charge him soon, or let him go. He's been there nearly twenty-four hours.'

'Do you know anything about the woman who made the claims?'

'A bit. She's called Frieda and she's rough, got several kids and her old man's doing time,' Frank said, his voice wavering. 'Stan used to empty her bins, and she set her cap at him at the end of last year, always coming out with a cup of tea for him and that.'

'Do the police know that?'

'Stan's bound to have told them now. Last Christmas Eve she came in here all dressed up, on the hunt for him.'

'What happened?'

'Stan was a bit drunk, he kissed her under the mistletoe and flirted a bit. The next day when he came for his Christmas dinner with me, he felt really bad about it. He said he'd only got to know the woman because her little girl used to chat to him, but he didn't really like her mother, and now he'd given her the wrong signals. I said he'd have to put her straight.'

'Did he?' Fifi asked.

Frank shook his head. 'You know what Stan's like, too much of a gent to be rude to any woman.'

'So she got her claws into him then?'

'Not in the way you mean. He didn't take Frieda out or anything like that, but he liked the little girl, and felt sorry for her cos she were a bit neglected. Next thing Frieda was tapping him up for a few bob when the kid needed new shoes and stuff. I reckon it must've got out of hand, because back in June Stan was getting the other blokes on the dust van to do the bins on that street so he didn't have to see her.'

'Do you think this is like "Hell hath no fury like a woman scorned"?' Fifi asked.

'I reckon so. I know Stan ain't seen her or the kid for ages, and if he really had done something to the child, Frieda would've screamed blue murder right away. The way I see it, she heard about what happened in the street, and thought she'd jump on the bandwagon and make some mischief for him.'

'Evil cow!' Fifi exclaimed. 'But did you tell the police this today?' she asked.

'Yeah, fat lot of good it did though. They see me and Stan as a team because we're mates. And of course there was that joke I made in the pub, they took that seriously.'

Fifi tried everything to cheer Frank up. She showed him her white arm, told him about *The Day of the Triffids*, and some of the more amusing things her mother had said during her visit. But it was impossible to make him either laugh or talk, and after a second drink she left to go home.

Once outside in the sunshine though, and just a tiny bit tiddly after two shandies on an empty stomach, she didn't want to spend the afternoon indoors. All at once she hit on the idea of going down to the council depot in Stockwell to see if she could enlist the help of one of Stan's workmates.

She had the idea that if she explained to them that he was in deep trouble, and that she thought this woman Frieda had made a false allegation, one of them might be persuaded to go to the police and tell them what they knew about her.

It was only one stop on the tube, and she asked a road sweeper for directions from there. Stan had told her once that the depot was just the place where the dust vans were cleaned and garaged, and that the refuse was dumped else-where. Yet as she turned into Miles Lane, a narrow, winding street of dilapidated small houses and workshops, the stench of rotting rubbish was overpowering.

The gate had a 'No Admittance' sign, but it was open so Fifi went in. Two young men stripped to the waist were cleaning a truck with hoses, and another two middle-aged men were sitting on the ground, with their backs against the wall of an office, having a cigarette.

Fifi walked hesitantly over to these two, ignoring the wolf whistles from the younger ones.

'I'd like some help, please,' she said, smiling flirtatiously, even though they were tubby, with thinning hair, and in very dirty overalls.

'Anything you want you can have, including me,' said the slightly bigger man, who had a squashed nose like a boxer's. He got to his feet. 'Bert's the name. I'd shake your hand but mine's too dirty to touch a pretty little thing like you.'

'Do you know Stan the Pole?' she asked.

The man's face tightened and he instinctively moved a step back, so clearly he knew Stan was in police custody. 'Yeah, we know 'im,' he said. 'What's 'e to you?'

'Just a neighbour and a friend,' she said. 'I want to help him because I know he hasn't done anything wrong.'

'Then 'e ain't got nothin' to worry about,' Bert replied.

'But a woman has claimed he molested her child,' Fifi said.

'So!' he exclaimed, and the fact he didn't display any shock or ask any questions suggested he knew exactly who she was referring to.

'I was hoping that someone here might go to the police station and tell them that what she's saying isn't true.'

''Ow do we know it ain't?' Bert's friend asked as he got to his feet. 'Stan's a weird bugger.'

'He's just foreign and different, not a child molester. I'd stake my life on that,' Fifi said. 'Do you know the woman who made the complaint? Her name is Frieda.'

'Might do,' Bert said, his eyes narrowing.

'Well, if you do, you must have an opinion about her?'

'She's a scrubber,' the other man chimed in.

Fifi smiled. She thought she was winning. Neither of these two men seemed very bright, but then Stan had once said that the biggest drawback of the job was the mentality of the men he had to work with.

'So did you know she was pestering Stan?' she asked.

'She's after anyfing in trousers,' Bert said. ''E were a mug giving 'er kid things, 'er ma must've thought 'er luck was in.'

'And he tried to avoid her, didn't he?' Fifi said patiently.

'Dunno, all we 'eard was that she 'ad the 'ots fer 'im,' Bert said. 'We used to take the mickey.'

'Would you go and tell the police that then?' she asked. 'Please! I know Stan would stick up for any of you.'

'We can't say nothin',' Bert said, and he looked down at the ground and shuffled his feet as if slightly ashamed. 'We been told not to.'

'Who by?'

'Daren't say,' he replied.

Fifi sighed. 'Just you two, or all the men here?'

'All of us.'

Fifi sensed she was beaten. She had no idea if what the man said was true, or if he'd made it up to get rid of her. But she clearly wasn't going to get much more out of him.

'Can you just tell me what road Frieda lives on then?' she asked. 'That wouldn't hurt, would it?'

'Whatcha want to know that for?' Bert asked.

'As you won't help Stan I thought I might be able to find someone there who would,' she said.

'Look, it ain't that we don't wanna 'elp 'im,' the other man said, glancing at his companion as if they shared some secret.

'I understand, you're afraid you'll lose your jobs.'

He nodded. ''E's an 'ard bastard, our boss, don't care that we got kids an' all.'

Fifi wanted to smile. He was so thick it hadn't occurred to him that he'd let slip who had said they were to say nothing. 'So just whisper what road, I'll find a way to do the rest,' she said.

'Jasper Street,' Bert said quickly. 'Now go afore the boss comes back and sees you.'

As Fifi walked back down Miles Lane, she wondered why the men's boss had warned them to say nothing about Stan. That was very odd – what possible reason could he have for demanding such a thing?

She was at the end of the lane, just about to cross the intersecting road, when a red Jaguar came along. The driver was slowing to turn into Miles Lane, and he looked right at her and grinned lecherously.

He was middle-aged, a big, wide-shouldered man with silver-grey hair slicked back from his tanned face. And Fifi knew she had seen him somewhere before.

She continued across the road but turned and looked back, trying to place him. He turned right and drove into the council depot.

Fifi walked on back to the tube station, but her mind was on the man. He could be the boss the men were nervous about, and she wondered if he had perhaps come into the Rifleman at some time with Stan.

But she couldn't imagine the foreman of a rubbish depot earning enough to have such a flashy car. She knew very little about cars but she was sure that was the latest model.

Outside the tube station Fifi paused again, wondering what she should do about Frieda. Ten minutes ago it had seemed such a good idea just to go there and have it out with the woman, but now she wasn't so sure. From what Frank said she sounded very rough, and she just might go for her. On top of that Frieda might report Fifi to the police, and that could get her into trouble. Nor did she know how far it was to Jasper Street, and she had intended to make something special for dinner tonight.

She wavered for several minutes before deciding it really wasn't her place to go banging on a stranger's door, and it might make things worse for Stan rather than better.

Once she was on the tube her mind kept turning back to the man in the red car. Dan always remembered people by their cars, but she wasn't sure she should ask him about this one as it would involve telling him about her visit to the depot. She knew he wouldn't approve, he'd say she was sticking her nose in other people's business and that might start another row. She didn't want anything to spoil her first evening without the plaster.

Back at home Fifi got out the ingredients for the fish pie she wanted to make. She'd cut the recipe out of a magazine some time ago. It looked delicious in the picture, and it sounded easy to make, even for her, as she was well aware she wasn't a very good cook.

While the fish was simmering in some stock, she made the pastry and the white sauce. But maybe she overcooked the fish because when she strained it, it looked more like grey soup. But she mixed it all into the white sauce anyway, put it into a pie dish and then placed the pastry on top. She made some decorative pastry leaves like in the picture, but when she put them on, the pastry began to sag down in the middle. Assuming it would rise as it cooked, she put it into the oven and went off to have a bath.

She was longer in the bath than she intended as it was so lovely to be able to immerse herself completely without the plaster on her arm. By the time she'd got out, she noticed that the whole house stank of fish, and worse still of burning. She rushed back and opened the oven to find the pie looking absolutely nothing like the one in the picture. It was only the edges that were burned, but the pastry hadn't risen, it had sunk even further into the filling and looked awful.

Undeterred, she prepared the vegetables and laid the table in the living room. She was sure it would taste nice even if it didn't look it, and Dan was always appreciative when he knew she'd made an effort.

By six she was ready, wearing Dan's favourite black dress, with her face made up. She turned the oven right down to its lowest setting and went over to the window to watch for Dan coming home.

Yvette came out of her house and hurried up the street. As always she was wearing one of her shapeless dresses, with a dull brown cardigan over it. It looked as if she was just going to the shop as she had a purse in her hand. As Yvette got to number 13 where the Boltons lived, John came out, and they stopped to talk.

Fifi had only ever spoken to John once or twice, and that was in the Rifleman when she and Dan first came to the street. He was in his late thirties, a big, handsome man with black hair, greying at the temples, vivid blue eyes, an engaging smile, and extremely sharp suits. It was whispered that he was a villain, and he certainly didn't appear to have a real job as he never emerged from number 2 before noon.

Vera, his wife, was a voluptuous red-head who worked as an usherette in a West End cinema. Someone in the street had told Fifi that their flat was very plushy, with thick carpets, expensive furniture and all the latest appliances, so the whispers about him were probably true.

Next to Dan, John was the best-looking man in the street, even Yvette had remarked on that. Fifi had seen her talking to him on several occasions, and although she expected it was only because Yvette made clothes for Vera some-times, Dan had often joked that the dressmaker had the hots for John.

She looked animated enough for that, her hands fluttering as if she were describing something to him. Fifi wished she was close enough to hear what they were talking about.

Suddenly Fifi's memory was jolted as John turned slightly and she saw his profile. She had the same view of him as when he waited for the door to be opened at the Muckles. It was some weeks ago, long before she had the miscarriage. But more importantly, his companion that evening had been the man she'd seen this afternoon in the red Jaguar.

While Fifi was busy studying Yvette and John Bolton, Sergeant Mike Wallis was talking to Detective Inspector Roper in his office.

'What's it going to be, guv?' Wallis said. 'Charge him or let him go?'

Roper lit a cigarette and drew heavily on it. He had been sitting at his desk for over an hour mulling over the evidence against Stan the Pole. But the man had been in custody over twenty hours now, and he couldn't keep him any longer without charging him.

'I don't believe that slag of a woman,' he said viciously. 'Okay, the Pole is a bit of an odd fish and he lied to us the first time round about where he was at the time of the murder. But he doesn't strike me as a nonce or a killer. Have you checked to see if Frieda Marchant's got any form?'

Wallis nodded, and got out his notebook. 'She has, two counts of receiving back in '61, and more recently shop-lifting. PC Coombs spoke to her neighbours who say she's a troublemaker, she neglects her kids, and she'll do or say anything for a few bob. I'd say that someone put her up to this.'

'So would I,' Roper sighed, loosening his tie and undoing the top button on his shirt. 'But who, that's the question? She's Alfie's kind of woman, not that much different to his missus, but he could hardly order her to make mischief for Stan from the prison.'

'She certainly has had some sort of relationship with Stan, and he admits some involvement with the kid, and buying her presents. I'm inclined to believe his story, that he just liked the kid and felt sorry for her, and this is Fat Frieda's revenge for him turning her down.'

'Thing is, can we believe his story about oversleeping on the day of the murder?' Wallis asked. 'Not one of the men at the council yard would admit he clocked Stan in that morning.'

'Well, they wouldn't,' Roper said, stubbing out his cigarette and lighting another one immediately. 'Anyone admitting that would get the sack. Besides, Stan's fingerprints don't match any of those from the bedroom of number 11, so I think we'll let the poor sod go. But let's put Fat Frieda under surveillance. If she was put up to this, she might go calling on them, and with luck it will be someone that was at that card game.'

'Tell me, guv, do you still think it was Alfie or Molly that killed the kid?'

Roper shook his head wearily. 'I dunno, Mike. I was a hundred per cent sure. But the more information we get, the more I doubt my own judgement. I almost believed Molly about Frank Ubley, for Christ's sake! She made it sound so bloody plausible. It was a stroke of luck for him that he'd gone into that flower shop by the tube station. It might have been a different outcome if the shopkeeper hadn't remembered him taking so long to choose flowers for his wife's grave. I felt bad that I'd even suspected the poor sod after that. Then this comes up about the Pole! So now . . .' He paused to grimace. 'Well, let's just say I'm even more confused. Alfie's the kind that would grass up his grandmother to save his own neck. So why won't he give the names of the men at that card party?'

'Is it worth bringing John Bolton in again?' Wallis asked. 'I know he couldn't have done it, but I got the idea he was holding something back.' He flicked back through his notebook to the notes he'd made when they interviewed Bolton before. '"*I just didn't like the company*," ' he read out, and looked at the older officer. 'That was what he said about the one card game he went to. He wasn't talking about Alfie, was he? I mean, they grew up in the same street, they were even pals as kids, so he already knew what he was like. So it stands to reason there was someone else there he didn't like. Reckon we could get him to tell us?'

Roper thought for a moment. He'd known Bolton for around twenty years and liked and respected him, even though he was a villain, for he had charm, humour and courage. Roper had been the arresting officer when Bolton was charged and eventually convicted of a robbery in Hatton Garden some eight years or so ago. Securing a conviction had been a feather in his cap as Bolton was a clever devil, always three steps ahead of the law. He remembered asking Bolton why he'd turned to crime when he could have succeeded in the business world.

'*All the doors were locked,*' he'd replied with a wide grin. '*By the time I'd learned to pick those locks, I didn't want to go in there.*'

'It's worth a try,' Roper said with a sigh. 'Maybe if we show him the pictures of the kid he'll feel revolted enough to name names.'

'Shall I pull him tonight?' Wallis asked.

Roper glanced at his watch and shook his head. 'Doubt he'll be in on a Friday night. Leave it till tomorrow.'

Chapter thirteen

When Dan hadn't come home by six, Fifi thought there must have been some delay on the tube, or his boss had kept him back to discuss something, but by the time it got to seven o'clock she was annoyed. *Emergency – Ward 10*, her favourite television programme, was on at eight, and she'd expected that by then dinner would be cleared away so she could relax.

At eight, because the dinner was getting dried up, she dished it up and put Dan's over a saucepan of boiling water, then ate her own.

The fish pie was absolutely awful, and that made her even angrier because she'd tried so hard to make something special. And still Dan hadn't come home.

The combination of worrying about where he was, the disappointment about the fish pie and thinking about the man in the red Jaguar, had stopped her enjoying watching *Emergency – Ward 10*. When Dan finally turned up at nine, she didn't wait to hear his explanation, and shouted at him that his dinner was ruined.

'That's probably just as well,' he grinned, making a comic display of sniffing the air. 'It stinks. I could smell it as soon as I opened the front door. What was it?'

'Fish pie, which I spent hours making,' she retorted, getting more annoyed by the second because he was so unconcerned about her feelings. 'I wouldn't have made anything if you'd told me you were going to the pub. It's a waste of my time and money.'

His grin vanished. 'I haven't been down the pub. I went to see a flat. I wouldn't have bothered, if I'd known you were going to be so crabby.'

'What flat, where?'

He shrugged. 'There's no point in telling you, I didn't get it. The landlady must've been to the same charm school as your mother, took one look at me and told me she'd already let it.'

The sarcastic reference to her mother on top of the ruined dinner was too much for Fifi. She looked scathingly at Dan. His hands and face had been washed, but his work clothes were covered in bits of cement, there was a jagged tear in his trousers with his knee showing through, and his boots were filthy.

'It wouldn't occur to you that maybe it would be a good idea to get cleaned up before going to see a flat? Nobody in their right mind would want to let a place to someone as dirty as you!' she shrieked at him.

'God, you sound worse than your mother,' Dan said, and wheeling round went out on to the landing. He took the plate of dinner off the saucepan and tipped it into the bin, plate and all. 'And you can stick your bloody fish pie,' he called back. 'I'll go and get something decent to eat where people don't judge me by my clothes.'

The moment the front door slammed behind him, Fifi wished she hadn't been so nasty. She was also embarrassed by the fish pie, because it really was stinking the whole house out. She retrieved the plate from the bin and washed it up, then took the rubbish down to the dustbin, hoping the smell would disperse.

When she came back up the stairs, she saw he'd left the

small canvas satchel he took his sandwiches to work in out on the landing, so she opened it to take his sandwich box and flask out to wash them. With them was a page torn from a newspaper, one advertisement circled.

'Two-bedroom self-contained garden flat in Barnes. Low rent for married couple in exchange for routine maintenance jobs in apartment block. Pleasant tree-lined avenue near river. Good references required.'

Fifi gulped hard. She understood Dan's reasoning now. As the landlady wanted maintenance work done, he had thought it would be fine to appear in his work clothes. He'd probably rushed over there full of hope, with the intention of giving her a lovely surprise if he got it. And she'd belittled him for it!

All at once she felt very ashamed of herself. He'd been at work since seven o'clock, but getting them somewhere better to live was more important to him than his dinner. No wonder he'd stormed off! She would have too if their roles had been reversed.

Dan came home after the pubs had shut. Fifi tried to apologize and ask him if he'd got something to eat, but he ignored her, stripped off his clothes and went to bed.

He was asleep within seconds, but because he'd got into bed without washing, smelling strongly of drink and cigarettes, and never even asked how her arm was without its plaster, she got angry all over again.

In the morning Dan got up at his usual time and left without a word, or even a cup of tea. As it was Saturday, she had wanted to know if he was working all day or coming back at noon, but he left so quickly she didn't get a chance to ask.

It wasn't until about eleven that morning that she thought

again about Stan and the man in the red Jaguar. Last night, long before Dan came home, she'd decided it wasn't a good idea to tell him any of it. Setting aside that he'd be cross she'd gone to Stan's depot, he wasn't likely to believe that the man she saw driving past was the same man she'd seen with John Bolton going into the Muckles'. He'd think she was becoming obsessive again and it might lead to a row.

But she knew she was neither obsessive nor imagining what she'd seen. That man in the Jaguar was definitely the same man she'd seen before. Maybe he wasn't Stan's boss, but he had some connection with the council yard or he wouldn't have been going in there. She felt it was her duty to go to the police with this, and she would go now and do the shopping for the weekend on the way back.

'Thank you for coming to us with this, Mrs Reynolds,' PC Tomkins said as he showed her out of an interview room at the police station. 'We'll look into it.'

Fifi was disappointed that Detective Inspector Roper hadn't been available for her to talk to. Tomkins had been nice, far nicer than Roper who could be curt, and he was young, no more than thirty, and quite attractive too. But to her disappointment he seemed to know very little about the case. She'd spilled out that she went to the council yard because she wanted to help Stan, and carefully repeated the conversation she'd had with the men there. She explained about seeing the man in the red Jaguar turning in there, and how her memory was jogged about where she'd seen him before when she saw John Bolton. But the young policeman had looked at her in the same faintly bemused way her father used to when she was making an excuse for why she was late home.

Maybe she'd talked too much? She did go on a bit about what a kind, good man Stan was, and how furtive the men at the depot had been. And even as she was explaining it all, she felt it all sounded weaker than it did in her head. Without any hard facts like the registration number of the red Jaguar, she supposed Tomkins couldn't really be blamed for thinking she was a bit hysterical, with an overactive imagination.

She had also been forced to admit that she'd only known Stan a few months, and Tomkins raised one eyebrow in a way that suggested he didn't think a few months was long enough to make a judgment about anyone's character. As she left she could imagine him laughing with his colleagues about nosy people who justified themselves by trying to be amateur sleuths.

On the way home she got some shopping, including a half-shoulder of lamb for Sunday dinner. Roast lamb was Dan's favourite meal, and even she couldn't mess that up. She was still very embarrassed about the stink of the fish pie, it was the first thing she'd noticed when she woke up. It was a wonder Miss Diamond hadn't complained.

As she got to the corner of Dale Street, Yvette came out of the shop with some shopping in her arms and smiled at Fifi.

'Ah! Ze plaster, they take it off,' she remarked. ''Ow does it feel to use your right hand again?'

'Strange. I keep forgetting to use it,' Fifi said, grinning and wiggling her fingers. 'I'm going back to work on Monday. It will be nice to get back to normal.'

As they walked down the street together Fifi asked her if she knew about Stan.

Yvette nodded. 'I saw 'im come home yesterday evening.

I theenk no charges 'ave been made. Those silly policemen! Stan could never hurt a child!'

'He's home? I've just been down to the police station,' Fifi exclaimed, shocked that Tomkins had let her pour out all that about Stan without telling her they'd let him go. 'Why on earth didn't they tell me? There I was pleading for him!'

'You went to plead for Stan?' Yvette asked, looking puzzled.

Fifi explained why she was there, telling her all about her trip to the depot and the man in the car. To her shock, Yvette rounded on her.

'You silly, silly girl,' she said. 'You must not get involved in this.'

'But I had to tell them that I'd seen the man before going into Alfie's,' Fifi said indignantly.

'No, you should not 'ave. It ees better to leave such things alone. These are bad men, Fifi. If they knew you were watching them they would . . .' She paused to make a gesture of slitting her throat.

Fifi laughed nervously. 'You know them then?' she asked.

Yvette caught hold of Fifi's arm. Her dark eyes blazed. 'I 'ave lived 'ere for long enough to understand when it is better to look the other way. You are like a child, Fifi. You weesh to meddle with everything. You tell people things best kept to yourself.'

Fifi was staggered by the woman's response. 'I only tell you things. I thought we were friends,' she said indignantly.

Yvette's face softened and she put one hand caressingly on Fifi's cheek. 'It is because you are my friend I weesh to prevent any harm to you,' she said softly. 'I 'ave told you many times you should leave this street. But you are still 'ere.'

'We are going, as soon as we can find somewhere to live.' Fifi felt as if she was being told off by her mother.

'That is good,' Yvette said. 'And when you go, tell no one where. Not even people you think are your friends.'

Fifi was so unnerved by Yvette's reaction that when she got home, she lay down on her bed for a while. Anyone else would have either told her she had an overactive imagination, or been hanging on her every word. But Yvette had sounded really scared, as if she knew absolutely everything about this business and was alarmed Fifi had stumbled on part of it!

Did she know the man in the red Jaguar? Was it him she thought was dangerous? Could she have still been in her flat when the murder took place and heard or seen something?

The police believed Yvette had gone out early that morning to do a fitting, and presumably they checked with Yvette's client as they'd checked on everyone else's alibi, Dan's included. But supposing they hadn't? Could she have been there?

Fifi told herself that this was impossible, yet her mind kept recalling things Yvette had said in the past, before Angela was killed. *'I have seen and heard many terrible things.'* What exactly had she seen and heard? Fifi had assumed at the time it was just fighting, maybe Alfie hitting Molly, even the kids getting a beating, the same sort of things almost everyone in the street had heard. But maybe it wasn't just that?

Everyone had remarked that it was odd Alfie wouldn't name the men at that last card game. Now Fifi had seen for herself the hideous squalor inside that house, she couldn't imagine anyone in their right mind wanting to spend an evening playing cards there.

What if the cards weren't the real attraction?

'No,' she whispered aloud as a hideous thought came into her mind. 'It couldn't be that!'

Yet Angela had been raped and murdered, that was fact. Why, if those other men had really been only drinking and playing cards, hadn't they come forward? Maybe Alfie was speaking the truth when he said he hadn't killed Angela, but he couldn't admit who did do it because he was too scared?

Just like Yvette.

Dan arrived home at half past one. Fifi had calmed down by then, even told herself that she was letting her imagination run away with her. She had decided that she was going to make it up with Dan as soon as he got home, whatever time that was.

When she heard him greet Frank jovially down in the hall, she took it that he'd decided not to work all day to meet her halfway and that pleased her. When he came bounding up the stairs in his normal manner she put the kettle on.

Yet as soon as his head popped up above the banisters as he reached the last landing and she saw a sort of furtive expression on his face, she knew something wasn't right.

He had a letter in his hand. 'For you,' he said, holding it out to her as he came up the last five steps, and Fifi immediately recognized the writing on the envelope as her mother's.

'That's funny,' she said, taking it from him. 'I didn't see any mail for me this morning when I went out.'

Frank always picked the letters up and put them on the shelf in the hall.

'Second post maybe,' Dan said, turning his head away. 'Or the postman put it through the wrong letter-box and they've just returned it.'

That explanation was too pat; he'd never been a good liar.

'Or you saw the Bristol postmark and picked it up on your way out this morning?' she suggested, looking sharply at him.

He gave the game away by blushing.

'Why, Dan?' she asked. 'Were you going to steam it open to see if she'd said anything about you?'

'No, of course not,' he said, but had the grace to look slightly ashamed. 'I just wanted to be with you when you read it to see if I was right.'

Fifi knew he was referring to his bet that her mother would invite Fifi home alone. 'Couldn't you just trust me to admit it, if that's what she did do?' she asked quietly.

'No,' he said. 'I couldn't, because I know you've got divided loyalties.'

Fifi turned her back on him and went into the living room, ripping the envelope open as she went.

Dearest Fifi, she read. *It was lovely to see you and your home the other day, your father was so pleased to hear the visit went well, and that we'd made a start on sorting out our differences. The boys and Patty were thrilled too, they are looking forward to seeing you again before long, they all have so much to say to you.*

I meant what I said about you and Dan coming for a weekend soon, but on reflection it would probably be for the best if you came alone the first time. There is still so much to be talked over, and we need to get that out of the way before we can really welcome Dan. I'm sure you'll understand what I mean.

Write soon,

All our love, Mum and Dad.

'Well?' Dan said behind her. 'Was I right or wrong?'

Fifi felt sickened that her mother had let her down, but

as she turned and saw Dan's smug 'I told you so' expression, she felt angry with him too.

'Wrong,' she lied. 'She only says how nice it was to see me and our home the other day.'

'So can I see it?'

'I've just told you what she said.'

'You've only told me part of it,' he said, and he lunged forward and snatched the letter out of her hand before she even saw him move.

'Give it back,' she shrieked. 'You've got no right to read my letters.'

He held it above his head, out of her reach, and read it.

'I rest my case,' he said as he handed it back to her. 'Just as I said, she wants you there all on your own. Once you've told her all my faults, it won't take her long to convince you that you'd be better off without me.'

Earlier this morning, before she went to the police station, Fifi had felt Dan was justified in walking out the night before, and she had been determined to tell him so when he got home today. She really wanted things to get back to the way they used to be, making each other laugh, being relaxed and happy together. When they first got married they had agreed that it didn't matter what anyone else thought or said about either of them. He said that he could live with her parents' attitude towards him, because he knew they had something together that was very rare and precious. She had promised him that she would never let her family come between them, and she believed she had kept her promise.

So she felt betrayed now, because after all they'd been through, he had decided to believe she was so stupid that she couldn't see how manipulative her mother was, and so weak that if she did go home alone, she would just bow under the pressure.

He had made sarcastic comments about her mother in the past, but Fifi had always laughed them off, understanding it was because he felt a little insecure, and she'd given him reassurance that he was the only important person in her life.

But now she felt angry that he couldn't see she had merely been protecting his feelings with this letter. She was the one who had been virtually cast out because of him. Dan had lost nothing at all. So how dare he get on his high horse about a situation which she had been trying desperately to improve?

'Perhaps I would be better off without you,' she snarled angrily at him in the heat of the moment, not stopping to think what she was saying. 'My life took a downturn the moment I married you.'

The goading, smug look he'd had seconds before vanished. She saw deep hurt replace it, and if she could have clawed back those words, she would have done.

'I didn't mean that,' she said quickly. 'I'm sorry.'

He raised one eyebrow and just stared at her, not saying a word. Then he turned on his heel and went into the bedroom.

She heard the sound of the wardrobe door opening, but thought he was just getting some clean clothes out to get changed. She decided it was better to leave it for now, and she began to lay the table.

She looked round as he came out of the bedroom, and to her consternation he was just standing on the landing looking at her, his duffel bag in his hand.

He looked exactly as he had when they first met. A bit grubby, hair in need of a wash, stubble on his chin, even the duffel bag was the same one. But he'd smiled all the time that evening, and now his expression was cold and unreadable.

'I'll be off now. I've left money on the chest of drawers for you. When you go back to Bristol drop a line to the site, and I'll come and get the rest of my stuff.'

'You're leaving me?' she asked incredulously.

'It's better for me to go now than pull you down even further.'

The hurt in his voice matched that in his eyes.

'Don't be ridiculous, Dan,' she pleaded with him. 'You know perfectly well I didn't mean it.'

'You did, and I can't really blame you either. It's true, I have pulled you down.' He was off down the stairs too fast for Fifi even to attempt to stop him.

'Come back, Dan,' she yelled, but the front door slammed and he was gone.

The shock was so great that she just stood on the landing like a statue. She couldn't believe it. She half expected him to come back in after a few moments and say it was a joke.

He surely couldn't leave her over something as petty as a letter. Could he?

As the minutes ticked by and he didn't re-appear, she realized he was deadly serious. It wasn't just that cruel and thoughtless remark, she knew that. It had been building throughout the strain of the past weeks. Her mother's visit, the letter, the way she treated him last night had all joined together in his head, and her angry words had just topped it off.

She collapsed on to the bed, crying. She could be strong as long as he was by her side, loving her, but without him she would fall apart.

Chapter fourteen

On Monday morning Fifi dragged herself reluctantly out of bed. She had spent the whole weekend alternately crying or looking out of the window in the hope that she'd suddenly see Dan coming down the street, and that everything would be all right again.

But by Sunday night she realized he wasn't going to come back, and all there was left was the post mortem, apportioning blame for all the incidents that led up to him walking out. She felt she was responsible for almost all of them.

The thought of going back to work today filled her with dread. The other girls were bound to question her about the miscarriage, and maybe about Angela's death if they'd read about Fifi's role in the papers. She couldn't talk to them about all that without revealing Dan had left her. If only she hadn't been so smug in the past about her happy marriage! It was always '*Dan does this*, or *Dan does that*,' as if he was Mr Perfect Husband.

She'd never admitted that her parents disapproved of him, or that their home was just two rooms in a seedy backstreet either, so how would she be able to explain why it had all gone wrong?

If she knew where Dan had gone, she'd have run to him yesterday and pleaded with him to come home. But she didn't know and had no idea where to look. He talked about the men he worked with often, but it was all about what they were like, their funny habits or interests, jokes they'd told him. He'd never said, 'Owen lives in So and So', or 'Jack comes up on the train from Catford.' Even if he had, what use would that be? London was a huge place, and she didn't even know his workmates' surnames.

It was tempting to skip work today and go down to the building site in Stockwell. But it wouldn't look good if she didn't turn up at work after having so much time off, and she'd need the job even more if Dan never came back. Besides, Dan had always insisted she wasn't to go to the site, he said it was no place for women. She guessed he would be even crosser with her if she showed him up in front of his friends and his boss.

All she could do was post the letter she'd written to him last night, and hope that by the time he got it tomorrow morning, he'd be missing her so much that he'd come straight back.

'Good to see you back, Mrs Reynolds,' Mr Unwin said as he came into the office and saw her at her desk. 'I hope you are fully recovered.'

Fifi thought Mr Unwin was a rarity in the legal world, genuinely kind and considerate to his staff, so very different to some of the brusque and heartless solicitors in the Bristol office. He was an ugly man, tall and thin, with a beak-like nose and very big prominent teeth, yet surprisingly he had a very beautiful blonde wife who appeared to adore him.

'Yes thank you, sir,' she replied, wondering how many more people would ask her that today, and how long she could keep up pretending she was fine.

Mr Unwin asked Beryl, the office junior, to bring him some coffee and then turned to Fifi again.

'Would you like to come in now for some dictation, Mrs Reynolds? I won't work you too hard today,' he said with a smile. 'I've got two letters I must get out, but once you've done those you can do some copy-typing or filing for the rest of the day.'

By lunchtime Fifi's arm and fingers were aching, but at least that gave her a good excuse for being less than vibrant. Some of the girls asked her to join them for lunch, clearly wanting to hear about everything, but she made the excuse she had some shopping to do, and went down to her favourite place by the Thames so she could think things through.

It was a warm but dull day, and the river looked grey and sluggish, just the way she felt inside. She remembered how joyful she'd been the first time she came to this spot. She'd been so excited to be by the famous river, to see all those landmarks like the Houses of Parliament and the dome of St Paul's Cathedral. She had really believed then that she and Dan would be together for ever, whatever life threw at them.

But without him, London had no romance, no excitement, it was just a huge, sprawling city that some people claimed was the loneliest place in the world.

She already felt unbearably lonely. Dan had once said teasingly that she didn't have any real friends in London, only acquaintances, and she'd find out the difference when she was in trouble. She'd been indignant at the time, running through about a dozen people she'd met since they'd come to London whom she classed as friends, and swore she knew they'd lend her money, give her a bed for the night or anything else she needed.

Yet now, when all she needed was a shoulder to cry on, someone who would listen and care, she couldn't think of anyone who would fit that bill. Yvette, Miss Diamond, Stan,

Frank, they'd all kind of distanced themselves from her recently. So she guessed Dan was right, they weren't real friends. Patty was the only person she knew she could rely on – she'd catch the next train up to London if Fifi called her. But she wasn't going to call her. If she did, her mother would know she'd won.

In her letter to Dan she'd explained that if he hadn't taken that letter to work with him, she would have read it, destroyed it and then written back to her mother to say they either came together for a visit or not at all. She had said that he did come first, she'd got along without her family for this long, and she could manage without them for ever if necessary. But she could not manage without him.

Fifi was bone-weary as she walked home from the tube station that evening. A full day back at work, after doing nothing for so long, had proved exhausting.

She stopped at the corner shop to get some bread. Mrs Witherspoon, the shopkeeper, was deep in conversation with Eva Price, the red-headed divorcee, but both women turned as Fifi walked in.

'Carry on if you were talking about me,' Fifi said sarcastically, thinking they'd heard Dan had left her.

'We weren't talking about you, dear,' Mrs Witherspoon said. 'We were just wondering what more could happen in this street.'

It was the tone of the shopkeeper's voice that jerked Fifi out of her own problems. Normally it was low, almost conspiratorial, possibly because Mrs Witherspoon spent a large portion of her day receiving and passing on gossip, but now it was shrill and frightened.

'We can't blame Alfie for this one, not when he's under

lock and key,' said Eva, looking even more troubled than Mrs Witherspoon.

'What's happened?' Fifi asked.

'You haven't heard?' Mrs Witherspoon asked. 'The police have been up and down the street all day!'

'I went back to work today,' Fifi said. 'I was just going home. It's not something to do with Dan, is it?'

'No, love. It's John Bolton. He's dead. They found his body in the river early this morning,' Eva said with a heavy sigh. 'Not an accident either. They've started a murder enquiry.'

Dan walking out had driven all the thoughts about the man in the Jaguar and John Bolton out of Fifi's mind. But this shocking piece of news brought them right back. 'No!' she exclaimed, suddenly feeling quite faint.

'Vera came in here for her fags this morning,' Mrs Witherspoon said, leaning her hefty bosom on the counter. 'She was going on about him staying out all night, said when he came home she'd be ready with the rolling pin. It were only a couple of hours later the police came. Soon as I saw the car I guessed something had happened to John. Poor Vera, there's some around here that's got no sympathy for her cos John was a villain, but to me she's just a woman who's lost her old man. I feel real sorry for her.'

'How awful for her,' Fifi said weakly. She could well imagine how she would feel if the police came to tell her Dan was dead. 'Have they got any idea who did it?'

'Don't think so,' Eva replied. 'They've been asking lots of questions, but John weren't the kind to talk about his business.'

'Some folk are saying his "business" was protection rackets,' Mrs Witherspoon said, her eyes glinting. 'If it were, then he deserves what he got. But it's poor Vera I'm worried about, she'll be beside herself.'

It was too much for Fifi. Suddenly she couldn't stay in the shop a moment longer. She put the money for the bread down on the counter, excused herself and rushed off.

As she opened the front door, Frank saw her from his kitchen.

'How did you get on at work?' he called out.

'Fine, thank you,' she said, wanting to get upstairs immediately because she felt so panicky.

'Have you heard about John Bolton?' he asked, and came down the passage towards her.

Fifi's heart sank. She couldn't be rude and rush away. 'Yes, just. Mrs Witherspoon told me. It's awful, isn't it? As if there hasn't been enough misery in this street already.'

'Common sense tells me it can't have anything to do with Angela's death.' Frank shook his head sadly. 'But what are the chances of two people living in the same street being killed within weeks of each other, without there being a connection?'

'There was a connection. John played cards at the Muckles',' Fifi said a little sharply.

'Yeah, but that's not much of one, and he certainly weren't there at the last game,' Frank said thoughtfully. 'Of course, he might have been able to finger the blokes that were there. Maybe they were afraid he'd blow the whistle on them?'

She couldn't continue talking to Frank, her legs felt as if they were about to give way. 'I'm really tired. I must go on up and see to the tea,' she said.

'You all right, love?' Frank asked, taking a step closer. 'You're as white as a sheet.'

'I just need to sit down and put my feet up,' she said, trying to smile.

'You make Dan go and get you fish and chips tonight,' he said, patting her paternally on the shoulder. 'And tuck yerself up in bed nice and early.'

Fifi felt even sicker then. Obviously Frank didn't realize Dan had gone. She certainly couldn't bring herself to tell him, not now when she felt so wobbly and tearful.

While Fifi was talking to Frank, Nora Diamond was in the bathroom rinsing out her stockings and she heard what was said. She quickly went into her living room and shut the door before Fifi came up the stairs because she couldn't face her.

She hung her stockings over the back of a chair to dry, then poured herself a large gin and tonic. She had already taken off her office suit and her girdle, and put on her housecoat, just as she did every evening when she got home from work. Normally she only had a small gin and sat down to watch the news before making her dinner, but tonight she needed a large one to steady her nerves.

Nora had heard the argument between Dan and Fifi on Saturday. She had been cleaning her living room with the door open. When Dan went rushing down the stairs she looked out of the window and saw him hurrying up the street with a bag over his shoulder.

Nora heard Fifi crying several times over the weekend. Her heart kept telling her to go up there and offer some comfort, but her head told her it was none of her business and that if Fifi needed help or someone to talk to, she'd call on her.

This morning Nora had watched Fifi from the window as she went off to work. She had looked elegant in a checked blue jacket, tight skirt and high-heeled shoes, her shiny blonde hair bouncing on her shoulders. The sight brought back memories of when her own heart was broken, yet she'd still done her face and hair and marched out to meet the world head on.

Nora liked both Dan and Fifi, so she didn't want to apportion blame to either of them. Whatever the causes of the breakup, it was a terrible shame. They'd been so good together.

But it wasn't Fifi and Dan's problems that bothered her tonight. It was John Bolton's death.

Mrs Witherspoon was better than the BBC at broadcasting trouble and disaster. Nora had only gone into the shop for a quarter of tea on her way home, and was immediately regaled with the news.

She was deeply shocked and horrified, but she had to control her emotions and react in the way Mrs Witherspoon expected of snooty Miss Diamond, a woman who was as unyielding and cold as her namesake.

In twelve years of living in Dale Street, Nora had learned that when her neighbours were puzzled by someone new, in the absence of fact, they invented something which suited them. Yvette was rumoured to have been a member of the French Resistance, Stan was sometimes a Polish war hero, but more often an illegal immigrant. When Fifi first appeared it was said she was a model, though this rumour soon died as Fifi candidly told the truth about herself.

Nora had been amused when she discovered that she was supposed to be a doctor who had been struck off. She could only imagine this was because in her first week here she'd given first aid to a man who had been knocked down by a car. In fact her limited medical knowledge had been gained during the war, when she was a volunteer nurse's aide in a hospital in Dorset.

She had chosen not to dispel this myth, however, because it proved to be a good smokescreen.

John Bolton was the only person who knew the truth about her. He had helped her when she had absolutely no one else to turn to, but by mutual agreement they had never revealed their connections with one another. Even Vera, his wife, knew nothing of it.

Nora sat back in her chair and closed her eyes. She never normally dwelt on the past. But John was dead, by tomorrow or the next day the newspapers would be digging up his lurid history, and she felt it only right to spend this evening recalling what he was like as a young man. He'd been compassionate and courageous then, a man whose looks, wit and intelligence could have taken him right to the top. Sadly he chose to become enmeshed in the criminal world, but even that hadn't stopped her feeling gratitude and affection for him.

She was thirty-one when she met him. It was 1950, shortly after Reggie had run out on her. She had reverted to her maiden name of Amy Tuckett, because she wanted to forget she had ever been Mrs Reggie Soames.

A friend in Plymouth had put her in touch with the owner of the Starlight nightclub in Soho. He was looking for a mature and classy woman to act as his manageress, and her friend thought she'd be perfect for the job. John was the head barman at the club.

Despite everything Reggie had put her through, she was still a head-turner in those days. She was overweight now, and she dyed her hair to cover up the grey, but back then it was a rich glossy auburn, and she had a perfect figure. People used to say she looked like Ava Gardner, and she copied the film star's famous hairstyle, swept back at one side with a cascade of waves down to her shoulders on the other.

Even in 1950, long before Soho became synonymous with vice and stripclubs, it still had a hardcore of criminal activity. But to Nora, who had spent almost all her life in Dorset, it was an exciting, sophisticated place and it was some weeks before she became aware of its seedier undertones. The club in Greek Street was elegantly appointed, with a clientele of aristocrats and very wealthy people. Her job was to greet them and make sure they had a good time, and to supervise twenty hostesses who kept the unattached men company for the evening.

Nora loved the job and took a pride in it. The hostesses got a fee for their entertainment services, and Nora got a proportion of each one. She went out of her way to know a little about all her girls, advised them on clothes, hair and makeup, and did her best to match the right girl with the right man. She was fair too, never singling out favourites who got all the work when the club was quiet, as she heard they did in other clubs. There was a rule that no hostess should go home with a customer, for the club could be closed down if it became a front for prostitution, and Nora was vigilant about this.

Released at last from all the anxiety and heartache Reggie had caused her, and earning around fifty pounds a week when as a secretary she would have been lucky to earn ten, her new life was good. Each night she met interesting, charming people, and she found a small, comfortable flat just a short walk from the club.

All the girls were half in love with John Bolton, the head barman. It wasn't just that he was only twenty-five, lean and handsome, while most of the regulars in the club were portly and well past forty, but he had an irrepressible sense of humour and great charm.

Just his looks were enough, for he had magnetic dark blue eyes, black hair and smooth olive skin. On Nora's first night he slipped her a double whisky with a wink, understanding she was nervous. It was he who told her which were the valuable punters and which ones were troublemakers. He also told her which girls needed encouragement, and the ones who were likely to give her grief.

For six months Nora was supremely happy. She stopped dwelling on her trust funds that had been plundered, the disgrace and shame Reggie had put her through. Sometimes she even felt strangely grateful, for she now had a far more fulfilling, glamorous life, and total independence.

But then one night three men came into the club. Big, tough-looking men with rough voices and faces that had clearly been moulded by fists, but wearing hand-tailored suits and gold watches. Such men were commonplace in Soho. They lived on the profits of vice, villainy or thuggery, but they were always big spenders, and usually behaved impeccably when they came to the Starlight.

These three men hadn't come for an evening's entertainment, however, they'd come to see her. They demanded to know where Reggie was, saying he owed them £15,000 for gambling debts, and they showed her an IOU signed by him.

Of course she told them that he'd robbed her and run out on her and that she had no idea where he was. But they said that as his wife, she would have to pay.

She just shrugged it off, told them it was nothing to do with her, and that she couldn't possibly be held responsible. When they left quietly, she assumed they'd accepted what she'd said.

But the following night, she'd just got into her flat in the early hours of the morning when the doorbell rang. She opened it, thinking it was the woman who lived above her, and there were the men again.

They pushed her aside and barged in, one holding her

back so she couldn't phone the police. They turned the whole flat upside down, pulling out drawers, going through the wardrobe, even the bookcase, and when they found nothing but £20 in her purse, they threatened her.

One of the men held her arms behind her back, while the leader, whom they called 'Earl', ran a knife menacingly down her cheek.

'You are a good-looking woman, and I expect you want to stay that way. So pay us and you can.'

She was terrified, instinctively knowing by the cruelty in his cold blue eyes that he'd enjoy scarring her for life. She cried and told them again and again that she had nothing but what she earned at the club. He said that for the time being he would settle for £50 a week, and he would be round to the club every Friday night to collect it. As the men left, taking the money from her purse with them, Earl turned at the door and smirked menacingly.

'Don't even think about going to the police or you'll find yourself waking up in hospital with your face rearranged. And don't try and run for it either. We'll soon track you down and make you regret it.'

Nora guessed that they had found out about her wealthy background and didn't believe that Reggie had taken everything. She realized, too, that if she'd taken an ordinary job in an office or shop, she would never have come to their notice. But by taking a position in a Soho nightclub, she might just as well have advertised herself in the national newspapers.

She didn't dare go to the police for fear of the men carrying out their threat, but she couldn't leave her flat and job either. For five weeks she paid them, each time pleading that she couldn't continue to do so as that was all she earned.

She was sick with fear and anxiety, she couldn't sleep or eat, and the few pounds she had tucked away for a rainy day were soon eaten up in living expenses.

But on the sixth Friday, Earl said that in future they wanted £100 every week, because at the rate she was paying it back she'd be on her old age pension before the debt was cleared.

She pleaded with him, insisted there was no possible way she could give him that much. But Earl just laughed at her.

'You're sitting on a gold mine,' he said with a sneer. 'You might be knocking on a bit, but there's blokes who'd pay thirty or forty quid to fuck you. So do it and stop snivelling. Next week we want a ton.'

John came over to her after they'd left the club. 'What's going on, darlin'?' he asked.

'Nothing,' she said, trying to smile, but she was so scared she was shaking.

'I know that crew,' he said, his usual wide grin disappearing. 'What have they got on you?'

She fobbed him off with a quip about one of them asking her for a date and getting nasty when she refused, but John wasn't easy to fool, and she felt him looking speculatively at her whenever she was sharp with one of the girls or a customer.

The following Friday night she was a bag of nerves. She didn't even have £50 to give them as she'd had to pay a month's rent.

They came in at nine, before the club got busy, went straight over to a table on the far side of the bar and beckoned to her. She was so scared of Earl that she could hardly manage to tell him that all she had for him was £40.

'You ain't listened to a word I said,' Earl said contemptuously. 'I don't like that. So get hustling, doll! You owe me and I'll be back to get it.'

She could barely walk out to the staff restroom, she was trembling so badly, and once in there she was violently sick. A couple of her girls came in and saw her, but she managed to tell them she must have got food poisoning.

She was still hanging over the toilet bowl when she heard John come up behind her.

'I never saw food poisoning come on just through talking to a rat,' he said, but he wasn't mocking her, his tone was kindly and anxious.

She had to tell him all about it, and he got a wet cloth and wiped her face, then hugged her and let her cry on his shoulder.

'I wish I could tell you they won't carry out their threat,' he said in a low voice. 'But I'm afraid they will. You see, it's not them your old man owed the money to, it's their boss. And they're as afraid of him as you are of them, so they have to get a result.'

'What can I do then?' she cried, realizing that John must know who their boss was. 'I can't get the money, I can't go to the police, and they'll track me down wherever I go! I can't live in fear like this.'

'I'll hide you,' he said. 'You'll have to leave the job and your flat. There's no way I can protect you while you're still around here. Now, do exactly as I tell you and you'll be okay.'

John's plan was that she had to go back into the club and act as if everything was normal. He said he expected they'd posted a lookout to make sure she didn't run for it. Meanwhile he'd work out a plan and tip her the wink when it was time to go.

Nora was on tenterhooks all night. The club was packed to capacity, every one of her girls dancing and drinking with customers, and as she mingled, checking that the bigger groups had enough drinks, smiling and chatting, making sure everyone was happy, she felt she was being watched closely. She was familiar enough with Soho by then to know that a powerful man who employed enforcers would also have informers and spies, and if John helped her, he'd be in the firing line next.

But John didn't come near her again, and by two in the morning when the band was close to ending their final set, she thought he must have had second thoughts about helping her. She was just chasing up a round of drinks for one of the bigger tables when Charles Lownes, a regular at the Starlight, came up and asked her to dance.

Charles was a bit of a joke in the club as he had the bearing and accent of an old Etonian. He always wore a dinner jacket, pleated-front dress shirt and bow tie. He was in his early sixties, and knocked back whisky as if he had hollow legs. Everyone assumed his wealth was inherited as he was usually one of the last to leave the club when it closed, and always seemed to be going off on little jaunts to Paris and the South of France, usually with a woman half his age.

Nora didn't often dance with customers, especially at the end of the evening when they were drunk, and she hesitated.

'Come on, my dear,' he said, leaning closer to her. 'John asked me to take care of you, and the only way I can do it is if you act as if you think I'm the answer to a maiden's prayer.'

Nora glanced over her shoulder. John was mixing a cocktail, and he looked right at her and winked, then looked away.

Charles was a good dancer, light on his feet, and as usual none the worse for the amount of drink he'd put away.

'Trust me,' he whispered in her ear. 'Whatever I say or do, go along with it.'

He kept up a show of trying to woo her right until the club closed, then said in a voice loud enough for everyone around them to hear that he was taking her somewhere for a nightcap. Nora thought this was because if the thugs saw her go with him they'd assume she'd taken their advice, and they'd be round in the morning to collect her earnings.

John was nowhere to be seen as she and Charles left the club. Duncan, one of the other barmen, had been left to lock up.

Outside in the street the night air was clean and crisp after the smoky atmosphere in the club, but there were still a great many people about, many of them staggering drunk. A cab was waiting for them, and Charles helped her in. Nora glanced out through the back window but couldn't see anyone watching them.

'Wimpole Street,' Charles told the driver, and as the cab moved away he sat back on the seat and put one finger on her lips as if warning her not to say anything about her predicament, for the driver might hear.

It transpired that Charles did live in Wimpole Street, but although he got the cab to drop them there, the minute the cab drove off he led her away. He took her to a mews at the back of neighbouring Harley Street, to a small flat above what had once been stables.

The flat was clean but very austere, the furniture nothing more than a bed, a couple of armchairs and a stove in the kitchen. Charles said it belonged to a friend who normally kept it for his domestic staff, but this friend was out of the country and had asked Charles to oversee some urgently needed repairs. Apologizing for the lack of comforts, he said he would be back in the morning with some food, but warned her she must not go out, answer the door to anyone or put the light on in the room at the front.

She spent over two weeks in that flat, nearly going out of her mind with boredom and loneliness. Charles came most mornings with food, a book or a magazine, and he also brought some toiletries and clothes as the sequined cocktail dress and high-heeled shoes she'd arrived in were incongruous in her new surroundings. He could never stay for more than a few minutes, and if he knew what was going on at the club in her absence he didn't tell her.

She was scared too. She would jump at any sudden noise, and with every car that drove into the mews she fully expected Earl and his men to be coming to get her.

On the twelfth day, Charles brought her a newspaper to read.

'Look on the third page,' he said with an impish grin.

The headline was 'Missing Hostess Abducted'. There was also a photograph of her, taken in the Starlight club.

She read with some amusement that on the night Charles brought her here, her neighbours reported they had heard her coming in around two-thirty in the morning, and some while later heard the sound of her door being forced, male voices shouting and furniture being knocked over and broken. When they looked out of their own front door, they saw two men half-dragging an injured person down the stairs who they assumed was Amy Tuckett.

Charles went on to tell her that he and John now knew that the man behind the bully boys was a man called Jack Trueman. Nora recalled meeting him just once in her first week at the Starlight, a big man with dark hair, strong, craggy features and cold eyes. One of the girls had told her he owned several clubs, casinos and the kind of hotels in Paddington that were used by prostitutes. Even she said he was a man to steer clear of.

John turned up later that day and told her Amy Tuckett

had got to stay missing. It was he who fabricated Nora Diamond, with false references and a National Insurance number. He jokingly called her 'the woman who never was', but cautioned her that if she ever broke her cover, she would be in very real danger. He said Jack Trueman was entirely ruthless, and he made sure that anyone who crossed him came to regret it bitterly.

The Ava Gardner hairstyle and the glamour-girl clothes had to go. Nora dyed her hair dark brown and put it up in an unflattering bun. Charles bought her a matronly navy blue costume and sturdy court shoes, and the transformation was complete. She became the formidable and very correct Miss Diamond.

Then, finally, she was able to walk out of that mews flat door, when John sent her to the vacant flat in Dale Street.

He knew it had become empty because he lived with his parents and two sisters at number 13. He thought it an ideal place because he could continue to keep a discreet eye out for her. At the same time he couldn't intervene on her behalf with Mr Capel, the landlord, because he didn't want anyone to know he had any connection with her. She told Mr Capel she'd just come up from Sussex to find work in London.

From the day Nora moved into Dale Street, if she ran into John they would just nod and smile like strangers. It was the only way it could be, but she would have given anything for his continuing friendship. She hated Kennington, the flat was awful, and at that time she had no money to decorate or make improvements, but it did feel safe with Frank downstairs, and a newly married couple upstairs.

John had managed to pack a few of her personal trinkets while he was waiting for the men to barge in and hurt her, but however touched she was that he'd done that for her, in reality she'd lost everything for a second time.

This time she had to begin again, finding a job without relying on her looks to give her a headstart. She would also always be looking over her shoulder, afraid of being recognized.

She had felt very alone when she first came to London, but there were people back in Dorset, friends, distant relatives and acquaintances, she cared about, and who presumably cared about her. But once Amy was gone, Nora could never contact any of them again. She cried as she burned her address book, for without her history, who was she?

Soon afterwards she got a job at the telephone exchange, and before long she was promoted to supervisor, in charge of eighteen young telephonists. In some ways it was very similar to her job in the club, except she was no longer a glamorous figure and she couldn't afford to let anyone get close to her for fear of revealing her true identity.

Nora had never lost her affection for John, despite her disappointment that he allowed himself to get sucked into crime. Even before he met and married Vera, and bought number 13 from his landlord, his name was linked with some of the most formidable and crooked businessmen she'd met in her Soho days. There was Peter Rachman, an unscrupulous slum landlord who charged sky-high rents to naive and frightened West Indian immigrants, Ronald Beasdale who was in illegal gambling, and Albert Parkin who ran protection rackets.

It was two years ago that she discovered John had become involved with Jack Trueman. There was an article in the paper about the new nightclub Trueman had opened in Soho, and a picture of the club's interior showing John as the manager behind the bar.

Nora knew John was smart enough to have concealed his identity that night in her flat when he'd thrashed Earl and his men. She knew too that he would never expose her either. But she was appalled to think John would go to work for such a man as Trueman. How could a man who had once risked his own life to help a vulnerable woman join forces with the thug who was responsible?

Yet looking at it realistically, she knew that John couldn't possibly have remained the same as he'd been a decade before. He had always wanted the 'good life', and he'd taken short cuts to get it. Everyone described him as a villain or a gangster, he'd been in prison, and probably done many bad things which had eroded his idealism. She naively hoped that he'd taken the club management job because he was trying to go straight; she knew it wouldn't be easy for a man who'd done time to find work.

That was certainly the way it looked. Almost every evening she saw him come out of number 13, wearing a dinner jacket and bow tie, and his car was back in the morning. She even heard the street gossip that Vera was happy again because he was home with her more – she'd had a miserable time while he was in prison.

Then one Friday evening over a year ago, she saw John and Jack Trueman going into number 11, with Alfie grinning at the door like a Cheshire cat.

The passing years hadn't changed Trueman that much, though his hair was silver rather than dark. She guessed he must be close to sixty, but he looked far younger and still very fit.

She didn't know which she was most shocked and appalled by, the thought of John consorting with a maggot like Alfie, or seeing the man she'd been told would maim her if he found her, right across the street. Terrified, she drew her curtains, locked the door and sat quaking in her chair, fully expecting the door to burst open any minute.

Yet by the following morning she was calm again. Clearly there was a good reason why John had brought Trueman to meet Alfie, and it had nothing whatsoever to do with her. She told herself that businessmen operating in Soho often had nasty characters like Alfie in their pay, and as John had grown up here in Dale Street and known Alfie all his life, perhaps he thought he could be useful to his boss.

She never saw John go into number 11 again after that night, but she had seen Jack Trueman several times, often in the company of a younger, swarthy man who was equally well dressed. She came to the conclusion that perhaps the men didn't mind slumming it if the stakes were high there or the card games were exciting. She wasn't at all happy about Trueman coming to the street, of course, every Friday night she was a bag of nerves, but it did spur her on to put her name down with several flat-letting agencies, and she hoped she'd be able to leave very soon.

To her shame she remembered feeling nothing but relief when she heard that the Muckles had been arrested. Not anger at what they'd done to their child, not even a tear for Angela, just relief because Trueman wouldn't be coming to the street ever again.

But now John was dead, and as Frank had pointed out earlier to Fifi, it was unlikely to be pure coincidence that two people from the same street had been murdered. Nora felt that something more than gambling must have been going on in number 11, and almost certainly John was killed because he intended to expose it.

She knew that she ought to go to the police right now and tell them about Jack Trueman, but they would ask why she hadn't come forward before. When she was interviewed after Angela's death she'd been asked if she knew or could describe anyone who attended the card games, but she'd told them quite brusquely that she wasn't in the habit of watching out of her window. To backtrack now was impossible. She couldn't name Trueman without explaining how she knew him and that would mean exposing her past and putting herself in danger.

She walked over to the window and looked out. There was a police car outside number 13. 'Poor Vera,' she murmured and her eyes welled up with tears of sympathy.

Frank spent the early part of the evening cleaning his kitchen and tidying cupboards, and only went into his living room when it was dark outside. He moved over to the window to draw the curtains before turning on the light, but paused as he saw Yvette coming out of her house. To his surprise she was hand-in-hand with a man.

After all the misery and anxiety of the past weeks, and the news of John's death today, the sight cheered Frank slightly. He liked the Frenchwoman and in all the years she had lived opposite he'd never known her to have a boyfriend. It was too dark to see if she was dressed up to go somewhere special, but it looked as if she was undecided about something, for she was pulling back.

Frank smiled as the man put his arms around her. Yvette had been living like a hermit for so many years that perhaps she was reluctant to go out. But Frank drew the curtains, not wishing to seem like a nosy neighbour, and he heard the car drive off seconds later.

He turned on the lamp and television and sat down, but as he reached for his pipe he thought he might go and knock at Stan's door later and suggest they went down to the Rifleman. He'd become almost as reclusive as Yvette in the last few weeks, and it was time he stopped this.

*

The following morning Fifi left the house for work at quarter past eight. She had hardly slept at all, for images of Angela, Dan, and even John Bolton's body being pulled from the river kept crowding into her head.

It was drizzling and rather cold, and as she walked up the street she thought gloomily of the winter months ahead. The windows in the flat were ill-fitting, the gas fire was ancient and inefficient, and she guessed she'd be frozen most of the time. If Dan didn't come home when he got her letter, perhaps it would be best to try to find a bedsitter, for being miserable but warm had to be better than being miserable and cold.

She was halfway to the tube when a blue car slowed right down and cruised alongside her. There were two men in it, both in their late twenties or early thirties.

'Hey, Fifi!' the passenger called out of the window. 'You are Fifi, aren't you? Dan said you were tall, blonde and beautiful!'

Fifi's heart leaped at Dan's name. Both men looked like workmen as they were wearing donkey jackets.

'Yes, I'm Fifi,' she said, stopping and bending down slightly so she could see the men better. The driver had dark red curly hair, and she thought he must be the carpenter Dan always called 'Red'. He looked a bit hard and surly. The other man had light brown hair and no real distinguishing features; he was unshaven, but he had a nice smile. 'How is Dan?' she asked.

'It is you! Thank Christ for that,' the man in the passenger seat exclaimed. 'We called at your house but you must have just left. We've seen at least six blondes so far, and two of them gave us a mouthful when we called out. I think they thought we were kerb crawlers. You see, Dan asked us to come and get you. He's been taken ill.'

Fifi was instantly thrown into a panic. 'What's wrong with him? Where is he?' she asked.

The passenger got out of the car and pulled his seat forward to let her get in the back. 'Hop in and we'll explain as we drive you there,' he said.

The rush-hour traffic was heavy, but the driver turned right off Kennington Road past the Imperial War Museum towards Camberwell.

The brown-haired passenger introduced himself as Martin, and the red-headed driver as Del.

'Some of us went out to do some work on Sunday for the boss,' Martin said, turning in his seat to speak to Fifi. 'It's out Eltham way. Your Dan weren't himself at all, but then he'd had a lot to drink on Saturday night. But come the evening he were worse and the boss said he'd better stay the night. Anyways, he weren't any better yesterday and couldn't go into work. The boss said he kept asking for you during the night, so he told us to come and get you and take you out there.'

Fifi was very alarmed. Dan was never ill, and he was also far too independent to dump himself on anyone, especially someone like his boss. He had to be seriously ill.

'Oh, my God,' she exclaimed. 'What is it?'

Martin shrugged. 'The boss said he had a kind of fever, high temperature and that. He's too weak to get up.'

'Did the boss call a doctor?' she asked.

'I dunno, but I expect so,' Martin said. 'He only called us and told us to get you.'

Fifi had no idea where Eltham was, what it was like or how far it was. But as she asked more questions about Dan and received only very brief, occasionally rather curt answers, she got the impression the men were a bit cross at being expected to act as a taxi.

On top of her anxiety about Dan, she was worried about not turning up at work too. It would look bad after only one day back. But Dan was her main concern, and she wondered if he could've slept rough on Saturday night and caught a chill. It had been wet and cold after all, and if he'd got very drunk he wouldn't have noticed. Suppose he'd got pneumonia?

'I thought Arnie lived in Essex,' she said, suddenly remembering something Dan had told her.

'Who?' Martin asked without looking round.

'The boss,' she said.

'Oh, he's not the top man,' Martin said airily. 'He's just the site manager. Ken's the real boss, but he don't come down the site that much, he's more on the planning side.'

'Oh, I see,' Fifi said, and lapsed into silence again.

They passed through New Cross and Lewisham, places she'd heard of but never been to.

'Are we nearly there now?' she asked as she saw they had left behind the Victorian terraces of Lewisham and were in a wider, more pleasant road with many trees and some newly built houses.

'Yeah, nearly,' Del the driver said.

All at once they were driving along a dual carriageway in semi-countryside. There were houses, semi-detached ones built probably in the thirties or forties, with attractive gardens, but fields behind them. It was the kind of area she expected a building-site boss to live in. It reminded her of Henbury back in Bristol.

All at once they turned off the wide road into a smaller one, then into a very narrow lane, with hedges on either side so she couldn't see where they were going.

It was only then that Fifi felt a twinge of unease. She

didn't know where she was, she had very little money on her, and she'd never met either of these men before today. Perhaps she shouldn't have got into the car quite so readily?

But she dismissed these thoughts as ridiculous. Of course they were taking her to Dan, why else would they come looking for her? It was wonderful that Dan wanted her with him, and once she got to his boss's house she'd be able to telephone the office and explain.

The lane was very muddy and went steeply uphill. Fifi sat forward in her seat, expecting to see a house at the end of it. But as they reached the top, all at once they were in a wide open space which went on for miles. All she could see was a big barn and a few sheds.

'Where's the house?' she asked. The rain was heavy now, drumming on the car roof, so perhaps this was why the barn looked so sinister and remote.

'Oh, the house!' Martin exclaimed. 'It's behind the barn, you can't see it from here.'

Fifi noticed he had a hard edge to his voice and she didn't like his furtive glance at Del.

Her heart plummeted as she realized she had been conned. The whole thing about Dan being sick was just a ruse to get her out here. Why, she didn't know, but she felt it was most definitely the kind of danger Yvette had warned her of.

Common sense told her she mustn't show she suspected anything. She must play along with them, and as soon as they let her out of the car she'd make a run for it.

But as Martin opened the car door, she looked down at her shoes. They were her favourite ones, with very pointed toes but comfortable, the heels only a couple of inches. She wouldn't be able to run in them, though, not on rough ground. Her skirt was tight too; they'd catch her in no time.

'Out you come then,' Martin said as he pulled forward his seat to let her out and held out his hand to her.

Del got out on his side, and skirting round the back of the car, he grabbed Fifi's free arm, making flight impossible anyway.

Just the way they held her proved her fears were completely justified. 'Dan's not here, is he?' she said bleakly. 'What's this about?'

'Don't you ever stop asking questions?' Martin said impatiently, not even looking at her. 'Come on or we'll get soaked.'

She tried to pull herself free, but they were holding her too tightly, and they frogmarched her towards the barn.

Fifi struggled, and looked around her desperately. It was just on nine in the morning, but there was no one in sight. Not a man with a dog, a farmer driving a tractor, no one. She couldn't see any house. There was a wood to her right, which possibly had a house beyond it, but nothing else, just acres and acres of stubble from wheat or barley that had recently been harvested.

The sheds and barn were robust-looking constructions. The barn was built of some kind of metal and on the door were two hefty chains and huge padlocks. She was really scared now; she could hear her own heart pounding and her stomach was churning. Martin held her tightly while Del unlocked the barn door.

'Please tell me what this is all about,' she pleaded with them. 'I haven't done anything to you. Why should you want to hurt me? Where is Dan? Why are you doing this?'

'Shut up, can't you?' Del said as he opened the big door,

then grabbed her right arm again. The barn was empty but for a couple of bales of straw, and she dug her heels in, refusing to walk until they told her what was going on.

They looked rattled, but they just caught her arms and dragged her across the straw-strewn floor towards what looked like a kind of big cage. 'This is where you'll stay until the boss decides what's got to be done with you,' Del informed her, and opening the door to it, pushed her through and locked it. 'Shout all you like, there's no one around to hear you. We'll be back later.'

'Don't go yet,' she pleaded with them, going up to the bars and holding on to them because her legs felt as if they would give way. 'Just tell me why. What have I done?' she asked, and tears ran down her cheeks.

She saw no sympathy in Del's face, just the desire to get back in the car and go. But Martin looked uncomfortable.

'There's some water and a blanket.' He pointed to the corner of the cage.

'Don't do this,' she cried out. 'My parents will lean on the police once they know I'm missing. I work for a solicitor, I'm not someone that can just vanish without anyone worrying!'

'You talk too much,' Del replied, looking at her dispassionately. 'Come on, Mart. Let's go.'

She screamed then, so loud she felt she could be heard for miles around. But it made no difference to them. They walked off, slamming the barn door behind them, and she heard the clank of the chain as they locked the padlock.

A few seconds later she heard the car drive off.

She didn't scream any more, she knew only too well there was no one to hear, and if she kept quiet, if someone did come by she'd hear them. But she couldn't stop herself crying, or cursing herself for the stupidity of getting into a car with people she didn't know.

By ten o'clock Fifi had gone right round the cage inspecting it, but found no weak spot in the bars or any implement which might help to free her. She thought the cage had been made for securing valuable merchandise, perhaps spirits, in a warehouse. It was constructed of steel, with a slightly raised wooden floor, and far too tough to break or bend. It was some ten feet square, and there were track marks to it from the barn door, which suggested a forklift had been used to place it here. It couldn't have been here long either, for there were no spider's webs or dust on it.

She had nothing remotely useful in her handbag; she'd already tried to pick the padlock with her nail file and the end had broken off. She didn't even have a book or a newspaper to pass the time with.

The barn was very big, taller than a double-decker bus, and gloomy because the only light came from horizontal narrow windows right up by the roof. There was enough space for dozens of tractors or other farm machinery, but the absence of anything, even rubbish, suggested it had been cleared out fairly recently and hadn't been used for anything since.

The mattress and the blanket on it were in good condition, dry to the touch and clean-smelling, as if they had only recently been brought here from someone's home. That at least suggested that whoever was behind her abduction wasn't entirely inhuman, but it might also mean he was intending to keep her here for some time.

Fifi sat down on the mattress and tried to think how long it would be before someone got anxious about her. At the office they wouldn't do anything. They couldn't phone her home, and as they didn't know Dan had left her, there was no reason why they'd find her absence anything more than irritating. Frank would wonder where she was when she didn't come home tonight, but it would be a couple of days before he found it worrying. Miss Diamond would be the same.

All Fifi could hope for was that Dan would get the letter she sent and go round to the flat. But he'd most likely think that she'd gone out straight from work with one of the girls from the office. Would he wait for her to come home? And if he did, might he think she was spending the night with another man?

Frank might tell him about the men calling this morning! He'd smell a rat at that, surely?

She sighed deeply as she realized they had almost certainly lied about that. If they meant her harm they wouldn't have presented themselves to a neighbour who could later identify them. They'd probably just waited in their car at the end of the road until they saw her.

However she looked at it, no one was going to be worried about her for at least two days, possibly longer. And even then, how would anyone find her? How would they know where to even start looking?

Yvette's warning kept reverberating in her head, and she had no doubt that this had something to do with her going to the police on Saturday. But how did they find out? And how did they know Dan hadn't been with her all weekend?

She mentally collated all the scraps of information she'd collected over the past weeks, and she realized that someone at Dan's work must be connected to Alfie and his card games. It was probably he who set up the attack in the alley, tipping off Alfie about what time Dan would be leaving the site. And when Dan said he'd walked out on her, this same man saw a golden opportunity to grab her.

But there were dozens of men working on the building site – any one of them could be one of Alfie Muckle's relatives or cronies. She wondered if Dan had ever talked about how she was always going on about the murder, or how she watched out of the window? She couldn't imagine him doing so, but maybe if he was growing irritated with her he had to let off steam?

But why snatch her? What possible use could she be to them? She'd already told everything she knew to the police!

As the morning slowly ticked by, Fifi became more and more frantic. People didn't get snatched or abducted for no reason, it was either to shut them up or to hold them to ransom. The latter seemed unlikely in her case; people in the street knew she was more or less estranged from her family, and they weren't rich anyway. Therefore the reason for her being here must be to shut her up.

She had to suppose John Bolton was killed because he knew too much. But what did they think she knew? Did they think she'd seen something more from her window?

Dan had often talked about the police tipping the wink to villains who had paid them. Could it be that the man in the Jaguar had been told she'd recognized him as one of the men who played cards at Alfie's?

That had to be it. Perhaps he was afraid she'd be called upon to pick him out in an identity parade.

Whatever their reasons for wanting her, there was a cold certainty about the way it would end. They'd have to kill her, for she could identify the men who had brought her here.

Just the thought of that brought her out in a cold sweat, and her heart beat faster. She wished to God she'd never gone to that council depot.

Chapter fifteen

Frank was washing up his supper things when he saw Dan come in through the front door. 'Hello, Dan,' he called out. 'First sighting of you in days. Been doing overtime?'

As Frank spoke, he left the kitchen and went down the hall towards Dan. He saw that the lad didn't look his usual glowing self. He was positively gaunt, with dark circles beneath his eyes.

'Yeah, overtime,' Dan replied, but he didn't look directly at Frank. 'Must go, things to do.'

Disappointed that Dan didn't want to chat, and a little concerned at his appearance, Frank watched him walk up the stairs, noting that he wasn't in his work clothes. Could he have lost his job and didn't want to admit it?

It was after seven and Frank hadn't seen or heard Fifi come in from work yet. She'd been behaving a bit oddly too; she hadn't gone out once at the weekend, and last night when he spoke to her about John Bolton, she barely responded.

'Maybe they're having a bad time,' he thought, going back into his kitchen to finish clearing up.

He was watching 'Z' Cars later, when there was a knock on his living-room door. 'Come in,' he called out, knowing it was Dan by the sound of his footsteps on the hall lino.

'Sorry to disturb you, Frank,' Dan said, putting his head

around the door. 'Fifi's not back yet. Did she tell you if she was going somewhere this evening?'

'No, she didn't,' Frank said. 'Come in, son, and shut the door. Didn't she leave you anything for your tea?'

'I'm not worried about that,' Dan said, coming in hesitantly. 'I just expected her to be here, that's all.'

Frank could see the lad was troubled. His eyes were dull and he had a slump to his shoulders. 'You two had a row?' Frank asked, seeing no point in being anything but direct.

Dan nodded miserably. 'I walked out on Saturday,' he admitted. 'I was so mad with her it seemed the only thing to do. I got a letter from her this morning at the site though, saying she wanted to make it up. But then I expect you know all this?'

Frank was deeply shocked. 'No, I didn't know. Fifi hasn't said a word to me,' he said. 'But it explains why everything was so quiet over the weekend. Now, don't worry about her not being here, she probably didn't expect you to come round immediately. She likely went off for a coffee and a chat after work with one of the office girls. Women do that when they're upset.'

'But she might have known I'd come straight here after I got the letter,' Dan said, his voice cracking as if struggling with his emotions.

Frank sensed Dan was close to breaking down. He looked as if he hadn't eaten or slept in days, so he told him to sit down and poured him a brandy.

'I'm going to make you something to eat,' he said firmly. 'You look all in, so you'd best have a bath and get into bed. She'll be home soon, and as I remember with June, the best way to make up is with a cuddle.'

An hour later, Frank was back in his chair watching television. He'd made Dan a quick meal of tinned stewed steak, peas and boiled potatoes, then packed him off for a bath. But it was after nine now, and Fifi still wasn't home. He couldn't help but be a bit worried himself as Fifi had often said she didn't like going out after dark without Dan. It also seemed unlikely that a coffee or cup of tea after work with someone from the office would turn into a night out.

Dan had told him what the row had been about, and said he had really thought Fifi would have a better life without him.

Frank had always been of the opinion that Fifi was like a fish out of water around here. Losing her baby, and then the trauma of Angela's death, was enough to shake the most solid of marriages. But whatever Fifi's parents thought of Dan, he was a decent, hardworking lad, and just to be with them both was to see how much they loved each other. So he gave Dan a little pep talk about all marriages having their sticky patches, and told him that he and June had blazing rows in the first couple of years they were married. 'But it's a mistake to walk out,' he informed Dan. 'You see, that leaves it all up in the air, even when you do come back and apologize. So the next time you have words, you drag all the old stuff out too. What you've got to do is talk it through properly. Fifi's been through a lot lately, you have to make allowances for that.'

They moved on to talk about other things after that and Frank told Dan about John Bolton.

'Jesus!' Dan exclaimed, his face blanching. 'That will have sent her right round the twist. No wonder she's not in, she probably thinks they'll be coming for her next.'

Frank had thought that was a daft remark at the time, but now he was sitting here on his own, his ears cocked for the sound of Fifi's key in the door, it didn't seem quite so ridiculous. People were saying that John had been killed because he knew too much about what went on at number 11. Fifi could have been spooked by that – after all, she was to be a key witness at Alfie's trial. He wondered if he ought to go upstairs and suggest Dan ring her parents in Bristol to see if she'd gone there.

'No, that'll just alarm him,' he murmured to himself. 'And Fifi wouldn't want her parents to know she and Dan were having problems.'

The darkness seemed to press in on Fifi as she lay huddled up under the blanket. She'd been doing all right until it got dark; after a spell of crying and feeling panicky and sorry for herself, she'd forced herself to climb the bars of the cage for some exercise. She felt quite proud of herself for having managed to swing hand over hand right along the top of the cage like a monkey, and she even did handstands to pass the time.

The exercise had made her more focused about all this too. She'd lain on the mattress, staring up at the rain on the barn window high above her, and carefully analysed everything she knew.

The police had never revealed any uncertainty about whether Alfie or Molly did actually kill Angela, that story had come from Johnny Milkins. Yet judging by the way they hauled in Frank and Stan, it looked as if they weren't totally convinced that the killing was down to the Muckles. Yvette's horror at Fifi playing amateur detective and her references to bad men suggested she knew something she hadn't disclosed. And just the way she spoke of it hinted that she wasn't talking only about the events of that last card game, but something which had been going on for some time.

The hideous idea that had formed in the back of Fifi's mind after speaking to Yvette on Saturday hadn't been fully erased, only put aside because of other events. But now John Bolton was dead, and she'd been abducted, it didn't look so far-fetched.

Had Alfie been allowing his card-playing friends to have sex with his daughters?

She had always wondered what possible attraction there could be for anyone spending Friday nights at number 11. In the past there had been screams, fights, loud music and raucous laughter. Weren't men who played cards for high stakes supposed to sit round a table in virtual silence?

Now she had aired that blackest of suggestions in her mind, the more she thought about it, the more certain she became.

Molly was a blackmailing slut, who neglected her children and allowed them to be physically abused. Alfie was completely amoral; rumour had it he'd given his older daughters children. She felt the couple were quite capable of selling or lending out their children for sex.

If it had been Alfie who raped and killed Angela, there would have been no reason for anyone else there on the Friday night to have been too frightened to come forward, for she wasn't killed until Saturday morning. In fact the vast majority of men, whatever their walk of life, would put aside all hard-held taboos about not grassing up a mate at such a heinous crime.

Yet if Angela had been passed around, and perhaps the two other Muckle girls as well, all the men were in it together, and they would be linked by an unholy bond. The ones who sat by and let it happen were as guilty as those who took part. So they'd all stick together, no one daring to break ranks. Fifi felt certain this was what had happened, but perhaps Angela was so traumatized by it that they feared she'd tell. So Alfie or Molly smothered her.

Fifi could only guess what happened after she'd been to the police with her information. Maybe they went straight to John Bolton to demand the name of the man she'd seen him with. They could have gone to the council depot and asked questions there, but either way she had no doubt it must have got back to the man with the Jaguar.

It had always seemed odd that Alfie hadn't named names, but was this only fear of reprisals? Perhaps he trusted the top man to find a way to get him off the hook for keeping his silence? Was that why Stan was put in the frame?

One thing was certain: if the Jaguar man was a villain, he was a powerful one if he could get John Bolton killed at a click of his fingers. She wondered why he hadn't got someone to make sure Alfie met with a fatal accident while in prison, as that would have been the surest way to keep his silence. And who would care? Everyone had always wanted him to be guilty and permanently out the way. But then there was Molly too! Fifi supposed two fatal accidents weren't feasible.

Working it all out in her mind did help stop Fifi from dwelling on what was going to become of her. But once daylight began to fail, and the men still didn't come back, she just fell apart.

It was so eerie and menacing in the dark. The wind was whistling around the barn, the rain drumming on the roof, and over and above that there were squeaking and rustling sounds which could only be mice or rats. She was so scared she felt she might die of fright.

Her stomach was rumbling with hunger, even though she doubted she could eat when she was so scared. She didn't dare try to sleep in case a rat ran over her. What if the men never came back? Suppose she just got weaker and weaker from hunger and thirst until she died?

It was like something from a film or a book. But people who got locked up like that always found some means of escape. She'd been over every inch of the cage, however, and there was no way out except through the door, and that was padlocked. They hadn't even left her a bucket as a toilet like they did in films; she'd had to pee in the corner of the cage and she couldn't bear the thought of how it would be when she wanted to do something more than pee.

And she couldn't wash or clean her teeth either. How could anyone do this to her?

Her anger became as strong as her fear. She hadn't done anything bad to anyone; she only went in to the Muckles' house because she was worried about Angela. She went to that depot to try to help Stan. Dan left her because she lied about what her mother said in that letter and she only did that to spare his feelings.

If she ever did get out of here, she'd make sure she looked the other way if she ever saw someone hurt or in trouble again.

Self-pity overwhelmed her, tears running down her face as she thought of the way her mother used to nag and criticize her. It was all Clara's fault; if she hadn't been so nasty about Dan they wouldn't have rushed into getting married. They wouldn't have ended up in Dale Street, and Fifi would never have known that there were people like the Muckles.

She blamed her father too. He should've stood up for her. All he did was bury his nose in the newspaper when her mother was ranting at her. He'd said he was sorry when she lost the baby, but those were just empty words if he didn't back them up with actions. Obviously he didn't love her and was glad she was out of his hair.

Then there were all those so-called friends back in Bristol!

Most of them she'd known since she was a child; they'd come to play with her, stayed to tea, even spent the night. Granted, she'd neglected them when she met Dan, but they'd done the same thing to her at times when they'd met a new man.

Why did they come round to the flat drunk that night if it wasn't just to sneer at her? Not a present, a card or even congratulations! Fine friends they turned out to be!

A sound outside stopped her silent angry tirade short. She could hear a car and see a chink of light through the barn door, which had to be headlights.

Was it the men bringing her food? Or someone else?

She screamed at the top of her voice, hoping it was the latter.

'Shut that racket,' a male voice boomed out in the darkness, and a torch was switched on.

Fifi blinked in the bright light, unable to make out who was behind it. But as it came closer, she saw that it was Del and Martin again, and they were supporting someone between them.

As they came closer, she realized by the clothes that the third person was a woman, and her head was slumped forward as if she were unconscious. 'Isn't one prisoner enough for you?' Fifi said sarcastically. 'What's she done to you?'

'Shut up or you'll get nothing to eat,' Del said sharply, and leaving Martin to hold the woman up, he came forward to unlock the cage door. 'Get over to the other side,' he ordered curtly, the beam of his torch sweeping round the cage.

As he turned to beckon Martin to bring the woman over, the torchlight passed across her face. Fifi was so stunned to see who it was that she remained rooted to the spot.

'Yvette!' she gasped.

'Get back,' Del warned her.

He came through the cage door backwards, holding Yvette under her arms and dragging her. Dumping her on the floor like a sack of potatoes, he left the cage immediately and locked the door behind him.

Fifi knelt down by Yvette. There was blood running down her cheek and she was out cold.

'What have you done to her?' she asked, looking to Martin who was standing watching her, the torch in his hand. 'Yvette wouldn't harm a fly, why hurt her?'

'She's not hurt, she's just had some knockout stuff to stop her screaming. She'll be fine when she wakes up,' he replied, his tone almost apologetic. 'Look, we brought you some food. And some more water too,' he added, pulling a bag out of his coat pocket.

Fifi didn't know whether she was more or less frightened by Yvette being brought here too. But she knew she had to hide her fear and try to make some sort of impact on these men.

'Why have you brought her here?' she asked more boldly than she felt. 'Are you going to bring in everyone from Dale Street? If you do, you might need a bigger cage.'

She was disadvantaged in every way – they were in shadow, whereas she was caught full on in the beam of the torch, and she knew she must look awful with her face blotchy from crying, and her skirt and blouse all creased up. Under the circumstances her appearance wasn't going to make a scrap of difference to how they treated her, but if she couldn't look good, she was at least going to have a stab at making herself memorable.

'Don't try and be funny,' Del said.

'Will you think I'm trying to be funny if I ask for a bucket to pee in?' she said with a wide, false smile.

'I'll get you one,' he said, turning away and walking towards the door.

Fifi was burning to examine Yvette, but being left alone with Martin was a golden opportunity to try to work on him.

Moving over to the bars, she put her hands through them. 'What did you bring me to eat?' she asked. 'I'm starving.'

He came right up to the bars. 'Just a pork pie and a cake,' he said with a rueful half-smile. 'It was all we could get.'

Fifi waited until she'd got the bag in her hand. 'Are you a child molester too?' she asked, looking hard at him. She knew she had no proof that this was what his boss was, for the conclusions she'd come to were only guesswork. But she had to say something to rattle a response from him.

He certainly didn't look or act like a would-be gangster. His light brown hair was cut into the fashionable college-boy style, and he was wearing what appeared to be a handknitted jumper under his donkey jacket. He might be brawny but she didn't think he was a cruel man; his eyes looked far too gentle.

'No, I'm bloody not,' he retorted, looking startled and puzzled by such a question.

'So why are you helping men who are?' she asked.

'Whatcha mean?' he asked, and the way the torch swayed in his hand suggested he was unnerved by her question.

Fifi thought it *was* possible he knew nothing of the murder in Dale Street if he didn't read newspapers or live in Kennington; none of the girls in the office had said anything about it. He could have been ordered to do this job without knowing what lay behind it.

'A few weeks ago a seven-year-old girl was raped and killed in Dale Street. Both Yvette and I live there, it was me who found the little girl. So whoever ordered you to bring us here is up to their neck in it, or they wouldn't want a couple of innocent women out the way. So you can't blame me for thinking you must be a nonce, if you work for one.'

She didn't know the word 'nonce' until Angela died. But since then she had heard people spit it out with utter disgust, and she knew the average man would want to tear apart, limb from limb, anyone with a leaning that way.

Martin looked at her in horror, his eyes wide and panicked. 'You've got it all wrong,' he said, gulping so hard his Adam's apple went up and down like a yo-yo.

The barn door opened and Del came back in.

'I haven't got it wrong, but I think you have,' Fifi said quietly but firmly. 'Think on it. Would your mother or your girlfriend be proud of you if they knew you worked for beasts that screw children, then kill them?'

Del was too far away to hear what she had said, but as he came into the arc of light he was scowling. 'What's she going on about now?' he asked Martin.

'I was just asking him how he came to have such a dirty job,' Fifi said airily. 'But I suppose if you're up to your neck in shit all the time, eventually you get to like the smell of it?'

'Is that supposed to be funny?' Del asked, and opening the cage door again, put a bucket in.

'Do you see me laughing?' Fifi replied and she asked Martin to shine the torch on Yvette while she knelt down beside her to examine her. To Fifi's relief, Yvette appeared to be in a deep sleep rather than unconscious from a blow, and the blood on her face was only from a scratch, not a real wound. 'Was a timid little dressmaker too much for you to handle? Is that why you've drugged her?' she asked indignantly, glowering at the two men.

343

'She'll sleep it off,' Del replied nonchalantly. 'Come on, mate, we're off,' he said to Martin.

Fifi sensed Martin was the weak link in this duo, so she looked straight at him. 'You ought to sleep on what you're doing,' she said warningly. 'Be a gangster if you like, but don't be the muscle for a murdering child molester.'

'What are you on about?' Del asked scornfully.

Fifi got to her feet and put her hands on her hips, staring impudently at the two men. She felt Del was a man who prided himself on being a hard bastard, she doubted he had a conscience. But she knew from things Dan had said that even the most cold-hearted of thugs didn't approve of child molesters.

'The man you work for is an animal that screws children and then kills them,' she said. 'If you do his dirty work for him, then you're as bad as he is.'

'You're round the bend,' Del exclaimed. He looked at Martin. 'She tell you that too?'

Martin nodded grimly, moving from foot to foot as if very uncomfortable.

'The boss said she were a lying bitch.' Del gave a humourless laugh. 'He could have told us she were mad as well!'

'I'm not mad, or a liar,' Fifi said evenly. 'I'm sane enough to see you two are being made a right pair of patsies. Can't you read? Angela Muckle's murder was in all the papers. I'm a witness because I found her. But don't take my word for it, check it out.'

'Listen, darlin',' Del said contemptuously, moving nearer to the bars. 'Shut yer gob if you know what's good for you.'

It was impossible to tell whether he knew the truth or not, as his face gave nothing away. But Fifi could see by his gorilla-like stance that he wanted to hit her; his hands were clenching into fists, and she was glad the cage bars were between them.

'Okay, but don't say you weren't warned,' she shrugged. 'I just hope you're being well paid, because you'll have to leave the country if you kill us. You see, we aren't like John Bolton, a villain no one cares about. You'll have every policeman in England on your tail, and you won't have any mates left once they find out you keep company with nonces.'

Del turned away, catching Martin by the arm. 'That's it, we're off,' he said. 'Fuckin' mad bitch.'

As they reached the barn door, Martin looked back over his shoulder. She couldn't see his face clearly enough to know whether she'd worried him or not, but the slight hesitation suggested she had.

The light went off, the door shut with a dull metallic thud, and she could hear the chain which secured it being clanked as they put the padlock on. Their car headlights beamed through the cracks around the door for a few seconds, then Fifi heard it roar away.

Her bravado vanished as soon as she was enveloped in darkness again. She sat down and shuffled on her bottom, her hands groping out in front of her for Yvette, and tears ran down her cheeks unchecked.

Dan had pointed out men like Del and Martin in the Rifleman, jokingly calling them 'London's wartime by-products'. He said that as boys of nine or ten during the war, they often weren't evacuated, and with absent fathers and often uncaring mothers they rarely went to school, spending their time marauding around London in gangs instead. These gangs became a substitute for a family as they looted bombed shops and houses or broke into homes while the owners were in the shelters. Their only code was 'Never grass, and stand by your mates'.

A couple of years of National Service honed their bully-boy tendencies still further. On their demob, with no education or qualifications, they chose a criminal life rather than manual labour. As Dan had pointed out, the fifties were a boom time for villains. The ones with sharp minds went into acquiring land and building shoddy new estates. Others opened clubs and pubs, or supplied hard-to-get luxuries. But for every entrepreneur, dozens of foot soldiers were needed to put the frighteners on, supply muscle and collect debts. The men at the top didn't dirty their hands.

Martin and Del were clearly two of those foot soldiers, and as such Fifi couldn't hold out much hope that Martin would help her. When it came to a showdown, men like him followed the pack.

As Fifi's eyes grew accustomed to the gloom, she finally saw the small mound that was Yvette and crawled over to her.

'Yvette!' she called out as she shook her, but the only sound in response was a little snore. Fifi realized she must get her on to the mattress so they could share the one blanket, for Yvette's skin felt cold and by morning she would be like a block of ice.

She found the mattress, hauled it over and rolled Yvette on to it. Then, lying down beside her, she pulled the blanket over them both.

'Fifi! Ees it really you?'

Fifi half opened her eyes at the familiar French accent. 'Yes, it's me, but I wish it wasn't,' she said sleepily.

She saw it was dawn, a weak grey light coming through the narrow windows at the top of the barn.

'But 'ow did we get here together?' Yvette asked. 'Did you rescue me from ze men? Why are we in a cage?'

Fifi might only have been here less than twenty-four hours, but it seemed like an eternity, and Yvette's accent, which Dan loved to mimic, was such a strong reminder of him and home. 'Can't we sleep a little longer?' she asked. 'Then we talk.'

'*Non*, we must talk now,' Yvette said. 'I do not understand.'

'Well, get back in here with me, it's freezing,' Fifi said.

Once Yvette was under the blanket with her again, cuddled up tightly to keep warm, Fifi explained how she got here, and how Yvette was brought later in the evening.

'What day is it?' Yvette asked.

'Wednesday,' Fifi replied. 'Now, tell me how they got you.'

'The man came on Monday evening,' Yvette said, her dark eyes very frightened. 'I was in the hall going to my kitchen when ze knock came on ze front door. If I had been sewing I would have looked out ze window first. But I opened ze door, and the man said he was a policeman and he wanted to take me to the police station. I say I have to get my bag and my coat first. I believe him; he looked like a policeman, wizout the uniform.'

She went on to say it was only as she got outside in the dark that she became nervous, for the car wasn't a police one. But the man caught hold of her hand and wouldn't let her go. When she struggled he put his arms around her and pushed her into the back of the car, then drove off.

'It was a long way,' she said. 'I think we go south because we didn't go over ze Thames. They take me to a house; it was small and very dirty. I cry and scream and the man hit me.'

347

'What did the man look like?' Fifi asked.

'He was big, more than six feet, with dark hair; ze other man was smaller, he 'ave a funny mouth.' She held up the side of her lip to show her teeth. 'Like this,' she said.

'They weren't the men who brought you here,' Fifi said thoughtfully. 'So did you hear them talking? Did they say why they wanted you?'

'They think I 'ave gone to the police and they ask what I tell them,' she said. 'I keep saying I never go to police, only answered questions when Angela die. But they do not believe me. All night they keep on. I 'ave to sit on a hard chair. I want to go to sleep, but they don't let me. So many questions, all the time.'

'What sort of questions?'

'About what I see. I tell them I was not there the day Angela die. They ask if I know John Bolton. If I talk to him. I say yes I talk to him if I see him in the street, but not about Angela. I talk to nobody about this.'

'Did you know John was found dead in the river?'

Yvette inhaled sharply, and stiffened beside Fifi. 'No! This cannot be!'

'He was,' Fifi said. 'I was told on Monday when I got home from work. It frightened me because I sensed it had something to do with Angela. You were right in telling me I shouldn't have gone to the police because I recognized that man in the red Jaguar as having been with John.'

Yvette didn't answer, and all at once Fifi understood why she had been captured.

'You had to tell them it was me who went to the police? Didn't you?'

'*Oui*,' Yvette said in a sad little whisper. 'They say they will cut off my fingers if I don't tell them. Wizout my fingers

I cannot sew. I think you 'ave Dan to look after you, you will be safe.'

While Fifi still didn't know how the men discovered that someone in Dale Street had been to the police, they obviously assumed it was Yvette because she lived right next door to the Muckles.

Fifi couldn't feel angry that Yvette had told on her. She knew she'd sing like a canary herself if someone was threatening to cut her fingers off. All she felt was deep, deep sorrow that through her, Yvette would have to be killed too.

'You are angry wiz me,' Yvette whispered brokenly.

'No I'm not,' Fifi said, putting her arm around the older woman. 'It's you who should be angry with me, you warned me to mind my own business enough times. This is my fault.'

'It will be okay,' Yvette said, kissing Fifi's forehead comfortingly. 'Your Dan, he will get 'elp for us.'

Fifi had to admit then that Dan had walked out, and that she hadn't told him about the man in the Jaguar anyway. 'It might be days before anyone misses us,' she finished up. She almost added that *they might be dead by then*, but she managed to stop herself in time.

'We mustn't panic,' Fifi said after a couple of minutes' silence. 'I haven't given up on Martin yet. He might help us.'

The day passed very slowly. The sun came out around eleven in the morning, slanting down through the narrow windows and making them feel warm enough to divide the pork pie in two and eat it. They decided to leave the cake, a large currant bun, until dusk, just in case the men didn't come back with more food. They dozed on the mattress, Fifi climbed the bars again and again for some exercise, and they talked a little, but although Yvette seemed to appreciate Fifi telling her about her childhood and her friends back in Bristol she was mostly silent, perhaps dwelling on what their end might be.

As it began to get dark, they tore the bun in half and ate it, then just sat on the mattress watching the patch of sky visible in the window grow gradually darker and darker.

'I was so scared when it got dark yesterday,' Fifi admitted. 'I don't think I could have stood a whole night alone.'

'The dark will not hurt you,' Yvette said, taking Fifi's hand in hers and squeezing it. 'It is people who hurt you.'

'But the mice and rats, I can't bear the thought of them,' Fifi admitted.

'They will not come near us,' Yvette said firmly. 'We 'ave not left one crumb of food for them. In ze rest of the barn there is bits of wheat, that is all they want. I would rather spend the night with a rat than a man who wishes to do me harm.'

They waited and waited, but Martin and Del didn't come and both women's stomachs were growling with hunger. Eventually they gave up hoping for food and lay down on the mattress. They were cold too. Yvette put her coat over the blanket, but it made little difference.

Fifi wondered if killing someone by starvation could be classified as murder, or would it be called 'misadventure' or some such thing if their captors claimed they'd been unable to get back? How long would it take? Two weeks, three? Or longer still? But she didn't voice her anxiety as she felt entirely responsible for their plight.

Fifi had a dream that she was lying on a beach sunbathing. She woke to find it was sunshine on her face, coming from the high window.

Yvette was standing up stretching; she turned and smiled down at Fifi. 'It does not seem so bad when the sun shines,' she said. 'But I weesh for a cup of coffee.'

Fifi looked at her watch and saw it was nearly ten. She was astounded she had managed to sleep so long, and remarked on it.

'I think ze body knows when there is nothing to get up for,' Yvette said. 'When I first came to England I used to sleep from Saturday right to Monday morning. It was cold; I had little money and no friends then. Sleep was good.'

Fifi got up and used the bucket while Yvette tactfully turned away.

'Why did you come to England?' Fifi asked after she'd had a couple of mouthfuls of water. 'Don't you have any family in France?'

'My mother died in the war,' Yvette said. 'I did not wish to have sad reminders.'

The crisp way she spoke suggested she did not want to talk about it, so Fifi took her comb from her handbag and began combing her hair.

'You have such pretty hair,' Yvette said, sitting down on the mattress beside Fifi. 'I always weesh I was a blonde. When the Germans came to Paris, some mothers bleached their girls' dark hair.'

'Why?' Fifi asked.

'To try and pass them for gentile,' Yvette said with a grimace. 'It did not work too well, many ended up with orange hair.'

Fifi was suddenly taken back to an event in her early childhood when she must have been six or so. She woke to hear her mother crying and went downstairs. Her parents were in the kitchen, and her father was holding her mother in his arms while she sobbed.

'You shouldn't have gone to see it,' her father was saying. 'I told you it would be too upsetting.'

Fifi had always been a great one for lurking in the hallway or outside rooms while grown-ups were talking. Her parents used to get very cross with her about it. But however much they said things like *eavesdroppers never hear anything good about themselves*, she could never resist it. But that night she ran back to bed, frightened by what she'd seen and heard.

That evening her mother had gone out to the cinema with her sister. They went out nearly every week together, and always before her mother would be laughing when she came in. Sometimes she'd hear her telling Daddy the whole story of the film.

The following morning her mother still had red, swollen eyes from crying and Fifi asked her why.

'Because I saw the most dreadful, terrible film,' she said.

A trip to the cinema was a huge treat for Fifi. She'd seen *Snow White*, *Dumbo* and *Bambi*, and she couldn't imagine how a film could be anything but wonderful.

'Was it sad like when Bambi's mummy died?' she asked.

'Much, much worse, because that wasn't real. This was a film about how a bad man killed thousands of mummies, daddies and little children.' Her mother's eyes filled up with tears again.

'Why did he kill them?'

'Just because they were Jewish.'

Fifi had no idea then what Jewish meant and it was years later before she learned about the Holocaust at school. It was only then that she realized her mother was upset that night years earlier because she'd seen the film which was made at the time the British and American troops liberated the concentration camps.

Fifi became almost morbidly fascinated by the whole subject. She used to go into the library and look for books about it. But whenever she asked about it at home she always got the same response. '*That was all over years ago. It should be forgotten about now.*'

It had often baffled her why kind, decent people like her parents could brush aside something as terrible as six million people being exterminated. She had wanted to know why no one seemed to be aware it was going on, how they reacted when they first found out, if they wanted to do something to help, or if they were just too stunned. She wanted to know, too, what happened to the surviving Jews and if they could ever forgive or forget.

She hadn't thought much about this in the last eight or nine years, but something about the way Yvette had spoken suggested she was Jewish, and that brought back all those questions she'd never had satisfactory answers to.

Turning to face her friend, she had to ask. 'Are you Jewish, Yvette?'

Yvette sighed deeply. 'Yes, Fifi, I am.' The way she said it made it quite clear it wasn't something she intended to discuss further.

Fifi had to let it go. She finished combing her hair, then offered to do Yvette's. Fifi had only ever seen her hair scraped back into a tight bun, until yesterday when the pins began to fall out, and it was quite a surprise to see that it was very long and thick, though sprinkled with grey.

Yvette had lost most of the pins, so Fifi suggested plaiting it, as she had a couple of rubber bands in her handbag. Fifi had always liked doing other women's hair, and Yvette seemed to relax as it was combed and plaited. They talked about how much they'd like to wash, clean their teeth, and have a cup of tea or coffee.

'You look like a schoolgirl now,' Fifi laughed when she had finished. She was about to say that Yvette should dye over the grey hair and have it cut into a bob, but she stopped herself just in time, and found her handbag mirror to show the older woman how she looked.

Yvette smiled at her reflection. 'This is how I wore it as a leetle girl,' she said. 'Mama would plait it as I ate my breakfast. Before I left for school she would tie ribbons on the end, but every day I lose one.'

'Me too,' Fifi smiled. 'My mother used to get really cross. She said once it was a waste of time trying to make me look pretty. I always thought that meant I was really ugly.'

Yvette patted her cheek. 'Mothers do not weesh to say their leetle girls are beautiful in case it make them vain.'

'Did your mother tell you that you have lovely eyes?' Fifi asked. 'They are like liquid dark chocolate, and your figure is so good too. Why didn't you ever marry?'

Yvette smiled. 'I never knew anyone ask so many questions! To get married it is not enough just to 'ave lovely eyes or a good figure.'

'But you are so nice,' Fifi said. 'A bit mysterious perhaps. I would think lots of men would fall for you.'

Yvette chuckled. 'So you theenk I am mysterious.'

Fifi grinned. 'Yes, but then men are supposed to like that.'

'I do not care what men like,' Yvette said a little sharply. 'I would rather be alone for ever than 'ave to live with a man. Look at 'ow these men treat us! No food, only one blanket. Another woman could not do that.'

The day passed even more slowly than the previous one, and with nothing to do but think how hungry they were, they grew snappy with each other. When Fifi began climbing up the bars for some exercise, Yvette complained. When Yvette rocked herself back and forward as she sat on the mattress, that got on Fifi's nerves.

'Stop it,' Fifi shouted. 'You look like you're going mad.'

'Stop what?' Yvette asked.

'Rocking!'

'I do not know what you mean,' Yvette retorted.

They ignored each other after that. Yvette lay down, curled up in a foetal position, and Fifi did exercises she remembered from ballet class, pretending to herself that the bars were the barre.

But as it gradually became dark, Fifi gave way to anger. She was hungry, cold and dirty and she felt she couldn't stand another moment of it.

'We really are going to die, aren't we?' she suddenly screamed out. 'Stuck here getting thinner and thinner until we're too weak to even stand. And you won't even talk to me to take my mind off it.'

'What do you want me to talk about?' Yvette said, looking surprised. 'You are such a child sometimes, Fifi, always ze drama.'

'It doesn't bloody well get any more dramatic than this,' Fifi snarled at her. 'I can't take it any more.'

Yvette got up and walked over to Fifi, putting her arms around her and holding her tightly.

'Hush now,' she said soothingly. 'Screaming and shouting won't make it any better.'

Fifi burst into tears, and Yvette led her back to the mattress, wrapped the blanket around her as though she was a small child and cuddled her close.

'How can you be this calm?' Fifi asked after a while when her sobbing had abated. 'Aren't you frightened?'

'Yes, I am frightened,' Yvette admitted. 'I am just as

355

hungry as you too. But I 'ave been very hungry and frightened before in my life, and perhaps this is why I seem calm now.'

'When you first came to England?'

'No, all I remember of that was the cold, not fright or hunger. But in Paris I was very scared, for every day the Germans come and round up Jewish people to take them away. We did not know then where they were taking them, but we knew it wasn't good. Sometimes my mama and I 'ad no food at all, for who needs a dressmaker when your country has fallen to the enemy?'

'Did the Nazis take you then?' Fifi asked through her sniffles.

'No, because Mama sent me away. She couldn't come with me, she had to sell what little we 'ad to pay for me to go. She said she would come for me as soon as the war was over.'

'Did she come?'

Yvette shook her head. 'The Nazis took her and she died on the train journey to Poland. They say there were so many people in each carriage that many could not breathe. It was bitterly cold too, and they 'ad no food or drink.'

Because of their plight Fifi could actually feel what it must have been like for Yvette's mother, whereas before this would have been just another horrible story that she could imagine, but without really grasping its stark reality. Mere words could not convey her horror and disgust that anyone could do such a thing to another human being, or how appalling it must have been for Yvette to discover her mother died in such a way. It was dark now and she couldn't see the Frenchwoman's face but she knew she was crying. 'I'm so sorry,' she whispered. 'I don't know what else to say. It's just too terrible.'

'Maybe it was better that she died there, before she see the camp,' Yvette said in a choked voice. 'She was at least with people she knew. I stay after the war is over, waiting for news, then when the Red Cross find her name on a list, I come here.'

Fifi thought of her own mother then. She could see her waiting outside the infant school gates with Patty, Peter and Robin sitting at both ends of the pram. Her mother would open her arms wide for Fifi to run to them, and she'd scoop her up and kiss her. How strange it was that such a lovely image should come into her mind now, when in the past she had chosen to remember only slights, arguments and all the negatives! Just a couple of days ago she was blaming all her misfortune on her family, and she felt ashamed of that now. She thought that if she ever got out of here she would make a determined effort to see all the good in her life, and forget the rest.

She remained silent for some time, holding Yvette in her arms, hoping that the warmth of her body would comfort her. But questions kept bobbing into her head; there was just so much more she needed to know about her friend.

'But what was it like for you during the war years? You must have been just a young girl?' she asked eventually.

'I was eighteen when it ended,' Yvette said with a catch in her voice. 'But I was not like a young girl any more. I think it would 'ave been better to die in the train with Mama.'

'Why? Weren't the people you were sent to kind to you?'

'Kind! They see me as just a young Jewish girl who can be sold to anyone with a few francs. You ask why I am not married. Fifi, I would sooner die than ever 'ave a man touch me again.'

Chapter sixteen

The air in the office of Trueman Enterprises was thick with cigar smoke. Jack Trueman was sitting back in a big leather swivel chair, a glass of whisky in one hand, gesticulating at Del and Martin with his cigar.

'I want you up in Nottingham pronto,' he said, his tone one of a man well used to giving an order and having it obeyed immediately. 'That slag is out of order, and you are to stay there until he knows it.'

Jack Trueman was close on sixty but he kept in shape by working out in a gym and swimming fifty lengths of his swimming pool each morning, so he looked far younger. Over six feet tall, with wide shoulders and a craggy face, he had never been considered a handsome man, but age had given him distinction. His dark hair had turned silver and he wore his handmade Savile Row three-piece grey suit and gold watch with the air of a man born to money. It was only his cockney accent that gave away his true origins, and the lack of warmth in his dark eyes warned people he was a human shark.

Anyone who had seen his mock Tudor mansion in Essex would be surprised he didn't run his large empire from a prestigious office suite in Mayfair. But the two small cluttered rooms above a bookshop in St Anne's Court in Soho, where he'd started from some forty years earlier, suited him just fine. He owned the building and ran the Mandrake drinking club in the cellar. Mirabelle's, a stripclub, the Bastille coffee bar and Freddy's nightclub, which he owned too, were all within three minutes' walk. But he also had full and part shares in many other businesses as diverse as garment manufacturers, restaurants, a couple of hotels in Paddington and gambling clubs in all the big cities.

It was the club in Nottingham he had a problem with. The manager had been creaming off the profits for some time, and he wanted Del and Martin not only to go up there and teach him a lesson, but to bring back what Trueman believed he was owed.

'Right, guv,' Del nodded. 'How bad are we to hurt him?'

'Bad enough that he won't try it again. But not so bad he'll need a hospital. He's good at his job, and he can keep it if he pays up. But if he don't –' Trueman made a sort of chopping gesture with his cigar, implying that they could lame or blind the man for all he cared.

Del went to the door as if to leave. Martin began to follow him but stopped abruptly and looked back at Trueman.

'What about the women?' he asked. 'They need food and water. Shall we go out there first?'

'You leave that to me, son,' Trueman replied with a grin which didn't reach his eyes. 'Get off to Nottingham now and quick about it.'

Martin hesitated. It was Friday, and they hadn't been out to the barn again since they took the second woman on Tuesday night. But Del tugged at his sleeve in a silent reminder it wasn't a good idea to argue with the boss.

Once down the stairs and out into St Anne's Court, Martin turned to his friend. 'Look, Del, we've got to go out there first,' he insisted. 'They'll be starving, and they've probably got no water left either.'

'In case you've forgotten, we gave the key back on

Wednesday, so we can't get in there,' Del said. 'So stop banging on about them, he'll have got someone else going out there. Not that the mouthy bitch deserves anything anyway.'

It was raining very hard, and neither Martin nor Del was exactly thrilled to be ordered to Nottingham on a Friday afternoon. Anywhere north of Watford felt like a foreign country to them, and by the time they'd done their business up there, they'd be forced to doss down in some fleapit before the drive home. That would mean they'd be shagged out for Saturday night, the busiest night of the week.

A couple of strippers from the Mirabelle came into the Court, huddled together under an umbrella. When they saw Del and Martin their faces brightened.

Most of the men they met in the club were middle-aged at least, and usually weirdos. To the strippers Del and Martin were white knights as they gave the girls some protection and dealt with troublemakers. Del took advantage of their admiration and trust, and often sold them amphetamines so they could lose weight and work longer hours. But then, Del took advantage of almost everyone, including Martin.

'Coming in the club later, boys?' the red-haired one asked.

'Not tonight, sweetheart,' Del said, flicking out his snowy-white shirt cuffs from his dark green mohair suit jacket. 'We're off on some business. Might catch you tomorra night, though.' He looked at Martin and jerked his head as the signal they had to go. Martin knew then that Del had already forgotten about the women in the barn.

Fifi, and what she'd told him, had been haunting Martin. Del insisted that she was talking a load of old cobblers and that the reason the boss captured her was because her old man had pulled a stroke on him and then legged it. The other woman was supposed to have kept the books in one of the boss's businesses, and she'd been ripping him off. Del said they were only being held until Dan Reynolds surfaced and the Frenchwoman had been taught a lesson.

But Martin didn't believe this. He'd already been told Dan was a bricklayer, he even knew where he worked, and as far as he knew there was no Frenchwoman employed to do the books in any of Trueman's businesses.

There was nothing remotely unusual about Martin and Del being sent to deal with a bloke who'd stepped out of line. That was a major part of their job. He'd be given a good kicking, locked up for a few days, and released once he'd learned his lesson about crossing Jack Trueman. But they had never captured and locked up a woman before. Women who upset Trueman, and they were invariably tarts, mostly got the threat of a face rearrangement. As far as Martin knew, that always got them back in line. He'd never yet been ordered to hurt a woman.

And whatever Del said, Fifi was no tart. Then there was that story about the kid being murdered. He'd gone through some old newspapers at his gran's last night, and there it was, just as she said.

Del even had an answer to the coincidence that the two women and John Bolton all lived in the same street. He said that the boss owned property there, and as Dan Reynolds, the Frenchwoman and John Bolton had all worked for him, they got the places as a perk. But Martin remembered that Bolton had owned his own house, and if Trueman did own any property in South London, it was the first he had heard of it.

As to the coincidence that the murdered kid lived in the same street as the others, Del said that was all it was, a coincidence and nothing to do with the boss. But to Martin, the whole thing stank to high heaven, and it seemed that Del had been around bad smells for so long he didn't notice them any more.

Martin had known Del since they were six-year-olds living in the same tenement block in Rotherhithe. They played together, played truant from school, even got sent to the same village in Sussex when they were evacuated.

Martin's gran always said that if he hadn't palled up with Del he'd be working in a bank now instead of doing what she called 'the donkey work for hoodlums'. It was certainly true Martin was far brighter than Del, and if he hadn't become so involved with him, he probably could have gone to grammar school.

But the war years bound him and Del together, starting when they ran away together from Sussex, got on a train and hid under the seats to escape the ticket inspector. From then on they were always up to mischief, and they got away with most of it thanks to the blackout and lack of parental guidance. Del's mum was always off somewhere with a fancy man while his dad was overseas, and Martin only had his gran. Martin often felt bad now that he'd worried his gran so much. She was a good sort, and she hadn't thought twice about taking him on when his mum died and his dad scarpered.

She was close on eighty now, and rehoused in a nice place in Dagenham, but she still grumbled about Del's influence on her grandson. She said Martin should come home at nights to her, rather than staying with Del and his missus Jackie in Hackney.

Martin always laughed when his gran said he would come to a sticky end. But deep down he thought she might be right. He wished he could make the break from his old pal and find a legitimate job, but he couldn't. Jack Trueman didn't like what he called defectors. That's what John Bolton had been, and he'd ended up in the river.

'What's up?' Del asked as they drove out towards Barnet. 'You ain't still worried about that bint, are yer?'

'No,' Martin lied. He knew Del had no tender feelings for women, not even Jackie. He would kill anyone who tried to take her from him, but he didn't value her as a person, only as a possession. 'Just a bit pissed off at having to go to Nottingham.'

'Yeah, it's a drag having to go on a Friday, but look on the bright side; you know what the birds are like up there, crazy about Londoners.'

Martin did know what the girls up there were like, still wearing their hair up in those huge stiff beehives and thick, pale makeup. He liked girls to look the way Fifi did, with clear, glowing skin, and long, loose silky hair.

Last Tuesday when they were sent to pick Fifi up they were told by Trueman she was a looker, but Martin hadn't expected anything so classy. She looked all clean and neat, the prettiest face he'd seen in years, and when she got into the car he could smell perfume like flowers, not the strong stuff most girls wore that made him gag.

She was brave too, standing up to Del. What on earth made her old man walk out on her? But that must've been true or the story about him being taken ill over the weekend wouldn't have made any sense to her. She must love him too, or she wouldn't have hopped in the car so readily.

It had to be bloody cold in that barn at night. She didn't even have a coat, only a little jacket. What if she or the other one got ill?

'I'm starving,' Del announced a little later as they reached

Barnet. 'Let's stop and go and get some fish and chips. They'll all be closed later on.'

Martin wasn't hungry, but he could do with a cup of tea. They'd been stuck in the office for ages and the snooty secretary didn't offer them one.

They parked up, found a fish-and-chip shop with tables to eat at, and both ordered cod and chips. Martin ate the fish but didn't want the chips, and when he felt in his pocket for cigarettes he found he had only one left.

'I'm just going to get some fags,' he said, getting up.

There was a newspaper shop just three doors down. Martin bought his cigarettes and a couple of bars of chocolate for later. He was just about to go back to the café when he saw the rack of birthday cards. It was his gran's birthday in a week's time, and he often forgot to buy a card in time to post it.

He was glancing through them, looking for the kind she liked with a soppy verse, when he saw a card that said 'Missing You'.

It had a teddy bear on the front with a tear running down its cheek, and once again he was thinking of Fifi.

'Come on, Fifi, do some exercises with me, that will make you warm again,' Yvette pleaded. She stood over the younger woman, who was lying on the mattress, and held out her hand.

'I haven't got the energy,' Fifi said weakly. 'I feel giddy when I stand up.'

Yvette felt giddy too. She'd had her last meal on Monday evening, not long before the man came and took her away. It was now Friday afternoon and she couldn't count half a pork pie and a bit of bun on Wednesday as a meal. There was only about two inches of water left in the bottle now and once they were forced to drink that she knew they would become really distressed.

In her heart Yvette believed they were going to be left to die. She had thought long and hard about it, and knowing what she did about the men behind all this, it made sense.

Why run the risk of being seen by someone coming out this way, of perhaps being outwitted as they attempted to kill them, when time alone would do it for them? It would be so much harder for the police to build a case against anyone when rain and wind had removed car tracks and any other evidence. She had no doubt that before using this barn, the men behind this had made certain that the owner wasn't going to turn up here for some time. The chances were their bodies would be completely decomposed by the time that happened.

Of course, only the most evil and cold-blooded person could let two people die of thirst and starvation, and she doubted that all the top man's henchmen and bully boys came under that category, but a powerful man would take that into consideration. Yvette had been taken by two different men to the ones that took Fifi. It would be easy enough to tell one set of men that the others were bringing them food. Yvette knew that when their bodies were finally found, none of the men involved were going to admit to any part of it, whatever their feelings. They would have to remain silent for fear of incurring a similar fate for themselves.

Yvette had often wished for death in the past, her life held nothing that she wanted to hold on to. She had no family to grieve, nothing to look forward to, and she'd gladly be released from her guilt. She didn't fear death in itself, but she was afraid of a slow and agonizing one.

She looked up at the bars above her. It would be so

simple to climb up there and use the belt on her skirt to make a noose to hang herself. She had seen a man hanged in France, and knew death came quickly.

But she couldn't do that, not with Fifi with her. Fifi believed the best of people, and she would want to hang on, convinced that no one could leave a couple of women to die of starvation.

Yvette couldn't share her optimism. It wasn't as if they could count on the police finding them. Even if Dan and Frank were convinced that something bad had happened to Fifi, and had demanded the police search for her, they weren't likely to come out this way looking. And it might be days before anyone realized Yvette was missing too. If the police couldn't squeeze the names of the men who'd been at his card game out of Alfie Muckle, there was absolutely no chance he'd do or say anything to help find her and Fifi. Besides, Alfie was a mere pawn in this game. If he wasn't safely in prison, he'd almost certainly be dead, as John Bolton was.

Yvette knelt down beside Fifi and tenderly stroked her brow. She had become so fond of the girl, and that affection had grown during the time they'd been locked up in here. It had been Fifi who had held things together, right up till today. She certainly wasn't the rather spoilt child Yvette first took her for. She thought of games to play to pass the time, they had sung and made up stories. She'd made Yvette correct her as she tried to speak her schoolgirl French, and she had used many long English words and made Yvette tell her what they meant.

At night it was Fifi who'd drawn Yvette into her arms to keep her warm, and she'd kept her fears to herself.

Even the way Fifi always wanted to know everything

about people didn't seem nosiness any longer, she was just curious to know what made them tick. She cared, and wanted to understand. Yvette thought that if there were more people like her, the world would be a far better place.

Fifi opened her eyes wearily and tried to smile. 'Dan will find us,' she said with conviction. 'I bet he's leant on everyone at the pub to find out what they know, and his mates at work will help too. You mustn't despair, Yvette. There's Martin as well, I haven't given up on him yet. He didn't seem so bad; he may have got in with a nasty crowd and maybe they've stopped him coming out here with food. But I'm absolutely sure he won't let us die here.'

Yvette's eyes filled with tears, for the younger woman's trust was so touching. 'I weesh I had your faith,' she said. 'But I 'ave seen such wickedness in my life that I doubt everyone.'

'Why don't you tell me about it?' Fifi asked. 'Come and lie beside me. We'll snuggle up under the blanket to warm each other. You and I are going to be best friends for life once we get out of here, because of this horrible time we've shared. So we shouldn't have secrets from one another, should we?'

Yvette was already very cold, the light was fading, and the prospect of yet another interminable night plagued with hunger pains, tantalizing visions of food and her limbs aching from scrunching them up to keep warm, was daunting. Telling Fifi about her demons might distract them both for a while, and maybe it might help the girl to see that the world wasn't the bright, beautiful place she believed it to be, and there couldn't always be a happy ending.

'I've kept my secrets for a long, long time,' Yvette warned Fifi as she lay down and cuddled close to her. 'It will be 'ard for me to tell you them, but you tell me all about you, and maybe you should know me too.'

Yvette began with how it was for her as a child, the father she never knew, the tiny apartment in rue du Jardin, and her mother constantly sewing.

'We were very poor,' Yvette said. 'Sometimes when Mama's ladies didn't pay her, we were hungry, but we had very happy times too. Mama used to like me to read to her while she sewed, and I make dresses for my doll from ze scraps of ze fine fabrics left over. On summer nights when it began to get dark and she couldn't sew any more, we would go out for walks down by ze Seine and watch the boats going past. We peep in the windows of the big houses, and stop outside grand restaurants to hear ze music. Mama always say she missed me when I was at school, but she was very proud because I was clever, always top of my class, she hoped that I would be able to get a good job and not have to work hard like she did.'

Yvette found herself slipping back to September of 1939 when she was twelve. She could see herself coming home from school with her friend Françoise, both skinny girls with olive skin, dark hair and eyes. They wore black wool stockings that slipped down in folds over their ankles, and their long plaits bounced and swung as they hopped over cracks in the pavements. People always thought they were twins because they were so similar, but Yvette thought Françoise was the prettier; she had dimples in her cheeks and perfect Cupid's bow lips.

At school their teacher kept talking about the war which had just begun, pinning up maps to show how the Germans were advancing through Poland, but it meant little to Yvette and Françoise, for Poland was so far away from Paris and neither of them had a father who would have to go and fight.

What Yvette remembered most about that time was the

food in the shops and the smells that went with it. Perhaps it only stuck in her memory because that was the last time for many years she would see such abundance. Rosy polished apples piled high, luscious purple grapes spilling out of boxes, peaches, carrots and vivid red tomatoes. Freshly baked bread and croissants, the marble counter at the charcuterie laden with dozens of different cheeses, ham and pâté. And so many autumn flowers too, tin buckets crammed with chrysanthemums, dahlias and purple daisies.

'It was Françoise who first told me that ze Nazis didn't like Jews,' Yvette went on. 'She 'ad relatives in Berlin, and they'd written to her mother to say they were trying to get away as Jews were being attacked and their businesses confiscated. But Françoise and me, we didn't really see ourselves as Jews, our mothers didn't go to the synagogue and they didn't keep up any of the traditions. To us we were just French, and whatever was happening in Germany had nothing to do with us.

'But by ze spring of 1940 I could see Mama was worried about something more than paying ze rent and whether ze war would stop her ladies having new clothes made. One day I ask her about it and she told me she was afraid for us.'

Yvette could remember having conflicting feelings as the Germans advanced closer and closer to France. There was a kind of raw excitement in the air, so many men in uniform milling around Paris, tales of heroism bandied around on street corners. To her and Françoise it was something like waiting for Christmas, so much anticipation and hope, yet because both their mothers were poor, there was also a faint dread as they were used to disappointment.

The casualties of war were already mounting, and the oldest people kept on recounting stories of the young men in their families who had died in the trenches of the First War. People married in haste without any of the customary ceremony and tradition. Young women who until then had been models of decorum were seen kissing young men passionately in public. The bars, nightclubs and restaurants all grew busier and noisier. Churches were packed on Sundays, and people stayed out on the streets as the days lengthened; maybe it was only to discuss the war or gossip, but to the two young girls Paris had an almost carnival atmosphere.

Sometimes Yvette and Françoise would go to the Gare du Nord to watch troops leaving on the trains. They were too young to fully understand the tears of sweethearts as they clung together, but old enough to want this heady drama for themselves. They threw flowers and waved handkerchiefs too. They even hoped that the war wouldn't end before they were adult enough to have someone to kiss goodbye.

But behind all this frantic activity throughout Paris, there was also a swell of anxiety and unease which grew steadily stronger through April and May. The teachers at school had very grave faces, and they seemed disinclined to show the Germans' advance through Holland and Belgium on their maps any longer.

Then at the end of May the whole of Paris was aghast as French and English troops retreated to Dunkirk. Church bells tolled and people flocked to pray that their menfolk were amongst those who were rescued from the beaches.

While everyone was still reeling from this disaster, the Germans were moving towards Paris. On 10 June the French government abandoned the capital because it could not be defended. While most citizens were glad their beloved Paris was saved from the destruction of siege and street fighting, they were still shocked and horrified to see the first advance units of German soldiers arrive in the city.

Yvette and Françoise slipped away to see the German horse artillery pass through the Arc de Triomphe, and all at once they understood the reality of war as they saw the cold, stern faces beneath helmets, and the long trail of horse-drawn gun carriages. Within hours Paris was fully occupied, and although France didn't surrender until 22 June, for Yvette, the day the first Germans arrived was the start of her war. She experienced her first real pang of fear, a foreboding that nothing would ever be the same again. Much later she was to see that day as the last of her childhood.

'You've made me see it all,' Fifi murmured against Yvette's shoulder. It was dark now, and she could no longer see her friend's face. 'But go on; did the Nazis come for you and your mother straight away?'

'No. But it was very frightening for everyone, Jews and gentiles. People were shot if they were caught in ze streets after curfew. The Germans walked into shops and demanded ze best produce, often refusing to pay for it. They would close businesses down, break windows, and often confiscated property. Just looking at them too boldly was enough to get punched or kicked.

'Mama said we must stay indoors and only go out to get food. But each day it grew harder to find any, sometimes we had to go a long way just for a loaf of bread, and the German soldiers were everywhere. We tried so hard not to be noticed, for they would call for you to stop and demand to look at our papers. Mama would slip out sometimes to talk to people she knew. I think now she must get word how bad it was for Jews in Poland, back in Germany and in

Holland. But she say little to me, only that she must get me away somewhere safe.

'When Françoise was sent away, I was jealous,' Yvette admitted. 'She had an aunt somewhere in the south to go to. I was lonely without her. Then a few weeks later Mama tells me I must go too.'

Fifi heard the catch in her friend's voice, and stroked her cheek to encourage her to carry on.

'You know, I can still see ze apartment, Mama's face, everything, just as if it were only yesterday, not twenty-three years ago.' Yvette sighed. 'But maybe that is because my leaving was so sudden.'

She closed her eyes as she remembered the last hours in the apartment, and she could see herself climbing the stairs, puffed from running home from school in the rain.

The staircase was stone, with rusting fancy ironwork banisters, and wound around the centre of the building. The only light came from a skylight up on the fourth floor, and from the front door when it was left open.

All the smells from the other apartments, and there were four on each floor, stayed trapped in the building in summer, a pungent warm soup of garlic, cheese, herbs, laundry soap and sometimes drains. Madame Chevioux, the widow who lived on the ground floor at the front, had the biggest apartment, and she lorded it over the other tenants because she was a relative of the landlord and collected the rents.

The tenants came and went frequently because of Madame Chevioux, but Yvette and her mother had lived up at the very top in the attic rooms since Yvette was just a baby. Mama smiled sweetly at the bully on the ground floor. She scrubbed the stairs all the way down every week, cleaned the bathroom on each floor, and occasionally made Madame a skirt or a blouse for nothing, just to ensure she wouldn't be evicted. Yvette had been warned a hundred times or more that she was never to be cheeky or rude to the woman, for cheap apartments were hard to get.

That day, as Yvette opened the door to the apartment, Mama looked round from folding some clothes on the table.

'I have some good news for you,' she said.

Mama was tiny; even at thirteen Yvette was a little taller than her. Françoise had once remarked that she looked faded, though until then Yvette hadn't noticed. But she was right; Mama had faded from the raven-haired, curvaceous beauty with doe-like eyes that Yvette admired in the photograph on the dresser. Now, her slender shoulders were rounded through bending over her sewing-machine, and her hair was more grey than raven. Even her eyes had faded; they appeared to have a milky film on them the way chocolate went if it was kept too long. She was thirty-five, which seemed very old to Yvette, and her face, though not lined yet, had a yellowish tinge.

'We're going somewhere!' Yvette exclaimed joyfully, for along with the clothes on the table was a canvas bag.

'Only you, my darling,' Mama said. 'I have found somewhere safe for you, until the Germans are gone.'

'But I can't go anywhere without you,' Yvette replied, the pleasure of a trip vanishing all at once. 'Why can't you come too?'

'Because you will be safer without me, and I have my living here.'

Mama didn't often speak in that firm tone, but when she did Yvette knew she mustn't argue.

'Where am I going?' she asked.

'To a country town. You will get plenty of food and fresh air, and it will be a good life. I will come for you as soon as I can.'

'Am I going soon?' Yvette asked.

'In a couple of hours,' Mama said. 'We will walk down to the market and you will be picked up there. I do not want Madame Chevioux to know you are going anywhere. I do not trust her.'

Yvette paused in her story, and Fifi realized she was crying silently.

'Was that the last time you saw your mother?'

'Yes,' Yvette said, her voice gruff with emotion. 'Yet I think in my heart I knew I was never going to see her or ze apartment again, for as I ate some bread and cheese and drank some milk, I seemed to soak up everything about them.

'I can see it so clearly still, the wood floor Mama paint with the varnish, the rag rugs she sew, and her old sewing-machine. Only one big room really, we 'ave a bed behind some curtains, and the table was huge so Mama could cut out her dresses. We 'ave a kind of sideboard under ze window; a big cushion on the top to make it like a window seat. When it was sunny I'd lie on it basking like a cat. I used to watch ze people in the street below too, and look out over ze rooftops to the dome of ze Sacré Coeur. Maybe ze apartment very shabby, but I never think of it that way.'

After a while Yvette continued, telling Fifi she and her mama were duly met in the market by Madame and Monsieur Richelieu. They seemed warm, charming people, a little older than her mama, and they said they were going to tell people Yvette was their orphaned niece. They lived in Tours where they had a boulangerie, and Yvette could help them in the bakehouse. They also promised they were going to continue with her education, and that by the time the war was over she'd be able to return to Paris to go to the university.

'I feel no suspicion about them,' Yvette said. 'I like them, so did Mama. They said it was best we didn't write letters to one another, at least for ze time being, in case they were intercepted. But Mama had ze address where I was going, so that didn't alarm me.'

'Don't tell me they were rotters!'

'They were. The worst and wickedest kind, for they duped Mama. But at first it was just like they say. We took the train to Tours; the papers they 'ad for me were checked and accepted. There was ze boulangerie, in ze centre of ze town, and I 'ad a little room next to theirs in their apartment over ze shop. Tante Grace, as she said I was to call her, fed me well, didn't work me too hard, and though I wasn't allowed out alone, I thought that was to keep me safe.

'But then one night about three months later, I was taken away by car. They must have drugged me for I remember nothing after eating my supper, and then ze motion of a vehicle. When I woke up I was in a room with bars at ze windows, and a woman came in to tell me that from now on I was her property.'

'What was this place?' Fifi asked. She had long since forgotten her hunger, the dark and the cold as Yvette took her back to France with her.

'A brothel,' Yvette almost spat out. 'Not that I even knew that word then, or what went on in them. I hadn't even started to menstruate or grow breasts. I knew nothing about the adult world. Just thirteen, a child still.'

Fifi gasped.

'I was made to bathe and wash my hair, and then I was given a nightdress to put on. I kept asking where Tante Grace was, and crying, but this woman she didn't even tell me 'er name, she slapped me, she say I am to do exactly what she tells me or be punished.'

Yvette relived that night again as she told Fifi about it. She could see the bare wooden stairs she was led down, the long gloomy corridor, and a door at the end of it. She was frightened, not by what lay ahead, for she had no knowledge of what was going to happen to her. But she was afraid of the woman, for she had a long bony face, sharp dark eyes, and her front tooth was missing, like a witch's in a fairy-tale book. She wasn't dressed like a witch – her dress was dark blue crêpe, and her blonde hair was set in tight waves either side of her head – but the hand that held tightly on to Yvette's forearm was like a claw, and the large ruby ring on her finger looked like blood.

The room she was led into was dimly lit, heavy tapestry curtains tightly closed, and sparsely furnished with just a bed and a couple of chairs. Sitting on one of the chairs was a man.

He was portly, and he looked old to Yvette, though he was probably around forty, and he wore a dark grey suit with a yellow waistcoat beneath it. He had a big, florid face with a double chin, and when he smiled as he saw her, she noticed he had wet, fat lips.

'You are sure she is intact?' he asked, looking Yvette over as if she were a prize sheep or pig. He was French, and a Parisian judging by his accent.

'I checked her myself. Not even hair on her fanny yet,' the woman replied.

It was that rude word that alerted Yvette to the nature of this man's interest in her, and she tried to shake off the woman's hand on her arm and run, but she was held too tightly.

The man got up from his chair and came over to her,

grasping her by both hands and pulling her to him. 'Come, my little flower,' he said. 'I want to look at you.'

Yvette screamed then, and it seemed to echo around the bare room. The man laughed, and picking her up, tossed her on to the bed.

'You can go now,' he said to the woman. 'If she's all you said, you'll get your bonus.'

Every second of that terrifying and painful ordeal was still imprinted on Yvette's mind. She could smell the man's breath on her face, feel the heat of his body through his clothes as he wrestled with her on the bed. There was such shame as he tried to look at her private parts and the pain when he poked and prodded at them. She tried to fight him off, but he slapped her hard, and pushed her down on the bed so violently that she thought he would kill her.

Then he unbuttoned his trousers, and such a fearsome thing reared out that she screamed again. She had only ever seen a little boy's penis, never a grown man's, and although a girl at school had once shown her a drawing of one, she'd thought it was a joke.

'He forced it into me, Fifi,' she whispered. 'I felt as if I was being split in two. I was trapped beneath him and the pain was too bad, like being burned with a red-hot poker. It seemed like hours he was ramming it into me. I think I may have passed out. I just wish I could have died there and then.'

Fifi cried with Yvette, as they held each other tightly and rocked together. All those questions she'd asked Yvette in the past, fishing as to whether she'd had a boyfriend or been married, and the jokes Dan made about the sexy French mistress, shamed her now. She wished she could find words to show Yvette that she not only fully understood her suffering but shared her pain.

Much later Yvette finished the story. She explained that she was one of many girls brought there. The brothel had been running for some years; most of the older girls had come to Paris to find work and had been lured by the promise of a bed and a meal. Some of them had not been little innocents; a few actually liked what they saw as an easy life. But the war had made it far easier for the owners to acquire much younger girls who were in great demand with their most decadent clientele. Desperate Jewish parents, terrified by the Nazis' hatred for them, wanted to find a safe haven for their children until the war over, and it was all too easy for unscrupulous people like the Richelieux to take advantage and make money out of their fear. Yvette had heard that young boys were taken to another house and used in a similar way.

Orphans who lived on the streets were picked up too and several girls had been brought over from North Africa. The African girls were the most pitiful of all as they were often unable to communicate with anyone else.

New acquisitions were kept under lock and key, controlled by fear until such time as they accepted that they were now whores, and were grateful for their board and lodging. But for the Jewish girls there was an extra dimension of fear, for they were told daily what would happen to them if they didn't please the men who came to use them. Enough information crept in from outside for them to know that trains left every day for Poland or Germany crammed with Jews being taken to labour camps.

In time, after many beatings and being starved and locked up naked in a cold room, Yvette knew the only way she would survive was to learn to smile and even pretend she liked what those terrible men did to her. Whether it was Nazi officers or slimy French collaborators she had to entertain, she stifled her feeling until eventually she felt she had none.

Most of the rooms had locked shutters on the windows, but not the attic rooms where the girls slept. Yvette would stand for an hour or more at a time staring out over the rooftops, looking for a landmark she recognized. But she couldn't see the dome of the Sacré Coeur or the Seine, so she had no idea what part of Paris she was in.

Occasionally one of the newest girls would escape, but word always got back that she'd been shot or found drowned in the river. It wasn't just trigger-happy German soldiers gunning down someone with no papers either; often the execution was carried out by one of the men who owned this place and others like it. So the girls didn't dare trust anyone, not even one of their own, for anyone might be tempted to turn informer if it got them out of a night with one of the more brutal or perverted customers. Yvette became outwardly like all the other girls, docile, amenable, grateful for any little kindness.

'But I was not like them in my 'ead,' she said with a sharp edge of defiance in her voice. 'I knew they would stay whores when ze war end, but not me. I kept it in my 'ead that I would come to England. In that house I did ze sewing, I knew I was good at it. If I had not had ze dream of England in my head I would have gone mad.'

Fifi could say nothing. She had profound sympathy and admiration for the inner strength Yvette must have had to live through such terrible experiences. Yet at the same time she could see that her friend hadn't really won her freedom by coming to England. She had remained in a kind of prison, exchanging the men who ruled her life back in France for equally demanding women here whom she served by making their clothes.

She had no real life of her own. She went out only to visit her clients, and her cluttered flat was probably very similar to the apartment she'd shared with her mother back in her childhood. An empty life without any love or joy.

All at once Fifi felt a surge of shame that she had so often felt hard done by. She really had nothing to complain about – she'd never known hunger or real fear until now. Poverty, sickness, homelessness, she'd never experienced any of them, or even true loneliness. No one close to her had ever died, and she was born into a good, loving family. Then there was Dan, her friend, husband and lover, who would probably die for her if necessary. So maybe her mother's disapproval of him was groundless, but mothers were the same the world over, they only wanted to protect their children.

Yvette's mama had let those people take her child away to what she thought was safety. If she had been faced with the alternatives of Yvette dying with her on the train to Poland, or going into the brothel, which would she have chosen?

Chapter seventeen

Dan shivered as he walked down Dale Street to the phone box on Saturday morning. There was a distinctly autumnal chill in the air even though it was only just the beginning of September, and that heightened his anxiety about Fifi. He was at his wits' end now; he had exhausted all possible places to look for her.

When he rang her office on Wednesday morning and found she had failed to turn up for work the previous day, and hadn't phoned in either, he knew something had happened to her. She liked the job too much not to let them know if she felt unable to work.

He phoned to see if she was at her parents' house, but she wasn't there either, and he could tell that Mrs Brown wasn't covering for her – no one could feign such anxiety.

After that he systematically asked everyone in the street when they'd last seen Fifi, and if she'd said she was going away. The last sighting was by Miss Diamond who'd seen her going off to work on Tuesday morning at eight o'clock. She said she was wearing a blue and white checked jacket and a navy pencil skirt, and she definitely wasn't carrying anything other than her handbag.

That was when he went to the police, but the minute he admitted that they'd had a row over the weekend, the police seemed to think she had just taken herself off to a friend's place. Even when Dan said she hadn't taken any clothes or washing things with her they showed no concern.

On Friday Dan had gone up to Chancery Lane to Fifi's office. He'd spoken to her boss, Mr Unwin, and to every single girl who worked there, but not one of them knew anything.

The only person he hadn't been able to talk to yet was Yvette. And now he was getting worried about her too. Mr and Mrs Balstrode, who lived above her, hadn't seen or heard her since Monday teatime, when she gave them a parcel she'd taken in for them.

He decided he was going back to the police station as soon as he'd telephoned Fifi's parents. They'd said last night that if they hadn't heard from her by this morning they were going to come up to London. Despite all the bad feeling in the past, Dan really wanted them here; he thought Mr Brown might be able to persuade the police to act.

As each day passed Dan had grown more frightened. Until John Bolton was found in the river and Fifi disappeared he had been totally convinced that Alfie killed Angela. He had never been able to understand why the police had been hauling in decent, law-abiding men like Frank and Stan who would never have crossed the threshold of that house. To him it had all been cut and dried, a hideous crime carried out by a maniac, and all the police needed to do was find the other card players and clear up the finer points like what time they'd left the house, and whether they'd seen any lead-up to the crime.

But in view of recent events he was now looking at all the many questions Fifi had raised in a different light, and wishing he'd taken her more seriously. While he still believed Alfie was the murderer, it was very clear that some other kind of criminal activity had been going on at number 11, and that John Bolton had known about it. If Bolton had been killed to silence him, maybe his killers believed Fifi knew something too.

The prospect of Fifi being murdered was too terrible to contemplate. She was his love, his life, everything. He'd said that last night to Mrs Brown, and broken down and cried. He wished he hadn't now; the woman would probably come to view that as yet another weakness. But she'd been surprisingly comforting and even sounded as though she cared about him when she'd asked if he'd had any sleep at all. As if he could sleep when his beautiful wife was in danger!

Dan came out of the phone box, turned up his coat collar because the wind was so cold, and began walking to the police station.

Mr and Mrs Brown had said they were leaving home immediately and they would stay in a London hotel until Fifi was found. Patty wanted to come too, but they'd said she was to stay in Bristol with her brothers, just in case Fifi phoned.

Dan was finally shown into an interview room with Detective Inspector Roper, the same officer who had taken Fifi's statement after she found Angela Muckle. It had taken Dan a while to convince the desk sergeant that this was the man he needed to see. Fifi hadn't actually liked Roper much, but she'd spent quite some time with him, and Dan didn't want to waste any more time talking to people who didn't know his wife.

The detective's suit was still as crumpled as it had been that day in August, and Dan wondered how such a small man had got a job as a policeman. He didn't look more than five feet seven, and he was in desperate need of a haircut and a dentist. His hair looked as though he'd had an electric shock, and his teeth were brown. But on the plus side, he did have a commanding voice and a firm handshake, and he had agreed to see Dan.

'I understand your anxiety, Mr Reynolds,' Roper said after Dan had explained that since last contacting the police he'd spent his entire time trying to trace Fifi without any success. 'But you said yourself you had a row and you walked out. You were gone the whole weekend! She could just be giving you a taste of your own medicine.'

'I might believe that of any other woman, but not Fifi,' Dan retorted. 'She isn't a tit-for-tat person. She wrote to me and begged me to come back. Why would she do that if she was going to run off?'

'To frighten you?' Roper suggested.

Dan shook his head. 'She isn't like that. She left for work on Tuesday morning but never showed up. She took nothing with her. Do you know any women who skip off for a few days without even taking their toothbrush?'

'She may have set off for work, and then changed her mind,' Roper said. 'She might have suddenly got it into her head to have a bit of a break to think things through.'

'You've met my wife,' Dan said, raising his eyebrows. 'You must have formed an opinion about her?'

'Yes, a very caring young woman. Intelligent and forth-right.'

'She's all those things,' Dan said. 'She's also nosy and impulsive. But above all she's a person who needs people and when she's troubled she likes to talk. She'd no more take off to some strange guest house on her own than fly to the moon!'

Roper shrugged. 'I've been called to see men who have been married for thirty years or more, then one day their wife just ups and goes without a word. Every one of them has always been convinced she's been killed or abducted. But the truth almost always turns out to be that the wife just got fed up or found a new man. I find that women are not as predictable as us men.'

'Fifi isn't predictable at all, but she's too caring to just light off without a word,' Dan retorted with indignation. 'And another thing! The Frenchwoman at number 12 has disappeared too. Of course that could be just coincidence, just like John Bolton's body being hauled out the Thames, but she hasn't been seen since Monday night.'

'Is she a friend of your wife's?'

'Yes, but then Fifi's everyone's friend.'

'Could they have gone off together?'

'Yvette never goes anywhere overnight,' Dan snapped, irritated that Roper hadn't even risen to his sarcasm about John Bolton's murder. 'Fifi might like Yvette, but she'd hardly be her choice of partner for a little holiday. The woman's a recluse; she's frumpy and a lot older than Fifi.'

'Has anyone been into the woman's flat to check it?'

'No. They'd have to break in. But you could do that.'

'Okay, I'll get someone round there. There is something I wanted to ask you, Mr Reynolds. The man your wife saw near the council depot last Friday – did you ever see him?'

Dan didn't know what Roper was talking about and said so.

Roper appeared surprised, then related how Fifi had come to the police station on the previous Saturday morning to report what she'd seen and been told at the depot. 'Apparently as she was leaving she saw a man in a red Jaguar, whom she had seen going into the Muckles' house with John Bolton some weeks earlier.'

'She didn't tell me about any of that,' Dan said in puzzlement. 'But then I suppose she thought I'd be angry she'd been down there poking her nose in.'

Roper nodded. 'So we have some proof she doesn't tell you everything,' he said dryly.

Dan ignored that little dig for a thought was flashing through his mind. 'This man! He could've been there at the last card party, one of the ones you haven't found yet. If he discovered Fifi saw him, he'd want her out the way, wouldn't he? And maybe Yvette knew him too, and that's why they've both disappeared!'

'Hold on, Mr Reynolds, I think you are getting carried away. As soon as your wife told us about this man, we followed it up. We have established that there are no employees at the depot who fit the description she gave us, and none of the men could confirm any such person had called there that day. Your wife might have been mistaken that he drove into the depot.'

'What about this Frieda woman who made the complaint about Stan? Have you checked her story out?' Dan asked with a touch of belligerence. It seemed to him that Roper wasn't doing anything much at all.

'We established that the woman is unreliable,' Roper said.

'Unreliable!' Dan exclaimed. 'I'd call her a bloody liar. But why did she make all that up if it wasn't to get the Muckles off the hook? Someone must have put her up to it.'

Roper shrugged. 'Believe me, we have checked her out thoroughly. We know now that her allegations were totally false, but so far it appears that she was acting on her own, a purely spiteful act against Mr Stanislav because he rejected her. But you didn't answer my question about whether you saw the man your wife described to us.'

Dan shook his head. 'Fifi's the one that watches out the window, not me.' He paused as another thought came to him. 'After Fifi came to see you, did you contact John Bolton about this man?'

'He was out when we called late on Saturday afternoon. Sadly we didn't get to speak to him before his body was found.'

To Dan that was confirmation. 'So he *was* killed because he knew the man's identity!' he exclaimed heatedly.

'Calm down, Mr Reynolds,' Roper said reprovingly. 'There is no evidence to support such a theory. As I'm sure you know, Bolton associated with dozens of shady characters and we are in the process of sifting through them right now. Go on home now, we'll send someone round later to check if Miss Dupré really is missing.'

Dan didn't like Roper's dismissive tone. 'I want you to start an investigation to find Fifi,' he said forcefully. 'Don't tell me to calm down either. My wife comes in here and tells you she recognizes a man who has been at number 11 and suddenly his mate is found dead, my wife disappears, and so does another neighbour. If that isn't enough to alarm me, I don't know what would be.'

Roper had a 'you're over-reacting' expression on his face.

'You must start an investigation,' Dan ordered him, putting his fists on the desk between them and leaning towards Roper. 'You can't let it just drift on. I know perfectly well she isn't tucked away making me sweat a bit. Someone's holding her.' He broke off as emotion got the better of him and his voice began to quaver and his eyes filled with tears. 'Please find her,' he begged. 'Before they kill her. Her parents are on their way here, at least let me be able to tell them you are pulling out all the stops to find her.'

Roper's expression softened then. He got up and came round the desk, putting one hand on Dan's shoulder. 'Okay, we'll start an investigation. We'll call in on you later to pick up a photograph of your wife. Do you have a recent one?'

'One from our wedding,' Dan said shakily, wiping his eyes with the back of his hand.

While Dan was at the police station, Martin was just waking up in a small hotel in Nottingham. Del was still sound asleep in the other twin bed. They hadn't got in till nearly three in the morning, and as the man they had been sent to sort out hadn't surfaced last night, they would have to stay here until he did.

Martin hadn't got a toothbrush, razor or clean shirt with him, but he could go and buy those things. What really worried him was Fifi. A sinking feeling in his gut told him the boss wouldn't bother to send anyone else out there to take the women food or water. Del insisted he would, but Martin wasn't convinced.

When he first started working for Trueman Enterprises six years ago, it was nearly all debt collection work. As most of the people they had to make pay up were toerags and weasels he'd never felt bad about what he did. But in the last six months there had been several jobs he felt uncomfortable about. He and Del were sent to torch a warehouse out at Dalston, and the night watchman Del clobbered ended up in hospital and would never work again. Then there were the Jamaicans in a house in Westbourne Grove that they had to evict. The poor devils were just chucked out on the street with their babies and small children. That was a scam and a half; they'd all been made to pay 'key money' to get the place, and they thought they were secure for years. God only knows where they ended up, they hadn't got any money, and most of the landlords in that area were every bit as unscrupulous as Trueman.

Martin put his hands under his head and lay looking at the cracks on the ceiling, wondering how he could get Fifi found without dropping himself in it. But there was no way. Trueman was smart and he played his cards close to his chest. Martin and Del were probably the only people who knew about the barn, and if the police raided it after an anonymous call, Trueman would soon realize who'd tipped them off and Martin would be dead meat.

As he lay there, his gut churning with anxiety, Martin remembered how when he was small, his gran used to make him say his prayers at night. He wondered if praying for a dog walker to go up by that barn and hear the women shouting would count as a proper prayer.

'If you can't do that, God,' he murmured, 'give me some other bright idea that won't involve me being found dead in the river.'

Clara and Harry Brown drank the tea Dan had made them as they listened to the latest developments. They were both stiff with tension, their eyes full of anxiety.

'After I saw Roper they came straight round here and got into Yvette's flat,' Dan said. 'They came over to tell me afterwards that they agree her disappearance does look suspicious. She'd left bread and milk on her table and was halfway through washing up her supper things when she left. It turns out Frank saw her with a man on Monday evening, but as there was no sign of a struggle indoors it looks like the bloke told her something plausible to get her out the house. Frank thought the man was cuddling her outside in the street, but in the light of her disappearance, he thinks he could have been wrong and the man may have been restraining her.'

'I can't bear it,' Clara burst out. 'I feel sick with fright.'

Dan nodded, grim-faced. 'Me too. But I keep blaming myself. If only I'd been here!'

Harry cleared his throat. 'If someone has snatched Fifi, it would have happened whether you'd been here or not,' he said evenly. 'She left here quite normally for work, but didn't arrive. So my guess is that she was abducted somewhere between here and the tube station. The people were probably lying in wait, maybe just along the main road. I'd also guess that they lured her into their car with some appropriate story.'

Dan was touched that Harry wasn't attempting to blame him. He'd thought he was a bit of an old duffer when he met him the first time, but he'd been wrong. The man had a sharp, logical mind.

'I can't see Fifi getting willingly into a car with someone she didn't know,' Dan said.

'Not even if they said you'd sent them to get her?' Harry asked.

'I suppose that might do it,' Dan agreed reluctantly. 'But they'd have needed to know me to make it believable.'

'Would they? I suspect if they were dressed like builders and said your name, perhaps even the site you worked on, that would be enough for Fifi,' Harry rubbed his hands on his face. 'We all know how impulsive she is.'

Clara began to cry soundlessly, tears cascading down her cheeks.

'I'm so sorry, Mrs Brown,' Dan said, and impulsively moved over to her, sinking to his knees in front of her and taking her hand. 'I know you don't think much of me, and something like this happening to her must just confirm your worst fears about me.'

She didn't brush his hand away. 'I can't blame you for this,' she said with a sigh. 'Fifi was always one for poking her nose into things she shouldn't. I told her a hundred times or more that her curiosity would get her into trouble one day.'

There was silence for a few moments. Then Harry cleared his throat again. 'She'd only been back at work for one day,' he said thoughtfully. 'So whoever did it hadn't had any time to watch her and find out her routine. No one would wait indefinitely in the hope she might come along the road, would they?'

Dan got off his knees and went back to his chair. 'Then maybe it was someone from round here, someone that's known her since before she was off work with her broken arm. They'd know about where I worked too.' He looked despairingly at his father-in-law. 'But there's dozens of people that know all that, Fifi talked to just about everyone. And she's the kind of girl anyone would notice.'

'Did she tell anyone about your row?' Harry asked.

'It doesn't look like it,' Dan replied. 'She didn't even tell Frank downstairs, and none of the girls at her work knew.'

'Did you tell anyone?' Harry asked.

'Well, I didn't actually talk about it, but most of the blokes knew I'd stayed with Pete over the weekend. A couple of them were taking the mick on Monday because I was miserable. Why d'you ask that, this hasn't got anything to do with our row, surely?'

'Well,' Harry said, and paused. 'It would be much easier to convince someone to hop in their car to see their husband, if they knew you hadn't been together just an hour or so before. I mean, if I was walking to work and someone told me Clara was ill or she'd had an accident, I'd say, "Hold on, she was all right when I left." Do you see what I mean?'

Dan nodded. 'So they'd really need to know both things. That we'd fallen out and that Fifi was back at work?'

'I'd say so. Did you tell anyone at work about that?'

'Yeah, I did,' Dan said. 'It was at dinnertime in the hut on Monday. I didn't have any sandwiches and Owen the chippy said I ought to nip home and make it up with Fifi and get some grub while I was there.'

'And you said she would be at work?' Harry asked.

Dan nodded.

'How many men heard that?'

'Owen, Pete, Roger, Chas.' Dan ticked them off on his fingers, his brow furrowed as he tried to remember who had been there. 'Oh, and Ozzie, five in all.'

'So why don't we give these five names to the police and get them to check if any of them have got criminal records?'

Dan looked aghast. 'I can't do that! Anyway, it couldn't have been any of them, they were all there on Tuesday morning.'

'Yes, but they could have passed the information on to someone else,' Harry said.

'Don't be silly, Harry,' Clara said. 'Why on earth would one of Dan's workmates want to pass on information about Fifi?'

'Well, they wouldn't under normal circumstances, but they might if they had some involvement with whoever killed Bolton.' Harry got up from his chair and went over to the window. He gazed out thoughtfully for some little time, then turned back to look at Dan. 'I know it's a long shot, but I still think we should speak to the police about it.

We'll go down there now, and while we're there I'm going to insist that they issue a press release on Fifi and Yvette being missing.'

Clara looked up at her husband fearfully. 'Won't that make it even more dangerous for Fifi?' she said in a quivering voice.

'A picture of Fifi in the papers might just jog someone's memory,' he said firmly. 'Without some help we'll just be looking for the proverbial needle in the haystack.'

Nora Diamond heard Dan and his in-laws' footsteps going down the stairs and went over to the window to watch them come out of the house. She wished she had gone into work today. She knew only too well that she only felt sick out of guilt, and staying home was making it worse. Especially when she heard Dan's visitors arrive.

She guessed who they were by the way they spoke. And she doubted they would have come here to see Dan unless they were frantic with worry about Fifi.

When Dan came down to her on Wednesday evening and asked when she'd last seen or spoken to Fifi, she had been a little offhand, but then she just assumed Fifi had taken herself off to a friend's because Dan had left her. Last night, however, she'd heard him telling Frank about all the places he'd been to search for her, and all at once she sensed the girl really was in danger.

Dan and his in-laws were walking up Dale Street now, and the mother's strong resemblance to Fifi was remarkable. It wasn't just the blonde hair, the height and slender figure, they also both walked with the same graceful glide. The woman took her husband's hand as they crossed the street, and there was something about the gesture which made Nora's eyes prickle with tears.

'Stop thinking about yourself and go to the police about Jack Trueman,' she said to herself.

But another voice inside her said that was a bad idea. She couldn't afford to risk her past getting out, and maybe he had nothing to do with this anyway.

'Talk to me, Yvette,' Fifi whispered in the dark. She was so cold, hungry and thirsty that she wasn't even sure whether it was Sunday night or Monday, and Yvette hadn't spoken or even moved for hours.

'What is there to talk about, Fifi?' Yvette replied, her flat voice reflecting her feelings of utter hopelessness. 'Except perhaps deciding 'ow much longer we wait before doing it.'

Fifi had been horrified when Yvette had suggested hanging themselves. While she could see her point that a quick death was far better than a slow one from starvation, she still had some hope it wouldn't come to that. It worried her too that Yvette had suggested she help Fifi do it first. While she understood that was meant in a kindly way, so Fifi wouldn't have to see Yvette dying, it still sounded so ghoulish.

'I'll never be able to do that,' Fifi said resolutely. 'Someone will have reported us missing by now. For all we know our pictures may have been in the papers, and someone may have spotted the car driving up here.'

'What is that expression you English are so fond of? "Pigs might fly!"' Yvette said scornfully. 'You tell me this place is hidden away and you see no one near!'

'I know, but there's still hope yet.'

'I 'ave no hope. Do you know what starvation is like? We will become too weak to climb those bars, and we will lie 'ere looking at them wishing we did it while we still 'ad the strength.'

Fifi already felt too weak to climb the bars, and even a whole twenty-four hours since Yvette first suggested it, when she was even colder, hungrier and more distressed, she still wouldn't entertain the idea. But then she still had some absurd faith left that Dan would find her.

It was so strange that now when she thought of Dan and her family, she could only think of the most endearing and lovely things about each of them. She could see Dan coming home with his wage packet and handing it to her trustingly. As long as he had enough for some cigarettes and the odd snack while at work, he never questioned where the rest of his wages went. She thought about how he wrapped himself around her in the night, how he smiled as soon as he opened his eyes. He didn't sulk, complain or envy other people. He was a truly happy man.

She remembered how intuitive and sensitive her father was. He was the one who made the best nurse when one of his children was ill; he got to the kernel of a problem immediately, and knew how to solve it. He was the quiet, calm one in the family, who didn't shout or rush about and rarely got worked up about anything. He had endless patience and he was never opinionated.

Robin was far more affectionate than Peter, but then Peter was more dependable. They were both so undemanding, happy to go along with whatever the majority of the family wanted to do.

Sweet Patty! She would give anything to be able to tell her sister just how much she loved her. All those nights of them giggling in bed, the covering up Patty'd done for Fifi right from a small child. She was a born diplomat, accepting and appreciating that not everyone was as uncomplicated or gentle-natured as she was.

But the biggest change in Fifi's opinion about a family

member was her view of her mother. The weaker and hungrier she'd become, the more she'd remembered good things about Clara. She'd also thought of all the things she'd done, often purposely, to annoy her.

When did she ever do as her mother asked? Even the rule about putting her shoes in the hall cupboard when she came in had to be disobeyed. If all six of them had left their shoes in the hall, what a mess it would have been! If her mother cooked chicken, Fifi wanted pork or lamb; she turned up late for meals, never washed the bath round, and when she was asked to put carefully ironed clothes away, she just dumped them on the bedroom chair.

She'd seen the light about some of these things once she was living with Dan, but it wasn't until now that she realized she had in fact treated her mother like a housekeeper, never asking how she was, what she'd done during the day, or even just thanking her for ironing and mending her clothes. She never offered to help around the house, get shopping or even cook a meal for her mother.

Looking back, she really must have tried her mother's patience. She argued about everything, and when she was younger, she never came home at the time she was told to. She never confided in her mother, never once suggested they went to the pictures or the theatre together. And Fifi was the one who started most of the rows because she would see a mere suggestion as an order or criticism.

It wasn't possible to forgive her mother entirely for not accepting Dan, but Fifi could see now that she'd put all those bad ideas into her mother's head by being so secretive about him in the first place. She was probably scared Fifi would get pregnant, and it would have been easy enough to tell her mother that she understood that fear, and reassure her she intended to wait until she was married. But she never really tried to talk to her mother at all; one sharp remark and she blew up. If she'd just enlisted her father's help, he might have been able to smooth things over.

Yesterday she had written all these thoughts about her family and Dan in the diary she kept in her handbag. She'd explained when and how she came to be brought here, and gave a description of Martin and Del. If she was to die here, someone might find the diary one day, and she hoped that it would, if nothing else, show that she valued them all.

But she wasn't prepared to die that easily, nor was she going to let Yvette give up.

'Taking your own life is a sin,' she said firmly. 'And it's cowardly. If you could survive all that terrible stuff during the war, you can survive this too.'

'You don't understand,' Yvette whined. 'I 'ave nothing to live for. My life holds nothing but hurt and sorrow.'

'It doesn't have to,' Fifi insisted. 'You could go back to working in a couture house, any one of them would be glad to have someone as talented as you. You'd be happier with other people around you, and you could find somewhere nicer to live. You're still young.'

'No!' Yvette cut her short. 'Don't you dare say I might meet a man and fall in love. This could never 'appen.'

Fifi hadn't intended to say that at all. Instead, she was going to suggest Yvette had a change of hairstyle, made herself some fashionable clothes and got out more.

'Life is precious,' she said instead. 'When we get out of here you'll see.'

Yvette sighed deeply, and Fifi thought she was trying to go to sleep again. But suddenly Yvette sat up, disturbing the blanket around them.

'What is it?' Fifi asked, thinking perhaps she'd heard something outside.

'It is no good, I theenk I 'ave to tell you,' Yvette said.

'Tell me what?' Fifi pulled the blanket round her again.

'That I killed Angela.'

Chapter eighteen

Late on Sunday evening Dan escorted his in-laws back to their hotel in Paddington.

'Stay and have a nightcap with us?' Harry suggested.

Dan really wanted to go home. His nerves were frayed and he could see that the hotel bar was full of foreign tourists. He didn't think he could stand their jollity, or the cacophony of different languages, but he was afraid he would seem churlish if he refused.

'Just a quick one then,' he said wearily.

It had been the worst weekend of his life. Coming face to face with Clara Brown again, with all the unpleasant things she'd said about him at their first meeting still ringing in his ears, was so hard. To be fair to her, she hadn't said one harsh word this time, even though he was sure she must be secretly blaming him for Fifi's disappearance, but the fear in her eyes and the tremor in her voice were somehow worse.

Harry had been easier to deal with for he was a logical man and he controlled his emotions. Every time Dan felt himself coming close to breaking down, Harry would put his hand down firmly on his shoulder, a silent message that they were in this together, bound by their love for Fifi.

They had spent most of Saturday hanging around at the police station, with Dan going through books of mug shots to see if he could pick out any faces he'd seen in Dale Street. In the evening they went into the Rifleman as Dan had the faint hope that by introducing the Browns to some of the regulars, some bit of useful information would surface.

Even if Dan had always had a close relationship with Harry and Clara, it would still have been difficult to cope with the strain of being constantly in their company. But to all intents and purposes they were strangers, and Dan had to be constantly on his guard. He felt he had to watch what he said, how he behaved, steer Harry and Clara away from alarmist and rough people. And he had to try to keep them optimistic, when he was in the depths of despair himself.

Today they had been interviewed by several reporters and that had distressed them all even more. At first the reporters had seemed so caring and sympathetic, but Dan had soon become aware that what they really wanted was juicy sensation. When Clara blurted out that Fifi had married Dan in secret, their eyes lit up, guessing at a family estrangement, and Dan had to step in to stop Clara from revealing things she'd be horrified to see in print.

The sky had been like lead all day, with a cold wind, and Dan had a constant picture in his mind of Fifi lying in a cold, dark place, terrified out of her wits. He had always thought he could cope with just about any situation life threw at him. But this waiting around, unable to do anything constructive to find his wife, was too much to bear.

They found a spare table and Harry ordered the drinks from a waiter. 'I'll just check if there are any messages,' he said as the waiter went off. 'And I'll quickly phone home too.'

Dan observed how Clara's eyes followed her husband as he walked back across the bar to the foyer and the phones.

She had held up well, but every time Harry went out of the room her eyes became full of panic as if she were afraid he would vanish too.

Dan knew now that he had been very wrong in thinking the Browns' marriage was more or less an arranged one, without real love. They had revealed their feelings for each other many times this weekend. Love was there, as sturdy as a rock, he'd noticed it in the way they fumbled for each other's hands when one of them became upset or frightened, the looks they exchanged, the little caresses. He felt somewhat ashamed that he'd once thought Clara's problems with Fifi were caused by jealousy.

He had also observed many similarities in their characters. Clara thought she knew best about everything, just as Fifi did. Clara was equally nosy, and she could act like a spoiled child too. She couldn't communicate with others as well as her daughter, and she was more dogmatic, but Dan felt that was largely because of her upbringing and the more sheltered life she'd led.

Yet he had also found much to admire in his mother-in-law. He liked her poise and her directness. Nor was she such a terrible snob as Fifi claimed. She reacted to bad manners with horror, but her attitude was the same whatever social group the ill-mannered person came from. She turned up her nose at people eating in the street, she thought the journalist asking her age was rude. Yet she treated people with lowly jobs, like the chambermaid in the hotel, waiters or taxi drivers with appreciation. In the Rifleman she had been charming. Even when Stan told her he was a dustman she didn't bat an eyelid and later remarked what a gentleman he was.

Clara had of course banked on her daughter marrying a professional man, and why shouldn't she? Her husband was one. But Dan realized now that it was Fifi who had created the frightening image of him in Clara's mind by being so secretive. If she'd only taken him home immediately, Dan felt Clara might still have been stiff and stand-offish at first, but her innate good manners would have demanded that she look for his good points.

He knew this because he could see it happening now. When the three of them went back to Dale Street early on Saturday evening, he had made tea and sandwiches for them, and he saw her watching in surprise when he laid the table. She clearly expected him to put the sandwiches and tea on the floor and tell them to 'dig in'. He might have done that once, but Fifi had trained him well.

Later Clara admired several things he'd made. '*You've made these with a lot of love, Dan. And a great deal of skill*,' she said approvingly. '*Harry is hopeless with his hands.*'

It wasn't an apology for judging him so hastily at their first meeting, but then he neither wanted nor expected one. It just pleased him that at last she was finding things in him to like.

The waiter brought their drinks, and when Dan got some money out of his pocket Clara waved it away. 'I'll put it on our bill,' she said.

They sipped their drinks in silence. Clara was looking at a group of American tourists at the next table. They had very loud voices and even louder clothes.

'London used to be full of very elegantly dressed people,' she said quietly. 'Even during the war everyone made an effort. But I haven't seen one smartly dressed person this weekend.'

'I have,' Dan said. 'There's you.' He meant it, she looked so neat and feminine in a navy blue costume with a white frilly blouse beneath it. He'd felt proud to introduce her in the pub as his mother-in-law.

She gave a weary little smile. 'I feel a wreck,' she said.

'Well, you don't look like one,' he said. 'Just very tired.'

She looked at him long and hard, and Dan braced himself for a sharp retort.

'I misjudged you, Dan,' she said softly and her eyes filled with tears. 'I'm so very sorry.'

He was so taken aback that he was tongue-tied, but as tears trickled down her cheeks he involuntarily moved forward in his seat, picked up a paper napkin and gently wiped her tears away as if she were Fifi.

'The past doesn't matter,' he replied, but Clara's eyes were so like Fifi's that it brought a lump to his throat.

'We'll have no future either if we don't get her back unharmed,' she said, catching hold of his hand with urgency. 'Tell me honestly, Dan, do you think she's already dead?'

'No, of course not,' he said quickly. 'I'm sure I'd know if she was, and besides, if they'd killed her, the police would've found her body by now.'

Clara's face relaxed for a minute, then tightened up again. 'Whatever could have gone on in that house?' she asked. 'It had to be something much more than just the one little girl being killed by her father.'

Dan nodded. 'I can't work out what though,' he said. 'Fifi was always saying that she found it puzzling that anyone would want to play cards with Alfie. I didn't really see what she meant. But now I wish I'd taken more notice of what she was saying, you know, talked to her about her feelings, then maybe she wouldn't have found it necessary to go down to that depot.'

'I've got a lot more to reproach myself with than that,' Clara said sadly. 'I should have been kinder when she lost the baby. I didn't meant to be nasty, but we had that long train journey, and she wasn't the least pleased to see me. I wish I could learn to curb my sharp tongue.'

'Fifi forgot about all that once you came to visit her. And whatever you'd said or done, it couldn't have prevented this,' he said to soothe her. 'If anyone's to blame it's me. I should have been more understanding after she found Angela, but I got irritated when she seemed so obsessed by it. All I could think about was working more so I could get enough money together so we could move away. If I'd just been there listening, maybe she wouldn't have resorted to snooping.'

'I doubt it, Dan,' Clara said. 'She always was a law unto herself. I never found a way to curb that curiosity of hers. I can remember dozens of times when she was still a child when I had to go searching for her. She'd slip out the gate when I wasn't looking and go exploring. Sometimes I'd find her in someone's garden, and she'd have gone right into their house if the door had been left open. She just didn't seem to have any normal sense of caution.'

Harry interrupted them by coming back and slumping down into his chair. 'No news,' he said sadly. 'Patty said that lots of the people she'd contacted to see if Fifi had been in touch with them had rung back to ask if there's any news. She said everyone was being very kind.'

Clara told Harry what she and Dan had been talking about.

'I want you both to stop blaming yourselves,' Harry said when she'd finished. He looked sternly at both his wife and Dan. 'We all know Fifi likes drama, and when there isn't one, she creates one. It's no good you thinking you shouldn't have taken her to London, Dan, you had to go, that was where the work was and a wife's place is at her husband's side. I'm just sorry that we didn't welcome you into our family. We were foolish and short-sighted. In the last two days we've seen for ourselves why Fifi loves you.'

Such a frank admission, and the affectionate and paternal way it was made, was too much for Dan after such a harrowing day and Clara's apology too, and all at once he was crying. He tried to stop himself but he couldn't, and he covered his face with his hands, appalled that he was showing himself up in public.

Clara got up and enveloped him in her arms. 'You poor boy,' she whispered as she rocked him against her chest. 'Stay here in the hotel with us tonight, we'll look after you.'

Her words were a comfort, for Dan couldn't remember anyone ever offering to look after him, not even when he was a child.

In that moment he saw the truth about Clara. She had a hard shell, that much was certain, she liked her own way, and she was stubborn. But the hard shell was there to protect the softness inside her, and she was just like any other good mother, prepared to fight to keep her children from anything that she perceived as harm. And that had once included him.

'Thank you, I appreciate it,' he whispered, pulling himself together. 'I'll be fine, just a temporary blip. But I'll go on home now. I feel closer to Fifi with all her things around me.'

They came out to the hotel foyer with him, and Clara hugged him and kissed his cheek. 'Try and get a good night's sleep,' she said tenderly. 'You never know, the police might have some good news by the morning.'

Harry embraced Dan too. 'We'll come over in the morning and go down to the police station together,' he said. 'Would you like me to go down to your work with you later on? You really must talk to your boss; you don't want to lose your job on top of everything else.'

Dan nodded. He hadn't contacted his firm since Thursday, and he knew he must, even though his job seemed unimportant right now. 'That would be good,' he said, and tried to smile. 'Sleep well and don't worry about me, I'll be fine.'

'Poor lamb,' Clara said thoughtfully as they watched Dan walk down the street to the tube station. 'I can see now why Fifi fell for him; he isn't the cocky, on-the-make thug I took him for at all.'

Harry put his arm around his wife's shoulders and drew her back into the hotel. 'I'm proud to have him as a son-in-law,' he said gruffly. 'He's made of the right stuff.'

As Dan was walking to the tube station, his cheeks still damp with tears. Fifi was sitting up rigid with shock at what Yvette had just said to her.

It was too dark to see her face; she was just a darker shape in front of her, with only the white of her teeth and the collar of her white blouse showing up faintly.

'You can't have killed Angela,' Fifi gasped. 'Don't be silly.'

'I did,' Yvette insisted.

'But why?'

'It was how you say? The lesser evil?'

'I don't understand. I don't believe you either; you couldn't kill anyone, certainly not a child,' Fifi said indignantly. 'And what do you mean by "a lesser evil"?'

A deep sigh came from the Frenchwoman, as if she were gathering her thoughts. 'Sometimes you 'ave to choose between two bad things. Like when you 'ave to choose to treat a very sick animal and maybe make it suffer more, or 'ave it put to sleep. Mama had to choose between sending me away or keeping me with her and maybe we both go to a camp. At theese times we try to choose the lesser of ze two evils.'

Fifi had a mental flashback to Angela lying naked on the bed with blood on her splayed thighs. She also had the image of Yvette being raped in the brothel in Paris.

'So you thought Angela would be used like you?'

She felt a slight movement as if Yvette was nodding her head. 'Right, well explain what happened that morning, from the beginning.'

'Eet started the night before,' Yvette said hesitantly. 'I hear ze men arrive. It is hot, ze windows open. I hear everything like I am in ze room.'

'Let's lie down,' Fifi said gently. 'It's too cold to sit here like this.'

She lay down and Yvette crawled towards her, then pulled the blanket over them both. Fifi waited patiently, afraid to rush Yvette because her breathing was laboured; whether this was because of the enormity of what she'd just confessed, or a symptom of her weakened condition, Fifi didn't know. She thought she ought to be frightened, yet strangely she wasn't.

'Do you remember how hot it was that night?' Yvette asked.

'Mmm,' Fifi replied.

'On hot nights when they had those parties I hate it because the men often use the garden like a pissoir. The smell it comes in my bedroom and kitchen. I was thinking theese when I hear them drinking and laughing, Molly is cackling like a madwoman.'

It was Molly's cackling that Yvette always found hardest to bear when they had these parties. The men's laughter was no different to the sounds from any crowded bar, but Molly's was shrill and maniacal.

At first the noise came from all the rooms on the ground floor, music from the front room, guffaws of laughter, shouted greetings from one man to another, clinking glasses and bottles from out in the kitchen, and now and then the children's voices mingling with the adults.

Earlier in the day, Yvette had overheard Alan and Mary talking excitedly about the trip to Southend the following day and around ten she heard Molly order them to bed with a few choice swear words and the warning they wouldn't be going if they came downstairs again tonight. She thought Dora and Mike went to bed too, as she didn't hear their voices again.

At about ten-thirty the entire party moved into the back room, which was next to her bedroom, and apart from the odd man going out into the garden to urinate, the noise lessened as they settled down for a game of cards. Yvette didn't mind the sound of cards slapping on the table, the odd creak of chairs, sighs and frequent expletives, at least that signalled this wasn't going to be one of those nights when more terrible things went on.

Yvette couldn't hear Molly's voice any longer either, but this wasn't in any way unusual – she could have been drunk in the front room or up in her bedroom with one of the men – but her absence suggested that cards was the only thing on the menu tonight.

She carried on with her sewing by the window in the front room, the curtains closed. She was tired but she knew it was futile to go to bed as the party would go on till the early hours of the morning and then it often became raucous once everyone was drunk and had lost interest in the cards.

Raised voices alerted her later that something unusual

was happening. Fights were common enough, bottles or glasses would be hurled, furniture turned over, and while she hated the noise and the menace of violence, at least she always knew it meant the party was drawing to a close. But this was something different; the men were drumming on the table, there was excitement in their raised voices.

Yvette wasn't in the habit of going to investigate anything going on next door. Over the years she'd learned the hard way what might happen. She'd had a full beer can thrown at her, been sprayed with urine, and just being spotted standing at her kitchen sink could result in screamed accusations that she was spying on them.

But her curiosity got the better of her, and she stole quietly out into the garden, keeping her head well below the fence that separated the houses. When she reached the bottom of the garden and the cover of the tree that overhung the back wall, she stood up on an old crate to see into number 11.

Her view of the Muckles' back room was uninterrupted, and as the lights in there were bright she could see everyone clearly, except for two of the men nearest the window who had their backs to it. There were six men in all, including Alfie, and the table was strewn with glasses, bottles, overloaded ashtrays and cards, with a heap of money in the centre.

Molly was standing, or rather posing seductively, by the door through to the hall, wearing a flimsy red negligee, with just underwear and stockings underneath, and she was holding Angela by the hand.

One swift glance at the men's leering faces, Molly's coquettish expression and Angela's look of complete bewilderment was enough for Yvette to know exactly what Molly was offering.

Her body or that of the child's, in exchange for the money on the table.

Had she not experienced the self-same thing herself as a child, she might very well have imagined Angela's presence was an accident, that she'd come down for a drink at an inopportune moment. But there was no mistaking the slathering hunger in the men's faces, and nothing else would create such a highly charged atmosphere, certainly not just Molly's body which could probably be bought for a bottle of drink.

'There's over two hundred quid in the pot,' one of the men yelled out. 'She ain't worth that much.'

Yvette began to tremble. She clasped her hands together and offered up a silent prayer that the men would denounce a mother who could sell her child, and leave hurriedly.

'Ones this young don't come cheap,' Molly said, then bending over she caught the hem of the child's nightdress and with a flourish whipped it off over Angela's head, leaving her stark naked.

'No, Mum!' Angela cried out, trying to cover herself with her thin arms.

Only a completely perverted beast could possibly have viewed the skinny little girl with her dirty face and unbrushed hair as an object of desire. Her ribs stood out like a relief map, her arms were like sticks of macaroni. But this was obviously what the men were feeling, for there was a buzz of appreciation. Overcome by a wave of both terror and nausea, Yvette got down from the crate and hurried indoors.

'I was sick again and again,' she whispered to Fifi. 'I 'ad feelings Alfie did theese to Mary, and I'm sure he also do it to his older girls when they lived there too. But Angela ees so leetle. She 'ave no breasts, no 'ips, just a small child. I should 'ave gone to the police right then, but I was too frightened and sick.'

Fifi felt sick herself. If she'd had any food inside her she was sure she'd have brought it up. She had formed the opinion that Alfie Muckle was allowing men to use his children, but thinking of something hideous like that in your own head could never be as horrifying as discovering those nightmare images were real.

'Do you know which man got her?' she asked.

'*Oui*,' Yvette whispered. She was trembling by Fifi's side. 'I did not see him but I 'eard his voice and I know it was ze big older man, who come so often. I know 'is name is Jack Trueman, because Molly she boast so often about this rich man who is her friend.'

The name meant nothing to Fifi, but it could very well have been the man with the Jaguar. 'So he took Angela upstairs?' she asked.

'I don't hear right away,' Yvette said. 'Later I go outside again when some of ze men are gone. I 'ope I am mistaken, you see, but then I hear the sound coming from the room at ze top. The old bed creak and poor Angela crying.'

Fifi shuddered. 'Then what?'

'I hear Angela crying in the morning. I think Molly must slap her to shut her up, and then I see ze whole family leave for their day out. I am, 'ow you say?, out of my wits.'

'Beside yourself,' Fifi corrected her automatically, seeing in her own mind the Muckles leaving the house that morning and her amusement at the spectacle of them all in holiday clothes.

'Yes, that is it, beside myself. I want to go in there and comfort her. I feel so badly for her. So I climb over ze back fence and go in.'

She described the filth she saw as she got into the kitchen, and Fifi was there with her, reliving every step of the way that she'd taken herself later that same day.

'I come to that top room and I open ze door, and there Angela is, suffering the way I suffered so many years ago. She had ze blood on her, her privates swollen and red. She look at me with theese big eyes, they say to me that she knows this is what she will get every Friday night, and even if I take her now, look after her and get 'elp, she will never forget. Just as I can never forget.'

Yvette made a kind of keening sound in her throat and began rocking herself.

'So what did you do?' Fifi asked, putting her arm round her and hugging her tightly. What she wanted to hear was something which didn't fit in with what she'd seen, for she still didn't believe Yvette was capable of killing the child.

'She didn't speak. I theenk she was in shock. I put my hand on her forehead. I say I 'elp her, but she is stiff, like she is paralysed. Just her eyes pleading with me, and it comes to me that she is asking me to kill her.'

She fell silent for a moment or two, and then when she did speak again her voice was suddenly cold, crisp and unrepentant. 'I pick up ze pillow and I hold it over her face. She didn't even struggle. Just her hands coming up like so.'

Fifi felt the fluttering of Yvette's hands even though she couldn't see them.

'It was quick. I wait till her hands go down, then I take the pillow away. She is dead and will never suffer that again. I go out on ze landing where there is cupboard; I find a clean sheet and put it over her. Then I go back to my flat.'

Too stunned to speak, and appalled as she was, Fifi could understand what made Yvette do it. She had no doubt that when she was confronted by the ravaged child, her mind flipped back to her own terrible experiences in France. Maybe after the first man raped her, Yvette had lain like that in the bed wishing for death.

What Yvette did, in her own mind at least, was an act of compassion. She was putting a fatally wounded animal out of its misery. Giving Angela what had been denied her.

'You understand now why I do not want to live?' Yvette said suddenly, breaking the silence. 'I 'ave theese on my conscience, I cannot forget. And now you are afraid of me too?'

'No, I'm not afraid of you,' Fifi said slowly. 'I can understand.'

She lay there silently for some little while. She felt sick and giddy, and she was frightened too by the enormity of what she'd been told. To think that all this had been going on just across the road to her. A seven-year-old child sold to the highest bidder! How could any mother be so depraved?

All through the summer she had been reading the juicy story of Christine Keeler, Mandy Rice-Davies and John Profumo, actually enjoying and being titillated by the scandal. But this far more terrible stuff had been going on right under everyone's nose.

'You are afraid,' Yvette said sorrowfully.

'Not of you,' Fifi sighed. 'I just wish you'd come over to me that night, or even the next morning, and told me what was going on. Then none of this would have happened.'

'But no one could understand what something like that could do to a leetle girl,' Yvette said sorrowfully. 'Once eet is done she have it in her head for life. They might give her a new home, buy her a bicycle and dollies. But it never go away.'

Fifi could neither agree nor disagree. All she wished was that day when Angela had been with her, she'd acted on her instinct and got outside help for the child. But she was too drained now to discuss it further. Angela was dead, let down by everyone – her parents, neighbours, doctor and teachers. Everyone who touched her young life had some responsibility, but it was too late to apportion blame now.

She tried to go to sleep, but her head was still whirling with what she'd been told.

'Why didn't the police find your fingerprints?' she asked suddenly. The police had taken hers, Dan's, Frank and Stan's and probably everyone else's they'd spoken to, to compare with ones they found in number 11. One of the biggest problems the police had had during this investigation was the number of fingerprints in the house, and many of them couldn't be matched to ones they had on record.

'I 'ad my rubber gloves on because I not like to touch anything in that house, eet is so dirty.'

Fifi remembered how she had scrubbed her hands after coming out of there, but she wouldn't have thought of putting on gloves before she entered. She thought a prosecuting lawyer would claim that made it a premeditated crime. 'I see. Were you in your flat all that day?'

'No,' Yvette said. 'I see you up in your window, and so I go out along the back wall like Alfie do. I get a taxi to my fitting. I know I will arrive at the time I was expected. I tell the police I left just after eight and went by bus.'

Yvette fell asleep then but Fifi was unable to. Just as it was difficult to credit anyone with taking the rest of their family for a day out after selling a seven-year-old to some pervert, so it was just as hard to imagine a woman doing what Yvette had done. Not so much the actual killing of Angela, that made a kind of sense, but for her to escape along a wall minutes later and spend the day doing a dress fitting seemed very calculated.

A cold chill crept over Fifi. Yvette had told her all this because she didn't believe they were going to be rescued. What if she woke in the morning, felt optimistic someone would find them and then regretted telling her? What might she do then?

'She wouldn't do that,' she told herself very firmly. 'And anyway Dan will find me. I know he will.'

On Tuesday morning Dan found it hard to get out of bed. The lack of sleep in the past week had finally got to him and he hadn't woken up at all during the night. As he lay there listening to still more rain against the window, and knowing the day ahead would hold nothing but more misery, he wanted to fall asleep again and have some respite from the nagging anxiety.

But he'd promised Harry and Clara he'd go down to the police station and see if there was any progress and then join them at the hotel afterwards. The story of Fifi and Yvette's disappearance was in all the newspapers the previous day, and they needed to stay where they could be contacted in case anyone phoned with some information.

Clara and Harry had come here yesterday and Clara sent Dan off to the launderette with his washing while she cleaned the flat. Harry said she always cleaned when she was upset, but Dan had found it upsetting to see her doing all the jobs Fifi had once done.

The woman in the launderette wanted to know everything. While Dan knew this was because she had often talked to Fifi and was just worried about her, he couldn't get out of the launderette fast enough, because he was now finding it hard to talk to people. Tears kept welling up and he found he got his words confused; in fact he had a job to string a sentence together.

It was good that Harry had gone with him yesterday to see his boss. Arnie Blake was a decent bloke, though short on humanity when he had penalty clauses hanging over his head. But Harry had a knack of putting things in such a way that anyone would feel obliged to go along with what he said. Arnie eventually told Dan he could have as much time off as he needed, and he'd still have a job to return to, but right now Dan thought if he didn't get Fifi back in one piece he'd be flinging himself under a tube train.

He had never experienced misery like this before. Throughout his bleak childhood, National Service, periods of sleeping rough, terrible digs and all the other black spots in his life, some of which were caused by women, he'd still managed to remain cheerful. But then with every other woman he'd ever been involved with he'd always kept a part of himself back. He'd given all of himself to Fifi; she was his sun, moon and stars. Without her everything was grey, and he missed her physically as if he'd had a limb cut off.

Reluctantly he got out of bed, washed, shaved and put on his trousers, but as he opened the wardrobe to get out a clean shirt and saw all the freshly ironed ones that Clara had hung in there beside Fifi's clothes, he began to cry.

He tried to laugh at himself but he couldn't. Fifi hated ironing shirts, and mostly she just ironed the collar and the front and hung them up hoping he wouldn't notice. To see them all perfect was absolute evidence she wasn't here, and to him confirmation she was never coming back.

He had cried several times in the last few days, but not like this. It was as though something had broken inside him and he could no longer suppress the pain and anguish. He banged the wardrobe shut but it made no difference;

everywhere there was evidence of Fifi – her hairbrush on the chest of drawers, the dressing-gown on the back of the door, her slippers by the bed.

He wrenched the dressing-gown off the door and holding it to his face he sobbed and sobbed. He could smell her Blue Grass perfume on the soft material, and the smell evoked memories of their wedding day and the first time they made love.

She was so innocent then, but so eager to please him. He'd never cared that she was a lousy cook, or that she didn't like ironing or clearing up, he would gladly have waited on her hand and foot as long as he could spend every night with her beautiful body close to his and those soft arms around him.

'Dan?'

At the sound of Miss Diamond's voice he took the dressing-gown away from his face and saw the older woman in the bedroom doorway. She was dressed for work in a suit, and she looked very anxious.

'I'm sorry to intrude,' she said. 'But I heard you crying and I was afraid you'd got bad news.'

The sympathy in her voice just made Dan cry harder, and all at once Miss Diamond had her arms round him, holding him tightly.

'It was just the shirts, and seeing Fifi's things,' he managed to get out. 'There's no news yet.'

She took his hand and led him still bare-chested down to her kitchen where she sat him down, saying she was going to make him a cup of tea. But he was still unable to stop crying and she stood by his chair, held him to her breast and let him weep, just silently patting his back as if he were a small child.

'You poor love,' she said after a little while. 'You've been so brave and strong for so long, but it's all got too much for you.'

Dan calmed down enough to say he mustn't stop her from going to work, but she waved that off by saying it didn't matter, she could always make the time up another day. She made him tea, then some scrambled eggs, and asked if there had been any response from anyone now Fifi's picture had been in the papers.

The tea and the eggs made Dan feel a little better, and he told her about what had gone on at the weekend and that Fifi's parents were staying in the hotel today and he'd go there later after he'd called at the police station.

'They don't seem to be taking the connection with John Bolton very seriously,' he said. It was surprisingly easy to talk to Miss Diamond; she was matter of fact about it all, and she didn't ask stupid questions or interrupt with irrelevant personal anecdotes the way most people did. She just sat there opposite him at the table and gently encouraged him to talk. 'I don't think they even believe there is a connection, even if it's as plain as day that there is,' he went on. 'They say they are investigating it, but they haven't told me one concrete thing they've done. They ought to be turning over all John's known associates, pulling people in, but as far as I can see they've done nothing.

'This bloke Fifi saw with the red Jag for instance,' he continued angrily. 'She saw him and John going into the Muckles' one Friday. Why can't they find him? How many people around here have got new red Jags, for God's sake! There can't be that many in the whole of London. It's obvious to me that Fifi was snatched because she'd been to the police about him, and you can't tell me she's the only person that could pick him out in a line-up! It can't be that fucking difficult either to find out who John worked with. I don't think they've even leaned on Vera.'

He blushed. 'Sorry about the swearing, Miss Diamond,' he said. The business about the car had really annoyed him. He'd asked Roper if they'd contacted all the Jaguar dealers in London and got a list of everyone who had bought a new red one in the past two years. Roper said there were men out there doing just that right now, but so far the only names they'd turned up were bonafide business and professional men.

'Miss Diamond is a bit formal, Nora will do,' she said, and half smiled as she ruffled Dan's hair. 'And what you're going through is enough to make anyone swear. I'm sure the police are doing their job, and they were over at Vera's on Sunday while you were out. But it isn't easy to get people to talk after what happened to John, they are too afraid.'

'Afraid of what?' Dan exclaimed. 'They don't have to give themselves away or shout it from the rooftops, all they need to do is whisper a name if they know it. They are bloody cowards!'

Nora's stomach churned at Dan's condemnation of the neighbours. She'd spoken to Frank Ubley on Sunday and he'd said all this had come out because people were too cowardly to stand up to the Muckles, himself included. Yesterday she'd called into the corner shop and overheard a couple of people discussing Fifi and Yvette's disappearance. Their view was that someone around here knew exactly who was responsible, and if the two women were found dead, they should be horsewhipped for not telling the police what they knew.

She had been stricken with guilt all last night, going over

and over it in her mind. But she'd told herself that she couldn't just go to the police and tell them she thought Jack Trueman was the man they wanted, not without telling them why. She'd come to the conclusion in the early hours of this morning that she should type an anonymous letter when she got into work. But faced now with Dan's distress and the serious danger Fifi and Yvette were in, she couldn't keep quiet any longer. As Dan had said himself, '*They don't have to give themselves away or shout it from the rooftops, all they need to do is whisper a name.*'

She took a deep breath. 'I can whisper a name,' she blurted out. 'The name of the man I think is behind it.'

Dan's expression was almost laughable, the kind of look he might give old Mrs Jarvis if she told him she'd helped in the Great Train Robbery last month.

'I know,' she said, hanging her head. 'You think I can't possibly know anyone dubious, but in fact I was married to a scoundrel once, and that's how I came to end up here.'

She had no intention of divulging her story to anyone, not even Dan whom she felt she could trust. 'If I tell you what I know about this man, you must promise me that you won't tell anyone you got it from me.'

He looked at her long and hard. 'I promise,' he said, then leaned forward in his chair, his expression boyishly eager.

'His legitimate businesses are mainly in Soho,' she said. 'John Bolton used to manage one of his clubs. I saw him go into the Muckles' several times, including that last card party.'

He gasped. 'And you kept this to yourself, even when a child was killed?'

Nora reeled at the contempt in his voice. 'Angela's death didn't appear to have anything to do with the card players. We all thought they'd gone home the night before Alfie killed her. It was only when I heard John was dead that I thought about this man again, and I've got good reason to be afraid of him myself, so I couldn't speak out. But now Fifi and Yvette –' She broke off as she began to cry.

'Okay,' Dan said. 'Just tell me his name.'

'Jack Trueman,' she said in a low voice. 'Please don't tell the police you got it from me.'

Dan let out a long low whistling breath and rubbed his hands on his thighs. She hardly dared look at him for fear he would attack her verbally. 'I'm sorry I'm such a coward,' she whispered.

Dan got up from his chair and put one hand on her shoulder. 'At least you finally told me. Thank you.'

Nora got up, afraid for Dan now because she could see steely determination in his eyes. 'He's a very dangerous man,' she said, her voice shaking. 'Be careful who you trust.'

She stood watching him as he went back upstairs, the muscles rippling in his bare young back. She was even more afraid then because she knew if Fifi was dead, Dan's revenge would be terrible.

As Dan was putting a shirt and shoes on, he heard Nora go down the stairs and leave the house. He guessed she'd rushed off because she was afraid he would come back down and press her for more information. Frank was frying bacon on the ground floor, and the smell wafted up, making Dan feel just a little queasy. He opened the bedroom window wide, and sat on the bed for a minute to compose himself.

There was no guarantee Nora was right in thinking that this man Jack Trueman had killed Bolton, or snatched Fifi and Yvette. And without telling the police where he got the name, and with nothing to back it up with, they were likely to dismiss it as poppycock. So how could he take this information to them and make them act on it?

Johnny Milkins' remark on Saturday night when he took Harry and Clara into the Rifleman came back to him then.

'I reckon one of the men that played cards with Alfie was a copper. It stands to reason. Alfie never got nicked for nothin'. He found out stuff that could only have come from the nick. And they ain't really pushing to find your Fifi, are they?'

Harry had dismissed Milkins' claim as utter rubbish, to him all policemen were above reproach. Dan knew that wasn't so, he was only too well aware that many of them took bribes from villains to look the other way, or at least give advance warning of raids. But he didn't believe any policemen, bent or not, would mix socially with Alfie.

Yet if this man Trueman owned nightclubs, it was quite likely he'd have a copper or two in his pocket.

So if there was a bent copper at the nick, and he got to hear what Dan had to say, would he tip Trueman off?

One side of his brain said he was being paranoid, but the other said he couldn't take any chances. A nervous villain with police on his tail might do anything. He'd certainly get rid of any evidence.

Dan got up from the bed and reached for his jacket. The first thing to do was to find out more about Jack Trueman.

Fifi woke to the sound of rain. She was warmer than usual and was about to close her eyes again when she realized the blanket over her felt thicker. She touched it, and found it was doubled over her, Yvette's coat on top.

She moved her head to look round, but couldn't see Yvette, and it was alarm that made her wake properly.

It was dusk. Another twenty minutes or so and it would

be really dark, and she realized she must have been asleep for several hours. Yvette had been acting very strangely in the morning, sitting well away from Fifi, rocking herself and muttering in French, while running the belt from her skirt through her hands as if it were a rosary.

Fifi had gone to her and put her arms around her, and told her to stop talking and to come and lie down to conserve her strength.

Yvette had looked at her strangely. 'I thought I was with Mama,' she said.

They had lain down together, and the last thing Fifi remembered before she drifted off was Yvette taking hold of her hand. 'Sleep, *ma petite*,' she had said softly as a mother might to a child. 'May the angels take care of you.'

Remembering those last words, it was all Fifi could do to make herself look round and up, for she instinctively knew what she was going to see and didn't want to.

Yet she still screamed when she saw her.

Yvette was dangling in space from the top rail of the cage, her brown belt tight around her neck. Her eyes were bulging horribly and her mouth gaping open as if in a silent scream. The slight breeze was making her body sway.

Fifi knew that if she was to get up, she'd faint, so she lay down again, shut her eyes tightly and pulled the blanket over her head.

It seemed incredible that Yvette had found the strength to climb up there, and the steely nerve not only to do what she intended but control herself enough to be quiet and not wake her friend. Even the place she'd picked was out of Fifi's line of vision from the mattress.

Yet even though Fifi wished she could be big-hearted enough to be glad Yvette's troubles were over, her whole being wanted to shriek at her selfishness for leaving her alone to die. But she was too weak to rage and shriek; she had got to resign herself to lying here while a dead body swung overhead.

Last night Yvette had whispered many things in the darkness, about how when the war was over, she and the other girls in the brothel were dragged out into the street where their heads were shaved because it was thought they collaborated with the Germans.

She spoke of walking by night towards Calais, sleeping in fields and barns by day so she wouldn't be seen, and rooting for something edible in fields and orchards which had been laid to waste by troops during the war. She was eventually rescued by a group of old nuns living in a ruined church. They nursed her back to health, sharing the meagre rations they had, and it was they who put her in touch with the refugee organization which helped her to get to England.

Fifi had thought she was telling her this to prove how long you could survive without food if you had the will to live, as she did then. But now it looked to Fifi as if she'd been trying to say she wished she'd just given up then and allowed herself to die.

Fifi felt compelled to look up again. The light was fading, ten more minutes and it would be pitch dark, and she felt she couldn't leave her friend dangling in space. She would have to force herself to climb up and bring her body down.

Just a week before she'd climbed up there as nimbly as a monkey, but when she tried to do it now, she found all her strength was gone. There was no power in her grip on the bars, her legs and arms had lost their coordination. This was evidence that the wasting process of thirst and starvation was well underway.

But she continued, her breath rasping with the effort. When she did finally reach Yvette and put one arm out to test her weight, she realized she was just too weak to lift her enough to unbuckle the belt around her neck, and she'd got nothing to cut it with.

Just touching her friend, feeling the stiffness of the body which had kept her warm all these nights made her cry and shake so much she nearly fell down. Every bone in her body ached, her vision was blurred and she knew it was the beginning of the end.

Somehow she managed to get back down and crawl back to the mattress, but the effort it took was so great that she could hardly manage to pull the blanket over herself again.

She would never be able to get up again; this was it, the last part of the slow slither into death. She recalled telling Yvette how she'd read somewhere that yogis in India could last for weeks without food or water by slowing down their breathing and lying quite still. Yvette had only smiled, so perhaps she had already made up her mind what she was going to do.

Fifi's mouth and throat were so dry she couldn't think of anything else. She knew too that even if she did hear someone outside, she couldn't shout. But it was the prospect of another night in here which terrified her most. She was sure that rats would descend on her, sensing she couldn't fight them off.

Chapter nineteen

Dan hesitated at the gate to Johnny Milkins' scaffolding yard. The rain had turned the ground into a mud bath, and a half-loaded flat-bed truck stood in the centre of it.

It wasn't the mud that deterred Dan, just the fear that if Johnny could give him the information he needed, he would feel compelled to act on it, alone and without police backup. Was he doing the right thing?

Johnny appeared in the doorway of his office at the back of the yard, his big face breaking into a welcoming grin as he saw Dan.

'Come on in, the water's lovely,' he yelled out. 'Or are you afraid of mucking up yer shiny shoes?'

Dan smiled despite his anxiety. The big man's humour was always a tonic. He sidestepped the worst of the mud and made it to the office.

'Just in time for a brew,' Johnny said, slapping Dan on the back. 'This pissing rain is buggering up my schedule. I had to send the men home. To tell the truth I was just thinking of going meself. Can't do a sodding thing in weather like this.'

Dan took off his mackintosh and hung it on a hook on the wall. The office was really only a shed, with as much mud on the floor as outside, and piled high with papers and boxes of assorted scaffolding joints. The walls were covered in pin-up pictures, many of which had moustaches and beards added, and on the floor was what appeared to be a large quantity of ladies' knitwear in a large open carton. Clearly something that had fallen off a lorry.

'Been trying on women's clothes?' Dan joked as Johnny plugged in an electric kettle balanced on an old beer crate.

'You caught me out,' Johnny said. 'Another few minutes I'd 'ave been dressed in a pink twinset. But don't tell no one. It don't fit me image.'

'I won't tell anyone if you promise you won't tell anyone about what I'm going to ask you,' Dan said.

'You want me to bung you a few bob fer the rent?' Johnny retorted. 'Or are you trying to tell me I'm a bloody loud-mouth?'

'Neither,' Dan said. He sat down on a chair with a broken back. 'It's just I know you've got a mate down the nick, and I don't want him to know about this.'

'Something about Fifi?' Johnny was suddenly serious. He liked Fifi, and Dan was pretty certain he'd do anything for her.

Dan nodded. 'Well, in as much as I may have got a lead on who's got her. But I'm scared to go to see Plod for the very reasons you brought up on Saturday.'

''Er dad didn't believe me, did 'e?' Johnny said and laughed, his huge stomach quivering.

'No, but I do. I want to know the SP on Jack Trueman. Do you know him?'

Johnny sucked in his cheeks and looked anxious. 'Only by his rep. He's an evil bastard,' he said. 'Not the sort of geezer I'd shake 'ands wiv. Whatcha wanna know for? Someone told you 'e might 'ave Fifi?'

'That's about the size of it.'

Johnny shook his head slowly. It wasn't an indication he

427

didn't believe it, more that he thought it unwise to take it any further. 'Who told you that?'

'I can't tell you, but believe me it's someone with their head stuck on straight and no reason to make it up.'

The kettle boiled and Johnny hurled the contents of a battered teapot out of the door, put a couple more spoons of fresh tea in it and filled it up, stirring it vigorously before answering.

'Okay, I reckon it's possible. John Bolton did work fer 'im some time back an' all,' he said, scratching his head thoughtfully. 'But then every face on the manor 'as done summat fer 'im at some time, even me. That's cos 'e gets is fingers in every pie. But I can't get the connection wiv Fifi.'

'Trueman was at the Muckles',' Dan said.

'Well, that bastard Alfie would arse-lick Old Nick 'imself if 'e thought there was something to be gained by it,' Johnny said, his genial face darkening. 'But it's fuckin' 'ard trying to imagine Trueman getting cosy wiv a maggot like 'im.'

'He has been there, several times, that's definite. Fifi told the Plod she'd seen him there with Bolton, only she didn't know the man's name.'

'Yeah?' Johnny looked worried now. 'When did she do that?'

'The day before Bolton was chucked in the river.'

'Shit,' Johnny exclaimed.

'So I want to know where Trueman hangs out,' Dan said. 'I can't wait till the Plod get their finger out. Fifi might be dead by then.'

Johnny looked hard at Dan, as if weighing up whether he should help him or not.

'Tell me, Johnny,' Dan said simply. 'I'm not asking you

to get involved. If he captures me I won't tell him where I got the info from, all I want is his address.'

Johnny poured tea into two mud-splattered cups, spooned some condensed milk and a couple of sugars into each and handed one to Dan.

''E's probably the 'eaviest, deadliest bloke in London,' he said, his voice subdued now, all humour gone. ''E's got an army around 'im 'an all. Everyone is shit scared of 'im. You can't take 'im on. It just ain't possible.'

'How old is he?'

Johnny shrugged. 'About sixty I'd say. 'E had the West End sewn up when I was still a nipper. Keeps 'imself fit 'an all.'

Dan was not going to be put off. To him a man of sixty, whether fit or not, could be induced to talk. All he needed to know was where to look for him, and he'd work out the rest of his plan when he'd checked that out.

'He can't be surrounded by his men all the time,' he said. 'I've just got to pick a moment when he's alone.'

Johnny nodded, then reluctantly said that the man had a big house near Brentwood in Essex. He listed the names of some of the clubs he owned and told Dan that he ran his empire from an office in St Anne's Court in Soho.

'That's all I need.' Dan drank down the last of his tea and got up, grinning wolfishly at Johnny. 'I'll get up there right now.'

'Don't, mate.' Johnny grabbed his arm. 'You can't, 'e's too big for you. Far too big fer me an 'all. I can't let you do this. I don't want you found in the river.'

'He won't be expecting one man to come after him,' Dan said, brushing down the jacket of his suit with his hand. It was the one he'd bought to marry Fifi and he'd worn it ever since Clara and Harry arrived in London so he'd look outwardly respectable. 'He might be tough-mob-handed, but I doubt he'll be as quick on his feet as me when he's on his own, and I'll be fighting for my wife's life, so it won't be easy to put me down.'

'You don't know what you're doing,' Johnny said with a sigh, but there was admiration in his blue eyes. 'Hang on a bit while I round up some of the lads to 'elp?'

'No, I'm not going to involve anyone else,' Dan said resolutely.

Johnny turned and opened an old filing cabinet, rummaged around under papers and drew out a cloth bag. 'If you must go at least take this'un,' he said, as he undid the tie. He removed some oiled rag and there was a small pistol. He put it in Dan's hand. 'It's in good working order, I've looked after it. Do you know anything about guns?'

Dan nodded, looking down at it. 'Yeah, I did my National Service. But I don't want it. I'd rather tear him apart with my own hands.'

'Don't be a prat, it'll be your life or 'is and this'll give you a fighting chance,' Johnny said as he reached back into the cabinet and brought out a box of cartridges.

Dan thought for a second and decided the man might be right, so he took them, loaded the gun and put it into his pocket, then gave the rest of the cartridges back to Johnny. 'Thanks, mate. I won't use it unless I have to. I owe you one.'

'All you owe me is to come back here in one piece,' Johnny said gruffly. 'Good luck, mate.'

It was still raining when Dan came out of Leicester Square tube station, and checking on a tourist map he found out where St Anne's Court was. Ten minutes later he'd been up and down it twice, and now he was perched on a stool in a coffee bar, drinking a coffee, smoking a cigarette and eyeing up the building opposite.

Trueman's office appeared to be above the dirty-book shop, and surprisingly the door that led to it was open, revealing a narrow, uncarpeted staircase which looked as if it hadn't been swept for years. He could see a fluorescent light on the ceiling of the office above, but not who was in there.

He could feel the hardness of the gun in his pocket, and he thought he ought to feel safer with it. But he didn't, he didn't like the feeling it gave him at all. What he wanted to do was punch the lights out of the man who was holding Fifi. Punch him and kick him until he told him where she was, then beat him some more, and only then, when he felt he'd maimed him for life, was he going to feel better.

There was a mirror on the wall beside him, and it seemed odd that the rage he felt inside didn't show on his face. He looked normal – clean-shaven, wearing a sparkling white shirt, a blue striped tie and his wedding suit. He didn't even look like a workman, more like a bank clerk.

But that was just as well, because he was going up into that office now, and he'd got to play at being an office worker who'd lost his way, while he checked the place out. He stubbed out his cigarette, smiled at the girl behind the counter, and walked out of the door and across the Court.

The tapping of the typewriter grew louder as he climbed the stairs. At the top was a half-glazed door. That was a further surprise as he'd expected the place would be like Fort Knox. He knocked, but opened it immediately and went in.

There was a woman of about thirty behind the desk wearing a red blouse. She was plain with glasses and straight, lank brown hair. She stopped typing and smiled. An open door beside her desk clearly led to Trueman's office, judging by the big leather swivel chair in there. It wasn't much of an office for a man with a sizable empire, and it was almost as chaotic as Johnny's.

'Can I help you?' the woman said.

'I'm the temp you booked,' Dan said. 'From Alfred Marks.'

She looked puzzled. 'We haven't booked a temp,' she said. 'Are you sure you've got the right address?'

'I hope so,' Dan said, giving her one of what Fifi had always called his winning smiles. He made a great show of feeling in his pockets, and finally pulled out the piece of paper he'd scribbled on earlier. 'Number six, St Anne's Court,' he read. 'That's right, isn't it?'

'Well, yes,' she said, frowning. 'But Mr Trueman didn't tell me to expect anyone from an agency.'

'Is he here to ask?' Dan asked, slipping off his wet raincoat and holding it over his arm.

'No, he's not I'm afraid,' she said. 'He doesn't normally come in until one. I can't phone him either because he's out at one of his businesses.'

'Oh dear,' Dan said, looking downcast. 'This isn't a very good start. I've only just come up to London and I was really pleased when I got offered this job straight away.'

Dan's Wiltshire accent had grown a lot less pronounced since he'd been working in London, but he laid it on thick for the woman. 'It would have been nice to work with you too.'

She blushed and dropped her eyes. 'Where are you from?' she asked.

Dan told her he came from Trowbridge, and played the country boy up in the big city for all he was worth, telling her how confusing he found London, and how expensive everything was. It seemed to do the trick as he could see her getting more relaxed and interested in him by the minute. He found out her name was Janice, and told her he'd got a room in Kentish Town and that he really wanted to work in a bank but he'd decided to do some temporary agency work until he'd found his way about.

'I was knocked out when they sent me to Soho,' he said, grinning at her like a Cheshire cat. 'It must be really exciting working here.'

She laughed. 'The Soho you mean doesn't get going till after the shops and offices close,' she said. 'I never see it.'

'Surely your boyfriend brings you up to the clubs and stuff at night?' he said.

'I haven't got one,' she said. 'But ordinary people like me don't come up here anyway. I don't think I'd like it much either, it's bad enough seeing the people who work at Mr Trueman's clubs and coffee bars during the day. None of them are my kind of people.'

Dan feigned innocent surprise that her boss owned such places, and asked her what these people were like.

'Well, they're a bit rough,' she said, clearly aware she mustn't be too indiscreet. 'Tough but dim men, women who've had a hard life.'

Through all this Dan was taking in everything in the two intercommunicating offices. Behind Janice's desk another door was open just wide enough to see into a small cloakroom. There was only the one way in and out, and the windows which opened on to St Anne's Court were overlooked on the other side by what looked like a disused storeroom.

'The boss runs clubs and coffee bars?' he exclaimed. 'I was told it was a packaging company, they said I'd be doing invoices.'

'I think you've got the wrong place then,' she said, looking very disappointed. 'This is Trueman's Enterprises. What name did they give you?'

He made a show of consulting his paper again. 'You're gonna think I'm a really dumb country boy,' he grinned. 'It's called Truscot's, not Trueman's. I'd better go and phone the agency and tell them they've given me the wrong address.'

'You can use this phone,' she said, indicating the one on her desk.

'I can't take advantage of a lady's phone,' he said. 'But do you get out for lunch? I'd like to buy you one for being so kind.'

He could see the delight in her eyes, and guessed she didn't often get chatted up.

'That would be lovely,' she said, blushing as red as her blouse. 'I can go when Mr Trueman gets here. I usually have to take letters to the post and go to the bank for him.'

'What does he do when you aren't here?' Dan asked.

She giggled girlishly. 'Swears at people down the phone mostly I suspect. Messes up the pile of letters I've left for him to sign, and fills the place with cigar smoke.'

'Doesn't sound as if you like him much,' Dan said.

She sighed. 'He's not an easy man to like. But he pays well and I run the place on my own most of the time. When I get back from lunch he usually goes out again, it's rare that we're both in here together for more than a couple of hours.'

Dan felt a surge of delight that he'd come to the one place where the man was vulnerable. He had expected that his office would be impregnable and full of people.

'Shall I meet you in Joe Lyons in Leicester Square? I know where that is,' Dan suggested.

'Okay,' she said with a shy smile. 'I'll have to go to the bank first so I won't be there till about twenty past I expect.'

'I'll wait however long it takes,' he said, looking right into her eyes.

'What about the other job? And you haven't told me your name.' She giggled.

'I'll suggest I start tomorrow, or at least well after two,' he said as he picked up his raincoat. 'And I'm Ted Baxter. But I'd better go now, I'm holding up your work.'

Dan went straight to an ironmonger's close by in Berwick Street and bought a length of washing line. In a secluded doorway he fastened it round his waist under his jacket. Then he went straight back into the coffee bar opposite Trueman's office again, and got a seat by the window so he could watch who came in and went out.

By eleven-thirty Dan had drunk three cups of coffee, eaten a bacon sandwich and pretended to read an entire newspaper. He'd seen a brassy-looking woman of about forty-five in a very tight skirt and high heels go up the stairs, and then come back down only minutes later. He thought she might be a manageress of one of Trueman's clubs. A bit later a teenage boy with a scar down his cheek went in and he wasn't long either. Then about twelve o'clock two men slightly older than Dan arrived. One had crinkly red hair, the other light brown, and both had the look of professional hard men with their expensive suits and broad shoulders. The red-haired one clearly fancied himself; Dan had noticed him admiring his reflection in the shop window, and he had an exaggerated swagger.

Dan was holding his breath now, willing the two men to come out because if Trueman arrived and they were still in there, he'd have to back off. Even with a gun he couldn't take on three of them alone.

At quarter to one the two men came down again. They

stood outside the door for a little while and seemed to be arguing about something. It was ten to one when they eventually moved away.

Trueman sauntered down the Court at five past. Dan knew it was him even before he turned into the office doorway just by the way he walked. It was an arrogant, head-held-high, get-out-of-my-way walk, and he stood out in the midst of office workers because of his height and size and his immaculate cream trench coat. As Johnny had said, he did look fit, and despite the greying hair seemed less than sixty. The gold watch glinting on his wrist had probably cost more than a house.

The coffee bar was filling up now with people on their lunch-hours, giggling office girls, businessmen and quite a few rough-looking types that Dan would put down as the dirty mac brigade fortifying themselves before going to one of the afternoon stripclubs.

Dan picked up a newspaper someone had left behind and hid behind it, in case Janice glanced in as she left the office. She came hurrying out at quarter past one, her handbag bulging with mail to be posted. He noted she'd put on some makeup and backcombed her hair.

It was time. His heart was thumping and he felt a bit queasy for he knew once he was in the office there was no turning back. He didn't know for certain that he'd got the right man, and Trueman could be armed too – he wouldn't have got the reputation of being tough for nothing. But the week of anxiety about Fifi had built up so much rage inside him that he wasn't going to think about what-ifs. He was going to get Fifi back come what may.

He closed the street door quietly as he went in, putting the lock on, and left his raincoat down there. Creeping up the stairs, he listened. The man was on the phone barking orders about a delivery of drinks. Dan could smell cigar smoke.

At the top of the stairs he paused, checked the rope was concealed under his jacket, patted the pocket where his gun was, took a deep breath and marched in. Trueman was in the inner office, tilted back in the big chair, his feet on the desk, and he'd taken off his suit jacket.

'I fucking well told you to deliver this a week ago,' he shouted down the phone, only glancing round at Dan briefly and indicating that he wouldn't be long. 'This will be the last order you ever get if you don't get it round there right now. You got that?'

He slammed down the phone and looked up at Dan. 'Bloody wankers,' he said. 'Couldn't run a piss-up in a brewery. What can I do for you, son?'

Dan walked towards the older man and stopped in the doorway of his office. 'I want my wife back,' he said in a measured tone, pulling out the gun. 'And if you give me the runaround I'm going to kill you.'

The shock on the man's face was almost laughable. His eyebrows shot up and he stared at the gun as if he thought he was seeing things. 'Your wife?' he repeated. 'I haven't got your bloody wife.'

For just a second Dan thought he might be wrong, but it was too late to consider that now. 'Fifi Reynolds,' he said. 'And you've got Yvette Dupré. Don't fuckin' piss around or I'll just shoot your leg for starters.' He took another couple of steps into the office and pointed the gun at the man's leg, still on the desk, wondering if he should shoot him anyway to speed things up.

'Get out of here,' the man roared, getting to his feet. 'You think you can come on to my turf and threaten me? I've eaten boys like you for breakfast.'

The fact that Trueman didn't persist in denying he had the women, or ask any questions, was enough proof for Dan that he had got the right man. He could see what Trueman was, a bully through and through. He'd grown so used to frightening people with his hired thugs that he'd forgotten that alone he was just another middle-aged man, and a cornered one at that.

'This gun is loaded, the door downstairs is locked, and your secretary won't be back for an hour at least,' Dan growled at him. 'I really want to hurt you, I'm dying to beat the shit out of you for taking my wife, so if you've got any sense you'll tell me where she is now.'

'I don't know what you're talking about,' Trueman said, but he looked scared now, taking a step back behind his desk.

'Sit down, you piece of shit,' Dan bellowed at him, taking a step closer.

Trueman's eyes were swivelling around the office as if looking for a weapon, but he did what Dan had ordered and spread his big hands out on the desk. 'You've got the wrong man, son,' he said. 'I run clubs, I'm a businessman.'

'Yeah, what business did you have in the Muckles' filthy den then?' Dan asked. 'You got your men to take my wife because you guessed she'd seen you going in there. A little girl was raped and killed there, what kind of business is that? Well, I got here before the police because I want my revenge. So tell me where she is, or as God is my judge I'll start shooting, first your hands, then your legs, and it will be some time before I finish you off altogether.'

Out of the corner of his eye Dan saw a thick walking stick propped up at the front of the desk and he guessed that was what Trueman was looking for. It was a flashy job, all varnished knobbly bits with silver on the handle. He leaped forward, grabbed it with his left hand and whacked it down with force on Trueman's hands.

The man yelped involuntarily.

'Tell me,' Dan insisted, lifting the stick again.

'You've got it all wrong,' Trueman said, but the power had gone out of his voice. 'I haven't taken her.'

Dan was past caring what he had to do to get it out of the man, so he hit him again, this time hard on the head.

Even if his left arm wasn't as strong as his right, by rights the blow should have smashed Trueman's skull. He reeled back in his chair, clutching at his head now, but although blood was seeping through his fingers, he wasn't knocked out.

Guns weren't Dan's thing. He wanted to feel the man's flesh beneath his fists. He put the safety catch on and slipped the gun back into his pocket, then leaped on Trueman, pulling him up by the shoulders and hammering his fist into his face. His nose almost exploded, and before he recovered from that one, Dan punched him in the mouth. He picked him up again, twirled him round and threw him over the desk, knocking off the lamp, papers and a box of cigars.

Dan had been a fierce brawler in his teens, he'd boxed too, and the years of bricklaying had given him iron muscles and stamina. Trueman was some four or even five stone heavier than himself, and although the room was too cramped for fighting, in his anger he tossed the older man around the office like a rag doll.

Trueman's false teeth shot out on to the floor and his whole face was a bloody pulp. He tried desperately to reach the door, but with one more power-packed punch Dan knocked him down again to the floor. He landed on his side.

Dan was on to him instantly, rolling him over on to his face and sitting astride him. He pulled the rope from around his waist, and twisting Trueman's arms up behind his back, he secured his wrists while the man was still reeling from the last blow.

He hit him several more times before he managed to get the man's knees bent back so he could secure his ankles along with his wrists. The finished effect was like a trussed chicken; the more he tried to move, the more it would hurt.

Trueman cried out with the pain, but Dan lit a cigarette and knelt on the floor beside him, looking right into his eyes.

'Tell me where she is,' he said, and held the cigarette to the man's temple. When he didn't reply Dan burned him and Trueman yelled out again. 'I'm not fucking about,' Dan warned him. 'You give me the address and I'll phone my mate to go and get her. Once I know she and the other woman are safe I'll let you go. Or at least let the Plod have you. But meanwhile I can just sit here and burn and burn you until your whole body's covered in them. And I'll enjoy it.'

As he put the cigarette close to the man's face a second time, Trueman yelled out, 'Don't do that, I'll tell you.'

Dan waited.

'I'll do a deal with you,' Trueman rasped out. 'I give you the address, you let me go. If you turn me over to the police my boys will get you and crucify you.'

Dan laughed then, relief that he really had got the right man flooding through him. 'You ain't got no power now, sunshine! You're just a nasty old fart with a lot to answer for. When word gets around I just breezed in here and did this, you'll look a right prat. You might be able to hire a hot-shot defence, but your so-called boys will desert you the moment you're nicked. So just give us the address and I'll stop making you squeal.'

There was some hesitation, but Dan only had to put the cigarette close to Trueman's face again and he began gabbling about a barn at Bexley. He even told Dan that the keys for the padlock on the barn door were in his desk drawer.

'Who's there with her?'

'No one, just her and the Frenchwoman.'

Dan opened the desk drawer. There were several bunches of Yale keys, but two smaller keys on a piece of cord looked as though they opened a padlock. He took all the keys anyway, just in case. There was also a car key with a Jaguar logo. He smiled to himself. 'Where's your car parked?' he asked.

'In Soho Square,' Trueman gasped out.

Dan got the registration number out of him, then stood looking down at the man. All he wanted to do was flee and get Fifi, but Trueman might be banking on that, and he was crafty enough to have given him the wrong address, especially if he knew some of his men were coming by later. Then there was Janice, he didn't like the thought of her coming back to this little lot. The whole office was upturned and Trueman's face was like something on a butcher's block.

He aimed one almighty kick at the man's ribs. 'Right now, tell me the truth about where she is. No more fucking about,' he yelled at him.

'It is the truth,' Trueman blubbered. 'The barn is up a track off Hurst Road, Bexley.'

'If she's dead when I get there I swear I'll make it my life's work to torture you,' Dan said, kicking him one more time for good measure. But he could wait no longer. He went into the tiny cloakroom, washed the blood off his face and hands, and then phoned Kennington police station. Roper wasn't there, but he spoke to Sergeant Wallis whom he'd met when he'd gone down to the station with Harry and Clara.

'I've got the man with the red Jag,' he barked out. 'His name is Jack Trueman and you'd better come and arrest him because he's just admitted he's got my wife. He'll need an ambulance too.'

Wallis tried to question him but Dan refused to be drawn. 'You just hold the bastard until I've got my wife,' he said, snapping out the office address. 'I'm on my way to get Fifi now.'

Hastily he wrote a note for Janice, to stick on the downstairs front door, telling her not to open the street door but to wait outside until the police arrived.

'The police will be here soon,' Dan said sweetly, grinning down at the pulp that had once been Trueman's face. 'If you haven't told me the truth about where my Fifi is, I'll make sure they don't get a doctor to look at you until you have.'

It was half past two as Dan slid into the driving seat of the red Jaguar. He had blood all over his suit, his knuckles were raw and bleeding and he was shaky. He didn't even know where Bexley was apart from it being south of the river, but he saw there was a map in the glove compartment, and he'd check it out when he got as far as the Old Kent Road. It felt as if it ought to be eight or nine at night, definitely the longest day he'd ever known. But with luck he'd be with Fifi in an hour.

Dan swore aloud when yet another turning off Hurst Road only took him into a row of houses with no drivable access to the fields behind them. The rain was making visibility poor, and he thought now he should have waited for the police instead of coming alone.

There were very few people around, and those he'd stopped and asked if they knew of a lane with a barn had just looked puzzled.

Hurst Road was far longer than he had expected, and he'd now been up and down it so many times he half expected a police car to turn up suddenly because someone had reported him behaving suspiciously. While that might appear to be the best thing, he knew what police were like – they'd probably ignore what he said, see the blood on him and haul him in for questioning.

Seeing a boy of about fourteen walking along Hurst Road with a greyhound on a lead, he stopped the car and got out.

'Do you know a lane anywhere off here that leads up to a barn?'

The boy was lanky and spotty, wearing an oilskin coat that was several sizes too big. He looked gormless.

'Yeah,' he said. 'Well, it ain't a lane so much, just a track. I go up it with the dog sometimes.'

'Would you take me there?' Dan asked, and reached in his pocket and pulled out a ten-shilling note.

'I got to get home,' the boy said, but he was looking at the note as if he wanted it.

'I'll take you back there afterwards,' Dan pleaded. 'Look, son, it's really important. I think someone's locked my wife up in this barn. I've been trying for ages to find it, and I'm getting a bit desperate now.'

The boy's face became more animated. 'Cor!' he said. 'You mean like they kidnapped her?'

Dan nodded.

'So will they have guns up there?' the boy asked. He didn't look frightened at the prospect, only excited.

But the mention of guns reminded Dan of the one in his pocket and that Trueman could have been lying when he said the women were there alone.

'I don't think so,' Dan said. 'But I'll just have to take a look first and see how the land lies. You can hide up with your dog, and if anything happens to me, you scarper and call the police.'

'Okay,' the boy said eagerly, clearly not bright enough to exercise any caution. 'I like your car, are you a gangster too?'

Dan had to smile; the Jaguar did look like a gangster's car. A bricklayer certainly couldn't afford one. 'No, we're the good guys. I'm Dan Reynolds, what's your name?'

'Clive,' the boy said. 'And my dog is called Lightning. 'Cept he isn't like lightning, he's really slow, that why my uncle let me have him.'

'Come on then.' Dan opened the car door. 'In you get, Lightning can sit in the back.'

Dan would probably have never found the lane without help; as Clive said, it was just a track, and as the start of it was beside an old house it just looked like access to the back of it. It was very muddy too, and all Dan could hope for was that he wouldn't get stuck.

Fortunately as they drove up it there were enough stones and weeds for the tyres to grip. It was very winding and overhung with trees. Clive remarked that hardly anyone ever came up this way because the farmer who owned it didn't like people on his land.

'But he died last year,' he said. 'They say they're going to build houses on it soon.'

'You'll come to it in a minute,' he added as they approached the top of the hill. 'The lane goes on down to the farmhouse behind the wood. But no one lives there now.'

'We'd better drive on past the barn first,' Dan said. 'Just to check if there's anyone around. If anyone stops us we'll make out we're looking for our other dog that's gone missing. Okay?'

All at once Dan saw the barn up ahead. In the grey light it looked menacing, but at least it stood in open ground, and he couldn't see any vehicles other than a rusty old tractor. Dan slowed right down, looking about. It didn't look as if anyone had been here for some time as there were thick weeds growing in cracks on the concrete in front of the barn and they weren't flattened.

'No one's here,' Clive said, sounding disappointed.

Dan had slowed down to a crawl. 'There could be men inside the barn,' he said, suddenly scared, realizing perhaps too late that he shouldn't have asked the boy to come with him. 'Can you run fast?'

'I won the five hundred yards at sports day,' Clive said proudly.

'Is there any way back to the road other than the lane we came up?'

'There's a path down there.' Clive pointed towards some bushes. 'That's the way I usually come up. 'Course you can't drive on it, it's only a footpath. And there's another lane out past the farmhouse, but that goes on to another road. That's like the proper way to the farm.'

'Right.' Dan nodded. 'We'll get out now, and you are going to go over by that path and call for the dog we've lost. I'm going over by the barn to do the same. Now, if anyone comes out and grabs me, I want you to leg it off down that path with Lightning and go and call the police. You tell them you met a man called Dan Reynolds who was looking for his wife Fifi. Tell them to come quickly. You got that?'

Clive nodded, his eyes gleaming.

Dan gave him the ten-shilling note. 'Now, what are we going to call the dog we've lost?'

Clive grinned. 'Tonto. That's what I'm going to call my next dog.'

'Good name,' Dan said. 'Now, just promise me you will run for it if anything happens.'

'I promise.'

'Right,' Dan said as he pulled up. 'That's it then.'

He was pleased to see the lad was obedient. As soon as he was out of the car with his dog he went straight over towards the bushes and began calling.

Dan went towards the barn.

'Tonto,' he called and then gave a piercing whistle. 'Come on, boy.'

As the door of the barn was padlocked and chained on the outside it was extremely unlikely that there was anyone in there with the women, but Dan wasn't going to take any chances.

He went right round the barn, continuing to call and whistle, but no one appeared. He tried to look inside the barn through a crack in the door, but it was too dark in there to see anything. He went back to Clive and told him he was going in. 'Get in the bushes in case anyone comes,' he said. 'I'll whistle if I need you.'

The second key on the cord he tried fitted the padlock and it opened easily, the chain falling to the ground with a clatter. Dan's heart was pounding like a steam-hammer and his stomach churning as he pulled the door open.

Although it was only around four in the afternoon the light was poor in the barn even with the door open. He pulled the gun out of his pocket just in case. There was a large cage-like construction ahead of him, but he was halfway across the barn before he saw Fifi lying motionless on a mattress inside it.

'No!' he yelled, thinking she was dead. 'Oh no, Fifi, you can't be!'

He shoved the gun back in his pocket and had the keys ready to open the cage, when he glanced upwards and saw Yvette. She looked like a huge bat swaying slightly in the breeze. All at once he was crying, his fingers trembling so hard he could barely get the other key into the padlock, but he finally managed it, dragged the chain out through the bars and flung it down.

He reached Fifi in two strides, knelt down beside her and wept. She looked like a very dirty angel, her blonde hair flowing out over the mattress and her face so thin, white and lifeless.

'No!' he roared out in anguish, flinging the blanket from her and scooping her up into his arms. 'I should have killed him too, the bastard. How could he do this?'

A kaleidoscope of images ran through his mind. Their first meeting in the coffee shop in Bristol, Fifi running to him barefoot across the Downs last summer, her hair like spun gold in the sunshine. In her cream suit and pink hat on their wedding day, with a smile as wide as the river Avon. Sitting up in bed on Christmas morning, with panda eyes from the previous night's mascara. And all the lovemaking, those long silky legs wrapped around him, kisses sweeter than he'd ever known before. He didn't want to live without her.

He sobbed as he rocked her, showering her dirty, cold face with kisses, his tears making rivulets down her cheeks. But all at once he felt a slight movement in his arms, and the tip of her tongue came out between her parched lips, licking at his tears.

'Fifi!' he exclaimed. 'You're alive!'

'Dan?' she croaked out, struggling to open her eyes. 'Is it really you?'

In that instant Dan knew utter bliss. Nothing had ever or could ever be that good again.

'Yes, baby,' he said through tears of joy, rocking her in his arms. 'It really is me. I'm going to take you home.'

'Dan?' Clive's voice came from the doorway of the barn. 'Is she there?'

All at once Dan remembered Yvette, and knew he mustn't let the boy see that.

'Yes. Go and get in the car. I'm bringing her out.'

'I knew you'd come for me,' Fifi whispered, her voice so cracked Dan could scarcely hear. 'You've never let me down.'

Chapter twenty

'I've found her,' was all Dan could manage to say to Clara when he telephoned her hotel from the hospital.

He didn't know whether to laugh or cry, to spin round the room or to get down on his knees and thank God. He certainly couldn't hold a sensible conversation.

'You tell them about it, I can't,' he said, handing the receiver to the policeman with him. 'Tell them I'll ring them later when I've gathered my wits,' he added, grinning like an idiot.

He walked down the hospital corridor from the private room where they'd put Fifi, and in a quiet spot away from other people he paused by a window overlooking the car park. The rain was still lashing down, and it was already almost dark though it was only about seven, but he felt he had been blessed today, and such a holy state should not be spoilt just yet with explanations.

He would never forget driving back down that narrow lane, Fifi slumped in the seat beside him, Lightning leaning his head over from the back seat, his long nose on her shoulder, Clive, also in the back, firing out questions.

It was from Clive's house that he phoned the emergency services, after giving Fifi her first drink of water. He thought it was funny how often people claim to be dying of thirst, when they really have no idea what it must be like. He certainly got the idea as he watched Fifi drink; she would've drunk a gallon if he'd let her, but he remembered from old Westerns that people got sick if they drank too much at once.

How he managed to speak coherently to the police, to say who he was, that there was a body in the barn, explain where it was, and that he needed an ambulance immediately to Hurst Road, he didn't know. But he'd barely drunk a cup of tea, and it was at the door.

He smiled as he remembered Jean, Clive's mother; just a very ordinary mum with a flowered frock and a tight perm. She was so startled when he burst through the door behind Clive, carrying Fifi in his arms. No doubt young Clive would be rabbiting on about it for weeks, driving his poor mother mad. He would have to phone her soon, explain and thank her properly, not to mention apologize for dragging her son into a potentially dangerous situation.

By the time the local police got to the hospital, Fifi had only managed to tell him that Yvette took her own life. He could tell by her expression that there was a tremendous amount more she wanted to say, but she was too weak. Dan felt much the same; he knew that very soon he would have to explain his part in all this fully to the police – all he'd told them so far was the barest essentials – but right now all he cared about was that Fifi was alive. The doctor had said she'd be fine in a few days as she was young and strong, and that was all that counted.

Dan felt a tap on his shoulder. It was the policeman again. A nice copper, middle-aged, fat-faced and fatherly.

'I've explained as much as I can to your in-laws,' he said with a warm smile. 'But given that I don't know much myself, that was difficult. They are coming over here now;

I've arranged for one of the officers from Kennington to bring them. Will you be up to talking to them? And would you like me to drive you back to Hurst Road to collect your car while we wait for them?'

Dan took a deep breath. 'It's not mine, it's Jack Trueman's. I think I told you he is the man behind all this. Did the Kennington police tell you if they picked him up?'

The policeman half smiled. 'Indeed they have. They said you doled out some very rough justice. That was foolhardy, you know, by all accounts he is a very nasty customer.'

Dan remembered then that he still had the gun in his pocket. He couldn't own up about it as it might get Johnny into hot water. He needed to get outside and hide it somewhere before the Kennington police got here, and he also wanted to get back to Fifi.

'I don't mean to be rude,' he said. 'But I'd just like to go outside and have a fag before I go back to see Fifi. I know you must want some proper explanations but I'm a bit shaky right now. Can it wait?'

The policeman put one hand on his shoulder in a gesture of understanding. 'Of course it can, son. You did a great job and she's safe now thanks to you. You go off now, and get yourself something to eat while you're about it; you look as if you haven't eaten for days either. Detective Inspector Roper will want to talk to you when he gets here, and you won't be much good to him if you're passing out with hunger.'

'Your mum and dad will be here soon,' Dan said as he sat down beside Fifi's bed some time later. He'd wrapped the gun in a handtowel he'd found in the toilet, put it in a plastic bag and hidden it behind a tree next to a hospital outbuilding. It would be safe enough there until tomorrow. He'd had a cigarette, a cup of tea and a bun, and finally persuaded the ward sister to allow him in to see Fifi.

But now he was alone with her, he couldn't find the words he wanted to say.

She looked so thin and pale, her eyes dull and her lips cracked, and a sudden rage had welled up in him that anyone could knowingly leave her to starve to death. She had been to hell and back, that much was certain, and it might be some time before she felt up to telling him about it.

The local police officer had said that he'd been on two cases where someone had hanged themselves, and both times he'd been a wreck after it. So what would it have done to Fifi? Yvette was her friend, not a stranger, and she'd been forced to stay there with the body, perhaps thinking she'd remain in the barn with it till she died too. He really wished that at least one of the men involved had been out at the barn; he would have enjoyed kicking his head in.

'It's so lovely to be warm again,' Fifi said. Her voice had been cracking when he found her, but it was only husky now that she'd had several drinks. The sister said she'd had soup and some rice pudding too. Fifi had apparently asked for more, but had been told she had to wait a while so they could be sure she had digested that properly.

They'd washed her, brushed her hair and promised that tomorrow she could have a bath and wash her hair. She said she felt fine again, but Dan knew that really meant she only felt a lot better, not that she was anywhere near back to normal.

'I thought you'd be asking me lots of questions,' she said. 'Are you still angry with me?'

'Angry?' Dan repeated in astonishment. 'Of course not. Why should I be?'

'Well, the last words we had before this were angry ones.'

'That was eleven days ago,' he reproached her. 'I forgot it all the moment I got the letter from you.' He told her briefly how he'd gone back to Dale Street that evening and suspected something was wrong straight away when she didn't come home.

'It seems so much longer than that,' she said, taking his hand and looking at the broken skin on his knuckles. 'I'm not even sure what day it is.'

'Tuesday,' Dan said. 'You were in that place a week. But it seemed like a month to me. I was frantic with worry. It wasn't until your parents arrived on Saturday that I really got anyone to take your disappearance seriously.'

The door opened and Clara and Harry came in.

'Darling,' Clara said, bearing down on her daughter, arms open wide to hug her. 'You can't imagine how wonderful it was to get that call from Dan, even if he didn't say much.'

Dan watched the family reunion closely. Fifi returned her mother's hug and assured her she was already feeling better, but there was still a slight chill there. She was warmer with her father, holding on to his hand while her mother spoke of the reporters, the endless waiting and her brothers' and sister's joy when she phoned them to say Fifi was rescued.

'Now we're taking you home just as soon as you can leave here,' Clara said bossily. 'You need good food and plenty of sleep to get your strength back.'

Fifi's face tightened. 'I'm staying with Dan,' she said.

Clara looked round at Dan, and he could only shrug.

'Dan can come too,' Harry spoke up. 'We certainly wouldn't want to separate you.'

'Of course Dan's coming, aren't you, Dan?' Clara turned to him, looking for his support.

'I'll go along with whatever Fifi wants,' he said. He was

surprised that Clara didn't realize that Fifi couldn't possibly know everything had changed while she'd been missing. She really ought to explain!

'Dan!' Clara said reprovingly, and he grinned.

'It's up to you, Ma,' he said. 'Fifi's a lot of things, but I don't think she's psychic.'

Like sun coming out from behind a cloud, Clara suddenly smiled as she realized what he meant.

She turned back to Fifi and caressed her cheek. 'Would you like me to introduce our new son-in-law? He's wonderful, everything we ever wanted for our daughter.'

The gaiety and joy in her voice made Dan's eyes well up. He felt like hugging Clara for she couldn't know what her words meant to him.

'You've made friends?' Fifi asked, her eyes lighting up.

'We made friends long before he became a hero.' Clara smiled. 'I know I always think I'm right about everything, but in Dan's case I was as wrong as wrong can be.'

'Daddy?' Fifi looked up at her father.

Harry gave a little chuckle. 'Well, I have to admit I found him amusing from the start, but I'd have created mayhem if I'd admitted it. We couldn't have got through this past week without him, Fifi, we are astounded by his courage, and we hope he'll always be a big part of our lives from now on.'

Fifi's eyes filled with emotional tears, and Dan was fighting his back.

'Do you know what he did?' Clara asked Fifi, her face full of wonderment. 'Detective Inspector Roper rang us before we left the hotel. Dan went all alone to see the terrible gangster that was behind all this, bearded him in his den, so to speak. He fought him and tied him up and forced him to admit where you were. Then he took the man's car and drove to find you. Isn't that just about the most marvellous, brave, romantic thing you've ever heard of?'

A couple of huge tears trickled down Fifi's face as she looked at Dan.

'Will you come home now?' Clara asked.

Dan nodded his agreement to Fifi.

'Okay, Mum, we'd love to.' Fifi sniffed back her tears. 'You don't know how lovely it was to hear you say all that!'

Dan felt the warmth in the air for the remainder of the visit. Perhaps her parents realized, as he did, that Fifi wasn't quite with it, because they didn't attempt to question her or speak of how frantic they'd been. To listen to her mother talking about the boys and Patty, a stranger would have thought she and Harry had just had a little holiday in London.

Dan was happy just to sit at the end of the bed, listening and watching. All Fifi needed right now was stability and affection. Tomorrow was quite soon enough for her to reveal what she'd been through. Perhaps she'd never want to talk about it.

The police officer who'd brought them here suddenly put his head round the door to ask the Browns if they were ready to go back to the hotel.

Clara looked anxiously at her daughter, clearly thinking it was too soon.

'You go,' Fifi said. 'And go back to Bristol tomorrow. I know you don't like being away, and Peter, Robin and Patty need you too.'

Dan saw then that she'd grown up a lot in a week. There was concern for them in her voice, tenderness in her face.

'We can't do that!' Clara looked scandalized.

'Of course you can, I'm already on the mend,' Fifi said

airily. 'There's no point in you two hanging around. Dan will bring me down when they discharge me. And I can phone you.'

Clara agreed, but her eyes were brimming with tears as she left. Dan guessed she felt just as he did, afraid to let Fifi out of her sight.

Detective Inspector Roper came in to see Fifi after her parents had left. He didn't ask any questions, just said how glad he was that she was safe, and wished her a speedy recovery. He went on to say he'd be back in the morning to talk to her. But he asked Dan to come outside with him for a few minutes.

In the ward sister's office, the first thing Roper asked was why Dan hadn't come to him about Trueman.

Dan saw no point in beating about the bush. 'I was afraid someone down the nick was leaking information,' he said. 'I couldn't take that risk.'

Roper frowned but didn't comment. 'So who told you about Trueman?' he asked.

'I heard a bloke in the pub talking about him, he said John Bolton had worked for him,' Dan lied. 'I asked around, discovered what he looked like, and that he had a red Jag. You could've found that out,' he added pointedly. 'And how come you never found his fingerprints in number eleven?'

'Surprisingly the man has no criminal record,' Roper said with some regret. 'He's been known to the Met for nigh on forty years, but they've never been able to pin anything on him, not even enough to get his prints. He didn't come into the frame for this because he doesn't normally extend his interests south of the river.'

'But Bolton managed one of his clubs!'

'Bolton had dealings with dozens of clubs.' Roper

shrugged. 'We were still checking them all out. What you've got to remember is that a man like Trueman controls people through fear. No one would risk passing us any information. But enough of that for now. How much has your wife been able to tell you about her abduction?'

'Nothing yet,' Dan said. 'Only that Yvette hanged herself. That must have been such a terrible shock that I'm not sure she'll ever get beyond that. So it's up to you now to find out why a powerful man like Trueman consorted with a piece of shit like Alfie. That's the bit that doesn't make any sense to me.'

Roper said he would be back in the morning to see Dan again, and hopefully Fifi would be up to talking by then too.

'Taking Trueman on was very courageous,' he said, looking up at Dan with an expression of awe and respect. 'Everyone in the force has nothing but profound admiration for you rescuing your wife. Please tell her from us that we will round up all those who were involved, and the investigation into Angela's death will be finalized and the guilty punished.'

After Roper had left, Dan asked the ward sister if it would be possible for him to stay with Fifi all night. He explained that he couldn't bear to leave her, and that he was afraid she might have nightmares. Sister was very sympathetic and said there was no need for him to sleep in the chair, she would get a camp bed sent up for him.

Fifi was asleep by the time Dan got back to her room, so he took the opportunity to nip out and get himself some fish and chips. When he returned Fifi was still sleeping so he lay down on the camp bed.

It was cosy in the small room with the blinds pulled down and the only light, above the bed, shining down on some scrawny flowers he'd bought from a barrow at the hospital gates.

Outside in the corridor it was quiet now visitors had left, only the occasional trundling sound of a drugs or drinks trolley, and nurses hurrying past. Dan knew he would have to go back to the flat tomorrow or the day after to get Fifi some clean clothes, and he supposed he ought to go and phone the Rifleman and ask them to give the news that Fifi was safe to Frank, Miss Diamond and Stan. But although he wanted to pass on the good news and relieve everyone of worry, he knew they'd all be upset about Yvette. She might have been rather odd, but she'd lived in Dale Street for a long time and people had become fond of her.

It was strange that he hadn't really reacted to her death. He was horrified of course to see her hanging there, that was bloody awful. But once he was out of the barn with Fifi he kind of switched off about her.

He was curious now though. When did she do it? Did Fifi try to stop her?

He really hoped that by tomorrow Fifi would have recovered enough to want to talk and ask questions, then he'd really believe she was on the mend. But he didn't know how he would explain how he found out about Jack Trueman without revealing Nora Diamond's part in it. Dan was curious himself now about what the man had done to her. But he didn't suppose she'd ever tell him. He wasn't sure he was prepared to tell Fifi about the gun either, he thought she'd be horrified to know he'd been walking about with it in his pocket.

So many questions that needed answering! And if he had a load, how many more would the police have tomorrow? He wished he could just scoop Fifi up now and whisk her off somewhere peaceful and beautiful.

He was not going to take her back to Dale Street, ever. Maybe it would be best to stay permanently in Bristol, so she never had reminders of all this again. It would be their first wedding anniversary on the 20th. What a terrible year it had been too! Surely it was time for something good to happen?

Fifi cried out suddenly, and Dan was off the camp bed and over to her in two seconds.

'It's okay, I'm here,' he said soothingly, gathering her into his arms.

For a second she looked as if she didn't know where she was, there was terror in her eyes. 'It was the rats,' she whispered. 'They were as big as cats and they were coming for me.'

'The only rat in here is me,' he said. 'And I'm the cuddly kind.'

She half smiled. 'It was so real,' she sighed. 'That's what I was most afraid of once I found Yvette dead. We used to hear them scuttling around at night, but we didn't actually see any.'

'So when did she do it?' Dan asked gently, moving round so that his back was supported on the bed rail while he held Fifi in his arms. 'Did you see it?'

Fifi shook her head and explained what happened. 'I think she went a bit mad at the end. She was talking in French, she said she thought she was with her mother. But that wasn't surprising after all she'd been through.'

Haltingly she began to tell him what Yvette had been through in Paris as a young girl. Dan was shocked, not just at the cruelty of it, but because he'd always had the idea Yvette was sort of born a spinster. He certainly couldn't imagine her in a bordello.

'I suppose she just didn't have anything to hang on

for,' he said. 'I mean, no one of her own looking for her.'

'It wasn't that,' Fifi said in a small voice. She turned to him and buried her face in his chest, clutching his arms tightly. 'Oh Dan, when she told me about it, it didn't seem real. Nothing did while we were in the barn. But now!'

She began to sob, a harsh sound which came from deep within her. Dan held her close, whispering endearments, reassuring her she was safe. He had expected that she'd break down once she thought over what she'd been through.

'What didn't seem real?' he asked after a little while. He thought it best to try to get her to talk. 'Do you mean Yvette's body hanging there?'

'No, that was terribly real,' she sobbed out. 'It was what she said.' Once again she buried her face against him.

Dan prised her from him, lifting her face and drying her tears with the edge of the sheet. 'So maybe it wasn't real then. Tell me and see what I think.'

'You won't believe it,' she whispered. 'I don't think anyone will.'

'Try me?' he whispered.

'She killed Angela.'

Dan almost wanted to laugh, and he might have done if he hadn't thought Fifi was losing her grip on reality. 'She couldn't have, sweetheart. Maybe she said she did, but she was obviously getting in a state. Maybe she meant it was her fault it happened because she hadn't reported the Muckles when she knew they treated their kids badly.'

'No, Dan, she really did do it,' she cried out.

As she began to tell him the story of that Friday night, the men arriving for the card game, Dan realized she was repeating what she'd been told by Yvette. At first he was just humouring her, listening but not taking it that seriously, but by the time she got to the part about Yvette crouching in her garden watching Molly offering Angela for sale, he knew this was what really happened. Suddenly it was almost as if he were there in that garden too.

'She heard the man upstairs with Angela,' Fifi sobbed. 'She said his name was Jack Trueman, and that's the name I heard you say to the policeman today. Is he the man you hit?'

'Yes.' Dan licked his lips nervously, feeling sick to his stomach that the man could hurt a child that way. 'Go on, what happened next?'

She continued with what took place the following day, right up to where Yvette put the pillow over Angela's face. 'She did do it, Dan, I know she did,' she sobbed. 'She even told me about getting the clean sheet to cover her.'

Dan was completely stunned. Had he known earlier today that it was Trueman who'd raped Angela, he wouldn't have stopped at just beating him up. He felt absolute disgust for the man and all the others who'd been there that night, and that made Yvette's part look almost kindly. But of course it wasn't. Yvette should have got help for the child the minute she knew what was going to happen. It wasn't her place to play God and decide the child would be happier dead.

'She must have been mad,' he exclaimed, so bewildered by what he'd heard, that seemed the only explanation.

'She called killing Angela the lesser evil,' Fifi said sorrowfully, clinging to Dan's chest. 'And I think she hanged herself because that was the lesser evil too.'

'Well, it saved her from a public trial,' Dan said grimly.

'No,' Fifi exclaimed, lifting her head to look at him. 'I know that wasn't her reason for it. She was a very moral person, I think she felt she must be punished. But starving to death with me would mean no one would ever know what she'd done. Even if we were rescued, it's doubtful she

461

would have been hanged, because of the circumstances. By killing herself, she took what she saw as the appropriate punishment.'

'Shit!' was all Dan could say.

They were silent for some time, Fifi lying in Dan's arms while he stared into space. He couldn't really think about the bigger implications of what Yvette had done, only about how this nightmare week would affect Fifi.

Suddenly she sat up, turning to look at him again. 'The question is, do I tell the police about it?' she asked.

'Well yes, of course,' Dan said.

'But if I tell them they'll have to let Molly and Alfie out, won't they?'

Dan looked at her in consternation. 'Why?'

'Well, they can't hold them for murder, can they?'

Dan saw what she meant. 'But selling your seven-year-old daughter must be a pretty serious charge.'

'What proof of that is there?' Fifi asked. 'Yvette's dead. Jack Trueman isn't likely to admit he bought and raped Angela. You can bet that anyone else there that night will deny it too. So what would there be left to charge Alfie and Molly with? They didn't kill John Bolton, nor did they abduct Yvette and me.'

Dan was impressed that she could think things through so well after such an ordeal, and he could see her point. Alfie and Molly were two people anyone sane would want locked away for ever. 'But if no one else admits to raping Angela, Alfie will get charged with it.'

'And what will he get for that?' Fifi asked derisively. 'Five years maybe? That's if they can even find enough proof to convince a jury he did it. Molly will be right off the hook, won't she? She'll cry and say how much she loves her children and that she didn't know what was going on. Before you could say Jack Robinson she'll be back in that house with her children!'

Dan thought Alfie would get a longer sentence than five years, and he didn't think Molly would manage to wriggle out of any responsibility that easily either, or get her children back. But he could see Fifi's point: there wasn't a lot of hard evidence against the Muckles, not since Trueman abducted Fifi and Yvette. If Fifi chose not to reveal what she knew, there would be a kind of poetic justice in them being hanged or banged up for life for the one thing they didn't actually do, when they'd got away with so much in the past.

'Okay. But if you keep quiet, where does that leave Trueman? I don't only want to see him go down for John Bolton's murder and your abduction. I want to see him pilloried for raping Angela.'

Fifi nodded. 'Yes, but even if I tell the police what really happened that night, unless someone else who was there that night confirms it, he'll get away with that,' she said wearily. 'He won't admit having any part in Bolton's death either, will he? That only leaves snatching Yvette and me.'

'And you can bet that right now, even in a hospital bed, he'll be working on some plausible story to cover that,' Dan said gloomily. 'And he's got enough money to hire a first-class defence.'

They fell silent for a while, both thinking deeply about the pros and cons of revealing what Yvette did.

'I think you must tell the truth,' Dan said reluctantly after some little while. Whichever way he looked at it, he didn't feel right holding back something so serious. 'Low as the Muckles are, you can't let them be convicted of murder when they didn't do it. You'd have it on your conscience for ever.'

'Molly doesn't have any qualms about what she does to

people,' Fifi argued. 'Yvette told her about the Paris brothel when she first came to England. She thought Molly was her friend then and she needed to talk about it. Molly blackmailed her with it, not asking for money as she did with Frank, but intimidating her so she would keep quiet about what she knew was going on at number eleven.'

'That's pretty evil, I agree,' Dan nodded. 'But Yvette could have moved away – no one with even a grain of common sense would just stay and put up with all that.'

'Don't judge her so harshly, Dan.' Fifi took his hand in hers and kissed it. 'She was all alone, she came to believe Molly had almost witchlike powers to track her down. What she'd been through in the war left her very damaged and with tremendous guilt. I honestly think she felt kind of cheated by not ending up in Auschwitz or Belsen.'

Dan nodded. 'Okay. But there's more to this than just pinning Angela's death on someone. Alfie and Molly were never innocent bystanders. Trueman and the other men who were there that night came to wallow in Alfie's sty because I suspect he provided them with kicks they couldn't get anywhere else. You said Yvette hinted that there were other young people there in the past. Don't you think that needs investigating and exposing? It might also shock Trueman's thugs enough for them to come through with information about him which might make certain he never comes out of prison either.'

'I suppose you're right,' Fifi said wearily. 'I just wish I'd never poked my nose into anything. I never will again.'

'Can I hold you to that?' Dan grinned.

Martin heard the news that Jack Trueman had been beaten up when he called into the Bastille coffee bar at five-thirty on Tuesday to collect the day's takings. Patsy, the little blonde manageress, called him into the kitchen out the back and broke the news.

'There were police all over the place earlier this afternoon and we heard an ambulance too, but we didn't think nothing of it. Then one of the girls from Mirabelle's come running in here, said the police had gone swarming up into the office and found Jack tied up and beaten to a pulp.'

Martin was so staggered he could only stare wide-eyed at Patsy. He even thought it might be a wind-up.

'Who did it?' he asked eventually.

'Well, Tricia was told by Janice that it was this good-looking bloke who came in the office that morning. He said he was going to meet Janice for lunch. But he didn't show, and when she got back to the office there was a note pinned on the door telling her not to go in, but wait for the police. They came soon after and they told Janice to go down into Mirabelle's while they investigated, and it weren't long after that the ambulance come and took Jack away.'

Martin immediately felt nervous because if this was the start of a turf war he knew Jack would expect all his men to retaliate hard and fast.

'It was to do with those two women that have gone missing, the ones that were in the paper,' Patsy said, tapping him on the arm because he didn't appear to be paying attention. 'Tricia reckoned the man was the pretty blonde one's old man.'

'You what?' Martin exclaimed. 'No, it can't have been!'

'Well, that's what she heard the coppers say,' Patsy retorted. 'But if Jack had got those women you'd have known about it, wouldn't you?'

Martin went all cold. He said he knew nothing about it, then, claiming he was in a hurry because he had other money to pick up, he took the bag of takings and rushed off.

He continued with his usual daily early-evening round of the businesses, collecting takings, putting them in the night safe at the bank, but his mind was working on two different levels. The higher level admired Dan Reynolds for having the balls to take on Jack Trueman and he hoped that by now Fifi and the Frenchwoman had been rescued. He even hoped Trueman was so badly injured he'd either die or have to retire.

But on the lower level he knew this meant he was going to be in serious trouble. Fifi could identify him and Del.

He met up with Del at nine at Cindy's, the stripclub in Greek Street. Del told him that he'd just heard a news bulletin on the radio. The women had been found out at Bexley. One had been taken to hospital, but the other woman was dead. It was also said a man was being held in custody.

Martin had to tell him what he knew then.

Del lost all his bluff and bluster. He looked very scared. 'I don't fuckin' well know what to do,' he exclaimed. 'I mean, do we carry on with the job? Or do we piss off out of here?'

'We won't get paid if Jack's in the nick,' Martin said. He meant that they might as well disappear now while they could.

'Yeah, but if we piss off and he gets out . . .' Del didn't finish what he was going to say. There was no need, they both knew what Jack would do to them.

'Well, I'm not hanging around here to wait till we're picked up,' Martin shrugged. 'I'm going home to me gran's. Until we know the score.'

'What's put the smile back on your face, sir?' Sergeant Mike Wallis asked as he came into the office and found his superior looking extraordinarily happy.

It was mid-morning on Thursday and Roper had been like a bear with a sore head all the previous day.

'I've just had Bow Street on the blower,' Roper grinned. 'Seems one of Trueman's gofers has been spilling his guts. I usually go along with the saying "There's no honour amongst thieves", but it seems this one doesn't like to see children or fair damsels being hurt.'

'You don't say!' Sergeant Wallis grinned. 'More like he knows it's going to come on top of him and he's trying to save his skin.'

'I don't give a toss what his reasons are, the result is all that matters. And you and I are off to Brixton to see Alfie Muckle.'

Almost as soon as the police got to St Anne's Court in answer to Dan Reynolds' call on Tuesday afternoon, a search warrant was issued for Trueman's house in Essex. But by the time the police got there, just a few hours later, the filing cabinet was empty, the safe was too, and the door was hanging open. Someone had beaten the police to the house and removed any incriminating evidence.

When John Bolton was found dead before Roper could question him about the man he was seen in Dale Street with, it had briefly crossed his mind that there might be a leak at the station, but he'd shrugged it off as being mere coincidence. Even when Dan Reynolds said that he hadn't gone to the police because he couldn't risk Trueman being forewarned, he only thought Reynolds was a trifle paranoid, which was to be expected under the circumstances.

Yet less than an hour later, as he looked at that empty safe, he had to concede Reynolds was right. Fewer than ten people knew that Trueman's house was going to be raided, and all of them were policemen. If the raid had been left to the following day he might have believed one of Trueman's stooges had just used his initiative on hearing he had been arrested. But the speed at which it happened told him otherwise, and Roper felt as if he'd been kicked in the belly.

On Wednesday morning he'd spent the morning at the Middlesex Hospital trying to get something out of Trueman. The man was handcuffed to the bed and an officer was posted outside the door, but Roper was still on tenterhooks expecting that Trueman's men would attempt to spring him. The man refused to speak, he just lay there like something out of a horror film, acting as if he was deaf and dumb. Roper had been tempted to continue Dan Reynolds' work; pain seemed to be the only thing that made some villains talk.

Then he drove over to the hospital in South London to interview Fifi Reynolds, and she dropped the bombshell that Angela Muckle was smothered by the Frenchwoman.

He had been convinced Alfie had killed Angela, and the prospect of him being hanged had brightened many a bad day, for the Muckles had been a thorn in his side for almost his entire working life. He had a file some ten inches thick with complaints about them, and there was no doubt they were involved to some extent with half the crimes committed on his patch. Yet each time he thought he'd finally got enough proof to put them away, some piece of new evidence or a rock-solid alibi always turned up, and his case against them fell apart.

Roper had felt he was high and dry this time. Even when a couple of red herrings, Stanislav and Ubley, were thrown into the investigation, he didn't allow himself to become downhearted. Fortunately there was no real evidence against them, and even the Muckles' brief wasn't too optimistic he could get them off. Bolton's body being found, then the abduction of the two women, muddied the waters somewhat. Clearly there was some other issue at 11 Dale Street that he hadn't picked up on. Yet through it all Roper hadn't allowed himself to be sidetracked from the real issue, that a small child had been raped and killed. Alfie, and hopefully his slagbag of a wife, would hang for it, that much he was sure of.

Then when he heard Jack Trueman was involved too, he felt as high as a kite. For almost as long as the Muckles had been plaguing him, Jack Trueman had been the man every senior officer in London wanted a chance to nick. They suspected he was involved in some way with half the serious crime in central London, but he was a clever bastard, always one jump ahead, covering his tracks carefully while flaunting his seedy but legal businesses. If Roper could nail him it would mean promotion and cause for celebration for all his men.

Then young Fifi spoke up about Yvette and said that it was Trueman who raped Angela, and all his hopes of putting Alfie and Molly away for good were blown sky-high.

The previous night he'd been in despair because he knew that as things stood he had nothing substantial against them. They were likely to get something for neglecting and failing to protect their children, but he doubted that would amount to much more than a year or so in prison.

As for Trueman, he'd undoubtedly wriggle out of responsibility for Bolton's death, and without an eyewitness, it would be well nigh impossible to prove he raped Angela either. Yvette had killed herself and that left only abduction charges to pin on the man; not much when Roper had hoped for so much more.

Fifi had said Yvette claimed there were other young

people who were sexually abused at number 11, but that was just hearsay. And they still hadn't discovered the identity of the other men who were there that night.

Last night he'd decided he was going to leave the force and move to another city. There was no way he could bear to watch Alfie and Molly set free to laugh up their sleeves at him and continue spoiling people's lives.

But this morning he got up and found the sun was shining again. It was even announced on the radio that an Indian summer had begun. That did seem like a good omen. Then he got the call that a man called Martin Broughton, who was one of Trueman's lackeys, had presented himself at Bow Street last night prepared to spill the beans.

Now Bow Street had a whole dossier on Trueman, details about his grubby empire that in the ordinary way they'd never get. And Roper had learned who had been informing here.

He'd never liked Inspector William Hall. Ex-public school bully and too flashy by half – no wonder he could afford to live in Barnes and drive a Zephyr 6. To think they'd all believed it was inherited wealth!

But he'd be pulled today too and suspended pending an investigation. But now it was off to Brixton. He'd even got some inspiration about how to trap Alfie.

'Walk into a door, did you?' Roper said sarcastically when Alfie was brought into the interview room by a prison officer. The man had two black eyes and he was limping badly. In the grey prison uniform he appeared small and insignificant and he had lost weight since he was arrested.

'Fight on the wing,' Alfie said with a feeble attempt at bravado. 'I tried to break it up and this is what I got.'

'No friends in here then?' Roper asked once Alfie was

seated opposite him and Wallis at the table. 'You ain't gotta lot anywhere else either. Your old woman keeps slagging you off, and so does Jack Trueman.'

At the mention of Trueman's name Alfie looked startled.

'Yup, we've got him,' Roper said gleefully. 'He's been singing like a canary too. Sez you sold Angela for two ton at the card party, and Molly reckons she pleaded with you to stop.'

Wallis glanced at Roper, almost certainly rather startled by such an outrageous lie. Trueman hadn't said one word as yet.

'That's a fuckin' lie,' Alfie roared out.

'What's a lie? That he wasn't there, or about Molly?'

'He were there all right,' Alfie growled. 'But it were Molly that sold Angie, I was too pissed to do anything.'

Alfie stiffened as he suddenly realized what he'd admitted, a hunted look coming into his eyes.

Roper was pleased to see Wallis sitting up straight now, a faint smirk on his lips.

'You don't have anything to fear from Trueman now,' Roper said soothingly. 'He's in hospital after a good kicking, handcuffed to the bed with an officer on the door. Soon as he's well enough to move he'll be inside. We won't bring him here of course, not if you give us a hand sorting out the last loose ends.'

Roper paused just long enough for that to sink in, then carried on. 'We've known for some time he was at your house that night. Molly told us she was having it off with him.'

'She told you that?' Alfie said incredulously. ''E wouldn't touch 'er with someone else's!'

'Come on, Alfie,' Roper wheedled. 'Molly's an attractive woman, you can't blame her for being tempted to go off and live with him, and he could give her a much better life than you could.'

Wallis blew his nose noisily, probably to cover up a snigger, and Alfie rose from his chair, clearly rattled. 'She's lying through her teeth,' he burst out. 'Jack Trueman likes 'em young, boys or girls. 'E wouldn't even look at an old boiler like 'er.'

'That's not what he told me.' Roper shook his head. 'He said when you were upstairs with Angela, he was screwing Molly in the front room.'

''E's fucking lyin'. I never went upstairs with Angela. It was 'im!' He bought her for two hundred nicker and shagged 'er.'

Much as Roper wanted the truth out of Alfie, it made his stomach churn to hear the man speak so flippantly of his daughter's rape. But he had to fight down his disgust and carry on. 'Come on, Alfie!' he exclaimed. 'You expect me to believe that? I've talked to you dozens of times and you've told me all sorts, but never that before. Are you just mad because he was screwing Molly behind your back?'

''E could screw Molly in front of me and I wouldn't care,' Alfie raged, white foam gathering on his lips. 'But I ain't gonna 'ave it said I touched our Angela, cos I didn't. I was so pissed that night I couldn't have got it up if Jayne Mansfield came in and begged me.'

Roper half smiled. Alfie had consistently denied raping Angela, the only part of his version of the events of that evening that was consistent. Yet even after learning the truth about who raped and who killed her, Roper had no intention of letting the louse off the hook. He wanted to get him so angry that he'd reveal more of his foul secrets.

'Trueman reckons you were frightened of Molly leaving you because she's the one that got you young birds.'

'She fuckin' got *'im* them, fer money,' Alfie exploded, banging on the table. 'And boys too. I likes real women, not some skinny little piece.'

Roper kept this up for some time, with each question bringing up some insulting and totally untrue statement that Trueman or Molly was supposed to have made. Alfie got angrier and angrier until he was close to bursting, then suddenly it all spilled out.

'I'll tell you how it really fuckin' was. I've been 'aving card parties on Fridays fer years, famous for it I was cos the stakes was always high and there was usually a few birds an' all. Then about a year ago Jack Trueman comes along and cos 'e's got those clubs an' all up West, Molly thinks he's the dog's bollocks. It don't take 'er long to work out what 'e likes, and that 'e'll pay well fer it. I told 'er the first time she brought a young bird back, barely fifteen she were, that this was big trouble, and soon 'e'd be wanting 'em younger still. But she wouldn't bloody well listen. Between the two of 'em, they'd got me by the short and curlies.'

Alfie ranted on for some ten minutes about how he tried to get the card parties back to how they used to be, but Trueman had only to wave a handful of notes at Molly and she'd jump to get whatever he wanted.

Roper felt this was probably true, but guessed Alfie had almost certainly done some criminal work for Trueman too, which made it impossible for him to complain or back off when Trueman began bringing other men with the same tastes with him for these evenings.

Alfie explained in his uniquely crude manner that Trueman and his mates liked one kid to share between them, because the watching was as stimulating to them as the actual sex. They didn't care whether it was boys or girls, as long as they were young. Molly provided them.

The youngsters, according to Alfie, were often runaways, attracted to London's bright lights. Molly found them roaming around Soho and befriended them, offering them a bath, a meal and a bed for the night.

Roper could well imagine what a plausible mother figure Molly could be when she put her mind to it. In the past she'd almost convinced him that she was a kindly, rather naive woman. Mike, Alfie's nephew, had also said he thought she was 'right nice' when he first went to live there.

Alfie said how she usually found a kid on a Thursday, made a fuss of him or her, even gave them new clothes, and then when Friday came she told them there would be a party that night. Before anyone arrived she'd give them a few drinks to relax them, and more often than not the kids thought the first overtures from one of the guests, someone taking them on their knee or giving them a cuddle, was just affection. At that point Molly would give them a drink laced with a few drops of sedative. Alfie claimed he had no idea what this was, all he knew was that she got the stuff from someone up in Soho.

'There was a lad one night, they buggered him one after the other till 'e was bleedin',' Alfie said indignantly. 'I couldn't stand it and I sez that's the end. But Trueman, 'e picked up a knife and said he'd cut off me cock and stick it in me mouth if I caused him any trouble. 'E meant it an' all. I got to 'ear that anyone who crossed 'im ended up disappearing.'

'You mean like John Bolton ended up in the river?' Wallis asked.

''E what?' Alfie exclaimed.

'You didn't know?' Roper said, well aware that Alfie was kept in isolation for most of the time for his own safety, therefore unlikely to hear any gossip or news. 'Well, I suppose you wouldn't hear in here. Sunday week it happened. They say he was about to grass up Trueman.'

To Roper's surprise Alfie looked genuinely upset. 'John were a good bloke, known 'im all me life,' he said, his lip quivering. ''E told me I were gettin' in over me 'ead with Trueman. Too right I was, look where I am now!'

'But he introduced Trueman to you, didn't he?' Roper asked.

'Naw, whoever told you that? It were some bloke Molly knew what brought Trueman round.'

'But Bolton was seen going into your house with Trueman.'

'Once 'e did, John 'ad done some job fer Trueman and John dropped 'im off at mine. I asked John to come in fer a drink fer old times' sake. 'E didn't stay long though.'

Roper felt this was true because John Bolton had said something similar when he was pulled in for routine questioning after Angela's death. He explained that he had hung around with Alfie as a kid and had freely admitted going to one card game back in June because of their past connection. He said he never repeated it though because he didn't like the way Alfie lived or what he had become. But he said he found it hard to blank the man entirely because his childhood pal had never stood a chance because of his family background.

'What d'you reckon Bolton was going to grass Trueman up about?' Roper asked.

''Spect 'e guessed what was going on.' Alfie had the grace to look a little sheepish. 'John didn't like stuff like that. Always were a bit of a gent, even when we was kids. There weren't no love lost between 'im and Trueman anyways. I 'eard Trueman sacked 'im from 'is club cos John wouldn't kowtow to 'im. See, John weren't nobody's man, know what I mean?'

That was exactly what Roper had always felt about John Bolton too. A rogue, but one with pride and a kind of honour.

Alfie went on to complain that meeting Trueman had ruined his life. He said his old mates stopped coming to the card parties, and Molly became greedier and greedier.

'She always 'ad 'er eye on the main chance, but once 'e came along she were impossible. Trueman knew 'ow to play 'er, 'e'd tell her she was beautiful and that, but it were only so she'd get 'im what 'e wanted.'

Roper found Alfie making himself out to be a victim a bit tedious; he preferred it when the man swaggered and boasted. But he sensed Alfie was getting things off his chest because he felt safe now Trueman was locked up and couldn't come after him. If Roper pushed him a bit harder, he might reveal even more.

'Molly said you buggered that young lad too,' Roper lied, almost believing it himself because he managed to say it so calmly. 'She said you couldn't even wait your turn.'

'She fuckin' what?' Alfie turned purple, his eyes nearly popping out of his head. 'I ain't a poofter. I only goes fer women. It made me sick just to 'ear 'em at it, bloody perverts. Then they expected me to stow it away fer 'em.'

Roper felt a prickling down his spine. Alfie wasn't the most articulate of men, and that last statement could have meant anything from comforting the abused lad to cleaning the floor. But Roper had a feeling it meant a great deal more than that. He glanced sideways at Wallis and saw he had reacted to it too. He was rigid, leaning forward on to the table, his eyes glued to Alfie.

'Molly told us the lad died,' Roper bluffed. 'She didn't tell us that you had to get rid of the body though. Where did you take it?'

For the first time since his arrest Alfie looked stricken with fear and an animal smell wafted from him. His mouth opened and shut again. Clearly he realized he'd dropped himself right in it.

'It's okay, Alfie,' Wallis said calmly. 'Molly told us about this ages ago. We haven't questioned you about it before because we were waiting to get Trueman in custody. Molly said it was you who killed him, but we don't believe that. It was Trueman, wasn't it? It's safe to tell us, he can't get at you now.'

Alfie was gulping so hard his Adam's apple looked likely to burst out of his throat. ''E never meant to kill 'im,' he blurted out. 'One of the blokes said they thought 'e just accidentally broke the kid's neck while 'e was 'olding him.' Alfie stood up, miming bending forward over someone and holding on to their neck. The mime made Roper cringe because it was clear Alfie had been an avid observer at this gang bang.

'One minute the lad were crying, the next he went all limp. He were dead.'

Roper felt sick, and even without looking at Wallis he knew he was in the same state. But they had to continue what they'd started now. A body along with a statement would keep Alfie and Molly in prison and hopefully Trueman would hang.

'And you were made to get rid of the body? Where did you take it?'

'I dunno exactly, it were dark and I don't know me way that far out in the sticks. It were way beyond Lewisham, I know that much. Trueman told Chas to drive us. 'E knew the way.'

477

Roper closed his eyes for a second. He felt he ought to be elated, for everything was falling into place. He was certain the place Alfie was referring to was the same place the two women were taken to. He also felt absolutely certain it would transpire that Trueman or one of his associates had bought that land when the farmer died.

Harry Brown had put forward the suggestion that one of the men at the building site where Dan Reynolds worked might have something to do with Fifi's abduction, and Roper had checked some of the men out. Charles Bovey, better known as Chas, didn't have a criminal record, but he was a well-known thug. And there were two complaints on record that he had sexually assaulted young girls, but in both cases the complaint had been withdrawn. Roper hadn't felt able to pull him in for questioning because there had been nothing concrete to tie him into Fifi's disappearance.

'Does Chas Bovey drive a black Daimler?' he asked almost in a conversational manner. He knew perfectly well that Chas had a green Consul, but two separate people had claimed to have seen a black Daimler in the street on a couple of Friday nights and he hoped to get the name of the owner.

Alfie shook his head. 'No, he's got a Consul.'

Roper feigned surprise. 'Molly said it was a Daimler!'

'She wouldn't know a Morris Minor from an 'earse,' Alfie said with a wolfish grin. He didn't even seem to be aware that he'd admitted being part of crimes that were beyond the pale. 'Maybe she's got mixed up with Trueman's mate, Tony Lubrano, 'e's got a Daimler, she were always asking 'im to take 'er up West in it.'

Both police officers pricked up their ears at the name Tony Lubrano. Like Trueman, he ran several shady businesses in Soho and was another man they'd been taking a keen interest in for several years.

'You could be right there, Alfie,' Wallis chimed in, lying with as much flair as Roper. 'Molly was talking about Tony being there that night, and we thought she said you went off in his car.'

'Yeah, 'e was there all right, but not 'is car. We went in the Consul.'

'When did this happen, Alfie?' Roper said.

Alfie looked at him suspiciously. 'Didn't Molly tell you that an' all?'

Roper gulped. He had started to think Alfie was a complete fool, and that was a mistake, for what he lacked in real brains, he made up for in low cunning. He had to keep the man sweet for a little longer, until he'd signed a statement.

'She did, but as she's lied about mostly everything, I just wanted you to confirm it,' Roper said in honeyed tones. 'My God, Alfie, I feel for you, she's trying to lay all this on to you. What on earth did you do to her to make her turn against you? I always thought you were rock solid.'

'I dunno.' Alfie shook his head sadly. 'But I ain't gonna let 'er blame me for all this. The gloves are off now. I ain't even begun to tell you yet what she can be like.'

Roper felt that he'd had more than enough for one day. He was sickened in a way he'd never been in his whole career as a policeman. The lad who died in such a brutal and horrific manner would probably turn out to be some young kid turned loose from a care home without any supervision. Unloved from birth, and with no one to mourn him now he was gone. And those other youngsters, what had happened to them after their ordeal? He could bet it had marked them for life.

But Roper couldn't stop now. They still needed the finer details, names and dates, to ensure Trueman, Alfie and Molly would never walk free, and the other men involved could be brought in and charged. He just hoped he could get through it without throwing up.

Two hours later, once outside the prison gates, the two policemen lit up cigarettes and stood silently for a moment gathering themselves.

They felt they had the truth at last, and a statement to go with it, but what they'd heard had disturbed and revolted them so badly they could barely look at each other. Wallis had said as they came away from Alfie that he doubted he'd ever be able to walk down Dale Street again without seeing the hideous images of what went on in number 11.

'I think it's time for me to retire,' Roper sighed. 'It just gets worse all the time. When I joined the force we nicked men that were just thieves. You could understand why because they were born into nothing, jobs were hard to come by and they had families to feed. But now you get stuff like this!'

'Did you see his face when he said they buried the body just before Christmas?' Wallis asked incredulously. 'He was so bloody gleeful that it snowed at New Year and it stayed around for weeks. He thought he was talking to men that had the same sick mentality as him!'

Roper shuddered. He felt he needed a bath in disinfectant to make sure none of Alfie's sickness had transferred to him. 'I'm not so sure I can feel proud of myself,' he admitted. 'I only got all that filth by lying to him. Now we've got to do the same to Molly. But I don't suppose she'll be such a pushover.'

'Were they both as evil as that when they met, or did they

make each other that way?' Wallis mused aloud as they walked to the car.

'I don't even want to think about that one.' Roper half smiled. 'If I did I might feel tempted to collect up all their children and grandchildren and kill them off to make sure the Muckle genes don't spread any further.'

Chapter twenty-one

'Your mum's watching us from the kitchen window,' Dan warned Fifi as she turned in her seat to kiss him.

It was a Sunday afternoon in mid-November and they were down the garden sitting by the summer house in a patch of sunshine. It had been raining incessantly for the last two weeks, but as today was dry and sunny, after lunch Fifi and Dan had volunteered to rake up the fallen leaves that lay like a thick orange and yellow carpet on the lawn. But halfway through the job they'd got bored and sat down for a rest.

'Let her watch,' Fifi murmured. 'I don't care.'

Dan returned the kiss, wishing he could whisk her indoors and go to bed for the rest of the afternoon. But he knew Clara would see that as a step too far.

'If only we had a place of our own,' he murmured, still holding her tightly. 'Shall I find us another flat to rent?'

'I don't think I can trust you with that job again,' Fifi joked.

They both laughed because here in the safety and seclusion of the Browns' garden, the recent events in London seemed just a bad dream.

Dan had found himself a job during their first week back in Bristol. It was with a local building company who did repairs and renovations as well as building new houses. Dan really

~ed it as he did a great deal more than just bricklaying. This week he'd been installing a bathroom, doing the plumbing and tiling, and on Monday he was starting on building a garage. His wages were almost as high as in London and the firm had so much work coming in they were turning some jobs away.

Fifi was doing temporary secretarial work for an agency at the moment while she kept her eyes open for a permanent job. She was fully recovered in every way now, eating like a horse, sleeping like a baby without any nightmares, and very happy to be back in the safety and comfort of her family home. It was Dan who suffered the nightmares and paranoia.

He liked living here. It was good to come home from work to a hot meal, and Clara was a fantastic cook. He got on well with Robin, Peter and Patty; Harry had become the father he'd never known. Even Clara with her strict mealtimes, the way she never trusted him to take his work boots off in the porch, or even wash his hands before meals, had become very dear to him. But it felt as though he wasn't really providing for his wife, and he still felt very guilty that he had taken Fifi to a place where she was exposed to so much danger.

They had a row after they arrived in Bristol because Fifi wanted to write to her old friends in Dale Street. Dan said it was dangerous for anyone to know where they were. She argued that if any of Trueman's men were intent on finding them, it wouldn't take much effort to do so anyway. She also said Frank, Stan and Nora Diamond all had enough troubles in their own lives without divulging their address to anyone else, and they'd be upset if they were just abandoned as if they'd meant nothing.

She was right, Dan knew that, but the image of the crimes committed in Dale Street wouldn't leave his mind. Or how he'd felt when he got to that barn and thought Fifi was dead. All he could hope for was that once all those terrible people had been tried and found guilty, he might be able to forget.

Detective Inspector Roper had waited until Dan and Fifi were home in Bristol before visiting them and taking their full statements, but he had telephoned since to update them with what was happening in the case.

The body of a teenage boy had been found buried near the barn, and although the forensic department had not yet finished their investigation, it was thought he was David Harvey, a fifteen-year-old runaway who had been reported missing in November 1962.

Jack Trueman had been charged with the boy's murder, rape of a minor, abduction, and a whole raft of other lesser crimes which had come to light during the investigation of his business empire. He was being held in custody to await his trial, and although he had tried to rally support from his old friends, associates and employees, Roper reported they had all turned their backs on him, and in the prison he was frequently attacked by other inmates.

Alfie had smugly believed that by turning Queen's evidence and giving the police a full and frank account of all the crimes committed at number 11, he would escape with just a short sentence. But when Molly found out that he would be a witness for the prosecution, she was so livid at what she saw as betrayal that she started talking too. She had revealed details of several robberies with violence he'd committed, the assault on Dan, and incest with his two oldest daughters. The latter was backed up with a statement from the daughters.

Roper was certain now that both Alfie and Molly would spend the rest of their lives in prison as on top of all their lesser crimes they were accessories to murder and had procured young persons for immoral purposes and endangered their lives. No judge was going to be lenient with a couple who had so little regard for even their own children and showed no real remorse at what their depraved behaviour had led to.

Seven other men who had taken part in some of the activities at number 11 had also been arrested. One was the gangster Tony Lubrano, who admitted helping in the burial of the teenage boy and disposing of John Bolton's body in the Thames. He claimed that Bolton was already dead when he was sent by Trueman to collect the body. But the amount of water in Bolton's lungs proved he had died of drowning and had only been stunned by a blow to his head before he went into the water, so he too would be tried for murder.

Dan wasn't entirely surprised when he learned that Chas Bovey, the labourer he worked with at Stockwell, was involved with Trueman, as he'd always known he had some very shady associates. When Harry had said someone from the building site must have been passing on information, the only man Dan felt was capable of it was Chas. But it was a shock to hear that he'd been present at several of Alfie's parties, that he'd driven the car with the teenager's body out to Bexley, and that his sexual tastes ran to young boys. The attack on Dan in the alley was clearly down to Chas tipping Alfie off too.

The remaining five men were present either on the night of Angela's rape or at the death of the young boy. They all used fear of Jack Trueman as the reason they hadn't come forward voluntarily but once arrested they were all too eager to spill out details about the nights in question. Roper had charged all of them with aiding and abetting, and concealment of a crime.

George O'Connell, the foreman of the council depot where Stan worked, was in the pay of Trueman too. He claimed it was Trueman's intention to have Alfie killed in prison, making it look like suicide, because he was afraid Alfie would implicate him. He had been unable to get this carried out as Alfie had been put in solitary for his own safety. O'Connell had bribed Frieda Marchant to make a false complaint about Stan in an attempt to draw the heat away from Alfie in the hope he would be put back amongst the other prisoners, and the original plan could be executed.

The two men who abducted Yvette had been found and charged; Delroy Williams and Martin Broughton, who took Fifi, likewise. But Broughton had been promised that the help he'd given the police would be taken into account when he was sentenced.

Mike Muckle had been almost beaten to death by other prisoners while held in Brixton; ironically he'd been mistaken for his Uncle Alfie. He was still in the prison hospital when Roper learned it was Yvette who killed Angela, so the charges of accessory to murder against Mike were dropped and he was transferred to a civilian hospital.

Roper had told Dan that Mike didn't appear to have played any part in the card parties, and as he wasn't very bright, in his opinion the lad was to be pitied rather than punished for having relatives like Alfie and Molly. He believed Mike would go straight now, as his spell in prison had frightened him so badly.

Fifi had asked Roper if he could find out how the three remaining Muckle children, Alan, Mary and Joan, were doing. He came back a few days later with the news that they were all doing surprisingly well in a small children's home in East Anglia. The matron had reported that they were very difficult to begin with, but right out in the countryside, with good food, kindness and no reminders of their former life, they had eventually settled down and seemed happy. Alan was reputed to be very good with animals, and said he wanted to work on a farm when he was old enough.

After hearing this news Fifi took the view that at least one good thing had come out of all the horror. She hoped poor Dora was happier too, wherever she was.

Both Dan and Fifi were very aware that the trial was likely to shake them up again, and that until it was over and sentences passed, they would be living in a kind of limbo. This was why they'd made no attempt to find a home of their own yet.

'If we did rent a flat it would take us far longer to save a deposit for a house,' Fifi said thoughtfully. 'So let's hang on here until after the trial, it's only about six weeks away.'

'As long as we do go then.' Dan grinned. 'My idea of a perfect Sunday is to spend it in bed with you, not raking up leaves. And I suppose we'd better get it finished now or your mum will get the tight face again.'

Fifi giggled. Clara was being almost too nice and it was beginning to get on her nerves. When she did do the 'tight face' as Dan called it, Fifi secretly hoped it would erupt into a row. Too much calm and serenity wasn't natural.

Yet finding out how distraught her family were when she went missing had made a huge impact on Fifi. She'd always thought she wasn't loved as much as Patty and the boys, and she'd often felt like an outsider.

On the first night home she gave her parents the notes she'd made about them in the barn. She'd thought it was important that they knew what she'd been thinking about during that time. Both of them had cried openly, the first time Fifi ever remembered her father crying.

'Just because you weren't easy like Patty was as a child didn't mean we loved you less,' her mother sobbed out. 'You were the one that made us laugh, you had a spirit that was all your own. Looking back, I often wonder if some of the problems you had were because I didn't have enough time for you alone. It was hard having four children in six years. Maybe I didn't let you be a baby long enough, and I was so anxious too, what with the war and your father away so much. But the oldest child always has the hardest time in a family, because they have to break new ground.'

Fifi had joked to Dan while she was still in hospital that she'd been through a mental spring-clean in the barn. All the old grievances had been pushed aside by good memories, she'd been able to see how much love she had inside her for her parents and how little she'd regarded their feelings in the past. She wasn't sure before she and Dan came back here to live that this change of heart was a permanent one; she suspected that at the first tiff she'd be back where she started.

But her parents' total acceptance of Dan, and indeed their affection for him, made Fifi so happy that it was impossible for her to backslide. Furthermore she found herself making a concerted effort to improve the relationship with her mother.

She'd stopped throwing her shoes down in the hall, she kept the spare room tidy, and she did a whole range of chores without being asked. She'd even got her mother to give her cookery lessons, something Clara had been telling her she needed for years and Fifi had claimed she didn't.

Yet Fifi really wanted a home of her own again. Being looked after and feeling totally safe was good, but she felt inhibited making love when her parents were so close by.

She wanted to cook for Dan, have her own things around her again, blast out music when she felt like it, and to have time alone too. There was something else as well, something Fifi hadn't even told Dan yet. She was pregnant again.

It must have happened soon after they got back to Bristol. There had been a couple of times when they forgot to take precautions. Fifi hadn't been the least concerned when her period didn't arrive, as the doctor at the hospital had said the shock of all she'd been through would probably disrupt her normal cycle. But then she began experiencing over-sensitive breasts and a faint nausea at certain smells, just as she had when she was pregnant before, and she knew what was causing it.

She had kept it to herself for many reasons: being afraid she might miscarry again; because her parents might see it as irresponsibility when she and Dan didn't have a home of their own. But mainly she felt Dan needed some respite from worrying about her. When they first returned to Bristol he'd hardly been able to let her out of his sight.

Two days ago she'd had it confirmed at the doctor's – their baby was due at the end of June. She intended to wait till Friday to tell Dan. They were going to a special family party in the evening, and if she told him just before, then they could announce it to everyone that night.

'Don't you go burning those leaves!'

Dan turned at Clara's shout from the kitchen door. He was trundling the loaded wheelbarrow towards the incinerator. 'Where d'you want them then?' he called back, making a comic face at Fifi.

'On the compost heap of course,' Clara replied. 'But mind you cover it up again!'

Dan began transferring the leaves from the barrow to the

compost heap, but the wind was getting up and blowing them around. Giggling, Fifi ran over to help him.

'I might have known she wouldn't trust me to light a fire,' he said glumly. 'I was looking forward to that part. Is she a secret pyromaniac? Will she wait till we've all cleared off tomorrow and then douse all this with petrol?'

'Don't be daft,' Fifi replied. 'They put all this stuff back on the garden when it's rotted down. You should know that. I thought you were a country boy?'

'Only when sex comes into it,' he grinned. 'Like rolling in the hay, or having it off in long grass.'

'Speaking of which,' she smirked lasciviously at him, 'if we hurry up we could nip upstairs for a while before tea. I'll tell Mum we're going to have a dress rehearsal for next weekend.'

This was the party when she intended to make the announcement about the baby. Everyone, including Harry's brother and Clara's two sisters and their families, were having a celebration dinner at the Grand Hotel. Neither Fifi nor Dan had been up to celebrating their first wedding anniversary in September but Clara had decided they should have a big party later on to welcome Dan to the family.

It was to be quite a grand affair, the men in dinner jackets and women in evening dress. Fifi had bought a frilly pink chiffon dress which she'd put on dozens of times in the past couple of weeks, but it was only yesterday that Dan had picked up the suit he was hiring.

'Brilliant idea,' he agreed, his dark eyes dancing, and he rushed to collect the last heap of leaves. 'Just make sure they don't all come bursting in to see how we look,' he shouted back to her.

All at once Fifi had to tell Dan her news. She felt just like all those leaves dancing around in the wind, too excited to stay still, let alone keep her secret for another five days.

She ran over to him, bending to scoop up a pile of leaves, and threw them all over him. He laughed as she ran away, and chased her towards the summer house. Catching hold of her and scooping her up into his arms, he said he was going to put her in the compost heap.

'No, you can't do that,' she said, wriggling in his arms. 'It isn't good for pregnant women!'

'You what!' he exclaimed, tightening his arms around her. 'Did you really say what I thought you said?'

Fifi giggled, because his dark eyes were wide with delight. 'Yes, I did. Little Reynolds will be here at the end of June.'

He put her on the ground then, but wrapped his arms around her tightly, kissing her all over her face. 'That's the best news ever,' he said. 'But why didn't you tell me before?'

'I've only just found out for sure, and I was waiting for a special occasion. I meant to tell you next Friday.'

'Every day with you is a special occasion,' he said, cupping her face between his hands and kissing her cold nose tenderly. 'But this is an extra special day.'

'We won't say anything to anyone else until Friday night,' she warned him. 'Maybe by then we'll have worked out some plan about where to live and how we're going to manage.'

'If I do some overtime, maybe work Saturdays, we'll scrape a deposit for a house together,' he said. 'There's always emergency plumbing work in the winter months.'

'Don't you start worrying again,' Fifi said firmly. 'It will all work out fine, I know it will.'

Fifi was walking back to her bedroom from the bathroom on Friday evening when she heard her mother let out a kind of wail downstairs. 'What is it, Mum?' she shouted down over the banisters. 'You haven't burned your dress, have you?'

Her father came out into the hall and looked up at Fifi. He was ready in his dinner suit, just waiting for his wife to tie his tie, and his face looked stricken. 'It's President Kennedy,' he said. 'He's been killed, shot by an assassin.'

Fifi's first thought was for herself: *why did it have to be today and spoil our party?* But she checked herself before she blurted that out, remembering her father had a high opinion of the President. 'Oh Dad, how awful!' she exclaimed. 'Ought we to cancel the dinner?'

'No, of course not,' he said. 'Our family is more important to me than a statesman, however much I admired him.'

A couple of hours later, Harry stood up after the waiter had taken all the orders. Everyone was talking about the assassination in Dallas and how President Kennedy died in his wife's arms in the open-top car.

'I know we are all shocked by John Kennedy's death,' he said, looking round the table at everyone. 'It's a terrible thing, a tragedy which will affect the whole world. But I'm going to suggest that we put it aside for tonight. This party to welcome Dan to our family is long overdue. Dan and Fifi's first wedding anniversary passed without any celebration because of the deeds of evil men. We shouldn't let more evil spoil our enjoyment of a family get-together.'

There was a cheer from his brother Ernest, and Robin made a little aside to Peter that he didn't much care what went on in America anyway. Patty put a warning finger to her lips to hush him – she knew their father was just holding his sorrow in check.

There were fifteen round the huge table. Ernest and his

wife Ann, who lived in Cambridge, and their two teenage sons, Robert and Michael. Clara's younger sisters, Rose and Lily, who both lived in Somerset, had decided against bringing their four children as they were too young to be relied on to behave, but their husbands, Geoff and Fred, were both there. Harry, Clara, their children and Dan completed the family group.

All the men looked very debonair in dinner jackets, and the women were glamorous. Clara looked particularly lovely in a midnight-blue shantung dress with a boat neckline and Patty was surprisingly chic in black velvet.

As the waiters removed the dishes after the main course, Dan got to his feet and tapped a fork on a glass for everyone's attention. A great deal of wine had been drunk with the meal and they were all very mellow.

'I'd like to just say a few words, if you can stand it,' Dan said. He looked down at Fifi's upturned face beside him and smiled. 'Being here with you all tonight means more to me than I can say. It's the acceptance that for better or worse I am Fifi's husband. I know it's been all worse so far, but things are improving – Clara's even stopped seeing me as a Teddy boy!'

Everyone laughed, including Clara, for they all knew that had been one of her favourite insults in the past.

Dan looked at Clara fondly. 'Teddy boys ceased to exist some eight years ago. If you want to move with the times, Ma, you're going to have to tell people I'm a rocker.'

There was more laughter, especially from the younger family members.

'Fifi and I have had what could only be called an eventful first year, but not all of it was bad,' Dan went on, looking round the table at each of the faces that were now his family

493

too. 'We got married because we couldn't bear to be apart, and a year and a bit on, we still feel that way. I hope we'll still be the same when we get to our golden anniversary.' He reached in his pocket and pulled out a small package wrapped in pink tissue paper. 'The actual anniversary day passed at the wrong time for me to make a grand gesture. Fifi told me that the first anniversary is 'paper'; so I gave her a card. But that makes me look like a cheapskate. Well, this was cheap too, but I did put a lot of effort into making it.'

He handed the present to Fifi, who quickly unwrapped it.

'Oh, Dan!' she exclaimed as she found it was a small papier mâché heart on a pink ribbon, decorated with tiny pink flowers. 'It's gorgeous. You couldn't have made it yourself!'

'I did,' he insisted, turning a little pink. 'If you don't believe me you can check your dad's shed tomorrow. All the rejects are still in there.'

As Fifi looked closer she saw each tiny flower had been cut out, perhaps from a seed catalogue, and stuck on, then the whole thing had been varnished so it looked like a Victorian heirloom. It was quite the most exquisite thing she'd ever been given, and even more precious because he'd made it without her knowing.

'Wait till I get you home,' she whispered in his ear. 'I'll show my appreciation then. But right now you'd better tell them the other news!'

Dan tapped a glass again. 'Just one more thing!' He looked round the table with a big smile. 'Fifi and I have some great news for you all. We're having a baby!'

Fifi had been watching her parents as Dan spoke; she saw the surprise on their faces, and waited to see if it was an

494

unwelcome one. But Harry leaped to his feet with uncharacteristic excitement, while Clara clapped her hands over her mouth and tears of joy welled up in her eyes.

'Whoopee!' Patty yelled. 'I'm going to be an auntie!'

'It was almost worth going through all those bad times for this,' Dan whispered to Fifi a little later. There was so much joy from everyone, excited discussions about names for the baby, whether a girl or a boy would be best. Harry said he thought he'd make a better grandfather than he had a dad, Clara was just smiling and smiling as if a long awaited dream had just come true.

No one had asked questions about where they were going to live, or did they know what babies really meant. They had all taken the news in the way Fifi had hoped for but not expected – that a new baby to join the family was a very special gift to them all.

Another hour later, everyone was a little drunk. The dinner had been wonderful, and as it had been years since Harry's brother and Clara's sisters had been together, they were making up for lost time catching up on all the news. Even Robert and Michael, the cousins, who had at first looked as if they were prepared for the most boring evening of their lives, were chatting and laughing with their relatives as if they were with their own friends.

The waiter served the coffee and petits fours, and after he'd gone Harry got to his feet again, this time a little unsteadily.

'Not a speech,' he said. 'I just wanted to say that Clara and I owe Dan a great deal. He not only took Fifi off our hands, he did it in such a way we didn't have to fork out for the wedding.'

Clara gasped indignantly. 'What a thing to say, Harry!' she exclaimed.

'It was a joke, dear,' Harry said with a sigh. 'Can't you hear everyone laughing?'

Dan was spluttering with laughter, he loved Harry's dry sense of humour.

'If I may go on?' Harry asked giving everyone a mock disapproving look over his glasses. 'Well, what I'd intended to say has been kind of upstaged by hearing I'm going to be a grandfather. So I'll just cut to the chase and remind you all again that the first anniversary is paper. I'm glad I'll be pushing up the daisies when their golden one comes round.' He handed Dan a large white envelope.

'What on earth is it?' Fifi said, looking curiously at her father.

'Open it and see,' he said.

Dan opened it and pulled out a glossy brochure of a new housing estate.

'Our gift is the deposit on one of them,' Harry said, then sat down rather heavily.

Dan just looked thunderstruck but Fifi realized it was the small estate of houses which were starting to be built around the time they got married. It was about a mile from her parents' home.

'You can go and choose the one you like,' Clara said helpfully. 'Just make sure you pick one with a south-facing garden.'

A year ago Fifi would have viewed this gift with grave suspicion. She certainly would have seen it as a method of controlling her. But she was older and a great deal wiser now. She knew it was given only because her parents knew she and Dan needed a permanent home of their own. They wanted her and Dan to be happy and secure, in a home with room for children, just as Harry's parents had done for them. And since her mother had very high standards, excellent taste and would have gone into everything – bus routes, schools and even the nearest doctor – Fifi could expect these houses to be as good as they looked in the brochure.

No more kitchens on landings, sharing a bathroom with strangers. She could even burn a fish pie and no one would be able to complain!

'That's so lovely of you,' she said, joyous tears pricking her eyes. She got up and ran round the table to hug and kiss both her parents. 'And even more wonderful now we're going to have a baby.'

'You'll have to be sensible and budget to keep up the mortgage repayments,' Clara said a little waspishly, but her eyes were dancing and Dan knew she wasn't feeling waspish.

'It is *so* generous and kind of you,' Dan said, getting up too and going over to embrace them both. 'I'll make sure you never regret it.'

Everyone around the table was trying to see the brochure, all talking excitedly at once.

'I don't like the design of some of the houses,' Clara said in her more characteristic sharp manner. 'They've put the kitchens at the front on some of them. I ask you! Who wants people to see into your kitchen?'

Dan picked up the brochure and looked at it. 'I think it would be a good thing for Fifi,' he said.

'Why?' Clara asked.

'Well, she could do the washing up while she's watching the neighbours,' he said.

'Dan!' Fifi exclaimed. 'You know I promised I'd given up being nosy!'

'A leopard can't change its spots.' He laughed. 'And I don't think I'd like you so much if you lost interest in watching people.'

Discover the gripping new novel from
number 1 bestselling author

LESLEY PEARSE

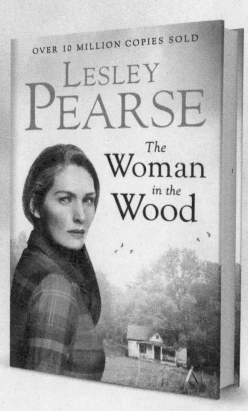

Read on for an exclusive extract…

I

West London, 1960

Maisy was woken by a piercing scream. Startled, she sat up in bed, assuming the sound was coming from the street. But then she heard the cry for a second time and realized it was coming from inside the house. It was her mother.

She rushed to her bedroom door and out on to the landing, then paused when she heard her father's voice travelling up from the floor below.

'Be quiet, Lily. You'll wake the twins and frighten them. I'm doing this for your own good.'

Maisy's twin brother Duncan came out of his room and joined her at the top of the stairs. 'What's going on?' he whispered.

Maisy put a finger to her lips to silence him and held his arm so he wouldn't run down the stairs. Their father, Alastair Mitcham, was a stern man who didn't take kindly to any interference.

'I don't want to go there! I'll get better here in my own home,' Lily Mitcham cried out. 'Don't make me go, Alastair!'

The pitiful pleading brought tears to both Maisy and Duncan's eyes, but they were only fifteen and a little afraid of their father, and they simply didn't know what to do.

'How many times have I tried to get professional help

for you? Each time you act the same way,' Alastair said, and the children heard the weariness and resignation in his voice and exchanged anxious looks. 'You aren't getting better; year by year you get worse. When did you last agree to go out of the house? I think that was two summers ago. You haven't even been downstairs for over a year.'

'But my back and legs . . .' she protested.

Alastair cut her short. 'There is nothing wrong with your back *or* legs, and well you know it. You can't hide behind a riding accident from some twelve years ago any longer. I'm sick of this, Lily. The only way I know to get you to face up to what really ails you is to take you to this place. Now, calm down, or I'll get the nurse who's waiting outside in the ambulance to come in and give you a shot of something.'

Maisy had heard enough. Despite her fear of her father and reluctance to drag her brother into trouble with her, she caught hold of his hand and pulled him to the stairs. Encouraged by her bravery, Duncan didn't try to pull back.

'Why are you sending Mother away?' Maisy asked when she was just a few steps above the first-floor landing.

Her father wheeled round. He was fully dressed in a suit and clearly hadn't heard them coming on their bare feet.

'This is nothing to do with you,' he snapped. 'Get back to bed, both of you.'

'She's our mother, so it has everything to do with us,' Maisy retorted. 'Where are you sending her? And why in the middle of the night? So the neighbours won't know? Or did you hope we wouldn't wake and you could make out she'd gone to stay with a relative for a holiday?'

It was the first time Maisy had ever stood up to her father. While he wasn't a violent man, he was so stern and forbidding that she and Duncan always did as he said. Her heart was racing and she was trembling, but even so she was determined to stick up for her mother.

'Don't let him send me away to an asylum,' their mother whimpered. 'It's cruel and horrible. I want to stay here.'

Shocked as she was to hear of her father's plans, when Maisy looked at her mother she realized why he was resorting to such drastic measures. Since she hadn't seen her mother's face clearly for many weeks, she hadn't been aware how much worse she had become. Her eyes were almost popping out of her head, and she was now so thin that the yellowish skin on her face appeared to be stretched over her cheekbones, with blue veins standing out on her forehead like thick crayon marks. Her brown hair was lank and greasy and her nightgown was very grubby. It was absolutely clear she needed help.

Right from when they were small children the twins had grown used to their mother being in bed most of the time. They had always been taken to school by someone else and she never took them for a day at the seaside, a picnic or even a visit to a park. It was all they knew and so they had accepted her claim that it was due to a riding accident.

'Father, don't do this,' Duncan said.

Still holding their mother's arm tightly, he turned to face them. 'I have to. She is ill. I never wanted you to know this, but she has been steadily getting worse and I'm afraid of what she will do. Just a few days ago she tried to drink some poison. Thankfully, Betty caught her just as she was about to swallow it and saved her life. But it doesn't bear thinking about what might have happened.'

Their mother tried to escape from her husband's grip, the expression on her face like a savage animal, teeth bared. Maisy instinctively took a step back, and Duncan took her hand.

'OK, Father,' he said, looking fearfully at his mother. 'But shall I go out and ask the nurse to come in to help?'

'Thank you, son, that would be best. Maisy, will you get your mother's dressing gown and slippers? She was struggling too much for me to hold them.'

A few minutes later the twins watched as the stout, middle-aged nurse, who had been waiting outside in the private ambulance, injected their mother with a sedative.

The effect was almost instantaneous. Lily stopped struggling and relaxed, and a vacant look came to her face. Alastair helped his wife into her dressing gown and put the slippers on her feet. 'That's better,' he said, kissing her cheek, a gesture that reassured the twins he really did have their mother's best interests at heart. 'Now, children, why don't you say goodbye to your mother and go back to bed? Whatever she may have said, she will be looked after properly, I assure you. It's a private home offering the best care available. Now I'm going to follow the ambulance in my car, and it will probably be a few hours before I get back. But don't worry, Betty will be in at breakfast time as usual.'

They watched from the sitting room window as the nurse helped their mother into the back of the ambulance. Their father started up his car and waited for the ambulance to move.

For a moment the twins said nothing, just stood at the window in the dark room like two statues.

Although no one had ever said openly that their mother was mentally ill, of late the twins had suspected there was something more to her mysterious illness than a riding accident from long ago. Everything about their home was different to other people's. Their parents slept in separate rooms, their mother had all her meals in hers, and sometimes they heard the sound of breaking plates and shouting. Betty the housekeeper always claimed their mother had dropped something, just as she always covered any strange noises by saying it was because she was in pain. Now it was all falling into place.

'That was horrible,' Duncan said eventually, his voice trembling. 'Not just for Mother, but for Father too. Still, I'm sure it's for the best. Shall we make some hot milk and then go back to bed? It's only half past two.'

'I never knew she was that bad,' Maisy said as they went down to the kitchen. 'I mean, I know she's always been poorly and a bit strange too, but I never thought she was . . .' She paused.

'Mad?' Duncan said. 'Neither did I, but then we've never known any different, have we? I'm sure they'll make her better; everything will be all right.'

Maisy poured some milk into a saucepan and lit the gas under it. Her brother was always the optimistic one, she thought to herself. She tended to be the opposite.

They looked alike, inasmuch as both had thick blond hair and deep blue eyes. But Duncan was taller than her, probably five feet six, while she was five three. He had a square face and a strong jaw, while Maisy's face was heart-shaped, with a dimple in her chin. She tanned easily to a golden brown while her brother was prone to freckles.

Their large, semi-detached home was in London's Holland Park. It had four floors, including the basement. It had last been decorated in Edwardian times, and though it must have been lovely then, it had grown very shabby over the years, and after the war decorating materials were hard to come by. Betty had told Maisy she'd overheard their father saying he wanted to sell it as it was too big and expensive to run. Betty thought it would be best converted into flats as so many other big houses in the area had been. The housekeeper had an opinion about everything, including that their mother was an attention seeker.

Because of the way things were at home, neither Duncan nor Maisy ever attempted to bring school friends back. They knew it would be embarrassing with a mother in bed all the time and a father who, when he was there, shut himself up in his study. Consequently they rarely got invited to anyone else's home. Their world was a very small one. A private school just the other side of the park, visits to the library and an occasional treat of the cinema. Fortunately they were close friends, and didn't think they needed anyone else.

They only had one close relative, Violet Mitcham, their paternal grandmother. She was a widow and lived in the New Forest, and she was as chilly as her only son. She only came to London to see them all once every couple of years. According to Betty she had never approved of Lily because she was so 'weak'.

The twins had very good memories of Grandmother Goldney, Lily's mother. They had been born in January

1945 in her house in Tenterden in Kent, where their mother had been living on and off for much of the war. Betty came from the town as well, and when they all returned to their London home Betty came with them as housekeeper. They went back to Tenterden for a month every August, but when they were eight Grandmother Goldie, as they had called her, died of pneumonia.

Their father had worked for the Foreign Office all his life. It was a reserved occupation during the war, so he didn't have to join up, but it took him away from home a great deal, which was why their mother spent so much time in Kent and the twins were born there. He never talked about what his job entailed, and though Duncan liked to pretend he was a spy, Betty pooh-poohed that notion and said he just did clerical work.

'What will happen now, do you suppose?' Duncan asked, bringing Maisy back to the present by pointing to the milk which was almost boiling. 'Do you think we'll just carry on the same?'

'Why would it be any different?' Maisy asked. She didn't want to be mean about their mother, but it wasn't as if she had ever done anything for them. 'For weeks now she's been asleep every time we went into her room. Looking back, I wonder if she was pretending to sleep because she didn't want to talk to us.'

'But why? And if it's true, how do you suppose she got like that?'

'I think if I was married to a man like Father I'd hide away,' Maisy said, semi-seriously. 'Let's face it, he's no fun. Have you ever heard him laugh? Whistle a tune, dance, crack a joke?'

'Now you mention it, I haven't. But let's go back to bed now. We've still got to go to school tomorrow.'

'Why don't we play truant for once?' Maisy suggested. 'We could go up to the West End and look in the shops, even go to the pictures in the afternoon to see something Father wouldn't approve of.'

'He said he was coming back here after taking Mother to that place. He might not go to work afterwards. I don't think we'd better.'

Maisy pouted. 'You're such a goody-goody. Watch out or you might end up like him.'

Dead to Me
Ruby and Verity become firm
friends, despite coming from
different worlds. However,
fortunes are not set in stone and
soon the girls find their situations
reversed.

Without a Trace
On Coronation Day, 1953, Molly
discovers that her friend is dead
and her six-year-old daughter Petal
has vanished. Molly is prepared to
give up everything in finding Petal.
But is she also risking her life?

Survivor
Eighteen-year-old Mari is defiant, selfish and has given up everythin in favour of glamorous parties in the West End. But, without warning, the Blitz blows her new life apart. Can Mari learn from her mistakes before it's too late?

Forgive Me
Eva's mother never told her the truth about her childhood. Now it is too late and she must retrace her mother's footsteps to look for answers. Will she ever discover the story of her birth?

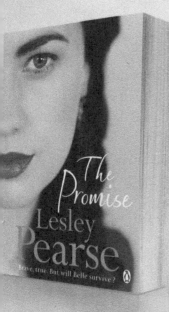

The Promise
When Belle's husband heads for the trenches of northern France, she volunteers as a Red Cross ambulance driver. There, she is brought face to face with a man from her past who she'd never quite forgotten.

Belle
London, 1910, and the beautiful and innocent Belle Reilly is cruelly snatched from her home and sold to a brothel in New Orleans where she begins her life as a courtesan. Can Belle ever find her way home?

Stolen
A beautiful young woman is
discovered half-drowned on a
Sussex beach. Where has she come
from? Why can't she remember
who she is — or what happened?

Gypsy
Liverpool, 1893, and after tragedy
strikes the Bolton family, Beth
and her brother Sam embark on
a dangerous journey to find their
fortune in America.

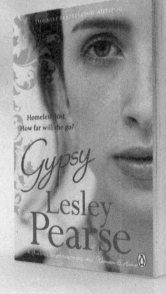

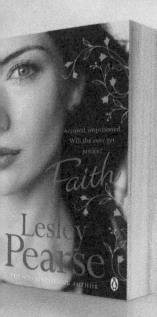

Faith
Scotland, 1995, and Laura Brannigan is in prison for a murder she claims she didn't commit.

Hope
Somerset, 1836, and baby Hope is cast out from a world of privilege as proof of her mother's adultery.

A Lesser Evil
Bristol, the 1960s, and young Fifi
Brown defies her parents to marr
a man they think is beneath her.

Secrets
Adele Talbot escapes a children's
home to find her grandmother —
but soon her unhappy mother is
on her trail . . .

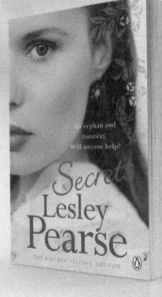

Remember Me
Mary Broad is transported to Australia as a convict and encounters both cruelty and passion. Can she make a life for herself so far from home?

Till We Meet Again
Susan and Beth were childhood friends. Now Susan is accused of murder, and Beth finds she must defend her.

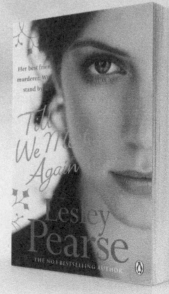

Father Unknown
Daisy Buchan is left a scrapbook
with details about her real mother
But should she go and find her?

Trust Me
Dulcie Taylor and her sister are
sent to an orphanage and then
to Australia. Is their love strong
enough to keep them together?

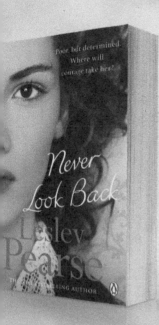

Never Look Back
An act of charity sends flower girl Matilda on a trip to the New World and a new life . . .

Charlie
Charlie helplessly watches her mother being senselessly attacked. What secrets have her parents kept from her?

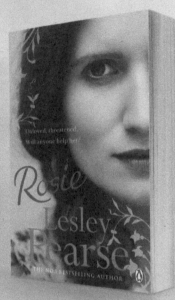

Rosie
Rosie is a girl without a mother, with a past full of trouble. But could the man who ruined her family also save Rosie?

Camellia
Orphaned Camellia discovers that the past she has always been so sure of has been built on lies. Can she bear to uncover the truth about herself?

How far would you go to discover your true identity?